The Rockwood

High upon the beautiful cliffs of the Devonshire coast,
Rockwood Castle stands. Cared for by the honourable Carey family
for centuries, the once proud castle is now crumbling into ruin.

Now a new generation of the Carey family is rising.
Burdened with debt but bound by love, can they save
their home and their family before it is too late?

In this spellbinding six-book series, Dilly Court opens
a door into Rockwood Castle - chronicling the
changing fortunes of the Carey family . . .

Book One: Fortune's Daughter

Abandoned by her parents, headstrong Rosalind must take
charge of the family. Until the appearance of dashing Piers
Blanchard threatens to ruin everything . . .

Book Two: Winter Wedding

Christmas is coming and Rockwood Castle has once
again been thrown into turmoil. As snowflakes fall,
can Rosalind protect her beloved home?

Book Three: Runaway Widow

It is time for the youngest Carey sister, Patricia, to seek out
her own future, away from Rockwood village. But without her
family around her, will she lose her way?

Look out for the rest of The Rockwood Chronicles,
COMING SOON . . .

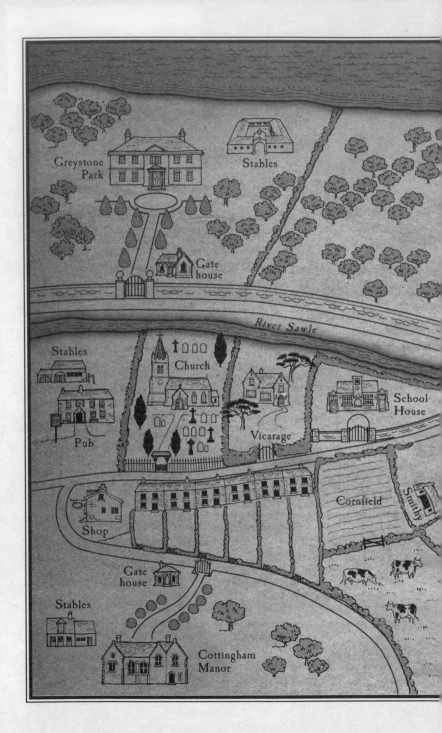

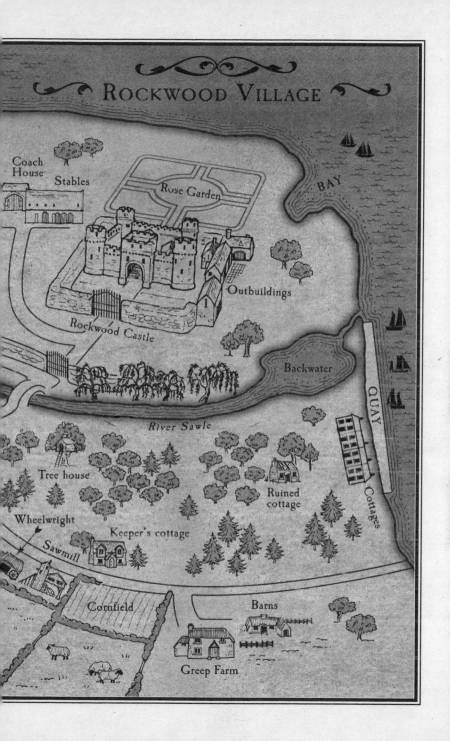

ROCKWOOD VILLAGE

Coach House
Stables
Rose Garden
BAY
Outbuildings
Rockwood Castle
Backwater
QUAY
River Sawle
Tree house
Cottages
Ruined cottage
Wheelwright
Keeper's cottage
Sawmill
Cornfield
Barns
Greep Farm

The Carey Family

Lady Hester Carey m Vice-Admiral Sir Lucius Carey m Lady Prudence Carey
(Née Dodridge) | (b. 1776) | (deceased)
(b. 1804)

Felicia Carey m Wilfred Carey
(b. 1806) | (1800–1851)

Bertram (Bertie) Carey | Rosalind (Rosie) Carey m Piers Blanchard | Walter Carey | Patricia (Patsy) Carey
(b. 1827) | (b. 1830) | (b. 1825) | (b. 1832) | (b. 1834)

Winter Wedding

Book two in

The Rockwood Chronicles

Dilly Court is a No.1 *Sunday Times* bestselling author of over forty novels. She grew up in North-East London and began her career in television, writing scripts for commercials. She is married with two grown-up children, four grandchildren and two beautiful great-grand-children. Dilly now lives in Dorset on the Jurassic Coast with her husband.

To find out more about Dilly, please visit her website and her Facebook page:

www.dillycourt.com
 /DillyCourtAuthor

Also by Dilly Court

Mermaids Singing
The Dollmaker's
Daughters
Tilly True
The Best of Sisters
The Cockney Sparrow
A Mother's Courage
The Constant Heart
A Mother's Promise
The Cockney Angel
A Mother's Wish
The Ragged Heiress
A Mother's Secret
Cinderella Sister
A Mother's Trust
The Lady's Maid
The Best of Daughters
The Workhouse Girl
A Loving Family
The Beggar Maid
A Place Called Home
The Orphan's Dream
Ragged Rose
The Swan Maid
The Christmas Card

The Button Box
The Mistletoe Seller
Nettie's Secret
Rag-and-Bone Christmas
The Reluctant Heiress

THE RIVER MAID SERIES

The River Maid
The Summer Maiden
The Christmas Rose

THE VILLAGE GIRLS SERIES

The Christmas Wedding
A Village Scandal
The Country Bride

THE ROCKWOOD CHRONICLES

Fortune's Daughter

Dilly Court

Winter Wedding

Book two in

The Rockwood Chronicles

HarperCollins*Publishers*

HarperCollins*Publishers* Ltd
1 London Bridge Street,
London SE1 9GF

www.harpercollins.co.uk

HarperCollins*Publishers*
1st Floor, Watermarque Building, Ringsend Road
Dublin 4, Ireland

First published by HarperCollins*Publishers* 2021
1

A catalogue record for this book
is available from the British Library

ISBN: 978-0-00-843552-3 (HB)
ISBN: 978-0-00-843553-0 (B)

Set in Sabon LT Std by
Palimpsest Book Production Ltd, Falkirk, Stirlingshire

Printed and Bound in the UK using
100% Renewable Electricity at CPI Group (UK) Ltd

For Team Dilly at HarperCollins, who have worked so hard, despite the pandemic, to bring my books to life.

Chapter One

It was one of those rare winters when snow had started to fall at the beginning of December. Rosalind could not remember a year when the preparations for Christmas had taken on such a seasonal feeling, but first, and even more important, there was her sister's upcoming wedding. Looking out of the drawing-room window across the snow-covered rose garden, she scanned the horizon for white sails set against the granite-grey sea, but there was no sign of her husband's ship returning from one of his interminable business trips abroad. It would be so disappointing if Piers was not at her side when her sister, Patsy, walked down the aisle to marry Alexander.

Rosalind sighed and turned back to the list she

had been checking. The arrangements for the wedding were far advanced, with only a few last-minute checks to be made. She laid her pen on the silver inkstand and sat back in her chair, stretching her cramped muscles. The comforting sound of apple wood logs crackling and spitting as the flames roared up the chimney all but drowned out the soughing draught that whistled through the ill-fitting windows of the ancient castle.

Just two short years ago it had been her own wedding that Rosalind had been planning with such meticulous care and excitement. Now it was Patsy's turn, but she was only eighteen and, in Rosalind's eyes, still too young for the responsibilities of marriage. Patsy was engaged to Captain Alexander Blanchard of the 46th Regiment of Foot. Rosalind smiled at the thought – they would be sisters and sisters-in-law, too. She turned her head at the sound of the door opening.

'There you are, Rosie. I knew I'd find you here, poring over yet another list. Surely all the organisation has been attended to now?' Patricia Carey tossed her blonde curls and subsided onto the damask-covered seat of the nearest chair. 'I'm exhausted. I've been standing like a statue for what seemed like hours while Meggie Brewer stuck pins into me.'

Rosalind laughed. 'She was only doing her job, Patsy. You wouldn't want to wear a wedding gown that didn't fit properly, would you?'

'No, of course not, but I'm worried. I haven't had a word from Alex. I don't even know where he is at present.'

Rosalind rose from the desk where she had been sitting and went over to give her sister a hug. 'Bridal nerves, Patsy. That's all it is. I expect I was the same before my wedding, but it was wonderful when it happened.'

'But you were marrying Piers. He visits that old china clay mine he owns in Cornwall, but he's never too far away. Alex could have been posted abroad and I wouldn't know.'

'Of course you would, silly. He would have sent a message to you one way or another. Besides which, he's now in the same regiment as Bertie, who is on his way here as we speak, if his last letter is anything to go by. I'm sure you'll hear from Alex in a day or so.'

'Bertie had better arrive soon – he's going to walk me down the aisle. If he doesn't get home in time I'll have to ask Walter to take his place. If he can tear himself away from his studies.'

'Please don't fret, Patsy. Walter would gladly stand in for Bertie if need be, but Alex and Bertie will probably arrive together.'

Patricia sighed. 'I'm sorry. I'm being selfish, as usual. You must be worried about Piers, too.'

'His ship is overdue, but it could be because of the weather and they've had to take shelter somewhere en route. I tried to persuade Piers to let Pedrick go in his stead, but Piers said that Pedrick might be a good manager at the clay mine, but he is no use when it comes to making business deals.'

Patsy shrugged. 'At least Alex doesn't have to travel the world promoting the china clay industry.'

It was on the tip of Rosalind's tongue to argue that Piers was a civilian businessman, and his brother risked his life for King and Country on a daily basis, but she thought better of it. Patsy was still her little sister and must be protected from the harsh realities of the world as much as possible, although heaven only knew what she might have to face as an army wife.

Rosalind managed a smile. 'Let's not argue. We have enough to do, what with the weather, the wedding and then Christmas. I'm just wondering if Lady Pentelow will decide to stay on and spend the festive season here as well.'

'I know she's Alex and Piers' grandmother, but she still scares me. I don't blame you for insisting on remaining here after you married Piers. I wouldn't want to live with her at Trevenor.'

'It's her home and she wouldn't welcome another woman taking over control of her household. We get on well enough, just so long as we're miles apart.'

'At least Aurelia will be here,' Patricia smiled smugly. 'I've beaten her to the altar – would you credit that? She was so sure that Hugo Knighton would propose and then he became engaged to Dorcas Mountjoy.'

'The Mountjoys are extremely wealthy and well connected. Hugo obviously has his eyes set on marrying an heiress. Perhaps Aurelia has had a lucky escape.'

'Yes, I shouldn't be mean. Aurelia is so pretty and vivacious she could have any man she wanted, and I have no fortune to recommend me, so I'm lucky that Alex loves me for myself.'

'Alex is a very fortunate man.' Rosalind returned to the small escritoire where she kept her lists and tidied them away. 'I'll finish this later. In the mean-time I'll go and check with Hester to make sure we haven't left anything to chance regarding the food and wine for the wedding breakfast.'

'If the snow gets any thicker it will prevent the guests from travelling. No one will come and it will be a disaster.'

This was so close to what Rosalind had been thinking that she avoided meeting her sister's anxious gaze. 'We won't worry about that just now, Patsy. Try to imagine how beautiful you will look in your new ivory silk gown with the fur-trimmed cape and bonnet. The whole village will turn out to watch when Gurney drives you to the village church.'

'I'll try,' Patsy said humbly.

'Good girl. Now I really should get on. I have some last-minute queries I need to discuss with Hester.'

Patsy pulled a face. 'We all love Hester, but what will the guests think when they find out that the

Dowager Lady Carey is still acting as our house-keeper, and she cooks for us if she gets a chance to oust Mrs Jackson from the kitchen?'

'Grandpapa was known as an eccentric, bless him. He didn't bother about conventions and I think he really loved her. At least Hester made his last eighteen months on earth the happiest he'd ever known.'

'I know you're right, but other people don't see it that way.'

'Well, they should. Hester is a good woman and Grandpapa really appreciated her tender care. I still miss him, and I always will.'

Rosalind left the drawing room and made her way to the blue parlour, which Hester had made her own. As their former nanny, housekeeper, cook and confidante, Hester had been part of Rosalind's life ever since she could remember. It had come as something of a shock when her late grandfather had decided to honour the woman who had kept his family together for so many years, but Rosalind was more than happy with his decision to marry Hester. Bertie, Walter and Patsy had taken a little longer to get used to the idea, but they all loved Hester and had warmly welcomed her into the family.

Rosalind knocked and entered without waiting for a response.

'The snow is coming down faster,' Hester said, gazing out of the window. 'I suppose Patsy is getting herself in a state about everything to do with the wedding.'

'Yes, of course she is, but can you blame her? I've tried to calm her down.'

'Meggie Brewer managed to get here from Exeter, so the roads must be reasonably clear. We can only hope that it stops snowing soon, and that Captain Blanchard gets here in time.'

Rosalind smiled. 'Really, Hester! You should call him Alex. He's asked you to often enough.'

'I'm still the same woman I was before your grandpapa honoured me with his name. Sometimes I wish I'd been strong enough to refuse and simply lived as his wife without putting the family to the shame of having someone like me with the title.' Hester rose from her seat and brushed the creases out of her black bombazine gown. She had been wearing deep mourning for the past few months and nothing would induce her to relieve its severity with even a ribbon or a bow. 'But I did love him in my way, Rosalind. He was a good and brave man.'

Rosalind smiled ruefully. 'He was courageous, but I don't think he was always good. Grandpapa was human and he loved life. You made him happy, Hester. That's all that matters. I just wish that you would stop working and take your proper place in the family.'

'I started in service when I was ten and I can't just stop. What would I do all day if I didn't manage the household and keep the accounts? I don't trust anyone to do it properly and honestly, and I miss my kitchen. I used to love cooking meals for you all, especially when we were so poor that we had to live off the land. It was a challenge.'

'Those days are behind us, Hester. Thanks to Piers, we're comfortably off.' Rosalind heard a sound outside and she was suddenly alert. She hurried to the window. 'I wonder who that could be. It looks as if we have guests.'

'There's only one way to find out, poppet,' Hester said, smiling. 'Perhaps a visitor or two will take Patricia's mind off her problems.'

'It depends who it is.' Rosalind crossed the room and opened the door. 'But I don't think it's Lady Pentelow – she always travels with a whole retinue of servants. I'll go and meet them. At least it means that the roads are still passable.'

Jarvis, like any good butler, was there before her, and he held the heavy oak door open, standing back as a blast of cold air laden with icy particles of snow hurled itself into the entrance hall. The ancient suit of armour nearest the door rattled ominously as if its former occupant was shivering, but Rosalind was used to the vagaries of the old castle and she automatically snapped the visor shut as she walked past. There was probably a simple explanation as to why the headpiece often looked as though it was smiling at some ancient joke, but when they were children Bertie had insisted that the spirit of Sir Denys Carey lingered on in his suit of armour. Rosalind had been terrified of it then, and even now, in the dim light of the evenings she averted her eyes when she walked past.

'Who is it, Jarvis? Can you see?'

'The snow is coming down too fast, ma'am. I can't make out who it is.'

Rosalind stood behind him, peering into the swirling whiteness. She could just make out the caped figure of the coachman, and a footman leaped down from the box to open the carriage door. Both men were iced with snow as if they were decorations on a Christmas cake, and clouds of snowflakes flew around them as they moved.

The first person to emerge from the carriage was a woman whose face was hidden by a thick veil and she was enveloped in fur. Close behind her a man alighted and took her by the arm to guide her over the slippery cobblestones. Rosalind recognised them instantly and ran forward, forgetting the adverse weather conditions.

'Mama, Claude, what a lovely surprise.'

'I was beginning to think we wouldn't make it,' Claude said breathlessly. 'The snow is piling up in drifts in the narrow lanes.'

Felicia Carey stepped into the hall and threw back her veil. 'I don't know why you're surprised, Rosalind. We're here for your sister's wedding. Nothing would prevent me from attending.'

'You didn't come to mine.' The words tumbled from Rosalind's lips before she could stop herself. Patsy had always been their mother's favourite. She was a younger edition of Felicia, with a mass of golden curls, although her eyes were violet blue, whereas Rosalind had inherited the hazel eyes of their mother and dark blonde hair from their late father, attributes that she shared with her brothers, Bertie and Walter. They were a good-looking family, but Patricia had the power to melt hearts if she fluttered her long eyelashes and would always be the centre of attention. Rosalind had learned at an early age that life was not fair and she loved her sister too much to be jealous. Even so, sometimes Mama's attitude rankled.

'That was unfortunate, my dear,' Claude said smoothly. 'But we were in Milan – your mama was singing at the world-famous La Scala opera house.'

'I'm sure you managed perfectly well without me, Rosalind,' Felicia said coldly. 'You were always an independent little creature, even as a child, whereas Patsy needs me.'

Rosalind stood aside as the coachman and footman brought in a mountain of luggage.

'It looks as if you've come to stay for a while, Mama.'

'May we continue this conversation somewhere warmer?' Felicia slipped off her fur-lined mantle and handed it to Jarvis. 'A cup of tea would be nice, with a tot of whisky to keep out the cold. I may be resting temporarily, but I have to look after my voice.'

Rosalind nodded. The reason for her mother's sudden arrival was now perfectly clear. 'Come into the drawing room. I'll send for refreshments and have your rooms made ready for you.'

'We will both share the master bedroom,' Felicia said firmly. 'Claude has asked me to marry him and I have accepted. Don't look so disapproving.'

'I'm not judging you, Mama. But Piers and I occupy the master bedroom now.'

'As your father's widow I take precedence over you, even if you are a married woman. I am the head of the household.'

'I think you'll find that the Dowager Lady Carey holds that position, Mama.'

Felicia laughed. 'Really? You expect me to kowtow to a servant who happened to wheedle her way into a mad old man's good books?'

'Hester deserves the respect due to her, Mama. You'll find that all of us agree on that.'

'As I recall, your husband was not above breaking the mores of society when it suited him. Where is he, by the way?'

'Piers should be arriving soon, Mama. He's been abroad on business.'

'I'm amazed that he was actually here for *your* wedding.' Felicia tossed her head. 'Don't look at me like that, Rosalind. I knew Piers Blanchard before you did and he took me in completely with his story about being the heir to the estate. A man who lies so glibly should never be trusted.'

Claude slipped his arm around her shoulders. 'Don't upset yourself, my love. Let's get you into the warmth with the benefit of some sustenance.' He gave Rosalind an apologetic smile. 'Your mama is exhausted after the long journey from Paris. We stopped there for a few days in order to visit the fashion houses.'

'I know my way to the drawing room,' Felicia said, walking off with her head held high. 'I lived here for many a long year when I was married to your father, Rosalind.'

Claude smiled apologetically. 'She doesn't mean half of what she says.'

Rosalind shook her head. 'You are too good for her, Claude. I know my mother so well – she says what she really means and the next minute she laughs and tries to pass it off as a joke. I'm past being hurt by her jibes.' She tucked her hand in the crook of his arm. 'Let's get you settled down by the fire and I'll make sure you have everything you need.'

'The weather really is closing in. I expect the roads will be impassable by morning.'

'That doesn't sound good, but please don't mention that fact to Patsy – she's anxious enough as it is. We can only pray for a thaw.'

They reached the drawing room in time to see Patricia leap to her feet and embrace her mother. 'Mama, you came. I knew you would.'

Felicia gave her a brief hug and then moved away, shaking out the creases in her travelling gown. Clouds of steam rose from her damp skirts as she sank down in a chair close to the fire. 'I'll probably catch my death of cold,' she said peevishly. 'I'm chilled to the bone and my voice will suffer in this abominable climate. If I had any sense I would live abroad.'

'No, no,' Patricia cried passionately. 'You must take care of yourself, Mama. I want you to be there when Alexander and I are married.'

'Where is the bridegroom?' Felicia glanced round the room. 'I hope he is here because the roads will soon be impassable.'

'He is on his way, Mama. Alex's regiment have been in the Eastern Mediterranean. It's a secret mission and none of us knows the exact details. Bertie is with him.'

'I always knew that Bertie would do something heroic. But are you sure you're doing the right thing marrying a soldier, Patsy?' Felicia folded her arms, shivering. 'It's so terribly cold in England and I can feel a draught.'

'You mustn't worry about me, Mama.' Patricia went down on her knees in front of her mother. 'It's lovely to have you at home again. You'll soon get warm.'

Rosalind sighed. 'I'll go to the kitchen and make sure a tray of tea is sent up immediately.'

'Don't forget the whisky,' Claude said in a conspiratorial whisper.

'I won't.' Rosalind smiled and hurried from the room. She made her way to the kitchen where she instructed Mrs Jackson to make up a tea tray, including a decanter of whisky. Having given Cook detailed instructions as to how Mrs Carey liked the bread to be thinly cut and lightly buttered, with a preference for potted meat rather than jam, Rosalind was satisfied that she had done all she could to keep her mother happy, at least for the moment. Thanks to Hester's foresight and years of experience, the beds in all rooms had been aired and made up in anticipation of the arrival of the wedding guests. Rosalind went to find Tilly and sent her to the west tower to light a fire in the room that Felicia and Claude were to share. Tilly scuttled off, eager to please and prove herself worthy of her recent promotion to chambermaid.

Walking slowly, Rosalind struggled to come to terms with her mother's sudden arrival. It had been a surprise, but then Felicia Carey never did what was expected of her. Rosalind was used to her mother's capricious temperament and although invitations had been sent, she had not expected her mother and Claude to accept. Felicia's presence created a problem. She had made it plain from the start that she considered Sir Lucius's marriage to his former housekeeper little more than an outrage and an insult to the family name. The thought of the two of them eyeing each other up like adversaries for the next three weeks or so was more than Rosalind could bear. She knew she must warn Hester, but how to do so without hurting her feelings was another matter. She found her, as expected, in the blue parlour.

Hester put down the garment she had been

mending and folded her hands in her lap. 'I'm glad your mama is here, if only for Patricia's sake, so don't worry about me.'

'But I do worry,' Rosalind said earnestly. 'I don't want you to be put in an awkward position, Hester. Mama didn't approve of your marriage to Grandpapa, and I know that nothing will change her mind.'

'Don't fret on my account. To be honest I think I agree with Madam Felicia, probably for the first time in my life. She's right: I don't belong at table with the rest of the family. I'll take meals in my room.'

'No, Hester. That's not necessary. I don't want you to be excluded.'

'What's the alternative, poppet? I've known your mama a very long time and while she's here I will keep out of her way.'

'It's all wrong,' Rosalind protested angrily. 'Mama will stay until Claude gets her a new booking and then she'll be gone again.'

'All I want is to be here with the family I love,' Hester said simply. 'I don't care about title and position. I'm still the same person I was before your grandfather and I were married. Let me do my job quietly and behind the scenes until after the wedding. When Christmas is over and your mama goes off on another tour, I'll think about taking my seat at the table.'

Rosalind rushed over to her and gave her a hug.

'You are the most wonderful person I know, Hester. But I can't allow you to do that.'

Hester stared at her blankly. 'It's my choice, not yours.'

'No. You're not going to be bullied into submission by anyone, least of all my mother. I know it sounds callous, but she's only here because she is between engagements, and it saves her the expense of staying in a hotel.'

'That's harsh, Rosalind. She is still your mother.'

'And I love her, but I'm not blind to her faults. Mama has never shown much interest in any of us, even Patsy, her favoured child. You, on the other hand, have always been here for us, Hester. You nursed us through our illnesses and you scolded us when we were naughty, and you were the one who bathed our cuts and kissed us better when we fell over.'

'I've always loved you all as if you were my own children, but that doesn't make me your mother. I don't want to cause any upsets, especially before the wedding.'

'I will be more upset if you hide away in your room as if you have something to be ashamed of. You are Lady Carey now and no one can take that away from you.'

'I would rather stay in the background and make sure that Patricia has a wonderful day to remember. Mrs Carey will rush off again when she gets the call to perform.'

Rosalind could see that Hester was not going to give in and, if she were being honest, it would be much easier to go along with Hester's plan. She shook her head. 'I don't like it, but you know Mama better than any of us.'

'Then you agree?'

'Yes, I do. But only until after the wedding. I want Patricia's happiness above all things.'

'And Captain Blanchard's, too?' Hester raised an eyebrow. 'You and he were very close a couple of years ago.'

'Don't bring that up again, please. I am very fond of my brother-in-law, and he did ask me to marry him, but I realised almost immediately that it was a mistake. I expect he's forgotten all about it, and so had I until you reminded me.' Rosalind turned away and walked to the door. 'I'd better make sure that the room is ready for Mama and Claude. They are engaged, by the way.'

'I'm surprised she didn't demand to have the master bedchamber.'

Rosalind left hastily. Hester knew them all so well, but she was wrong about Alex. That brief affair of the heart had been over for a long time. Piers was the man she had loved since their first encounter when they were both children. She had never forgotten the boy who had come ashore with the smugglers, and had shielded her from the hail of bullets raining down on the beach from the preventive officers on the clifftop. Next day he was gone, but he had returned many years later and now they were man and wife. She hoped that one day in the not-too-distant future they would have a family of their own, although this was not the time to think about herself.

She made her way to the largest guest room in the west tower where Tilly was adding coals to the fire. There was a definite chill in the air, but Rockwood Castle was notorious for draughts and ill-fitting windows.

Tilly scrambled to her feet. 'It'll soon warm up, Mrs Blanchard. I'd have lit it hours ago if I'd known your ma was coming.'

'I didn't know myself,' Rosalind said, smiling. 'Make sure they have plenty of coal and logs, Tilly.'

'Yes, of course, ma'am. Shall I start unpacking Mrs Carey's things? Jarvis didn't seem to think she had brought her maid.'

'Yes, make a start, if you will.'

Rosalind left Tilly to complete her tasks and she braced herself to face her mother again. She could only hope that Patricia would not fall prey to their mother's less-than-optimistic view of life. There was sure to be something wrong, whether it was the fact that Alex and Bertie had not yet arrived, or the minor irritation of being allocated the second largest bedroom in the castle.

Rosalind entered the drawing room to find her mother and Patricia chatting happily about the wedding arrangements, while Claude sat by the fire, reading a copy of *The Times*. He looked up and she could tell from his expression that something was wrong.

'Come and look at this, Rosie,' he said in a low voice.

'What is it, Claude?'

He brushed a stray strand of silver hair back from his forehead and held up the newspaper, pointing to an article on the front page. 'That's your brother's regiment, isn't it, Rosie? And Alexander's, too?'

'Yes, Claude. Alex was in the 32nd Regiment of Foot, but he was transferred to the same regiment as Bertie. They were due to return to England two days ago.'

Claude pointed to the small print, which swam before her eyes.

'The 46th Regiment of Foot were on their way back from the Mediterranean when their ship ran aground in the Bay of Biscay during a storm. It says there were many casualties.'

'No! I don't believe it. Surely we would have heard if the worst had happened?'

Claude fingered his waxed moustache nervously and lowered his voice. 'From what I've read I'm afraid it doesn't look good, my dear.'

Chapter Two

'Don't say anything to Patsy,' Rosalind said urgently. 'That is their regiment but it doesn't necessarily mean that Alex and Bertie were on that particular vessel.'

'It doesn't say how many survived, or even the number of injured.'

Rosalind leaned over to read the small print. 'But the soldiers and crew were taken to Brest – that's in northern France, isn't it? Someone in charge must have the list of casualties.'

'I imagine that the army will notify next of kin.'

'Don't say that, Claude. It makes my blood run cold to think about it.'

'We know nothing for certain.' Claude glanced out of the window. 'If this weather continues I don't think anyone will be travelling very far. I think postponement is going to be the only answer.'

'I won't rest until I know they are safe.'

'What are you two whispering about?' Felicia demanded.

'We were talking about the weather, Mama,' Rosalind said hastily. 'I hope it stops snowing soon or it will make travelling very hazardous, if not impossible.'

'What are you saying?' Patricia jumped to her feet. 'Alex will make it, even if he has to dig his way through snowdrifts.'

'Of course he will,' Rosalind said firmly. 'He has Bertie to help him, too.'

'You don't think the adverse weather will prevent our guests from coming, do you, Rosie?' Patricia clasped her hands together, her eyes magnified by tears.

'Of course not.' Rosalind made an effort to sound convincing. 'Can you imagine anything that would keep Lady Pentelow and Aurelia away?'

'No, I suppose you're right. Mama and Claude made it here.' Patricia sank back onto her chair with a sigh.

'I wouldn't miss your wedding for anything, my love.' Felicia reached for the decanter and poured a generous measure of whisky into her tea. 'This is purely medicinal, so don't look like that, Claude. I'd almost forgotten how cold this ancient pile can be in the winter. It's a wonder that Sir Lucius lived to such a grand old age.' Her smile faded. 'Where is Hester, by the way? I hope she won't presume on the fact that my late father-in-law chose to make an honest woman of her.'

'Hester took great care of him in his last few months, Mama.' Rosalind handed the newspaper back to Claude. 'However, she is very conscious of your feelings and she has decided to keep her distance during your stay.'

Felicia tossed her head. 'I should think so, too. She is a servant and always will be. They have a different way of looking at things from us, Rosalind. You would do well to remember that. Keep them in their place and the household runs smoothly. Treat them like an equal at your peril.'

Rosalind was tempted to argue, but she managed to control the urge. She knew from experience that nothing would change her mother's mind once she had made it up on any subject.

She rose to her feet. 'Your room should be ready now, Mama. I'm sure you would like to go upstairs and rest before dinner.'

'I'll go when I'm ready, thank you, Rosalind. By the way, I need someone to take care of me while I'm here. My maid, Smithers, abandoned me to marry some totally unsuitable fellow – an Italian who owned a restaurant near the cathedral in Milan. It won't last, and I told her so, but she was adamant that he was the love of her life.'

'I hope she'll be very happy,' Rosalind said firmly. 'Tilly has unpacked some of your garments, Mama. She's very young and still learning the duties of chambermaid, but she is very willing.'

'I suppose she'll do for the short time we intend to stay here. Winter in England is abominable. We plan to leave as soon as the festive season ends.'

'Really, Mama? Where are you off to next?' Patricia asked eagerly.

'I don't know yet. Claude handles all my business affairs. I dare say he has something in mind for me.' Felicia turned to him with an expectant smile. 'Preferably somewhere warmer than this foggy little island.'

'Not at present, my love. Although I'm considering Paris.'

'I do so love Paris. If you girls had not bound yourselves in matrimony you might have accompanied us to the city I adore. I could have found you rich husbands.'

'I'm perfectly happy with Piers,' Rosalind said sharply. 'And Patsy loves Alex. He's a fine man.'

'I'm sure he is.' Felicia did not sound convinced. 'But there is no sign of the prospective bridegroom as yet, and where is your husband, Rosalind? Surely he ought to be at your side, helping with the preparations for your sister's wedding? Or is the china clay business more exciting than married life?'

'It's the whisky talking, Rosie,' Claude said hurriedly.

'What did you say, Claude?' Felicia stood up, swaying slightly.

'I said I think you've had quite enough to drink, my love. You should rest before dinner. It was a long and tiring journey.'

'But at least we are here.' Felicia leaned on him as he proffered his arm. 'Which is more than I can say for Piers Blanchard and the rest of his family.'

'Come along, my love.' Claude gave Rosalind an apologetic smile. 'Are we in the usual room, Rosie?'

'Yes, Claude. The guest room in the west tower. Dinner will be at seven o'clock. We still dine early here in the country.'

'Perhaps we should have employed Smithers' Italian chef gentleman friend and brought them with us,' Felicia said darkly. 'At least we would be sure of good food, and I would have an experienced maid.'

Claude propelled her from the room, allowing the door to swing shut behind them.

'Oh dear.' Patsy sighed. 'Mama is going to hate everything. I knew she would.'

'It's just her way,' Rosalind said hastily. 'As Claude said, it was the whisky talking. Mama is exhausted and she'll be in a better mood when she's had a nap. I don't think she'll find anything to grumble about in Mrs Jackson's cooking, and Hester will make sure that only the best is served from now on. We're not relying on Bertie to go out and shoot a rabbit or a brace of pheasants for our supper.'

'Alex and Bertie should have been here days ago. I'm getting really worried now.'

'It's the weather, Patsy.' Rosalind crossed her fingers behind her back. It was only a half-truth, but for all she knew Alex and Bertie might not have been on the ship that was wrecked off the coast of France. They could arrive at any time. 'I'm sure they'll turn up soon.'

'Maybe Alex has changed his mind. He's been gone for months and he was in love with you before you married Piers. Maybe he still is.'

'Patricia Carey, you can stop that silly talk right away. Alex just *thought* he was in love with me, but it was a passing fancy. I'm very fond of him, and I'm sure he returns the affection in a brotherly way, but he's chosen to spend the rest of his life with you.'

'I'm scared, Rosie,' Patricia said tearfully. 'I was excited by the prospect of being an army wife and following my husband wherever he was sent, but now I'm not so sure. How will I cope in a foreign land without you?'

'You'll have Alex, Patsy. That's what being married is all about. Then eventually you'll have a family of your own to love and care for.'

'That scares me, too.' Patricia shot her a sideways glance. 'I worry that I might become a mother too soon. But you've been married for over two years and you haven't had a baby yet.'

'These things happen in their own good time,'

Rosalind said stoutly. She was not prepared to admit the disappointment she felt when her hopes were raised, only to be dashed each time she thought she might have conceived. If they had a child she was certain that Piers would spend more time at home, and he might even allow Pedrick to manage the mine on his own. Sometimes she felt that the business came first and she came a poor second. But that was unfair: Piers provided handsomely for them and he was keeping two households. He understood her love for Rockwood and had never reproached her for wanting to live in her ancestral home. He also realised that his grandmother ruled the household at Trevenor and would never relinquish her position to a younger woman. Piers was a good husband.

'Did you hear what I said, Rosie?'

Patricia's impatient voice broke into Rosalind's reverie and she came back to earth with a start. 'I'm sorry, I was miles away. But you mustn't worry about anything, Patsy. I'm sure that all brides have second thoughts so close to the wedding, but it's just an aggravation of nerves. When you see Alex again you'll know why you promised to marry him.'

'I hope so, Rosie. I just want to know that he's on his way. It worries me that we've heard nothing.'

Rosalind slid the newspaper beneath a cushion on the sofa. 'We have just over a week before the wedding. Alex will be here and so will Bertie.'

'You're right, of course. I'm just allowing my nerves to get the better of me.'

'There's nothing we can do other than wait. You should follow Mama's example and have a rest before dinner. I'll send Tilly to do your hair and then Mama won't be able to find anything to criticise.'

'You're so sensible, Rosie,' Patricia said with a reluctant smile. 'You always know what to do and what to say. I wish I were more like you.' She left the room and Rosalind retrieved the newspaper. The article blurred before her tear-filled eyes as she read it over and over again. She tore it into strips and threw them onto the fire, watching the paper curl and blacken in the flames. At least Patsy would not come across the terrible news by accident, but the destruction of the evidence did nothing to dispel Rosalind's fears. She had to keep busy and she returned to the escritoire to check her lists yet again. She was poring over them when Claude entered the room.

'Did you tell her?' he asked breathlessly. 'It doesn't bode well, Rosie.'

'I couldn't. She's in enough of a state without adding to her worries.'

'We don't know how long it took for the newspaper to get hold of the story. I'm sorry to be such a Job's comforter, but I can't help thinking that the groom is not going to make it for the wedding.'

'I know, but how can we find out? Or do we have to wait until the day of the ceremony?'

'I think we should wait for another couple of days.'

'Even supposing they're back in the country. The same goes for my husband. I don't know where he is at present. He was due home a day or two ago, but the ship might have been forced to seek shelter from the same storm, and anchored somewhere along the coast.'

'Try not to worry, my dear. There's nothing that any of us can do. We will just have to be patient, and try to keep up Patricia's spirits. That's one thing your mama is very good at.'

Rosalind eyed him curiously. 'Really?'

'When Felicia is on stage all eyes are on her. She commands the attention of the audience. I'm sure if you confide in your mother she will rise to the occasion, and Patricia will not have a moment to brood.'

Next morning Rosalind looked out of her bedroom window and was dazzled by the brilliance of the sun's reflections on a blanket of white snow. The storm had passed and there was a feeling of calmness in the cold air. Tilly had lit the fire but it barely took the chill off the room, and the water Rosalind poured into the flower-patterned bowl on the wash-stand cooled rapidly. She dressed hastily and wrapped a woollen shawl around her shoulders before she went downstairs to the dining room. To her surprise Claude and Felicia were already seated at table, tucking into bacon, eggs and devilled kidneys.

Felicia looked up and smiled. 'It appears that the

weather is on our side after all, Rosalind. The guests should be able to travel and I am ready to take charge of the wedding preparations.' She picked up a small silver bell and rang it.

Molly Greep appeared seconds later, as if she had been hovering outside, waiting to be summoned. She looked from Rosalind to Felicia.

'My coffee is cold and we need more toast.' Felicia waved her away with a flick of her hand.

'Thank you, Molly. That will be all for now.' Rosalind went to the sideboard and helped herself to buttered eggs before taking her place at the foot of the table, noting with a wry smile that her mother was seated at the head with Claude on her right.

'Did you hear what I said, Rosalind?' Felicia asked impatiently. 'I am taking charge of arrangements from now on.'

'I don't think that anything has been left to chance, Mama,' Rosalind said mildly.

'Nonsense. This old ruin is about as welcoming as the crypt of St Paul's. I can feel the ghosts from the past shuddering at the thought of guests arriving to such a bleak welcome. I've sent a message to Coaker, assuming he is still managing the grounds-men and gardeners?'

'Yes, Mama. He is.'

'I've told him to cut down holly and ivy, and we need a huge Christmas tree in the entrance hall, as well as one for the drawing room. Really, Rosie, I don't know why you haven't attended to decorating the reception rooms. That girl who's waiting on table – I don't know her name – I've told her to instruct Hester to have the decorations brought down from wherever they are stored these days.'

'The girl is Molly Greep. She's Farmer Greep's daughter and I'm training her as housemaid, but Hester is no longer a servant, Mama. You may not approve but I would ask you to treat her with the respect she deserves.'

Felicia bit into a slice of buttered toast. 'You know my opinion on that matter. I refuse to talk about it. Anyway, there are more important matters to attend to. I'm assuming that the guests will be arriving very soon. I want the castle to appear to be welcoming, if that's at all possible.'

'My dear, I don't think you quite realise the seriousness of the situation,' Claude said gently. 'It's possible that not even the groom will get here in time.'

'I would have persuaded Patricia to think again before she agreed to marry an army officer, but it appears that fate is on my side.' Felicia smiled smugly as she selected another slice of toast from the silver rack.

'Patsy loves Alex.' Rosalind filled her cup with coffee. 'She is fully aware of the difficulties she might face.'

'Don't be ridiculous. She's still a child, with no more knowledge of the outside world than a newborn baby. I sincerely hope that the groom does not show up on time, but we will be prepared for all eventualities. In the meantime I will do my best to change her mind for her.'

Rosalind looked round at the sound of the door opening, but it was only Molly with the coffee and more toast. She set them down close to Felicia and backed away.

'Did you pass on my instructions to those concerned? I'll know if you are lying.'

Molly bobbed a curtsey. 'Yes, ma'am.'

'That will be all, thank you, Molly.' Rosalind gave her an encouraging smile, which faded as she turned back to glare at her mother. 'Mama, please remember that you are a guest here these days. You will confuse the servants if you start giving them orders.'

'I'll thank you to remember that you have no real position in this household, Rosalind. Bertie inherited the title and the estate, and as his mother I am perfectly entitled to run things as I see fit. You and your husband are allowed to reside here thanks to your brother's generosity, but Piers Blanchard owns Trevenor, and that is where you should live.'

'Let's not go into that, my love,' Claude said nervously. 'I'm sure that Rosalind is fully aware of her position, and it really is none of our business.'

'That's where you are wrong, Claude. I lived in this crumbling edifice for many years after I foolishly agreed to marry Wilfred.' Felicia pushed her plate away and sat back in her chair, with a faraway look

31

in her hazel eyes. 'I gave up a wonderful career for what I imagined was true love.'

'But you've resumed your calling now, my love,' Claude said hastily. 'You are a star in your own right.'

'I was a child of fifteen when my talent was first noticed, Rosalind. I joined the opera company in London and I sang in the chorus at first, but I had my first major role when I was barely sixteen.'

'You were a child prodigy.'

'Yes, Claude, I was, and my greatest regret is that I married young and was burdened with an errant husband and constant child-bearing.'

'There are only four of us, Mama,' Rosalind said sharply. 'Some of the families in the village are far larger.'

'Don't compare me to the peasants, Rosalind. I was born a lady and I'll thank you to remember that.'

'Yes, Mama.'

'Don't roll your eyes, Rosalind. If I pulled a face when I was a girl, my governess used to say that if the wind changed I would get stuck that way.' Felicia rose to her feet. 'I'm going to the morning parlour. I hope there's a good fire burning because this room feels like an ice cave. If you happen to see Coaker, send him to me there.' Felicia marched out of the room without waiting for a response.

'I didn't mean to annoy her,' Rosalind said, sighing. 'But I can never please Mama, no matter what I say.'

'She's a very sensitive woman, Rosie. You have to know how to handle her.'

'I take your word for it. But what are we going to do, Claude? The guests will start arriving to-morrow, if the roads are clear.'

'I know it sounds flippant, but I suggest we deco-rate the Christmas tree when Coaker finds one large enough to suit Felicia. I think we should concentrate on making the place as festive as we possibly can. The only alternative is to tell your sister the truth.'

'I suppose you're right, but it's going to be difficult to keep cheerful in the circumstances.'

Claude laid his hand on her shoulder. 'You can do it, Rosie. Your mama is a great actress as well as a talented singer. Perhaps you've inherited some of her dramatic skills.'

'It's not funny, Claude.'

He smiled sadly. 'I know, my dear, but we must try to keep the news from them for as long as possible in the hope that all will be well.'

'I agree. I'll find the decorations and try to act as if everything is normal, at least for a day or two, but if we don't hear anything from Alex or Bertie soon I will have to tell Patsy about the newspaper article. I burned it last evening, by the way.'

'You did the right thing, my dear. We mustn't jump to conclusions.'

'I'm going to speak to Hester. She always gives me good advice.'

'And I'll go to the parlour and see if I can assist Felicia.'

'You're too good to her, Claude. She tramples all over you.'

He smiled. 'Maybe I like it like that, Rosie. Your mother is a good woman, despite her little ways.'

Rosalind watched him as he walked out of the room and she smiled to herself. She had not thought much of Claude when she first met him in her mother's dressing room at the opera house, but as she had come to know him better she had changed her mind. Claude was flamboyant and a larger-than-life character with his extravagantly pomaded silver hair, waxed moustache and dandified appearance, but a kinder and more loyal man she had yet to meet. He had supported her mother throughout the ups and downs of her career, and he never had a bad word to say about anyone. She was smiling in spite of the seriousness of the situation as she went to look for Hester.

Rosalind found her in the linen cupboard, checking items off a list.

'Hester, why are you doing that? You should leave such menial tasks to Annie. That's what she's here for.'

'Assistant housekeeper!' Hester said, curling her lip. 'Annie Hannaford is only seventeen. She should be serving in her father's shop. What qualifies a young girl to take over such important duties?'

'Annie will never learn unless you allow her to take over some of the simpler tasks, Hester.'

Hester placed the list on the shelf and stepped out of the linen cupboard. 'I suppose you're right, but I've been doing this for more years than I care to remember. I'm not the sort of person who can sit by the fire and embroider or read a book.'

'Neither is my mother, I'm sorry to say. She is determined to put her mark on the festivities and she's sending Coaker to cut down two fir trees and as much holly and ivy as he can find. Mama wants the Christmas decorations. Do you remember where we stored them last year?'

'Yes, of course. I supervised it myself because I wanted it done properly.' Hester shot a sideways glance in Rosalind's direction and smiled. 'All right, I know what you're thinking, but in this instance it's a good thing because I expect I'm the only one who knows that they are tucked away in the top room of the north tower. I'll fetch them now.'

Rosalind laid a restraining hand on Hester's plump arm. 'No, you won't. I'll go, and I'll take Tilly and Molly with me. The girls can carry the boxes and I'll supervise.'

'Do you want me to lock myself in the linen cupboard until your mother leaves for her next engagement?'

'Don't be cross, Hester. It was your idea to keep out of the way. I wanted you to take your rightful place, if you recall.'

Hester bowed her head. 'Yes, I'm sorry. But I knew that your mama would not approve and I didn't want to spoil Patricia's wedding preparations with a family disagreement.'

'The truth is that the wedding might have to be postponed.'

'Postponed? Why?'

'Claude showed me a newspaper article reporting a serious incident involving a troop ship. We don't know if Bertie and Alex were on board, but there were serious injuries and the survivors were taken ashore in the north of France.'

Hester frowned thoughtfully. 'But that's just supposition, Rosalind. They might be on their way home and have been delayed by the snow.'

'Yes, that's right, which is why we haven't told Patsy. But as each day passes it gets more and more likely that they won't arrive in time for the wedding.'

'There is still a week to go before the ceremony, although the guests who are staying here will start arriving very soon.'

'Yes, that's true and the rooms are ready. Everything depends on the state of the roads. I don't want to panic, but if Bertie and Alex were on that ship . . .'

'Best not to think that way, poppet. Perhaps your mama is right after all, and we should concentrate on making the castle as festive as possible. I'll get the younger ones to assist me in putting up the swags of holly and ivy, and perhaps you can persuade Patsy to help you decorate the tree. We must keep ourselves occupied and hope for the best.'

'You're right, and Walter can stop studying for once and do something useful. He might be in his second year at Cambridge, but he spends even more time with his head in a book.'

'I keep telling him he'll ruin his eyesight if he goes on like this, but you know your brother: he doesn't listen to anyone other than his tutors.'

'He'll have to pay attention to me now. He can help to bring the decorations down.'

'I'll go to the kitchen and make sure that Mrs Jackson has everything in hand.'

'I'm never going to persuade you to give up working am I, Hester?'

'Probably not, my pet. But perhaps you understand now that keeping busy is important if you are not to fret. After all, you must be worried about your husband. You haven't mentioned him in all this, but he's overdue, isn't he?'

'Piers isn't in danger, at least not as far as I know. I'm sure it must be the bad weather that's delaying his return. Pedrick would have contacted me if anything had happened to the ship.' Rosalind tried to sound positive, but she was as worried about Piers as she was about her brother and Alex. She left Hester to carry out her inspection of the kitchen, knowing that there would be ruffled feathers, but perhaps that was not a bad thing. At least Hester could be trusted to make sure that everything was done to a high standard that even Lady Pentelow could not fault.

Rosalind went to the library and dragged Walter away from his studies. They ventured up to the chilly north tower where the rooms were rarely used except for storage. The Christmas decorations were all packed neatly in tea chests and Walter carried the heaviest down the spiral staircase, leaving Tilly and Molly to bring the smaller boxes.

Rosalind followed with some of the more fragile pieces, but she came to a halt by the oriel window that overlooked the bailey courtyard. James, the footman, rushed out to open the great iron gates, and a carriage drawn by a pair of matched greys rumbled across the snow-covered cobbles. It was followed by another vehicle and a cart piled high with luggage.

'Walter,' Rosalind cried, leaning over the banister rail, 'I think Lady Pentelow has arrived.'

He looked up and groaned. 'Now I'll never get any peace. She may be Piers' grandmother, but that woman interferes with everything.'

'Never mind that. She might have heard from him or Alex.' Rosalind abandoned the box of decorations and ran down the last flight of stairs.

Chapter Three

Lady Pentelow sailed into the entrance hall, leaving a trail of snowy footprints on the marble tiles. She took off her fur cape and thrust it into Jarvis's arms.

'We've had the most abominable journey. Why your sister chose to get married at this time of year is quite beyond me, Rosalind.'

Rosalind smothered a sigh. 'Welcome to Rockwood, Lady Pentelow.'

'We've been travelling for three days,' Lady Pentelow said peevishly. 'I've had to sleep in unaired beds and consume questionable food.' She glanced round the unadorned space. 'You haven't bothered to make the place look welcoming.'

'That's all in hand. We weren't expecting you until tomorrow at the earliest.' Rosalind crossed her fingers behind her back. It was a lie, of course. She had known that the party from Cornwall would be arriving very soon, but she had more to worry about than putting up a Christmas tree. 'Won't you come to the drawing room, Lady Pentelow? I'll send for refreshments.'

'I'd rather go to my room. I suppose it is ready?' Lady Pentelow glanced over her shoulder as her granddaughter breezed into the hall. 'Don't loiter, Aurelia. Where is Simms?'

'She's helping Grainger, Grandmama. They're making sure that our luggage is unloaded carefully.' Aurelia turned to Rosalind with a wide smile. 'How lovely to see you again, Rosie. I still can't quite get used to thinking of you as Piers' wife, but that's because we see so little of each other.'

'As you've discovered, it's a long journey to Trevenor, and I'm kept very busy here.'

'Is there another reason why you can't travel?' Aurelia said pertly.

'Not yet, but you will be among the first to know when you're to become an aunt.'

'Aunt Aurelia! I'm not sure I like that.' Aurelia tossed her head and her glossy dark ringlets framed her oval face. She made a *moue*. 'It makes me sound like an old spinster.'

'That's something you will never be,' Rosalind said, smiling. 'You are not going to be left on the shelf, Aurelia. Hugo Knighton was a fool to choose Dorcas.'

'Our engagement was never official,' Aurelia said with a careless shrug. 'I was the one who broke it off, anyway.'

Lady Pentelow clicked her tongue against her teeth, frowning. 'You were well rid of that silly young man, Aurelia. He was not good enough for you. The Knightons are parvenus; your ancestors came over with Duke William. Anyway, why are we standing in the freezing entrance hall? Piers might have made improvements to this old ruin, but they are not apparent in this weather. Is this your idea of hospitality, Rosalind?'

It was useless to argue. Rosalind had learned that long ago. 'Follow me, if you will. It's nice and warm in the drawing room.'

'Where's Patsy?' Aurelia demanded eagerly. 'I want to see her now.'

'Where is Piers?' Lady Pentelow added, gazing round as if expecting him to materialise from the shadows. 'Why isn't he here to greet us?'

'I was hoping he might be with you.' Rosalind's voice broke as suppressed anxieties threatened to overwhelm her.

'Why would he be with us?' Lady Pentelow demanded crossly. 'He's your husband and he chose to live here in this crumbling old castle rather than Trevenor, his ancestral home.'

'Just a moment, Grandmama,' Aurelia said anxiously. 'Why isn't he here, Rosie?'

'He went on a business trip and I've been expecting his ship to return for days now. I thought perhaps they had taken shelter in St Austell Bay and he might be with you at Trevenor.'

'I suppose you're about to tell me that Alexander is also missing?' Lady Pentelow threw up her hands. 'I'll be very annoyed if we've had a wasted journey.'

'Alex hasn't arrived yet and neither has my brother. I'm hoping that with all three of them it's just the bad weather that's delaying their arrival.' Rosalind headed for the drawing room without waiting for a response. Her nerves had been on edge before the arrival of Lady Pentelow and now they were frayed to breaking point.

'What's wrong, Rosie?' Aurelia caught up with Rosalind as she entered the drawing room. 'Has something happened to Alex?'

'I hope not. I don't know any more than you do, but please don't say anything to Patsy. She's in a state about everything anyway.'

'What is it that you aren't telling us?' Lady Pentelow demanded, peeling off her gloves. 'Why isn't Alexander here?'

'I don't know, and that's the honest truth.'

'But you suspect something.' Aurelia caught Rosalind by the wrist. 'Tell me, Rosie. I'm not a child, and I want to know.'

'Please take a seat and I'll tell you all I know.' Rosalind tugged at the bell pull. 'There was an article in *The Times* regarding a troop ship that had gone aground off the coast of France during a terrible storm in the Bay of Biscay. I have nothing to confirm, nor can I refute the possibility that my brother and Alex were on board, but I am worried. Now you know, but as I said, please don't mention a word of this to my sister.'

'Why not?' Lady Pentelow unpinned her fur hat and laid it on a side table with her gloves. She sank down in a chair by the fire, glaring at Rosalind as if she was at fault. 'If your sister is old enough to be married, then she should be mature enough to cope with this situation. You can't treat her like a baby for ever.'

'Are you talking about me?' Patricia burst into the room. 'What have you been saying, Rosie? There's something you're not telling me. I know it.'

Aurelia slipped her arm around Patricia's shoulders. 'Patsy, sit down. Your sister has been protecting you with good reason, but I think you ought to know. What do you have to say to that, Rosie?'

Rosalind opened her mouth to reply but at that moment the door opened again and Felicia marched into the room, followed more slowly by Molly. 'I found this girl loitering outside the door. Do I take it you'd rung for her, Rosie?'

'Yes, I did. Please bring refreshments for our guests, Molly.' Rosalind turned to Lady Pentelow. 'Would you prefer tea or coffee, ma'am?'

'Coffee will do, and cake if there is any. I seem to remember your cook, Hester, made very good cakes.' Lady Pentelow hesitated, raising her hand to cover her lips. 'I'm sorry, I forgot that she had been elevated by a convenient marriage.'

'That is a subject we do not discuss,' Felicia said

coldly. 'My late father-in-law was not in command of his senses during the last ten years or so of his life.'

'That's not fair, Mama.' Rosalind turned to Molly with an encouraging smile. 'Just tell Cook that coffee and cake are required in the drawing room.'

Molly bobbed a curtsey and scuttled off, closing the door quietly behind her.

'I can see this is going to be an eventful stay,' Lady Pentelow said with a wry smile. 'Are you party to the deception, Felicia? Or did Rosalind take it upon herself to keep the truth from you *and* her sister?'

'I don't know what you're talking about.' Felicia looked from one to the other. 'Rosalind?'

'Please sit down and I'll tell you all I know.' Rosalind laid her hand on Patricia's shoulder. 'I wanted to keep it from you, Patsy. It's just possible that Alex and Bertie were on the troop ship that foundered off the coast of France.'

'What are you saying?' Patricia shook off her sister's restraining hand. 'Why didn't you tell me before? Were they on that ship or not?'

'I didn't say anything because we only found out from a newspaper that Claude brought with him. That really is all I know, Patsy.'

'But were they all saved? Were there injuries? What did it say, Rosie?'

'There was nothing specific.'

'Where is the newspaper? I want to see it.'

'Yes, we should read it for ourselves,' Lady Pentelow said gravely. 'You might have missed something.'

'I burned it.' Rosalind met her sister's angry gaze with an apologetic smile. 'I wanted to save you the worry, Patsy. It didn't give any more details, I promise you.'

'How do I know that you're telling the truth?' Patricia's voice rose an octave. 'You might think you're protecting me, but I'm not a child, Rosie. My fiancé was probably on board, and our brother. How can you remain so calm?'

'I'm not calm. I'm just as worried as you are, but until we have definite news there's really nothing we can do.'

'Nothing? Of course there's always something to be done. I want to travel to France to find Alex and Bertie. You should have thought of that – you were always the clever one.'

'For a start, we don't know for certain that they were on board, and even if they were, the article didn't say where the crew had landed. There is nothing we can do, Patsy. If there were, don't you think I would have taken steps to discover the truth?'

Patricia paced the floor. 'I don't know anything any more. I don't know what to do.'

'Why don't we go to your room and you can show me your wedding gown?' Aurelia said gently. 'Rosie's right, you know, Patsy. There's always hope. You don't even know that Alex was on that ship.'

'Why aren't you worried? He's your brother. And where is Piers? Why isn't he here to help us?'

Felicia stepped forward. 'You're getting hysterical, Patricia. I suggest you go to your room with Aurelia, as she suggests. Even if the boys were on that ship, it doesn't mean that they suffered any injuries. I'm anxious about Bertie, but creating a scene isn't going to help.'

'Alex would have been here by now if he could, or he would have sent a message somehow. It's all gone terribly wrong.' Patricia ran from the room, Aurelia hurrying after her.

'I'm sorry,' Rosalind said softly. 'I wanted to spare her that until we had some definite news.'

'The whole thing is a disaster. If you'll excuse me, Lady Pentelow, I want to speak to my fiancé.' Felicia walked slowly to the door, but she hesitated, glancing over her shoulder. 'Rosalind will see that you have everything you need.' She left the room.

Rosalind had a feeling that her mother was enjoying the drama of the situation despite her genuine concern for her son and daughter. She glanced at Lady Pentelow and was met with a stony stare.

'You could have sent word and saved us the trouble of travelling in such inclement weather, Rosalind.'

'They could still turn up at any moment, ma'am. Piers promised me that he would be home in time for the wedding and for Christmas.'

'I didn't know that my grandson had gone abroad. He tells me nothing these days.'

Rosalind was suddenly aware of footsteps and the rattle of china. She moved swiftly to open the door for Molly, who was carrying a tray laden with coffee and cake. 'Put it on the side table. That will be all for now, thank you.' Rosalind waited until Molly was out of earshot. 'Let's get one thing clear, Lady Pentelow. If you persist in criticising everything and causing trouble, I'll be forced to ask you to leave. You wouldn't behave like this if Piers were present, and I won't put up with bullying in my own home. Do I make myself clear?'

Lady Pentelow stared at her in wide-eyed astonishment. 'I beg your pardon, Rosalind. Do you dare to speak to me in that insolent manner?'

Rosalind filled a cup with coffee and handed it to her. 'There is no need for us to fall out. We should be supporting each other in this time of crisis.'

'I didn't approve of you marrying my grandson, and the passing of time has not changed my opinion.'

'I'm sorry you feel like that, Lady Pentelow, but Piers and I are happily married.'

'So you say, but where is he? A devoted husband would be at your side at a time like this.'

Rosalind snatched up the silver knife and stabbed it into the cake. 'Would you like a slice of seed cake, ma'am?'

Lady Pentelow glared at her as if about to refuse, but she seemed to relent, and she accepted the plate with a grudging nod.

Good manners prevented Rosalind from leaving the room, whatever the temptation. She sat down and poured herself a cup of coffee, while Lady Pentelow forked cake into her mouth, rendering herself speechless for a while at least.

Rosalind was trying to think of an excuse to leave when the door opened and Hester walked boldly into the room. She nodded to Lady Pentelow. 'Good morning, Lady Pentelow.'

'Hmm.' Lady Pentelow eyed her frostily.

'What is it, Hester?' Rosalind asked eagerly. 'Has the post arrived?'

'Not yet, but Coaker has brought two fir trees, Rosie. Would you like to choose which one you want for this room?'

Rosalind put down her cup and saucer and jumped to her feet. 'Yes, of course. You'll excuse me, Lady Pentelow. As you said, the festive spirit here is somewhat lacking. We are about to put that right.' She followed Hester to the great hall where Coaker was erecting a huge tree while a slightly smaller one was propped up between two suits of armour.

'It was a ploy to get you out of her clutches,' Hester said, chuckling. 'Molly told me that you were alone with the good lady, and I thought you might need rescuing.'

'You're an angel, Hester. She doesn't like me; she never did, although I believe she did try at first, but in her eyes no one would be good enough for Piers or Alex. Anyway, there's no call for her to be rude and ignore you. You are Lady Carey now and you should receive the respect due to your position.'

'It doesn't worry me. It's what I would expect from someone whose family money came from trade. She has no call to set herself up so high above others. That woman should be grateful that her grandsons have chosen to ally themselves to the Careys.'

'We'll forget her for the moment and decorate the tree. That's something I always enjoy.' Rosalind walked over to where Coaker was surveying his handiwork. 'That's a splendid tree, Abe. And the one for the drawing room looks equally good. You may put that one up when Lady Pentelow goes to her room, which will be soon, I think. In the meantime I suggest you go to the kitchen and charm Mrs Jackson into giving you a cup of tea. She might even let you have some cake.'

Abe nodded and grinned. 'I'll do that, Miss Rosalind.'

'What is the weather like now, Abe? Any sign of a thaw?'

'Aye, it's certainly warmer today and the snow was soft under foot.' Coaker picked up his cap and shambled off in the direction of the kitchen.

'What are you thinking, Rosie?' Hester put her head on one side. 'I know that look.'

'If the thaw really has set in and we don't get a sudden freeze, the roads should become passable quite quickly. If it's humanly possible I know that Alex will get here in time for the wedding.'

'And if he doesn't?'

'I don't know, Hester. There's nothing we can do, which makes me feel so helpless.'

'Take my advice and keep Patricia occupied. There are the two trees to decorate, for a start, and there's a big pile of holly and ivy in the flower room. We'll get through this, Rosie.'

At dinner that night Rosalind had a feeling that her mother was plotting something with Claude. They kept exchanging conspiratorial smiles and Felicia seemed to have forgotten her dislike of Lady Pentelow, going out of her way to include her in the conversation. Rosalind was suspicious and by the time they reached the end of the meal she was convinced that something was afoot.

'I think it's time the ladies withdrew,' Lady Pentelow announced, about to rise from her seat, but Felicia shook her head.

'Not now, ma'am. Claude and I have been discussing the present situation.' Felicia turned to Patricia with a tender smile. 'We know how worried you are, darling. Anyone in your position would be fraught with anxiety, but we have a suggestion.' She held up her hand as Patricia attempted to interrupt. 'No, let me speak. The wedding is booked and the guests are on their way here from all over the county, weather permitting. Claude and I will take your place at the altar, Patsy, darling. We intended to be married very soon and it's a pity to cancel the nuptials and all the arrangements that have been put in place. So we will get married and when Alex and Bertie get home you can have your day.'

There was a moment of silence before Patricia jumped to her feet with a cry of anguish. 'Mama, how can you even think of such a thing? Alex promised to be here in time and he will be.'

'My darling, it doesn't seem likely. Claude has confirmed what Rosalind told us about the newspaper article. I pray that Alex and my son are unharmed, but they are in the army and they can't do as they please. The chances of them getting here in such a short time are so remote that the only alternative would be to cancel the wedding and disappoint a great many people.'

'Do you really intend to take their place, Mama?' Rosalind demanded angrily. 'Have a thought for Patsy's feelings.'

'You can't take my wedding away from me,' Patricia sobbed. 'That's cruel, Mama.'

'It's unacceptable.' Lady Pentelow rose to her feet. 'My grandson would not approve.'

'Alexander is not here,' Felicia said sharply. 'He could have been here had he tried harder.'

'That's not fair, Mama.' Rosalind stood up and went round the table to hug her sister. 'Can't you see that this is upsetting Patsy? She's been sick with worry and you're making it worse.'

'I agree.' Walter pushed back his chair. 'I thought better of you, Mama. And you, Claude. Why did you allow her to do this?'

Claude shook his head. 'I can understand how you all feel, but surely it's a common-sense solution? The wedding was due to take place in a few days' time. There's no sign of the bridegroom and we have no way of communicating with him, even if we knew for certain where he is at present. Think of your mother for once, Patricia. Allow her to have her day, and yours will come soon enough when Alexander returns. If you cancel all the arrangements people might think you were jilted.'

Patricia covered her face with her hands. 'It's all so unbearable. I think I might die.'

'Nonsense.' Rosalind gave her a hug. 'That's silly talk. It's a postponement, after all, not a cancellation, and I'm sure people will understand. We can't go on waiting for news each day and getting more and more despondent when we hear nothing. I don't like the idea, but it has some merit, if you think about it.'

Patricia twisted free from her grasp. 'It doesn't. It's horrible and I hate you all for even considering it.' She ran from the room.

'I'll go after her,' Aurelia said hastily. 'I know what it feels like to be jilted. I'm the best person to be with her right now.' She followed Patricia from the dining room.

'Do you really think it's a good idea, Mama?' Walter eyed his mother angrily. 'You've really upset Patsy. Shame on you.' He stood up abruptly and walked out, leaving them staring after him.

Lady Pentelow shook her head. 'I don't know what you expected after making such an announcement, Mrs Carey, but I can't say I blame your son and daughters for the way they took the news.' She rose to her feet. 'This always was a strange household and you yourself are not a good example to your children.'

'What do you mean by that?' Felicia demanded.

'You live with this fellow openly. You abandoned your family to follow your own path without a thought for them. No wonder they have turned out as they have.' Lady Pentelow stalked out of the dining room, almost knocking over James as he was about to enter.

'Claude, say something,' Felicia cried, fanning herself vigorously. 'Are you going to stand by and allow me to be insulted?'

Rosalind turned to James. 'Not now. Come back later. I suggest you sleep on it, Mama. Maybe Alex and Bertie will turn up in time, and you, as always, will have put yourself first.'

'Don't lecture me, Rosalind. Let me remind you that you married a man who had been involved with smugglers at a very young age. More than that, he threatened to take away your inheritance and leave you and your brothers and sister destitute.'

'Piers never intended to evict us from our home,' Rosalind said hotly. 'His involvement with the gang came about because he was trying to save his father from going to prison. His father broke the law and Piers went out of his way to put things right.'

'Well, he's not here now, is he? Maybe your husband has run off with another woman,' Felicia said spitefully.

'That's quite enough, Felicia.' Claude had been silent until now but he was obviously angry and his sharp tone made Felicia turn to stare at him in astonishment.

'Claude?'

His stern expression relaxed into a half-smile. 'Harsh things are often said in the heat of the moment, my love. We are all tired and things will probably look better in the morning.'

Felicia eyed him coldly. 'I'm sure they will and I intend to go ahead with my plan. You must rise early and Gurney can take you to Exeter where you will get the train to London.'

'What are you talking about, Mama?' Rosalind asked wearily. 'Why send Claude to London?'

'He must visit Doctors' Commons and purchase a special licence so that we can be married instead of Patricia and her errant fiancé.'

'What will you do if Alex arrives in time, Mama?'

'If he does, we'll have a double wedding. My mind is made up. Claude has been wavering and shillyshallying for too long. It's high time we were legally wed.'

Rosalind turned to Claude. 'You don't want this now, do you?'

'It seems I have very little choice. But I would say that it costs a minimum of twenty guineas, Felicia, my love. If we spend that much on a licence it will mean that Paris is out of the question.'

'Then you will find me a part in London. I really don't care, Claude. But tomorrow you will do as I say or I will want to know the reason why. I'm tired and I'm going to bed.' Felicia rose from her seat and marched out of the dining room.

'Are you going to do as my mother says, Claude?' Rosalind asked anxiously. 'I mean this whole idea is mad. If we assume that Alex can't get home in time, what will the guests think if the wedding is all about my mother and you? What will it do to Patsy?'

Claude looked away. 'You know your mama as well as I do, Rosie. Do you imagine that anything I might say or do will make her alter course?'

'But it's not right.'

'I will go, Rosie. I'll get the licence to keep your mama happy, but I will use my time in London to visit the War Department in Whitehall. If anyone can give me information as to the fate of your brother and Alexander, I should be able to get it there.'

'That would be wonderful, Claude. Not knowing is the worst thing.'

'I agree, and it's one of the reasons I've decided to travel to London tomorrow. If I leave very early in the morning I should be back by nightfall, depending on how bad the conditions are further east.'

'I can't thank you enough for doing this.'

'I only wish I could do something for you, Rosie. You must be worried sick about your husband, but you never complain.'

'I am, of course, but his visits abroad often take much longer than anticipated. In a way I've grown used to never knowing when Piers will arrive.'

'Even so, I'm sorry for what Felicia said earlier. She had no right to upset you like that.'

'You don't have to apologise for my mother. I'm used to her ways, Claude. She often speaks out of turn and is usually very sorry for it afterwards. I don't expect anything else from her, if I'm to be honest.'

'If I have time I plan to call in at the Opera House on my way from Doctors' Commons to Whitehall. The manager is an old friend, and he might have a part to offer your mama in one of the future productions. With that and the special licence, it should guarantee to keep her happy for quite a while.'

'You spoil her, Claude.'

'She didn't have a happy start in life. Her mother performed at The Eagle in the City Road, London. She died of consumption when your mama was fourteen, leaving her to make her own way. That's how her talent was spotted at such a young age. She makes light of the hardships she suffered, but they were very real, I can assure you.'

'She's never spoken about her early years. All we've ever heard about were her successes. She never mentioned her parents.'

'I'm not sure she ever knew her father, or even who he was. I believe her mother was quite free with her favours, but it's easy to judge harshly. I can't begin to imagine how hard it would have been for a young woman to earn her living by singing in public houses or even on street corners. Your mama raised herself from the gutter to live in a castle.'

Rosalind smiled and shook her head. 'Even that didn't make her happy. But thank you for telling me all this. It does make it easier to understand her a little better.'

Claude drank the last of his wine. 'I should go to bed if I'm to be up early in the morning.'

'I'll send James to the stables to tell Gurney to be ready, but we'd better keep the fact that you intend to visit the War Department a secret from the others. I don't want to raise Patsy's hopes only to have to dash them again should there be bad news.'

Chapter Four

Claude did not return that evening as Rosalind had hoped, and there was still no word from either Piers or Alex. Felicia` was determinedly planning her wedding and Patricia refused to leave her room, despite attempts at persuasion from Rosalind and Aurelia. The trays of food that Hester lovingly prepared to tempt Patricia's appetite were sent back to the kitchen untouched, and by the next morning Rosalind was beginning to worry about her sister's health. An air of gloom hung over the castle, making a mockery of the beautifully decorated Christmas trees, the swags of holly and ivy and the bowls of richly coloured chrysanthemums that had arrived from Greystone Park. The accompanying note from Sir Michael, wishing Rosalind the compliments of the season, confirmed the fact that he had long forgiven her for spurning his advances. She toyed with the expensive sheet of writing paper, reading it for a second time. 'Hester, I have an idea.'

'I hope it's a good one, poppet. Your sister will waste away if she carries on like this.'

'If anyone can talk sense into Patsy it will be Christina Greystone. They were always close, even when Sir Michael took against me. I'm going to ask Gurney to saddle up my horse and I'll ride over to Greystone Park this morning. The thaw seems to have set in and the roads should be passable.'

'Shouldn't you wait for Claude to return from London? Maybe he'll have good news.'

'But what do we do if he hasn't any information about Bertie and Alex? I can't sit back and watch while my sister starves herself to death. Mama says she'll eat when she's hungry, but Patsy isn't a six-year-old. She's afraid that something has happened to Alex, and the prospect of Mama and Claude getting married in her stead is simply too much for her.'

'But will Christina be able to do anything? Aurelia has tried, as have you, but Patricia won't even allow me into her room.'

'Have you any better ideas? Sir Michael has a seat in Parliament and maybe he can use his influence with the War Department to find out what's happened to Bertie and Alex. That's if Claude has not had any success.'

'I really don't know, but perhaps it will do you good to get away from here for an hour or two.

How you keep patience with Lady Pentelow is beyond me. If she continues to carp and criticise everything I might forget I'm a lady now and tell her a few home truths.'

Hester's comical expression made Rosalind laugh in spite of the dire situation. 'Don't do that. I have to bite my tongue when she's being difficult, but she will be returning to Trevenor in the near future.'

'None too soon for my liking.'

'Remember you're Lady Carey now, Hester. I don't want any fights when I'm out.'

'Will you tell your mama where you're going?'

Rosalind shook her head. 'I doubt if she'll even notice that I'm not here. I won't be long. I can't stay at home doing nothing.'

The roads were passable with care and Rosalind's sure-footed bay mare seemed to know the best path to tread with very little guidance. Greystone Park looked even more impressive as it rose from the snow, its red bricks warmed by the winter sun. A stable boy came running from the coach house and led Sheba away. Rosalind stamped the snow off her boots as she mounted the steps and the heavy oak door opened before she had a chance to raise the lion's-head door knocker. If Sir Michael's butler was surprised to see Rosalind he was too well trained to show a flicker of emotion.

'I would like to see Sir Michael, if he is at home, Foster.'

'Of course, Mrs Blanchard. If you would care to wait here?'

Rosalind paced the floor. She would have to tell Sir Michael everything, but perhaps that was a mistake. The whole village would know soon enough that Patricia's wedding to Alex was postponed and that Felicia Carey and her manager would be taking their place. She was trying to think of an excuse to leave when Foster reappeared. Whatever doubts she felt, it was too late now, and she was left with little choice other than to follow him to Sir Michael's study.

He rose to his feet, smiling. 'Rosalind, this is a delightful surprise. Do take a seat.'

'I came to thank you for the beautiful flowers, Sir Michael. It was a kind thought.'

'I'm glad you like them. Our kitchen garden has produced an excess of blooms this year, or so I'm told.' He put his head on one side, eyeing her curiously. 'But that isn't why you're here, is it? A note would have been enough.'

'No, you're right.' Rosalind clasped her hands in front of her. 'You've probably heard that my brother and brother-in-law have not yet returned.'

'You know how things are in Rockwood village, Rosalind. I don't listen to gossip, of course, but Christina did mention it at breakfast this morning. With the wedding being imminent she is worried about Patricia. Do you plan to postpone the ceremony?'

'That would be the obvious choice. However, things have changed.'

'In what way? I don't understand.'

'My mother intends to ask the vicar to perform the ceremony as arranged, but it will be for herself and her manager, Claude de Marney.'

Sir Michael's eyes widened. 'Your mother is taking Patricia's place?'

'I don't need to go into details, Sir Michael. The truth is we don't know what has happened to Bertie and Alexander. We think they were on a troop ship that got into trouble off the coast of France and they may have landed near Brest, but we have no more information.'

'And you were wondering whether I could help?'

'Claude went to London yesterday, intending to get a special licence to marry my mother, but also he said he would try to get some information from the War Department.'

'Was he successful?'

'I don't know. He hadn't returned when I left to come here, but if he didn't succeed I would be very grateful for your help.'

'I am always ready to assist you in any way possible, but there's something else, I can tell.'

'Patsy won't come out of her room and she refuses to eat. I wonder if you will allow Christina to come to Rockwood and speak to her. They were always close and Patsy might find it easier to talk to Christina.'

'I don't wish to sound unkind, Rosalind, but surely your mother is the person to deal with Patricia? It seems that she is exacerbating the situation by her actions.'

'Mama can see nothing wrong in what she's doing, Sir Michael. She simply cannot understand why Patsy is so upset.'

'I'm sorry to hear that.' Sir Michael resumed his seat behind his desk. 'Families can be very difficult, as I know from past experience, but that's another story. I'm sure that Christina will be only too happy to help, if she can.'

'And if Claude has no luck with the War Department, could you give me any advice? I really don't know what to do next.'

'Parliament is in recess for the Christmas period. I had not planned to travel to London, but I will write to the War Department and see if I can find out anything more than you know already.'

'Perhaps Claude will bring news. I hope so, anyway.'

Sir Michael reached for the bell pull. 'I can see by your outfit that you rode here. However, I'd prefer to send Christina to Rockwood Castle in my carriage. I expect Sylvia will want to accompany her. Do you mind?'

'Not at all. May I speak to them?'

'Of course.' Sir Michael looked up as Foster entered the study. 'Are my daughters in the drawing room?'

'No, Sir Michael. I believe they are in the long gallery.'

Rosalind stood up. 'I know the way.'

'Send for the chaise, Foster. My daughters will be visiting Rockwood Castle.' He rose to his feet. 'I'll accompany you to the long gallery, Rosalind.'

She would have preferred to go on her own, but Sir Michael had agreed to help them and she managed a polite smile. 'Thank you, sir.' She left the study, making her way through the oak-panelled corridors to the entrance hall and Sir Michael fell into step beside her.

'I know you are a happily married woman, Rosalind, but do you ever regret turning me down?'

'What sort of question is that, Sir Michael?'

'Your husband seems to spend a great deal of time away from home. That must be hard for you to bear.'

'Piers has a business to conduct. I have no complaints.'

'And yet it's almost Christmas, your brother and brother-in-law are missing, but Piers still has not returned to support you during this difficult time.'

Rosalind came to a halt, clutching the banister rail so hard that her knuckles showed white beneath her skin. 'That is none of your business, Sir Michael. Perhaps I made a mistake in coming here today, but I thought we were old friends.'

'We've had our ups and downs, but I've known you since you were born. I think that entitles me to make a sound observation. I'm sorry if I caused offence.'

'Would you mind if I went to speak to the girls on my own? I'd find it easier to tell them what has happened if you were not present.'

'I can see that I've upset you. I am sorry, Rosalind. Please speak to my daughters. I know they will want to help.' Sir Michael turned away and descended the stairs, leaving her to make her own way to the long gallery.

Christina and Sylvia were playing with a ball, endangering the priceless statues that graced the long gallery, but they stopped when they saw Rosalind.

Christina hid the ball under a chair. 'Papa doesn't approve of us playing games in the long gallery. He's afraid we might break one of his precious figurines, so I hide the evidence.'

'Have you come to luncheon?' Sylvia asked eagerly. 'Can you stay awhile?'

'We heard that Alexander and your brother have not returned,' Christina said cautiously. 'Is it true, Rosie?'

'I'm afraid so. We think they might have been on a troop ship that foundered in the Bay of Biscay. The crew were taken ashore, but that's all we know so far.'

'Poor Patsy,' Christina said sadly. 'She must be distraught.'

'She is and that's why I came here today. She refuses to leave her room and she won't eat. Please come to Rockwood and talk to her. She might listen to you, Chrissie. After all, we don't know anything for certain.'

'Alex and Bertie could arrive at any moment,' Sylvia said hopefully. 'They might be on their way but have been delayed by the weather.'

'Surely the most sensible thing would be to postpone the wedding,' Christina added.

'Yes, of course, but the fact is, our mother has decided to take Patsy's place at the altar. She says it would be a shame to cancel the arrangements at such short notice.'

Christina and Sylvia exchanged horrified glances.

'I think I'd lock myself in my room if that happened to me.' Christina rolled her eyes. 'Your mama is extremely thoughtless, Rosie. I hope you don't mind me saying so.'

'I agree, but that's how she has always been and she won't change. I've tried to convince Patsy that she will have her day when Alex returns, but she thinks everyone will be laughing at her if the wedding takes place.'

'I'll be very angry if I hear any gossip,' Sylvia said firmly. 'We'll come with you, won't we, Chrissie?'

Christina nodded. 'Yes, of course.'

'That's wonderful. I think talking to both of you will help Patsy to see things differently. Your papa has sent for the carriage. I came on Sheba, so I'll go on ahead and wait for you at home.'

'Does your mama want us to be her bridesmaids?'

Sylvia asked, frowning. 'It would be a pity to waste our new gowns.'

'For heaven's sake, Sylvie, don't be so naïve.' Christina tossed her head. 'Really, could you say anything sillier? Of course we'll wear our gowns, but we'll wait until Patsy marries Alex.'

'I knew I could rely on you for sound common sense, Chrissie,' Rosalind said, smiling.

Despite the luxury and warmth of Greystone Park, Rosalind sighed with relief when she walked into the great hall of Rockwood Castle. The chill of winter permeated the old stones, and there was always the slight smell of damp that no amount of lavender polish could completely eradicate, but it was home. Even the rusty suit of armour seemed to welcome her with a toothless grin. She closed Sir Denys's visor as she walked past. 'Good day to you, sir,' she said softly. 'You might find the current situation amusing, but I don't.'

She looked up to see Jarvis hurrying towards her, and she handed her fur-lined cape and gloves to him. 'Has Mr de Marney returned?'

'Yes, Mrs Blanchard. He's in the drawing room.'

'Thank you, Jarvis.' Rosalind could not wait to find out if Claude had any news and she went straight to the drawing room, but she came to a halt in the doorway, hardly able to believe her eyes. Claude was standing by her mother's chair, but she looked past him. Walter was grinning broadly and standing next to him was a tall young man in army uniform with his cap tucked under his arm. His golden brown eyes gleamed with pleasure and his generous mouth curved into a smile.

Rosalind's heart missed a beat. 'Bertie!' She ran to her brother and threw her arms around him, holding him so tightly that he protested.

'Hold on, Rosie. What have I done to receive such a welcome?'

'We didn't know if you were alive or dead,' she said, halfway between tears and laughter. 'There was an article in *The Times* about a troop ship that came to grief off the coast of France.'

'That was us, but as you can see I'm here and I'm unhurt.'

'It takes more than a shipwreck to kill a Carey,' Walter said, chuckling. 'He's taken us all by surprise, Rosie.'

'Yes, indeed.' Felicia raised Claude's hand to her cheek. 'Bertie and my dear husband-to-be arrived together.'

Rosalind glanced round the room as if expecting to see Alexander hiding behind a column. 'But where is Alex? Why isn't he here?'

'I'm afraid he was injured,' Bertie said warily. 'But he's being well treated in a French hospital.'

'Was he badly hurt? Have you told Patsy?'

'He has a broken leg, and he can't be moved until the doctors say so. I haven't been to see Patsy yet. We only got here a short while ago.'

Claude cleared his throat. 'Hester has gone to give Patricia the good news.'

'My daughter won't speak to me,' Felicia said crossly. 'I don't know why, especially when I have something really lovely to tell you all.'

Rosalind knew exactly why her sister wanted nothing to do with their mother, but she knew it was pointless to say anything. 'What is it, Mama?' she asked wearily.

'The vicar called to see me while you were out. He said he will be pleased to conduct our marriage ceremony, even though it's such short notice. I did promise that Claude would give a generous contribution to the church's restoration fund, but it's all settled and Claude has come home with the licence. So all is well and Patricia will soon get used to the idea.'

'Let's hope so, Mama.' Rosalind turned to Bertie. She was so happy to see him unharmed, although he was pale with fatigue and dark shadows underlined his eyes. She drew him down onto the sofa beside her. 'Tell me everything. What happened to you? How did you meet up with Claude?'

'We met on the railway station,' Bertie said with a hint of his old wry humour. 'I don't know who was more surprised.'

'Isn't it wonderful to have Bertie safe and sound?' Felicia clapped her hands. 'Now we will all be together for our wedding, Claude.'

Bertie eyed his mother, frowning. 'Do you really

intend to go ahead with the arrangements, Mama? Don't you think in the circumstances it would be better to wait until after Christmas?'

'No, why should we? Oh, if you mean Patricia will be upset by it, she will be so delighted to know that her fiancé isn't badly injured that she will forget to be angry with me.'

'Will you please tell me the whole story?' Rosalind said impatiently. 'You said that Alex is in hospital. Where is it exactly?'

'It's outside a town called Brest. We were crossing the Bay of Biscay in a violent storm when our ship was in collision with another, and both vessels were driven onto the rocks. It was a nightmare and I really thought I was going to die, but eventually we were rescued and taken ashore in an armada of small craft.'

'We must bring Alex home,' Rosalind said thoughtfully. 'Surely the army will help?'

'There's something else I should tell you, Rosie.' Bertie's smile faded.

'What is it?' Rosalind was suddenly nervous. She could always tell when Bertie was keeping something from her. 'Tell me, please.'

'Piers was a passenger on the other ship. He was amongst the survivors, but his condition is grave. They are both in the same hospital.'

Rosalind stared at him in disbelief. 'Are you sure it was Piers?'

'Yes, I saw him and I spoke to him, although I'm

not sure how much he could understand. He has a head injury, Rosie, and inflammation of the lungs, or that's what I understood from the doctor in charge. Although you know me, my knowledge of French is very limited.'

'You were never a good student,' Felicia said casually. 'At least Piers has survived, Rosalind. There's no need to look as if it's a tragedy. He'll recover, no doubt, and come home when he's well again. It's a pity he won't be here for the wedding, but now we can go ahead without upsetting Patricia.'

'Mama, you can't mean that?' Rosalind said slowly. 'Haven't you any feeling for others?'

'Don't be impertinent, Rosalind. You might be a married woman, but I am still your mama.'

'Patricia's fiancé is in hospital in a foreign country and my husband is seriously ill. I will not apologise for speaking my mind.'

Claude laid a restraining hand on Felicia's arm as she was about to jump to her feet. 'I was sorry to hear about Piers' illness, Rosie. At least he's in the right place. Bertie assures me that it's a good hospital.'

'He's getting the best care,' Bertie added quickly. 'I told them that money was no object when it came to my brother-in-law's wellbeing.'

'Thank you, Bertie.' Rosalind stood up. 'I'm going to see how Patsy has taken the news.' She walked purposefully to the door. 'By the way, Christina and Sylvia will be here soon. Perhaps you could entertain them for a while, Claude? They can see Patsy later.'

'I'll come with you.' Bertie followed her from the room. 'Are you all right, Rosie? I know it must have been a shock to learn that Piers is in hospital, too.'

'I've been so worried. I knew that something awful must have happened to keep him away for so long, especially with Christmas so near.'

Bertie slipped his arm around her shoulders. 'I had permission from my commanding officer to return to Rockwood to tell you about Piers. I couldn't do anything in France, but now I'm back in Devon we can work out a way to bring them both home.'

'He's very ill, isn't he? You don't need to pretend for my sake, Bertie.'

'Yes, I won't lie. His condition is very serious.'

'I don't want you to tell the others.'

'What are you going to do? I know that look.'

'I want you to make enquiries at the quay. I'll pay handsomely for passage to France. I'm not going to leave Piers and Alex in a foreign hospital. I'll bring them home even if I have to do it by myself.'

'I'll help you. I have a short leave of absence, but I have to return to my regiment soon.'

'Don't say a word to anyone, especially Patsy. She can't know what we're planning.'

'I agree. I won't say a word.'

Patricia was sitting up in bed, sipping a cup of hot chocolate.

'You're feeling better,' Rosalind said with a sigh of relief.

'I am, but I'm cross with Alex for not letting me know sooner.' Patricia placed the cup back on its saucer and laid it on the side table. 'I'm still not happy about Mama and Claude taking my wedding away from me.'

Bertie perched on the edge of the bed. 'That's a bit unreasonable, Patsy. You would have to postpone the wedding anyway, unless of course you plan to travel to France and marry Alex in his hospital bed.'

'You're not funny, Bertie. I'm glad to see you, of course, but you could be a bit more sympathetic.'

Rosalind shook her head. 'I think the time for sympathy has passed. You should get up, have a wash and get dressed. Christina and Sylvia will be here any minute now and they won't want to see you looking like this. Alex has suffered a broken leg and you should be glad that his injuries weren't more severe.'

'Don't lecture me, Rosie. I have a headache.'

Bertie stood up. 'It seems to me that you're enjoying the attention, as always, Patsy. Get up and try to look happy for Mama and Claude. Put a brave face on it and let them make use of all the preparations, or are you going to behave like a spoilt child for ever?'

Patricia's blue eyes welled with tears and her pretty mouth drooped at the corners. 'You're mean, Bertie.'

Rosalind was about to step in to prevent an argument when a tap on the door made her turn away. 'Come in.'

Christina and Sylvia burst into the room. Christina laid a bunch of hothouse lilies on the side table. 'You poor thing, Patsy. How you must have suffered, but at least you have some good news now.'

Sylvia laid a basket of oranges on the coverlet. 'We didn't have time to get anything more interesting, but these are from our orangery.' She sat on the edge of the bed. 'You look awful. You need cheering up.'

Patsy managed a watery smile. 'I'm bearing up, but Bertie is being horrible. You're lucky to have each other and no brothers to bully you.'

Christina shot a sideways glance at Bertie and her cheeks flushed prettily. 'I don't know . . . I think you're lucky to have such a handsome brother.'

Bertie laughed. 'I hope you'll save the first dance at the wedding for me, Chrissie.'

Her blush deepened. 'Of course.'

'We'll leave you to chat,' Rosalind said hastily. 'See if you can persuade Patsy to get dressed, Chrissie.'

'I'll see you at dinner, Patsy.' Bertie leaned over and kissed the top of her head.

Rosalind waited for him outside the room. 'Patsy will get her grand wedding when Alex is fully recovered, but I'm really worried now, Bertie. Is Piers' life in danger?'

'All I know is that he's in good hands. Alex is there to keep an eye on him.'

Rosalind shook her head. 'I'm worried, Bertie. Everything you say makes me think I should leave as soon as possible.'

'You can't think of going before the wedding, surely? Mama would never forgive you.'

'And I would never forgive myself if Piers took a sudden turn for the worse and I wasn't there to comfort him.'

'If you go to France you'll have to take Patsy. She'll be desperate to see Alex.'

Rosalind walked on slowly. 'I don't know about that.'

'You'll have to tell her what you're planning.'

Rosalind stopped outside her bedroom door. 'Bertie, stop putting obstacles in my way. I have to change out of my riding habit now. We'll talk later.'

'All right, but think about it, Rosie. Another two or three days isn't going to make much difference. Speaking selfishly, I would love to spend some time at home with my family, especially at Christmas.'

'You don't have to accompany me, Bertie. I'm quite capable of coping on my own. I just need to find a boat to take me straight to Brest. Anything else would take too long.'

Rosalind opened her bedroom door and went in, closing it before Bertie had time to argue. Her mind was made up. Nothing would keep her away from her husband and the man she had once thought she might marry. Both of them were dear to her and she could not bear to think of them suffering on their own in a foreign country.

She changed quickly into a blue tussore afternoon gown. As always in times of need or family crisis it was Hester to whom everyone turned and today was no exception. Rosalind found her, as she had expected, in the blue parlour.

'It is good news, isn't it, poppet?' Hester said, pouring tea into two cups.

'It's wonderful that both Piers and Alex survived, but Bertie thinks that Piers' condition is serious. I must go to him, Hester.'

'Do you mean right away? Before the wedding?' Hester added milk and passed the cup and saucer to Rosalind.

'As soon as I can find a boat whose skipper is willing to take me to France.'

Hester sipped her tea, eyeing Rosalind over the rim of the cup. 'And I suppose you want me to use my influence with the fishermen to find someone willing to take us to France?'

'I was hoping you would, but I'm going on my own, Hester.'

'Oh, no, you're not, poppet. If you take on that hazardous journey you're not going alone. I'm coming with you, and that's that!'

Chapter Five

The remaining patches of snow gleamed palely against the night sky, but the village slept as Rosalind and Bertie circuited the wood, making their way to the quay.

'I hope that Harry Mudge is waiting, as he promised,' Rosalind said in a low voice. 'I might not be able to get away so easily next time, should we have to postpone this trip.'

Bertie held out his hand to help her across a stile. 'Mudge is a reliable fellow, unlike his cousins.'

'Jacob and Seth will be locked up in the county prison for a long time to come. They were lucky not to be transported when they were convicted of smuggling.'

'Wait for me,' Hester caught up with them, gasping for breath. 'I'm not as young as I was.'

'I'm sorry,' Rosalind said guiltily. 'I don't want Harry to think we've changed our minds.'

'You don't have to do this, Rosie.' Bertie relieved her of her valise. 'You could come home with me now, and no one will be any the wiser.'

'This is the only way,' Rosalind said, sighing. 'I know you mean well, Bertie, but Piers is ill and at the mercy of strangers. I can't sit at home and leave him to suffer.'

'Mama will be upset that you're missing her wedding.'

'I doubt if she'll even notice I'm not there.'

'What about Patsy? I'm not sure I'll be able to deal with her tantrums on my own. I'd feel safer facing the Russian Army.'

'You'll cope admirably,' Rosalind said, chuckling. 'And Patsy will come round eventually. Come on, Hester. We have to do this for Piers and Alex.'

They made their way carefully across the clifftop, heading for the well-worn steps that led down to the fishermen's quay. A chill wind slapped at Rosalind's cheeks and her full skirts hampered her progress, but she was undeterred. Bertie went first, guiding Hester, followed by Rosalind. A shadowy figure was waiting for them on the quay wall.

'There's Mudge. I've paid him for his trouble.'

'Thank you, Bertie. I couldn't have done this without your help. I'm sorry to leave you with all the recriminations you're bound to get from both families.'

'I'm a soldier – I've been through worse. I'll just have a word with Mudge and then we'll get you two aboard, but you can still change your minds. I won't think any the worse of you for that.'

Rosalind shook her head. 'I'm going to France, Bertie. Hester must do as she wishes.'

'I'm coming with you, poppet,' Hester said firmly.

'That's settled then.' Bertie strode off and Harry Mudge walked slowly to meet him. After exchanging a few words Bertie turned and beckoned to them.

'Come on, Hester. Let's hope the sea is calm to-night.' Rosalind was suddenly nervous, but she made her way carefully over the slippery ground to greet Mudge with a cheerful smile. 'Good evening, Harry.'

'Evening, ma'am. It's a fine night, but it might be a bit choppy mid Channel.' He helped her into the boat before turning his attention to Hester. 'You next, miss.'

She allowed him to help her onto the deck. 'Did I tell you I'm not a good sailor, Rosie?'

'No, but thank you for warning me.' Rosalind waved to Bertie. 'Goodbye. Wish us luck.'

He answered with a cheery wave.

'I'm going to cast off now, ma'am,' Harry said politely. 'I suggest you two ladies go into the saloon. Me and the boy will do the sailing. The wind and tide are on our side so we should make good time, but once we make landfall in Brest you'll be on your own. You still have time to change your minds.'

Rosalind glanced up at Bertie, who was standing

on the quay, watching them. She shook her head. 'Just get us there, please. But I won't forget what you're doing for us.'

'To think I nearly married into that family.' Hester wrapped her cloak more tightly around her plump body. 'Jacob Lidstone courted me for years, but it was all a pretence. He was as guilty as his cousins.'

'They're paying the price now, Hester, and you had a lucky escape.'

'Your dear grandpapa kept me safe, Rosie. I could tell him everything and he always understood, even when his mind was going.'

'You'd best find cover, ladies,' Harry said gruffly.

'Let's do what he says and keep out of his way.' Rosalind gave Hester a gentle push towards the somewhat grandiosely named saloon, which in fact was just a small cabin built amidships, but at least it was shelter, and as the vessel edged its way out to sea Rosalind was very grateful for protection from the wind and spray. Hester began to feel sick quite soon, and Rosalind gave her the bucket that Harry had thought to provide as it was too danger-ous to allow Hester to wander around the deck in the dark. Eventually Hester seemed to recover a little and dozed off, leaving Rosalind to snatch a couple of hours' sleep.

They were put ashore next morning and Rosalind used the smattering of French that she had learned from her old governess, Miss Brailsford, to give a cab driver instructions to take them to the hospital on the outskirts of the town. There was a small café nearby where they drank coffee and ate sweet pastries before venturing into the hospital, which turned out to be part of a convent.

Hester posed as Alexander's mother, although the nun on duty eyed her suspiciously when she gave her name as Lady Carey. However, Rosalind stepped in to confirm Hester's title and she demanded to see her husband. Eventually a younger, fresh-faced nun was summoned and she led them to a large ward with a high vaulted ceiling and stained-glass windows. The smell of dampness and incense mingled with the strong odour of carbolic. The male patients lay listlessly in their narrow iron beds, following every move that Rosalind and Hester made with curious stares. The silence was broken by the occasional groan, and Rosalind found herself tiptoeing towards the bed where Alex lay with his right leg encased in plaster. He met her eager smile with a dazed look in his eyes, which had dulled to moody umber in the half-light.

'Am I dreaming? Are you real, Rosie?' His face was pale with the skin drawn tightly across his high cheekbones, but his smile was genuine. 'Is Patsy with you?'

'She's made herself ill with worrying about you, Alex,' Rosalind said tactfully. 'She wasn't in a fit state to make the sea journey.'

He pulled a face. 'That doesn't sound like the Patsy I know. I imagine she is more upset that the wedding has had to be postponed. It would take a miracle to get me back to Rockwood in time.'

'Don't worry about that now. You can make it up to her when you're fully recovered.' Rosalind moved closer. 'Are you in much pain?'

'Not unless I try to move, but how did you get here?'

'I hired a fishing boat to bring us from Rockwood,' Rosalind said in a low voice.

He shook back a lock of honey-coloured hair and reached out to hold her hand. 'You are a wonderful woman, Rosie. I can't believe that you got past Sister Mary-Grace. She's very strict about who may or may not visit patients.'

Hester cleared her throat. 'We told the nurse on duty that I'm your mother. It was the only way we were allowed to see you.'

'I have permission to visit Piers, but they warned me that he is very sick. Have you seen him, Alex?' Rosalind leaned closer, aware of the other men in the ward straining their ears as they tried to catch a word or two of the language that was presumably foreign to them.

'They tell me that he has a head injury and a lung infection. I haven't been able to get out of bed to visit him. Thank God you're here, both of you.'

'Are they feeding you properly?' Hester glanced over her shoulder. 'All the men look very thin and so do you, if it comes to that.'

He pulled a face. 'The food isn't wonderful and

there's not much of it. I've been dreaming of your Madeira cake, Hester, and pigeon pie, or rabbit stew.'

Rosalind could see the young nun hovering in the background. 'I have to go now, Alex, or I won't be allowed to see Piers, but I'll be back.'

'Promise me you won't leave without telling me, Rosie.'

'Of course not. We're here and I intend to find somewhere we can stay while you are both in hospital. Hester will tell you what's been going on at Rockwood, and I'll come back when I've seen Piers.' Rosalind squeezed his fingers gently. She turned to the nun, who glided off, indicating that she should follow.

Piers was in a small room with a slit window in the stone wall, allowing a single shaft of light onto the pristine white coverlet. The narrow bed, a chest of drawers and a wooden chair were the only furniture in the room, which seemed more like a prison cell than a place to offer comfort or encourage a feeling of wellbeing. His head was bandaged and he lay with his eyes closed and his arms folded on his chest. A shiver of apprehension ran through Rosalind's whole body. Her much-loved husband looked as though he was already dead and laid out ready for the undertaker. She shot an anxious glance at the nun, who gave her an encouraging smile.

'Your husband is in a stable condition, Madame.'

'You speak English?'

'A little.'

'May I know your name?'

'I am Sister Dominique.'

'Have you seen any improvement, Sister Dominique?'

'You would have to ask a more senior nursing sister, Madame Blanchard.'

'Language is a problem,' Rosalind said with a rueful smile. 'Is there a doctor present who can tell me more about my husband's prognosis?'

'Not at the moment, Madame, but Father Laurent is here. Maybe he can help you.'

'I would like to speak to him.'

'If you would like to sit with Monsieur Blanchard, I'll see if I can find Father Laurent.' The nun smiled and left the room.

Rosalind pulled up the chair and sat down. She reached out to touch Piers' hand, but his skin felt hot and clammy and she drew back swiftly. His breathing was ragged and he seemed feverish. His dark hair had been shorn close to his head and his skin was sallow. Rosalind wanted to speak to him but it would be foolish to have a conversation with a man who was so deeply unconscious.

'Madame Blanchard.'

Rosalind jumped to her feet. She had not heard the door open and she found herself facing an elderly priest. His face was grave but his eyes were gentle and he motioned her to sit.

'You came all the way from England, Madame?'

'I hired a fishing boat to bring us to France. I was desperate to see my husband, Father.'

'He is lucky to be alive; others were not so fortunate.'

'I'm so grateful for the care he's received, but can you give me any information about his condition? Is he really getting better?'

'He was close to death when he was brought here, Madame. The doctors and the nuns have worked miracles to bring him this far. I believe his lung infection is improving but he has not regained consciousness, and that is a concern to us all.'

'But he's out of danger?'

'That is in the hands of God, but we pray for his recovery every day. No doubt your presence will help.'

'He doesn't know I'm here.'

'Perhaps if you talk to him he will hear you, or he will feel your presence. We know very little about injuries to the head. Sometimes patients made remarkable progress.'

'Are you saying that some people never recover completely?'

Father Laurent nodded, folding his hands across his chest. 'I have seen such cases, but we must hope and pray that Monsieur Blanchard will regain his senses quickly. In the meantime, Madame, have you anywhere to stay? You said that you had only just arrived in France.'

'Yes, we arrived early this morning. We need to find suitable accommodation.'

'I'm afraid all the inns and lodging houses are full to capacity. Those whose ships were wrecked have taken all the available rooms, and many of the able bodied are camping in tents while they await the arrival of a suitable vessel.'

'I am here with my mother-in-law. We must find accommodation quickly as we have nowhere to sleep tonight.'

'I see.' Father Laurent stroked his chin, eyeing Rosalind thoughtfully. 'There is a property which is owned by the Church, but the last tenant passed away some time ago. The Château Gris is very near, but you might not consider it suitable.'

'We would be most grateful for anything,' Rosalind said earnestly. 'But I don't know how long we will be staying.'

Father Laurent smiled. 'That is in the hands of the Lord, Madame Blanchard. I will go now but I will return when I have made the necessary arrangements with the housekeeper. The nuns will look after you until then.' He glanced at Piers, shaking his head as he left the room, which was not an encouraging sign.

Rosalind sank back on the chair. 'I'm here, Piers. I don't know if you can hear me, but I'm not leaving until you are well enough to return home with me. I don't care how long it takes.' She closed her eyes but opened them again at the sound of footsteps.

'I've brought you some coffee, Madame.' Sister Dominique set the coffee bowl on the chest of drawers. 'Father Laurent will return soon.'

'Thank you,' Rosalind said, smiling. 'You are very kind.'

'I think your mama would like to see you. Perhaps when you have drunk your coffee you will go to her?'

'I will, thank you again.' Rosalind lifted the coffee bowl to her lips and sipped the strong black coffee. She watched for signs of recognition when she spoke to Piers, although it was obvious that he was too deeply unconscious to hear her voice. It was heartbreaking, but she knew she must be thankful that he was still alive. She finished her coffee and replaced the bowl on the chest before leaning over to kiss Piers on the forehead. 'I'll be back soon, my darling,' she whispered, biting back tears. She straightened up and took a deep breath. This was not the time to weaken; she must put a brave face on things if only for Alex and Hester's sake. She made her way back to the male ward.

'Piers is much better than he was, according to Father Laurent, the priest who came to speak to me. And the good news is that he thinks he's found us somewhere to stay. If it's suitable I hope you will soon be able to move in with us, Alex.'

'That would be wonderful, Rosie. I can't tell you how much I long to be out of here, even though they've been very kind to me. I know that my men are waiting for a ship to take them back to England, and I was dreading being stuck here on my own.'

'You wouldn't want to leave your brother alone in a foreign country, would you?' Hester said sharply.

'Of course not but, from what the nuns tell me,

Piers hasn't regained consciousness. He doesn't know where he is and perhaps he's the lucky one.'

'He will get better,' Rosalind said firmly. 'We'll get him to a hospital in London, if all else fails, but I want to speak to his doctors. Father Laurent was helpful, but he's a priest, not a medical man.'

'We'll find a way to take him home as soon as they say he can be moved.' Hester stood up and stretched. 'I've sat around for long enough. I'm going to find one of those holy ladies and ask them where we can get some food. I don't know about you, Rosie, but I'm starving.'

Alex chuckled and his eyes gleamed with golden lights, crinkling into laughter lines at the corners. 'You'll be lucky to get a bowl of thin soup and a chunk of bread for luncheon. The nuns share their food with us, but we get better rations in the army.'

'Ah, here comes the angelic young woman,' Hester said cheerfully. 'She understands English but I have difficulty knowing what she is saying to me. Can you help, Rosie?'

'Leave it to me.' Alex questioned the young nun in rapid French and listened carefully to her response. He smiled and nodded. 'Sister Dominique says that a guide has come to take you both to the château. I'd give anything to be able to leave here now and go with you.'

Rosalind leaned over the bed and kissed him on the cheek. 'We will get you out of here very soon. That's a promise.'

Alex grasped her hand. 'I trust you implicitly, Rosie. I know you'll do what's best for all of us, and money is not a problem. Pay them whatever they ask for their château, although I don't hold out much hope it's as grand as that word implies. It could be a tumbledown old barn of a place with no glass in the windows and a leaking roof, for all we know.'

'I'll come back this evening, if they'll let me,' Rosalind said earnestly. 'I'll tell you the worst then.'

The Château Gris perched on the edge of a precipitous cliff like a bird of ill omen. The Gothic Revival building had taken its name from the grey stone used in its construction, with four small turrets pointing up into a pewter sky. Despite the fact that it was mid-afternoon the light was fading fast, creating cavernous shadows beneath the gnarled trees and overgrown shrubs in the front garden. Father Laurent led the way along a twisting path slashing at overhanging branches with his furled umbrella. Rosalind followed him at a distance, hoping desperately that the interior of the château was more welcoming. A single glance at Hester's tense expression was enough to convince her that they were sharing a sense of foreboding.

However, Father Laurent appeared to be unaware of anything amiss as he waited for someone to answer his knock on the metal-studded door. It opened to reveal a small, plump woman with a pale face and grey hair swept back mercilessly into a neat bun. A silver chatelaine laden with large iron keys hung from her waist, giving her the appearance of a prison warder rather than a welcoming housekeeper.

'Madame Planche,' Father Laurent said, smiling. He continued in rapid French that Rosalind could not understand. Madame answered with a few curt words and walked away with hunched shoulders. It did not take an interpreter to translate. Her actions indicated clearly that they were unwelcome.

'Madame is more than happy to have you stay here for as long as you wish,' Father Laurent said hastily. 'You might find her manner a little abrupt, but she has a heart of pure gold. Come along, ladies.'

Rosalind had a feeling that Father Laurent was the eternal optimist who saw goodness in even the most disagreeable people.

Madame Planche led them along a wide corridor with a well-worn flagstone floor, and walls painted dark blue, creating a sense of eternal night. A strong smell of garlic and sour wine emanated from a room where the door had been left ajar, sending a shaft of flickering candlelight across their path. Rosalind caught a glimpse of a man wearing a red velvet robe. He was sprawled in an armchair with his feet resting on a low table, which was strewn with empty wine bottles and pools of red wine.

'Who is that, Father?' Rosalind said in a low voice. 'The house appears to have a tenant.'

'Oh, that is Monsieur Delfosse. Don't worry about him. He won't bother you.'

'Does he live here?'

'He's Madame's brother. He does the maintenance work around the château, and tends the grounds.'

Hester sniffed audibly. 'He doesn't seem to be doing much at the moment.'

'The château has been without a tenant for some time now and has fallen into a state of disrepair.' Father Laurent met her frown with a smile. 'Perhaps your presence will remedy that.'

'I think you should pay us to stay here,' Hester said icily. 'I'm sure there must be an alternative.'

'Don't be hasty.' Rosalind laid her hand on Hester's shoulder. 'Father Laurent said that all the accommodation locally has been taken by the army.'

'It doesn't say much for this place if the British Army refused to stay here. It's huge and it's cold and it smells funny.'

'The rent is very reasonable,' Father Laurent said hastily. 'And it's very near the convent, so it will be easy for Madame Blanchard to visit her husband.'

Rosalind nodded. 'That is an important consideration, Hester. I think we should take it. After all, we need somewhere to stay and it's so close to Christmas. I don't think we have much alternative.'

Father Laurent closed the door on Monsieur Delfosse. 'I think Madame wants to show you the drawing room, Madame Blanchard.'

The drawing room was just as cheerless as Rosalind had suspected. Tall windows in the Gothic style of architecture were draped with heavy red velvet curtains, and the cumbersome mahogany furniture was upholstered in a similar fabric, as was the horsehair sofa. Two cavernous armchairs were placed on either side of a fireplace that would not have looked out of place in Rockwood Castle. Twisted iron candlesticks on the mantelshelf matched the heavy chandelier, creating a bizarre note in comparison to the rest of the room.

Madame Planche launched into a speech that was clearly supposed to impress, speaking rapidly and accompanying her words with exaggerated hand gestures.

Father Laurent listened attentively, nodding in apparent agreement. 'Madame says that this is the best room in the château. It was so beloved of the late tenant that in her last few months she had her bed moved in here.'

Hester's hand flew to her mouth. 'She died in this room?'

'No, she was moved to the hospital across the street at the very end.'

'She probably haunts the place,' Hester said in an undertone.

'Madame would like to know if you wish to take up the tenancy.' Father Laurent looked from one to the other. 'You seem a little uncertain.'

'I don't think we have any choice,' Rosalind said reluctantly. She could hear sleety rain beating against the tracery on the windows and it was almost dark. She tried to convince herself that a fire and candlelight would make all the difference. 'Please tell Madame Planche that we will take the château for a month.'

'That's too long,' Hester protested. 'Surely we will be able to book passage to take us home sooner than that.'

'You didn't see Piers. He is very ill, Hester. I hope we will be able to return to England sooner, but it's best to be careful.'

'I don't see people queuing up outside to take the place on.' Hester glared at Madame Planche. 'Tell her we need a fire in all the rooms we're going to use, Father. And plenty of good wax candles. I won't put up with tallow.'

Father Laurent turned to Madame Planche, speaking to her in such a pleasant manner that Rosalind suspected he was putting Hester's commands in a much more persuasive way. He listened attentively to her answer, smiled and nodded.

'Madame says that you will have to hire a servant to wait on you. She is here to look after the property only. She also asks for the rent in advance, which I think is quite normal.'

'It seems that what we need most is someone who can speak English,' Rosalind said warily.

Madame wrote something on a notebook that she produced from a pocket in her apron and handed it to Father Laurent. He passed it to Rosalind. 'That is the rent for a month. I gather that it is for the rooms only. It does not include meals or coal and candles.'

Hester peered over Rosalind's shoulder. 'Robbery,'

she said sharply. 'The woman is taking advantage of our situation.'

'Hush, Hester.' Rosalind folded the paper and tucked it into her reticule. 'I will pay what she asks, but what can we do about taking on a servant, Father? It's getting late and we need food and heat.' She took out her purse and selected a half-sovereign. 'I only have English money, Father, but this is gold and I think it will more than cover our rent, and perhaps some coal and candles to start off with.'

Father Laurent took the coin. 'Madame is a simple woman, but she understands the power of gold. I think the least she can do is to provide you with heat and light.' He turned to Madame Planche, holding the coin just out of reach, as he spoke. She shot a calculating glance at Rosalind but she nodded and held out her hand. With the money clutched in her fist she hurried from the room.

'She will light a fire in here and in your bedrooms, and she will provide you with candles but you will have to look after yourselves.' Father Laurent lowered his voice, glancing anxiously over his shoulder as if expecting to find someone eavesdropping. 'I should warn you that Madame Planche is a notoriously bad cook. Need I say more?'

'No, indeed. Thank you for the warning, Father.' Rosalind examined the contents of her purse. 'Do you think you could help us to find a maid, who understands English, Father? I can afford to pay someone and we need to eat.'

'Of course, Madame Blanchard. As it happens I do know a young woman who would be more than willing to earn a little extra, and she speaks English quite well.'

'I hope she's not related to Madame Skinflint,' Hester said, sniffing. 'I'm hungry.'

Father Laurent walked swiftly to the doorway. 'Don't worry. The young lady I mentioned has been trained by my housekeeper. Agathe Boudon was left at the convent when she was a baby, and brought up by the nuns. She came to me when she was twelve and has been with us ever since. She is now a young woman and she will serve you well during your stay.'

'Thank you, Father,' Rosalind said earnestly. 'I don't know what we would have done without your help.'

Father Laurent looked round the room and shuddered. 'I hope I've done the right thing by bringing you here, but I had very little choice.'

'I'm sure we'll be perfectly all right,' Rosalind said stoutly.

'I don't want to worry you, but I suggest you lock your bedroom doors at night.' Father Laurent backed out of the room and his footsteps echoed eerily on the flagstone floor, fading into the distance.

Rosalind walked over to the bell pull and tugged at it.

'What are you doing?' Hester demanded nervously.

'I want to see our bedchambers. If they are too terrible I'm not staying here a minute longer.'

Chapter Six

'Well, I suppose the bedrooms will do. At least we're next to each other.' Hester slumped down on the sofa. 'This is the most uncomfortable piece of furniture I've ever had the misfortune to sit upon. Those beds didn't feel much better, and I'm wondering when the sheets were last washed.'

'It's only temporary,' Rosalind said automatically.

'Well, I don't think you should have paid all that money. Madame Planche is making a fortune out of us. Even the priest said he wasn't sure whether he'd done the right thing by bringing us here, and then he told us to lock our bedroom doors.'

'I know this isn't what we're used to, but what choice do we have?' Rosalind glanced out of the window. 'It's terrible weather and at least we have a roof over our heads. We will have to make do, Hester. Perhaps, when it stops sleeting, we could go to that café where we had breakfast and get something to eat.'

Hester opened her mouth to respond, but at that moment the door creaked open and Delfosse shambled into the room. He was carrying a brass coal scuttle, filled with coal, and a sack of logs, which he tipped into a large wicker basket by the fireplace. Rosalind turned away from him as a miasma of stale wine and strange-smelling tobacco smoke threatened to engulf her. Hester pulled a face and moved to a seat by the window while Delfosse attempted to light the fire, his efforts accompanied by grunts and mutterings. Rosalind was glad that her knowledge of French was limited, but it was obvious that his words were not meant for sensitive ears. He succeeded in getting the fire going after a while, although smoke continued to belch into the room, sending a shower of sooty flakes into the air. He struggled to his feet and picked up the sack, eyeing Rosalind with a frown. She attempted to thank him, but he answered with something like a growl and stamped out of the room.

'I *will* lock my door tonight,' Hester said with feeling. 'And it's even more important for you to do so, poppet. That man is an animal.'

Rosalind chuckled. 'I think that's unkind to animals.' She held up her hands as Hester uttered a cry of protest. 'I know it's not a laughing matter, but if I don't see humour in the situation I'm afraid I will cry. At least we have a fire of sorts. I suggest we go out now and get some food. When we've eaten I'm going to sit with Piers for a while, if the nuns will let me.'

A timid knock on the door made them both turn with a start.

'Come in,' Rosalind said warily.

A young woman entered the room. Standing in the shadows she looked almost spectre-like in her dull grey coat, her face a pale oval and escaping from her bonnet, a wisp of hair that was so fair, it was almost white. Clutched tightly in her hands she held a large basket, covered with a crisp white cloth.

'Excuse me, Madame. Father Laurent sent me to help you.'

Rosalind experienced an almost overwhelming desire to give her a hug. 'You must be Agathe.'

'I am, Madame.'

'Then you are most welcome,' Rosalind said earnestly. 'I am Madame Blanchard and this is my companion, Lady Carey.'

Hester acknowledged Agathe with a friendly smile. 'We would be very grateful for your help, my dear. We need to buy food, but I don't know whether Madame Planche will allow me to use her kitchen.'

Agathe's pale blue eyes darkened. 'Madame Planche will do as Father Laurent wishes.'

'That's good to know,' Rosalind said hastily. 'But our most urgent need is for something to eat.'

'Madame Fournier, Father Laurent's housekeeper, instructed me to give you this. She said that Madame

Planche would not feed you, and if she did it would cost you twice as much as it's worth.'

Agathe placed the basket on a low table and Hester plucked off the cover. 'Roast chicken,' she said excitedly, 'and it's still warm, Rosie. There's bread, too, and butter.' She sniffed suspiciously. 'I think that's cheese, but it smells off.'

Rosalind glanced over Hester's shoulder. 'I'm sure it tastes delicious. Anyway, I do hope this wasn't intended to be Father Laurent's supper.'

'I'm sure he has plenty to eat,' Hester said firmly. 'Look, Rosie, there are apples and there's something wrapped in a paper poke.'

'That will be coffee, Madame,' Agathe said shyly. 'I will take it to the kitchen, with your permission, and I will make coffee for you.'

'If you have trouble from Madame Planche you must tell me,' Hester said firmly. 'I won't stand any nonsense from that person.'

'Yes, Madame. I will bring you plates and cutlery.' Agathe curtsied and hurried from the room with the poke of coffee in her hand.

'Now I know the meaning of "heaven-sent",' Hester said, licking her lips. 'If it weren't bad manners I would eat all this with my fingers.'

The food was so delicious that Rosalind ate far too much, and the cheese proved to be as tasty as she had hoped. With a full stomach and a warm fire to return to, she felt much more optimistic as she walked over to the hospital, accompanied by Hester. It was dark and the rain had stopped but the temperature had dropped dramatically and ice was beginning to form on the puddles. The sister on duty informed them that evening visitors were only allowed in a small number of cases, but Rosalind refused to leave without seeing her husband and eventually they were both granted permission to see Piers and Alex, but only for a short time.

Piers lay motionless in the narrow bed. In the flickering light of a single candle he looked deathly pale, and Rosalind felt a cold shiver strike through her whole body. She leaned over the bed and kissed him tenderly on the forehead as she might have done to a sleeping child, but he remained unresponsive. She took a seat at his bedside and talked softly, telling him about the eerie château and the strange couple who were supposed to take care of them. After what seemed like a very short time, Sister Dominque came to tell her that it was time to leave. Rosalind raised Piers' hand to her lips before resting it back on the pristine white sheet.

'I'll come tomorrow, my love,' she said in a whisper, her voice choked with unshed tears. 'I'll leave now, but first I'll say good night to Alex.' She walked past Sister Dominique, pausing briefly to thank her.

It was a relief to see Alex looking remarkably cheerful despite his immobilised leg. He gave her a beaming smile. 'Come and sit with me for a moment before they descend upon us like avenging angels. The nuns don't want their strict routine disturbed by visitors.'

'You look tired, poppet,' Hester said sympathetically. 'Is there any change in Piers' condition?'

Rosalind shook her head, unable to speak.

'Sister Dominique told me that the next few days will be critical,' Alex said in a low voice.

'She tells you everything, does she?' Hester eyed him curiously.

'I don't think she was meant to say anything, but I have ways of charming information out of people, even nuns.'

'You always thought highly of yourself, Alex,' Rosalind said with a reluctant smile. 'At least some things never change.'

He reached out to take hold of her hand. 'Keep up your spirits, Rosie. Piers is tough and he's not going to give in to this, but he won't want to see a sad face when he wakes up.'

'That's right,' Hester said briskly. 'He's survived so far, and he's in the best of hands.'

Alex squeezed Rosalind's finger. 'Hester's been telling me about the haunted house across the street. I think the sooner I move in with you the better. I don't like the sound of that fellow Delfosse.'

'I think he's harmless enough,' Rosalind said with more confidence than she was feeling. 'Madame Planche seems able to handle him.'

'Well, make sure you lock your bedroom doors

tonight. If the priest told you to do that he must have a good reason.' Alex glanced from one to the other. 'Maybe you ought to share a room, at least until you're sure that Delfosse doesn't wander round the corridors in the early hours of the morning. I'd come to your rescue, but it's a long way to hobble on one leg.'

Rosalind laughed. 'We do need you with us, Alex. The sooner the better.'

Hester glanced over Rosalind's shoulder. 'There's a nun marching towards us, Rosie. I think we're about to be sent on our way.'

'I'm sorry, Alex. I wanted to stay and talk to you,' Rosalind said hastily. 'There's so much to tell you about what's been happening at Rockwood.'

'Hester told me that your mother and Claude are getting married. I can imagine how Patsy must have reacted to that, but there's nothing I can do about it from here. Anyway, it's so good to see you, Rosie.' Alex shot a wary glance at the nun. 'I would kiss you, but I don't think Sister Mary-Grace would approve.' He winked and grinned mischievously.

Rosalind was tempted to ignore the sister's presence and hug Alex, but she did not want to jeopardise their ability to visit every day. She merely smiled and patted him on the cheek. 'Good night, Alex. I'll see you tomorrow.'

'Good night,' Hester said briskly. 'Sleep well, Alexander.'

'The only person who calls me Alexander is Grandmama, and she reserves that for when I've really upset her. Good night Rosie, good night Hester. Don't forget what I said about locking doors.' He held up his hands. 'All right, Sister Mary-Grace. I'm going to sleep now, like a good boy.'

Rosalind left the ward with a memory of the brilliant smile that Alex directed at the nun, whose stern expression had softened and a delicate flush had made her look almost pretty.

'That young man would charm the devil himself,' Hester observed as they walked the short distance to the château. She shot a sideways glance at Rosalind. 'He had you under his spell not so long ago. You might need to keep your guard up now, Rosie.'

Rosalind shook her head. 'That was more than two years ago, Hester. I love my husband and I do love Alex, but like a brother. He's engaged to my sister, unless you'd forgotten.' She made her way through the clutching fronds of brambles and the tangle of overhanging branches to the front door.

'I hope he remembers that,' Hester said darkly. 'For both your sakes.'

The door opened and Delfosse stood aside, holding a lantern to light their way. Rosalind shuddered. By daylight the old house had seemed forbidding and gloomy; now, in the hours of darkness it felt positively frightening. 'Thank you, Monsieur,' she said firmly. 'We won't be needing you again this evening.'

He grunted and ambled away, taking the lantern with him, leaving them little choice other than to follow the vanishing path of light. He opened the drawing-room door and walked off without saying a word.

'I could do with a cup of hot chocolate,' Hester said gloomily. 'Maybe it was a mistake to allow Agathe to return to the priest's house to sleep.'

'I could hardly ask her to stay with Madame Planche and her awful brother.' Rosalind walked over to the fireplace and took a spill from the jar on the mantelshelf. 'At least we have a good blaze to take the chill off the room.' She held the spill in the flames and lit several candles. 'I don't know about you, Hester, but I'm ready for bed.'

'I'm not staying down here on my own. I'll come with you.' Hester snatched up a candlestick. 'You lead on. I'm not sure I remember the way.'

Rosalind had to rely upon her memory, but everything looked different in the darkness, with deep menacing shadows at the end of long corridors. The wide treads of the staircase creaked with every step, and the galleried landing was uncarpeted so that each footfall echoed off the high ceiling. Their rooms were on the second floor, the larger of which had been allocated to Rosalind.

As she entered her bedchamber Rosalind could hear waves breaking on the distant shore, but when she went to look out of the window she was met by a wall of darkness. Sleet hurled itself against the panes, tapping and scratching like sharp fingernails.

'I'll say good night, then,' Hester said reluctantly.

Rosalind shivered despite the fire that blazed up the chimney. 'Lock the door, Hester. Would you mind sleeping in here tonight? It's a big bed and I promise not to kick you, if you agree not to snore.'

Next morning they were both up early.

'I hardly slept a wink,' Hester said grumpily.

'Neither did I, because you were snoring.'

'I don't snore.'

'It doesn't matter.' Rosalind moved to the window and drew back the curtains. The garden was iced with snow and the bare branches of the trees were spangled with hoar frost. She could see traces of a formal design, but even beneath a thin blanket of snow it was obvious that the grounds were overgrown and that nature was trying to reclaim the land. They were nearer the edge of the cliffs than Rosalind had imagined and the sea was a restless grey, flecked with white horses.

'It's freezing in here,' Hester said crossly. 'I'm going to find Delfosse and tell him to light the fires, the lazy good-for-nothing. We're paying enough rent, goodness knows.'

'I think we need to get some form of agreement with Madame about the use of the kitchen, too. We can't afford to eat out all the time, and similarly we can't rely on Madame Fournier to send us food. Perhaps Agathe could take us to the market to buy provisions.'

'All in good time.' Hester shrugged off her nightgown, reaching for her chemise. 'I wish I'd brought more clothes with me. I thought we would be here for a few days at the most, but having seen Alexander, and from what you said about Piers, I think we're going to be staying for quite a while.'

Madame Planche stood in front of the ancient range, arms akimbo, glaring at Agathe, who was acting as interpreter. Madame spoke volubly, leaving Agathe to translate.

'Madame says that this is her kitchen and she does not want any interference from outsiders.'

'Please tell her that we require the use of the range at agreed times during the day in order to prepare our food,' Rosalind said firmly. 'She cannot argue against that, and if she does we will have to ask Father Laurent to intervene.'

Agathe turned to Madame, who responded verbally, accompanied by waving hands.

'Madame agrees,' Agathe said eventually. 'But you have to provide your own food and pay extra for the coal in order to keep the range going.'

Hester shrugged. 'She drives a hard bargain.'

'We're not in a position to argue, Hester, much as I would like to.'

'What do we do about breakfast?' Hester asked plaintively. 'I'm starving and I would love a cup of tea.'

Rosalind turned to Agathe. 'We need to purchase provisions. Could you help us?'

'Of course, Madame. Shall I make coffee first? I've brought some rolls with me and a few of Madame Fournier's pastries. She is most concerned for your wellbeing.'

'I thank her from the bottom of my heart,' Rosalind said earnestly. 'I don't know what we would have done without you and the kindness of Father Laurent and his housekeeper.'

Madame Planche sighed heavily and Rosalind took this as a hint to leave the kitchen. 'We'll be in the drawing room, Agathe. I hope that Monsieur Delfosse has lit the fire.'

After breakfast Rosalind sent Hester to the market with Agathe. She would have liked to accompany them, but she needed to see Piers and she went straight to the hospital. His condition was unchanged, as she had feared, and Sister Dominique could not tell her anything more than she already knew. Rosalind sat with Piers for a while, and she made an effort to talk to him, but it seemed futile speaking to someone who was deeply unconscious. In the end she braved the wrath of Sister Mary-Grace and went to see Alex. The men in the other beds eyed her with varying degrees of interest, although most of them seemed too sick or too preoccupied with their own problems to pay much attention to her.

Alex greeted her with an engaging smile. 'You ran the gauntlet to see me, Rosie. I always knew you were brave.'

She pulled up a chair and sat down. 'I expect I'll be sent out when one of the sisters sees me, but I've just spent some time with Piers. He doesn't respond at all.'

'He's no worse, at least that's what Sister Dominique told me this morning. It's just a matter of time,' Alex said gently. 'Don't give up now.'

'I'm trying to be positive, Alex. But he looks so ill.'

'I won't deny it, Rosie.'

'How are you, Alex? Don't tell me that you're fine, because I can see that you're in pain.'

'No, really, as long as I keep still it's all right. It's only when I forget that I get a sharp reminder. More important, how are you?' He eyed her keenly. 'You look tired, Rosie.'

'I shared a bed with Hester because we were both nervous. She snores, although she won't admit it.'

'Is it the château itself, or are you afraid of that man Delfosse?'

She shrugged. 'I suppose we were just exhausted and we allowed our imaginations to take control.'

'Nevertheless, I'm going to ask my commanding officer if I can move to the château. I can't do much in my present condition, but I can shout louder than you.'

'I can't deny that it would be a comfort to have you with us. Hester and I could take good care of you.'

He laughed. 'I warn you I'm a very demanding patient, but seriously, I think it would be a good thing. I'm sure that in the circumstances there can be no objection.'

'That would be wonderful, but simply moving you across the road might make your injury worse.'

'That's a risk I'm prepared to take. I'll heal quicker if I'm with you, and Hester, of course,' Alex added quickly. 'You are my family, Rosie. And I don't like the thought of you two alone in that place with such strange people. Besides which, it's nearly Christmas and I was dreading being here on my own.'

His crestfallen expression went straight to Rosalind's heart and once again she had to resist the temptation to hug him. 'Whose permission do you need, Alex?'

'Colonel Munday. He's staying at the local inn.'

'If you promise to speak to your doctor, I'll find the colonel and explain the situation to him. It would be wonderful if we could all be together for Christmas and, who knows, maybe Piers will have regained consciousness by then. It's only three days until Christmas Eve.'

'Which should have been my wedding day,' Alex said with a wry smile. 'Patsy will never forgive me.'

'Nonsense. She understands.' Rosalind spoke with more conviction than she was feeling and she avoided meeting his gaze. Alex had a way of knowing when she was not telling the truth. She rose to her feet. 'I'll go to the inn now and hope that the colonel is there.'

He caught her by the hand as she was about to

walk away. 'Take Hester with you, Rosie. The town is crawling with soldiers and seamen. You shouldn't go out on your own.'

'All right, I will. Now let me go, and I'll be on my way.'

He tightened his grip. 'Promise, Rosie. I know you: you'll do as you think fit. Promise you'll take Hester with you.'

She met his anxious look with a reluctant smile. 'I promise. Now please may I go?'

He released her with a sigh. 'Come back later, Rosie.'

'I will, Alex. I'll come with good news.'

A fitful sun had pushed its way between ominous dark clouds and a sharp breeze blew in from the sea as Rosalind stepped outside onto the pavement. She glanced across the street but the château looked just as uninviting by daylight. The thought of going back there on her own was so daunting that she decided to walk into town where she hoped she might meet Hester and Agathe. It was not exactly breaking her promise to Alex, it was simply stretching the limits a little. She did not know where to find the marketplace, but she went the way they had come from the harbour. The pavements were slippery and people were going about their business hunched against the cold and muffled up so that only their eyes were visible. Alex's prediction that the town was crawling with soldiers and sailors seemed to be mere supposition, but as Rosalind approached the inn, she was aware of raised voices speaking English, and loud laughter, even though it was only mid-morning. She hesitated outside the door, tempted to go inside and ask for Colonel Munday, but wary of breaking her promise even further.

'What you doing out here in the cold, darling?' A voice behind her made Rosalind turn with a start to find two soldiers standing uncomfortably close to her. She tried to edge away but they pinned her to the door.

'That's not very friendly to the foreign visitors, is it?' The older man grinned, breathing brandy fumes into her face. 'Come inside, love. We'll make sure you have a good time.'

'No,' Rosalind said anxiously. She would have protested more but they thrust her into the building without bothering to gain her permission. She tried to talk to them but the noise from the bar and the tables set around the large room drowned her attempts to reason with them. They were both the worse for drink, as were the rest of the rowdy customers. The landlord was busy serving, but a disturbance close to the fireplace distracted her captors for long enough to give her a chance to slip away. She pushed her way to the bar and grabbed the landlord's arm.

'Monsieur, I am English. I need to see Colonel Munday.'

The landlord stopped what he was doing to stare

at her in astonishment, but by this time the men had realised their mistake and they barged through the crowd to reach her.

'She's with us, landlord.'

Rosalind shook her head. 'No, I am not. Let go of me or I will report you to Colonel Munday.'

There was a sudden silence in the room and the men backed away. 'She's English, you fool,' the younger man growled.

'I am, and you two are a disgrace to your uniform.' Rosalind held her head high. She turned back to the landlord. 'Colonel Munday – is he here?'

'Who wants to know?'

A stern voice from the narrow staircase made Rosalind turn her head. She knew from the uniform that this was the man she sought and she edged her way towards him. 'Colonel, I need to speak to you urgently.'

He glanced round at the now largely silent crowd of drinkers. 'You men are a disgrace. Get back to your quarters and sober up.' He glared at the two men who had manhandled Rosalind. 'You two, report to your senior officer. You will be facing charges. I do not condone this sort of behaviour, especially in a foreign country where we are guests.'

Rosalind watched them as they sidled out into the street, all their bravado and bullying tactics cut to shreds by their superior officer. 'Thank you, Colonel.'

Colonel Munday led her to a table by the fire.

'*Café au lait, s'il vous plait, Patron.*' He sat down opposite her. 'Now then, ma'am. Might I ask who you are and why are you wandering the streets on your own?'

'My name is Rosalind Blanchard. My husband is in a critical condition in the convent hospital, and my brother-in-law, Captain Alexander Blanchard, is also on a ward there.'

'I know Blanchard, of course, but that doesn't explain why a lady like yourself is out in a foreign town unaccompanied.'

'Please don't tell Alex,' Rosalind said hastily. 'He made me promise not to go out on my own, but I was hoping to meet my companion and our maid. Then I was accosted by your men outside the inn.'

'For that I apologise, Mrs Blanchard. Why did you want to see me?'

'Lady Carey and I have rented the château opposite the hospital, hoping to be able to take Alex and my husband home when they are well enough. We can take care of Alex but he said that he needs your permission to leave the hospital.'

'He has to have permission from the doctors, ma'am. But you're right, I need to know where he is, too. I believe he was going to be married before Christmas.'

'Yes, Colonel. Alex is engaged to my sister, but, of course, the wedding has been postponed.'

'That's a pity, but life in the army is never predictable. However, I have no objection to Captain

Blanchard being moved such a short distance.
Ultimately it is a matter for the doctors to decide,
but thank you for coming to see me.' He looked up
as the landlord brought bowls of steaming coffee.
'*Merci, Patron.*'

'Thank you, Colonel.' Rosalind sipped the coffee.
'This is very good.'

'You must allow me to see you back to the château,
Mrs Blanchard. I will call in at the hospital when I
have seen you safely home.'

Chapter Seven

It was finally agreed that Alex could be moved to the Château Gris the day before Christmas Eve, but this in itself created a problem. Rosalind had considered turning one of the small parlours into a bedroom for Alex, but that presented difficulties due to his lack of mobility. After a brief discussion with Hester, Rosalind instructed Delfosse to bring a bed from upstairs and place it between two tall windows in the drawing room. Hester and Rosalind shifted furniture around so that there was a table close to the bed and chairs set on either side. During a quick and slightly nervous exploration of one of the turret rooms they found a hand-painted Japanese screen, which would give Alex a little privacy, as well as a washstand complete with china jug and basin. With Agathe acting as interpreter, Delfosse was again persuaded to move the items to the drawing room, which he did accompanied by the now familiar muttering.

The next problem to overcome was the fact that the cumbersome plaster hampered Alex when he attempted to rise from his hospital bed. Colonel Munday suggested that stretcher bearers would be the answer, and he supervised the move himself. Father Laurent had followed them from the hospital, carrying the few possessions and articles of clothing that Alex possessed. He was still wearing a flannel nightshirt and a dressing robe in faded crimson velvet trimmed with an extravagant fur collar, which someone had donated to the poor. However, the sudden exposure to the bitter cold and the unavoidable jolting caused Alex a great deal of pain, and it took all their efforts to transfer him from the stretcher to the bed, even with the assistance of Delfosse.

Rosalind greeted Colonel Munday with a grateful smile. 'Thank you so much, Colonel. We couldn't have done this without your help.'

'Don't mention it, my dear Mrs Blanchard. Alex sustained his injury during combat with the sea, which is a ferocious enemy. It was the least I could do.'

Rosalind laid her hand on Father Laurent's arm as he was about to leave. 'Don't go yet, Father. I believe that Christmas Eve is the main feast day in France, so I wondered if you and Colonel Munday would like to join us here tomorrow for a festive meal. Madame Fournier is invited, of course, and Agathe.'

Colonel Munday's ruddy skin darkened to a deeper hue. 'What a kind thought, ma'am. I'd be delighted to join you.'

Rosalind smiled. 'That's wonderful. What about you, Father? I know you'll have church services to conduct but we'll take that into consideration. Do say you'll come.'

'I think that would be a very good thing to do.' Father Laurent nodded approvingly. 'We will be delighted to join you, Madame Blanchard.'

'I'll have to fight Madame Planche for use of the kitchen range,' Hester said grimly.

'It's Christmas, Hester. We'll ask Madame and her brother to join us, too.'

'I'll have to go to market again,' Hester protested.

'Agathe and I will go with you.' Rosalind clutched Hester's arm. 'We'll do it together. Please, Hester, say you will.'

Alex had been silent during the conversation, lying back against a pile of pillows, but he raised his head with an attempt at a smile. 'Don't I have a say in all this?'

'Of course you do.' Rosalind hurried to his bedside. 'It's for your sake as much as anything, Alex. After all, tomorrow should have been your wedding day. We ought to mark the occasion in some way.'

'I'm glad Patsy can't see me now,' Alex said with a wry smile.

'I think you look quite regal in that velvet robe.

You only need a crown and you could be a king holding court,' Rosalind said cheerfully. 'Anyway, Alex, your leg will heal and we'll all travel home together. Piers will recover. I won't allow him to die.'

Alex reached up to stroke her cheek. 'He wouldn't dare, Rosie.'

'That's right. I'll sit with him when I return from the market, and I'll tell him he simply must get better.'

Colonel Munday smiled. 'You would make an excellent general, ma'am. I salute you, and I look forward to joining you tomorrow.'

'One o'clock, Colonel,' Rosalind said confidently. 'We'll have hot rum punch, exactly as my grandfather used to make at Christmas. We might be far from home, but we'll raise a glass to our loved ones.'

To Rosalind's surprise, Madame Planche accepted the invitation to join them for dinner next day. She even delegated Delfosse to help them carry the shopping back from the market. He obeyed reluctantly, as usual, but his presence as he lumbered along behind them acted like magic, clearing the crowds and keeping undesirables at bay. One look at him and even the boldest of the men roaming the streets kept their distance. Rosalind decided that Delfosse had his uses after all. When they returned to the château with baskets spilling over with all the good things necessary for a merry Christmas, Rosalind left Hester and Agathe to put everything away. She checked on Alex first, but he was sleeping peacefully and she placed the screen around his bed. Still wearing her outdoor clothes, she made her way to the hospital to sit with Piers for an hour. She was growing accustomed to talking to him without feeling ridiculous, and she told him about their plans for the next day, even going into detail about the two fine geese they had purchased for the Christmas feast. At one point she thought she saw his eyelids flicker and she jumped to her feet, moving closer to the bed while she waited for another sign. Nothing happened and she fought back tears of frustration and disappointment.

'Piers,' she said angrily, 'stop playing games and wake up. You know you can hear me.' She sighed, shaking her head. 'Tomorrow is Christmas Eve. The best present you could give me is to open your eyes. I'm going now, but I'll be back in the morning.' She leaned over and dropped a kiss on his forehead.

When she awakened next morning Rosalind remembered that not only was it Christmas Eve, but it was the day that Patsy should have been walking up the aisle with Alex. Whereas now she would have to attend the wedding as an onlooker, there to witness their mother's marriage to Claude. Rosalind could only imagine the scene at the castle with all the family tensions bubbling to the surface, and no one in overall charge of the arrangements. She pitied

Bertie and Walter having to bear the brunt of their mother's frustration and Patsy's tantrums when things did not go quite to plan. It was the first time in Rosalind's life that she would be spending Christmas away from Rockwood and it felt very strange. She slid out of bed, not wanting to wake Hester, who had still not plucked up the courage to sleep in her own room. It was bitterly cold and the fire had burned away to a pile of ash. Agathe's first chore in the mornings was to light the fires but it was still early, judging by the dark sky with just a hint of dawn light filtering through the window.

Rosalind washed quickly in icy water and dressed with equal speed. She lit a candle and was on her way downstairs when she almost bumped into Agathe, who was staggering beneath the weight of a full coal scuttle.

'I'm sorry, Madame. I am a little late this morning.'

'I'm up early. I couldn't sleep a moment longer.'

'I've given Monsieur Alex some coffee, Madame. He called out to me as I was clearing the grate. I hope I did right.'

'Of course you did. Thank you, Agathe. I'll go to him now.' Rosalind quickened her pace, heading for the drawing room. The newly lit fire had taken the chill off the gloomy room and she could just make out Alex's bed by the window.

Alex raised his head. 'Rosie, is that you?'

'Agathe said you were awake. Are you in much pain?'

'A bit, but she makes good coffee.'

'Sister Dominique gave me some laudanum for you to take if the pain was too bad.'

'I'm all right for now, but to tell the truth I'm starving. Does that fierce woman who keeps house allow you in the kitchen?'

'We have an understanding,' Rosalind said, chuckling. 'Not a very good one, but we've called a truce today, or so I hope. I'm hungry, too.' She moved to the bed and plumped up the pillows.

Alex caught her by the hand as she was about to back away. 'Thank you for everything, Rosie. You can't imagine how grateful I am to be out of that hospital ward.' He raised her hand to his lips. 'You smell wonderful,' he added, smiling.

'It's called soap and water, Alex.' Rosalind withdrew her hand gently. 'Perhaps you would like me to help you to wash later.'

'I think I can manage that on my own, but thank you for the offer,' Alex said with a wry smile. 'Will you have breakfast with me, please? Before Hester and Agathe take over and start ordering me about.'

'I know you love all the attention, Alex. So don't pretend otherwise.'

'I like it when you make a fuss of me, Rosie.'

She knew he was teasing, but there was a look in his eyes that she remembered only too well. 'I have better things to do than to pamper you, Alexander.' Rosalind hurried off without waiting for his response. She could still feel the imprint of his lips on the back of her hand, but a small voice in her head warned her to take care. All the old feelings she had harboured for Alex were in danger of rising to the surface, and she could tell by the warmth in his hazel eyes that she held a special place in his heart. Fate had thrown them together, but neither of them was free to resume their old relationship. She was a married woman with a sick husband who needed her, and Alex was spoken for.

Rosalind made her way to the kitchen and found Delfosse sprawled in a chair at the table with his head in his arms. His snores echoed off the high ceiling, rattling the metal utensils and copper pans that hung above the range. Rosalind ignored him and went to investigate the cold room and the spacious larder. Hester had been busy the night before, plucking, drawing and preparing the geese for the table, and she had made an attempt at making a plum pudding from ingredients that came to hand. The smell of cinnamon and nutmeg filled the air, evoking memories of past Christmas dinners, and Rosalind's mouth began to water. That aside, she knew she must concentrate on making breakfast, and she remembered that Alex liked porridge.

She worked with a will and set a tray with everything they needed, including a pot of Madame Planche's strawberry preserve and thick slices of toast.

Alex raised himself on his elbow when she placed the tray on the table by his bed. 'Is that porridge? Real porridge with cream and sugar.'

'It most certainly is. I made it to Hester's exacting standards, I hope.'

'Can you help me to sit up, Rosie?'

Somewhat reluctantly she moved to his side and he placed one arm around her shoulders. The nearness of him was even more unsettling and Rosalind had to steel herself to remain calm and unflustered. His breath on her cheek was warm and brought memories of their brief romance flooding back.

'Count to three,' Rosalind said firmly, 'and I'll try to lift you.'

He rested his head momentarily on her shoulder. 'All right. One, two, three . . .' He groaned with pain as their combined efforts slid him up the bed into a semi-recumbent position. 'Well done, Rosie.' He leaned on her a little longer. 'Let me get my breath back.'

'It's all right, Alex. Take as long as you need.'

He made an attempt at a smile. 'I can't wait to taste the porridge.' He withdrew his arm slowly. 'Thank you, my angel. I hope I didn't hurt you.'

'No, of course not.' Rosalind moved away quickly. 'Cream and sugar, just how you like it.'

'You remember.'

'Of course. I'm the big sister. I look after everyone.' Rosalind handed him the steaming bowl of porridge.

'That smells so good. You will sit with me, won't you? I feel like a leper stuck here away from everyone.'

She pulled up a chair. 'Of course I will. We're up

123

before anyone, apart from Agathe, and she's busy stoking fires. Delfosse must have drunk himself into oblivion last night. He's draped over the kitchen table, snoring like a pig.'

Alex frowned. 'He hasn't bothered you, has he?'

'No, not in the way you mean. Hester and I were scared of him at first, but I think he's harmless, and Madame Planche keeps him in order.'

'She's not very good at it if the fellow is dead drunk. The sooner I get back on my feet the better. If he lays a finger on you, Rosie, I swear I'll be off this bed in seconds and he'll get a good thrashing.'

'Eat your porridge, Alex,' Rosalind said, laughing. 'You need to build up your strength first.'

'You're right. I need spoiling like this every day. This porridge is excellent, and that looks like strawberry jam. If it's half as good as the one Hester makes it will be wonderful.' He scraped the bowl clean and licked the spoon. 'Thank you, Rosie.'

She looked up and felt herself drowning in his gaze. More than two years of marriage to Piers were in danger of being swept away by the resurgence of old emotions. She loved her husband, of course, but his obsession with the clay mine in Cornwall and his long business trips had taken their toll on their relationship. Even so, she was loyal and shocked by her unexpected reaction to Alexander's charm.

'It should have been your wedding day, Alex,' she said abruptly. 'I wonder how Patsy is feeling.'

'She will dance at your mother's wedding and

probably outdo my sister when it comes to flirting with eligible bachelors,' Alex said casually.

'Don't you care?' The question came out before she could stop herself.

'Of course I do, but I've been away a long time. To be honest, I wonder if Patsy will be upset because she wants to be my wife, or because she is no longer the centre of attention. Am I being unfair, Rosie?'

'I don't know, Alex. You could be right, but the only way to find out is for you to be with her again. It would be too late once you are married, so maybe some time together is what you both need.'

'Are you happy, Rosie?'

The question came as a shock and she answered mechanically. 'I am, or I will be when Piers is out of danger.'

'Yes, of course.' Alex reached for a slice of toast. 'This is very pleasant, Rosie. Do you think we could rise early and share breakfast every day?'

She found herself relaxing, her anxiety calmed by his easy charm. 'I don't see why not. Although Hester won't approve.'

'That will make it even more fun. We'll go back to the lives we have planned soon enough. Let's enjoy this precious interlude.'

Rosalind smiled. 'You are a bad influence, Alex.'

'What were you thinking of?' Hester demanded crossly.

'We had breakfast together, that's all.' Rosalind

handed the tray of crockery to Agathe. 'I was up early and Alex was awake and hungry. What would you expect me to do?'

'I'm not fooled by that innocent look, Rosalind. What would your husband say if he knew you were paying so much attention to the man you almost married?'

'Alex and I were never formally engaged. All right, Hester, I did once imagine myself to be in love with him, as I admitted before, but it was over a long time ago. Alex and I are friends, and when we get home eventually he'll marry my sister.'

'Hmm.' Hester shrugged. 'I know you believe that, but we're in a foreign land amongst strangers. Alexander is a charmer and we've been through this before. Take care, that's all I'm saying.'

'You worry too much,' Rosalind said lightly. 'Now, I'm going to wrap up and go across the road to the hospital to spend some time with Piers. It's Christmas Eve, Hester. Let's do what we can to make the best of things. You have to trust me.'

'Oh, I trust you, poppet. It's Captain Alexander Blanchard I don't trust.'

Rosalind knew it was useless to argue with Hester, who seemed to have the power to read minds as well as hearts. She wrapped a warm cloak around herself and braved the cold to cross the road to the hospital.

Sister Dominque greeted her with a calm smile. 'How is the gallant captain today, Madame Blanchard?'

'He is very grateful to everyone here for what they have done for him,' Rosalind said tactfully. 'He seems quite cheerful and determined to follow the doctor's instructions to the letter. Is there any change in my husband's condition?'

'I am afraid not, Madame. Do you need me to show you the way to his room?'

'No, don't let me take you away from your work. I'll find him.' Rosalind walked off purposefully, making her way through the echoing stone-flagged corridors, past the now familiar male ward and ending up at the door of the room where Piers was receiving treatment. She opened it and stepped inside to find everything exactly as she had left it the day before.

'Good morning, my love,' Rosalind said in a low voice. 'It's Christmas Eve and we've moved Alex over to the château. I hope it won't be too long before you wake up and the doctors allow you to come home, too. We're all waiting for you.' She hesitated, hoping to see a flicker of his eyelids or the slightest movement of his fingers, but he remained motionless. She tried again, describing the meal that they were preparing and all the people who were going to share the festivities with them. In the end she found herself babbling about anything that came into her head. After what seemed like an eternity she rose to her feet and kissed him on the cheek. It was heartbreaking to see the man she had married turned to a living statue by a tragic accident. She felt guilty for recoiling from him when perhaps she should have taken him in her arms and attempted to breathe life into his inert body. The contrast between Piers and Alex, who despite his injury was bubbling over with life and warmth, was so marked that she was suddenly angry.

'This is all your fault, Piers Blanchard,' she said in a low voice. 'Perhaps if you'd stayed at home more, instead of devoting all your time to business, you wouldn't have ended up like a dead fish on a marble slab.' She backed away from the bed. 'If you'd shown me more consideration I wouldn't find my old feelings for Alex coming back to haunt me.'

She left the room and hurried past Sister Dominique. One word of sympathy from anyone would be enough to make her break down the iron reserve she had built up since finding Piers in such a dire state. She crossed the street and entered the garden but she was still struggling with a maelstrom of emotions, and instead of letting herself into the château she fought her way through the undergrowth to what must once have been a pleasure garden. Patches of snow remained beneath the shrubs and the paths were overgrown with weeds and the trailing fronds of ivy. Thorny shoots of brambles clutched at her skirts, but Rosalind shook free of them and kept walking with no particular aim other than to get away from a situation where she was virtually helpless. She crossed what must once have been a lawn fit for a game of croquet but was now hummocky

with coarse tufts of couch grass, and she headed
blindly for a hawthorn hedge. She could hear the
waves beating on the shore at the foot of the cliffs,
and she had a sudden longing to climb down to the
beach, as she had done so many times at home.

She found a gap between tangled branches, but
she missed her footing on the icy ground and began
to slide helplessly towards the edge of the cliff. She
clutched at anything within her grasp but the more
she fought to regain her balance the quicker she slid
towards the precipice. Then, suddenly she was jerked
backwards, the breath knocked from her lungs, and
then the world turned upside down as she was flung
over a man's shoulder. She hung helplessly, bumping
up and down against his booted legs as he strode
onwards, regardless of the snapping branches and
grasping thorns.

'Put me down,' Rosalind gasped in between
sobbing breaths as they skirted the lawn and the
shrubbery, ending up in the cobbled yard at the back
of the château. She found herself unceremoniously
dumped on her feet.

Delfosse grunted and stomped off, entering the
château through a back door. Rosalind took a
moment or two to smooth her ruffled garments
and pat her hair in place before fastening her
bonnet, which had come untied during her somewhat rough rescue. She followed Delfosse into the
maze of corridors, which would have been the
domain of the servants in the old days, but were

now empty and sending back mocking echoes of her footsteps. Rosalind passed the open scullery door where Agathe was washing dishes in the stone sink. She walked on and entered the kitchen where Hester had her sleeves rolled up and her arms white with flour as she kneaded bread dough.

'What happened to you?' Hester demanded. 'Why did you come in that way?'

'I wanted some fresh air,' Rosalind said weakly. 'I've been to see Piers and he's no better. I think he's dying, Hester.'

'Now, now, don't talk like that, poppet. You mustn't give up hope.' Hester eyed her curiously. 'That doesn't explain the state of you. Your hair is all over the place, your skirt is torn and there's mud on your hem.'

'I almost had an accident. I didn't realise how slippery it was. I fell and was sliding towards the edge of the cliffs when Delfosse saved me.'

At that moment Madame Planche burst into the kitchen. 'My brother tells me you were roaming round the grounds, Madame. That was foolish.'

Rosalind stared at her in amazement. 'You speak English.'

'When it suits me, yes. Madame de Gris entertained many foreigners like you, and I found it necessary to learn the language. I only speak it when I have to, and now is the time. Do not go beyond the pleasure garden, if you must go out at all. The cliff is falling away into the sea.'

'I won't go out there again,' Rosalind said hastily. 'Please thank Monsieur Delfosse for saving me.'

'You were lucky he saw you or you wouldn't be here now.' Madame Planche tossed her head. 'I have told him to light the fire in the grand dining room. With so many people you cannot eat at a small table in the drawing room. Madame de Gris would turn in her grave.'

'But Alex can't move,' Rosalind protested.

'Delfosse will carry him and we will place two chairs together to support his leg. You must set the table, but I will unlock Madame's silver and best china. It is Christmas Eve, after all, but tomorrow we go back to normal.'

'I'm very grateful, Madame,' Rosalind said earnestly. 'I'm sure Father Laurent will appreciate the trouble you've gone to.'

'I should hope so.' Madame Planche poked her finger into the resting bread dough. 'You need to get that into the oven quickly, Madame.' She marched out of the kitchen, slamming the door behind her.

'I preferred it when she only spoke her own lingo,' Hester said grimly. 'I don't want to hurry you, Rosie, but I'd be grateful for a hand with the preparations for our festive dinner. Keeping busy will help you to stop worrying about your husband.'

'I'd better see if Alex needs anything first.'

'He's perfectly all right. I took him hot water and he's had a wash and shave, so there's nothing you can do for him at the moment. There'll be plenty of time to chat later.'

Rosalind smiled reluctantly. Hester could be relied upon for good sound common sense and sometimes it was comforting to follow instructions rather than to be the one giving them. She did as Hester suggested and threw herself into helping with the preparations for the meal.

When the table in the dining room was laid and the food prepared, Rosalind went to her room to change into clean clothes. They had travelled light, but she had packed one of her favourite shot silk taffeta gowns, which changed from crimson to blue as it caught the light. It was, after all, Christmas and they were entertaining in style, even though Piers could not be with them. She put her hair up and fastened it with a pearl and amethyst comb. Now she felt in the spirit of the season and she went downstairs to the drawing room, ready to receive their guests.

'You look beautiful, Rosie,' Alex said softly.

'Merry Christmas, Alex.' Rosalind turned away hastily and began preparing the Christmas punch exactly as her grandfather had done every year. 'The guests will be here soon.'

'I should be doing that for you,' Alex said, sighing.

'Maybe next year. Everything should be back to normal then,' Rosalind said. 'You will be married to Patsy, and Piers will be fit and well again.'

'I hope we'll all be together, but if the trouble

continues in the Crimean Peninsula I'm afraid I will be sent there.'

Rosalind sliced an orange and dropped it into the mixture of rum and brandy, adding a generous amount of sugar and lemon rind. 'Don't say that, Alex. If you go to the Crimea that means Bertie will be there, too. I can't bear the thought of losing either of you.'

'Rosie—' Alex started to say something but was interrupted by a loud crashing on the door knocker. 'Our guests are eager,' he said, laughing.

'Agathe will let them in.' Rosalind was about to lift the kettle from the trivet in front of the fire to add hot water to the punch when Agathe burst into the room.

'Madame, a nun from the hospital is at the door. She says you must come quickly.'

Chapter Eight

Rosalind reached the front door to find Sister Dominique standing outside, shivering with cold.

'Sister Dominique – my husband . . .'

'He opened his eyes, Madame. He is conscious.'

'Has he spoken?'

'No, Madame. But Sister Mary-Grace sent me to fetch you. The doctor is with your husband now.'

'I'll come right away.' Rosalind spun round at the sound of footsteps and saw Hester hurrying towards her. 'Piers is conscious. I'm going to the hospital.'

Hester snatched a cloak off the hallstand and thrust it into Rosalind's hands. 'Put that on. We don't want you to catch your death of cold.'

'Thank you, Hester.' Rosalind wrapped it around her shoulders as she hurried after Sister Dominique, who was already halfway up the path, moving swiftly and silently like a dark shadow. Rosalind could hardly breathe as she entered the sickroom for the second time that day. Sister Mary-Grace was standing at the foot of the bed with the doctor.

'Madame Blanchard,' Sister Mary-Grace said with one of her rare smiles. She turned back to the doctor, speaking in rapid French and he responded with a nod.

'How is he?' Rosalind demanded anxiously. Piers looked disappointingly the same as when she had left him.

'Madame, you will forgive my English. It is not good, but your husband shows signs of recovery from the head injury.' The doctor, whose lined face was pale and wan with dark shadows underlining his weary eyes, gave her a vague smile. 'His lung infection is no worse, which is a good sign.'

'Thank you, Doctor,' Rosalind said earnestly. 'Does that mean he will be able to come home soon?'

'It is in the hands of God, Madame. But there is hope now.'

'I can't thank you and the sisters enough.'

'It is what we do, Madame.' The doctor turned to Sister Mary-Grace, speaking to her in a low voice. He listened to her response before picking up his medical bag and hurrying from the room.

'May I stay with him for a while?' Rosalind asked urgently.

Sister Dominque translated the question, receiving a nod from Sister Mary-Grace, who made haste to follow the doctor.

Rosalind moved closer so that she could hold Piers' hand. 'Will he hear me if I speak to him, Sister Dominique?'

'It can do no harm, Madame. I will be back later to check on Monsieur Blanchard.' Sister Dominique let herself out into the corridor and a blast of cold air rushed into the room.

Rosalind was overcome with shame when she recalled her outburst earlier and she leaned over to kiss Piers gently on the lips. 'You must get better now. When you are well enough we'll take you to the château, and then I hope we will be able to go home.'

Piers' eyelids flickered and he opened his eyes, staring at her blankly without any sign of recognition, which was the harshest blow of all. He closed his eyes again with a sigh, and Rosalind clutched his hand, holding it to her heart. 'You are on the mend, Piers. Next time I come here perhaps you'll realise it's me, Rosie, your wife.'

She stayed with him for a while, hoping that he might respond to her presence again, but he seemed to have lapsed into unconsciousness and there seemed little point in staying. She left the hospital, having made Sister Dominique promise to let her know the moment Piers opened his eyes again.

The smell of hot rum punch wafted round the entrance hall as Agathe let Rosalind into the house. She held her hand out to take Rosalind's cloak. 'How is Monsieur Blanchard?'

'He is getting better, Agathe. Or at least he opened his eyes, but he didn't know me. However, the doctor seems hopeful.'

'It is a Christmas miracle, Madame.'

'Yes, of course it must be.' Rosalind cocked her head on one side at the sound of laughter emanating from the drawing room. 'Are the guests here?'

'They are all very merry, Madame. The drink is making everyone happy.'

'Then you must join us, Agathe. We are all going to sit round the table together.'

'Madame Fournier will not approve.'

'Leave her to me. It's my house for the time being and I say that we all eat together at one table.'

Rosalind walked purposefully to the drawing room. Colonel Munday had put himself in charge of the large china bowl in which Rosalind had mixed the punch, and he was busy ladling the heady concoction into cups, there being no equivalent here to the punch glasses that the family used at Rockwood. Madame Planche had refused to allow them to put hot liquid in the late Madame de Gris's delicate wine glasses, but that did not seem to make any difference to the drinkers. The punch was obviously going down very well, if the flush on Father Laurent's cheeks was anything to go by. He was seated by the fire, chatting amicably to Madame Planche, who in turn was responding with a genuine smile. Madame Fournier, however, seemed to be having difficulty in communicating with Delfosse, who was at the sullen stage of intoxication. Rosalind met Alex's questioning look with a smile but she was accosted by Hester before she had a chance to cross the floor to speak to him.

'Well? Is it true? Agathe seemed to think that Sister Dominique had good news.'

'Piers opened his eyes once while I was there, although I don't think he recognised me. The doctor seems hopeful.'

Colonel Munday handed Rosalind a cup of punch. 'This will bring the colour back to your cheeks, ma'am. I couldn't help overhearing. We should drink to your husband's speedy recovery.'

'Thank you, Colonel. I'm afraid he has a long way to go.'

'Here's to his continued improvement.' Colonel Munday raised his cup and drained the contents in one large gulp. 'Excellent punch, Mrs Blanchard.' He turned to Hester. 'Allow me to refill your cup, Lady Carey.'

Rosalind left Hester to deal with the colonel and she edged her way past Delfosse and Madame Fournier, who seemed to be having an argument.

'Well?' Alex said, smiling. 'I believe it's good news.'

'At least he was conscious for a few seconds. The doctor seemed to think it's a good sign, but Piers didn't recognise me.'

Alex grasped her hand. 'I'm sorry, Rosie. I know how you must be feeling, but it's a start. Neither of us is much use to you at this moment, are we?'

'You are shameless, Alexander,' Rosalind said wearily. 'I'm not going to satisfy your vanity by answering that question.'

'But I can try to make you laugh.' His smile faded. 'And I can listen if you want to talk about it, Rosie. You know that, don't you?'

She glanced over her shoulder at the sound of footsteps and, seeing Hester advancing towards them, she freed her hand from Alex's warm grasp. 'What is it?'

'We're going to serve the food before the guests are too drunk to know what they're eating. Delfosse will carry you into the dining room, Alexander. I think we need to make a move before the creature gets to the falling down stage of drunkenness.'

Alex sighed. 'The sooner I can master walking with crutches the better.'

'You will join us, won't you?' Rosalind asked anxiously. 'Although you can have your meal here, if you'd rather.'

'No, I'll suffer the brute manhandling me, but only if I sit next to you, Rosie.' He gave Hester a mischievous smile. 'She keeps me in order, Hester.'

'Someone has to,' Hester said, sniffing. 'Come with me, Rosie. Agathe can't manage on her own and I don't want Madame Planche interfering in the kitchen.'

Rosalind handed her untouched cup of punch to Alex. 'Drink this,' she said in a low voice. 'It will deaden the pain.' She followed Hester to the kitchen where she was met by the delicious aroma of roast goose, and plum pudding steaming gently over a saucepan of hot water.

The guests were seated around the great table in the dining room, which was lit by all the spare candles that Rosalind had been able to find. It was mid-afternoon but it was dusk outside and the roaring log fire crackled and spat in the enormous stone fireplace, entertaining the party with a miniature firework display. Delfosse had brought half a dozen bottles of claret from the cellar and he saw to it that Alex's glass was never empty. Rosalind could tell from Alex's ashen cheeks that he was in a great deal of pain, but she knew better than to fuss over him. She could feel Hester's gaze upon her and she met her look with an attempt at a casual smile.

The meal began with vegetable soup followed by the roast goose, which Hester carved expertly. There were roast potatoes and parsnips, with a large dish of buttered cabbage, and rich gravy. All this was followed by plum pudding and brandy butter. It was a very traditional English Christmas dinner, but their French guests seemed to enjoy it and even Madame Planche found little to criticise. Colonel Munday could not praise the cooks enough and he ate until his face was as red as the claret in his glass.

Father Laurent had to leave soon after they finished eating as he had services to perform and Madame Fournier accompanied him. Colonel Munday fell asleep in his chair, and Delfosse was just sober enough to carry Alex back to his bed in the drawing room. The last Rosalind saw of Delfosse was when he and Madame Planche staggered off to their own quarters, each carrying a bottle of claret.

Later, when all the dishes were washed and put away, and Colonel Munday had left for his lodgings, having drunk several cups of black coffee, Hester fell asleep by the fire and Agathe went to her room to relax until it was time for her to attend midnight mass. Rosalind doubted whether Madame Planche and Delfosse would be going to church. Perhaps they would rise early, and gain favour with Father Laurent by attending the first mass on Christmas Day. At least their Christmas Eve dinner had been a success. Rosalind made coffee for herself and Alex, and took a tray to the drawing room.

'Are you in much pain?' she asked gently.

'I'm sore, but it was worth it. I'm just not suited to lying around in bed all day, Rosie. You know that.'

She poured the coffee. 'Yes, I do. If the pain is too bad I have the laudanum that Sister Delphine gave me for you.'

'Maybe later. Let's enjoy this quiet time together.'

Rosalind handed him a cup. 'The sooner we get home, the better, Alex.'

'Are you afraid of being alone with me?'

'How could I be afraid of you? If anything I'm scared of myself.'

'Why is that?'

'We know each other too well.'

'I was a fool to let you go.'

'I love Piers, and I believe you love my sister.'

'Can I not love both of you?'

Rosalind put her cup and saucer back on the tray. 'You should get some rest now.' She half rose to her feet but his hand shot out, and he pressed her back onto the chair with effortless strength. 'Don't run away, Rosie. I'd never do anything to hurt you. I love you and I always have, and I think you love me, too.'

She gazed down at his fingers encircling her wrist. 'It's the wine talking, Alex. Don't make me say something we'll both regret in the morning.'

He released her, shaking his head. 'I think you've answered me, Rosie. If you can't bring yourself to deny it that means you feel the same as I do. I won't ask you again if it upsets you, but I had to know.'

'Piers will recover and then we'll go home. You will marry Patsy and you'll return to your regiment. All this will be just a memory, Alex. It's an interlude in our lives that can never have a happy ending for either of us, at least not with each other.'

'It's Christmas, Rosie. Will you give me a kiss – a Christmas gift that will last me for ever?'

Rosalind glanced at Hester, who seemed to be asleep with her chin resting on her chest. 'I don't think that's a good idea.'

He slid his arm around her shoulders and drew her gently towards him. 'A Christmas kiss. What harm can there be in that?'

She looked into his eyes and saw herself mirrored in his dark pupils and she allowed him to pull her into his arms. Their lips met in a kiss that blotted out time and meaning. His mouth claimed hers in a delight that was both exciting and so familiar that she could not help but respond with equal passion. Her whole body seemed to melt in his arms and her hands caressed his cheeks.

'Rosalind Blanchard, what do you think you're doing?' Hester's irate voice made them pull apart.

Rosalind gazed at her blankly, her mind and body still consumed with desire that had set her senses aflame. Alex clutched her hand and they were both trembling.

'This has nothing to do with you, Hester,' Alex said angrily. 'This is our business, not yours.'

Rosalind raised his hand to her cheek. 'Hester's right, Alex. We shouldn't have done that.' She turned to look him in the eye. 'But I'm so glad we did.'

'Rosie, what are you saying?' Hester demanded angrily. 'Have you lost your senses?'

'It won't happen again.' Rosalind brushed Alex's hand with a tender kiss before releasing it. 'We both know it was wrong, but we couldn't help ourselves. Neither of us has forgotten where our loyalties lie – I'm married to Piers and Alex is going to marry my sister.'

'Keep telling yourself that,' Alex said in a low voice, 'but it doesn't alter anything, Rosie. You belong to me, heart and soul. You'll never change that.'

'That's quite enough of that,' Hester said sternly. 'It's the drink and the festive season that's brought this on. Tomorrow you'll both suffer from the memory of it. I think you ought to go to bed now, Rosie. I'll make Alexander comfortable.'

Rosalind stood her ground. 'No, Hester. I know what you're doing, but I'm a grown woman now. I love you, but you can't protect me for ever. I'll make my own mistakes and I'll pay for them. Thank you for everything you've done today, but I think you should go to bed. You've earned a good rest.'

Hester opened her mouth as if to protest but she seemed to think better of it and she marched out of the room without saying a word.

'It's time you stood up to her, Rosie,' Alex said seriously. 'She's a good woman and I know she loves you like a mother, but she mustn't be allowed to run your life.'

'It grieves me to speak sharply to her, but this is between us, Alex. It's no one's business but ours, and neither of us wants to hurt the people who love us.' Rosalind managed a weak smile. 'It's Christmas, we should try to be happy. At least you and Piers are safe and your leg will mend. I just hope Piers makes a full recovery.'

'I hope so, too.' Alex leaned back against the pillows. 'You should try to get some sleep, Rosie. You were up early, and I don't need anything more tonight. That's the advantage of being permanently in a nightshirt and dressing robe. I don't have to bother with boots and buttons, but tomorrow I'm going to get Delfosse to make me a pair of crutches. I've had enough of being an invalid. I'll get back on my feet, if it kills me.'

Delfosse obliged, but only after being paid handsomely for making two wooden crutches that were not exactly works of art, but were strictly functional, which was all Alex had wanted. He persevered with them even though every movement hurt, but he was determined to become mobile.

In the days that followed, Hester did everything she could to prevent Rosalind and Alex being left on their own, and nothing Rosalind could say would persuade her to act differently. Alex found it amusing, and he treated it like a game, snatching a kiss whenever Hester had to leave the room or if her back was turned. Rosalind tried to reprimand him, but she knew that their brief reunion could not last, and soon enough they would return to the lives they had planned.

She could not quite bear to let Alex go, at least not until it became absolutely necessary, but despite her feelings for him her first loyalty was to Piers and she visited him every day. He had regained consciousness and he recognised her eventually, but he was still very unwell. There was little that Rosalind could do other than sit and talk to him, but even that seemed to exhaust him, and the sister on duty would urge her to go away and come back later. Rosalind prayed for a miracle and on New

Year's Eve when she visited the hospital she was met by a smiling Sister Dominique.

'Madame Blanchard, the fever has broken. Monsieur is still very weak but he has been asking for you.'

'Thank God,' Rosalind said fervently. 'May I see him now?'

'Of course, Madame. You know the way.'

Rosalind burst into the room. 'Piers. You're better.' She rushed over to the bed and grasped his hand.

He gave her a weak smile. 'I think the fever has left me.'

'Sister Dominique seems to think so. It's such a relief. Now all you have to do is to recover completely. You've been very ill, my love.'

'I can't believe that you're here in France. Sister Dominique tells me that you arrived before Christmas and you've been to see me every day.'

'Don't exhaust yourself by talking, Piers. Save your strength and as soon as the doctor says it's safe for you to be moved you can come to the Château Gris to recuperate before we take you home.'

He pulled a face. 'You make me sound like a helpless infant.'

'You will be very weak, but we'll soon rectify that. Hester is here with me and Alex is at the château, too.'

'They tell me he broke his leg when his ship was wrecked. I don't remember any of it, Rosie. My memory is a complete blank.'

'Perhaps that's just as well. It must have been terrible, but you're safe now and I'm here to make sure you continue to progress well. I have so much to tell you, but perhaps not now.'

He closed his eyes. 'I am a bit tired, but I do want to hear it all.'

Rosalind glanced over her shoulder as Sister Dominique entered the room. 'I think the sister would like me to leave you, but I'll come back later.' She leaned over the bed and kissed him gently on the lips. She left the room hurriedly, unable to look Sister Dominique in the face as a feeling of guilt assailed her, and as she left the hospital to cross the street she kept telling herself that she loved her husband. What she felt for Alex was a passing fancy brought about by the situation in which they found themselves. The two brothers were so different from each other that it seemed impossible for her to be torn between them. Alex was her old love, but Piers was her husband and her future, and when they returned to Devon everything would be as it was before.

She was met by Alex, who had managed to get as far as the entrance hall on his crutches. He came to a halt, balancing precariously on one leg and a crutch. 'Look at me, Rosie. I'm walking again.'

'So you are.' Rosalind smiled in spite of everything. 'Don't overdo it, Alex.'

'You know me: I won't give up until I can run a mile on these wretched things. Well, perhaps not a mile, but I can move about without too much difficulty. It's a start.'

'Piers is much better,' Rosalind said hastily. 'He

was able to talk to me quite rationally, and the doctors are very pleased with his progress.'

'That's excellent. I might hop over to see him in a day or two.' He chuckled. 'Don't look at me like that, Rosie. I'll be sensible, but seriously, I am glad my brother is on the mend.'

Rosalind was about to reply when Hester came bustling towards them. 'Is that true? Is Piers really out of danger?'

'Yes, Hester. He's making rapid progress. I hope to be able to bring him here soon and then we can plan our return to England.'

'I've grown quite fond of the old haunted château,' Alex said cheerfully. 'Rockwood will seem quite tame after living here for a while.'

'I think it's time you made your way back to the drawing room. You don't want to overdo things, Alexander.' Hester stepped in between him and Rosalind. 'I can't wait to get home myself. When do you think they will allow Piers to leave the hospital, Rosie? We could look after him very well.'

'We'll just have to wait and see what the doctors say.'

Alex swung round on his crutches and started back towards the drawing room. 'We should celebrate. It's New Year's Eve and both my brother and I are on the mend, so what better reason for a party?'

'I haven't recovered from all that work on Christmas Eve,' Hester said irritably. 'You need to rest. The sooner you get back to your regiment the better for all of us.'

'Hester!' Rosalind stared at her in disbelief. 'That's unkind.'

'No, poppet. It's not wrong to want everything to get back to normal. Being confined to this weird old house is affecting you and Alexander. I can speak out because I love you as if you were my own daughter, and Patsy, too. I don't want to see either of you broken-hearted.'

Alex stopped and turned back to face her. 'I've been very patient with you, Hester, because I know you love Rosie, but so do I and we are adults – we make our own choices. That said, neither of us wants to upset those who love us, so you'll just have to trust me to do the right thing.' He swung round on his crutches and marched off with surprising speed towards the drawing room.

'Hmm.' Hester shook her head. 'I think he believes what he says, but I know you both very well. Sometimes good intentions are not enough.'

'Don't say any more,' Rosalind said crossly. 'Alex is right. We'll have a special meal tonight and a bottle of Champagne. I'll take Agathe and go to market. This is a celebration, Hester. Piers is on the mend and soon we'll be returning to our normal lives at Rockwood. The old year is on the way out and tomorrow we start afresh. I mean that.'

'I hope you do, for all our sakes. I'll find Agathe and send her to you.'

*   *   *

149

On her way to market Rosalind spotted Colonel Munday coming out of the shipping office. He greeted her with a wide smile. 'Good morning, ma'am.'

'Colonel Munday. You look very pleased with yourself.'

'I've just had confirmation of a ship due to arrive tomorrow morning to take the rest of my men back to England. How are you, ma'am? Is your husband showing any improvement?'

Rosalind smiled and nodded. 'Yes, he is and this evening we're having a New Year's Eve dinner. You would be most welcome to come and join us, if you are not otherwise engaged.'

'It's my last night in France. I would be delighted.'

'Then we'll see you at about seven, if that's convenient?'

'Thank you, ma'am. That will be excellent.' Colonel Munday tipped his hat and walked on.

'Come, Agathe,' Rosalind said with a smile. 'We'd better get to market before everything is sold out.'

'Madame Planche will expect to be invited.' Agathe pulled a face. 'And Monsieur Delfosse. You know she can be very difficult if she feels she's being left out.'

'Then we'll invite them both. What do you suggest we serve, Agathe?'

'Oysters, if there are any left in the market, and Champagne.'

'Bread and different cheeses, too. Then we don't have to cook. What a good idea.'

The informal meal was a great success. Delfosse had been called upon to shuck and prepare the oysters, which Rosalind did not particularly enjoy but she knew from past experience that Alex had a fondness for them. Colonel Munday also displayed a liking for them, as did Delfosse, and Madame Planche ate so many that Rosalind feared she might be ill. Hester preferred the bread and cheese, and after a couple of glasses of Champagne she became quite cheerful and more like her old self. Rosalind was careful to avoid showing any preference for Alex's company and she devoted herself to keeping Colonel Munday entertained. She also drank freely of the Champagne and the colonel had brought with him a bottle of Calvados.

Agathe had declined the offer to join them, but she waited on them at table and left shortly after she had brought them their coffee. Madame Planche brought out the best brandy goblets and shortly before midnight Colonel Munday rose from the table to propose a toast.

'I want to thank you for entertaining me so royally, and I look forward to seeing you back on duty as soon as your broken bones heal, Alex. You're a fine officer and you will be missed by your men, so I hope you are fit enough to return soon. I would like to raise a toast to Mrs Blanchard for her hospitality and kindness, and to the health of Mr Blanchard, whom I have yet to meet.'

Alex raised his glass to Rosalind, but she glanced away quickly, aware that Hester was watching their every move. Later, when Madame Planche and Delfosse had returned to their part of the château and Colonel Munday had said his last goodbye, Hester took a candle to light her to her room.

'You'd better go before me, Rosie,' she said firmly. 'I'll fall asleep as soon as my head hits the pillow. I don't even mind sleeping on my own now.'

'Good night, Alex,' Rosalind called over her shoulder as she mounted the stairs. She would have liked to kiss him good night, but she had made a firm resolution to resist the overwhelming attraction she felt for him. She kissed Hester on the cheek. 'Good night, Hester.'

'Good night, poppet. You're doing the right thing.' Hester went into her room and closed the door.

Rosalind sighed as she entered her own room and set the candlestick down on the table by the bed. She undressed slowly, standing in front of the dying embers of the fire. She reached for her nightgown and was about to slip it on when she heard her door creak open.

'Did you forget something?' She spun round to see Alex standing in the doorway.

'What do you think you're doing? Go away.' Rosalind backed into the shadows.

'You don't mean that, Rosie.' Alex edged into the room, closing the door behind him.

'Of course I do. What are you thinking?'

He swayed on his feet. 'Do you mind if I sit down?' He moved awkwardly towards the bed and slumped onto it with a groan. 'This isn't how I imagined it would be. I'm sorry.'

'So you should be.' Rosalind turned away to slip her nightgown over her head. 'I'll help you down the stairs, but you must go back to your own bed.'

He nodded. 'You're right. I just wanted to be close to you – I shouldn't have come.' He lay back against the pillows closing his eyes.

Rosalind moved nearer. 'Are you in a lot of pain?'

'Yes, and before you say anything, I know it serves me right. Blame the wine and the Calvados.'

She perched on the edge of the bed, brushing his fair hair back from his forehead. 'No, I blame you, Alex. This is your fault entirely.' She pulled the coverlet over him. 'Go to sleep.'

He opened his eyes. 'You're letting me stay?'

'Only if you behave yourself. If I try to help you down the stairs we'll almost certainly disturb Hester, and that's the last thing I want.'

'I may never get another chance to be with you like this,' Alex said sleepily.

'We had our chance to be together two years ago, Alex. It's too late to change our minds now.' Rosalind went to sit by the fire, but she became cramped and cold, and in desperation she climbed into bed, keeping as far apart from Alex as was possible. She sank into a deep sleep, comforted by his nearness and the warmth of his body.

Chapter Nine

'That must never happen again, Alex.' Rosalind placed his breakfast tray on a small table by his chair in the drawing room. 'If we'd come down a couple of minutes later we would have met Agathe on the stairs.'

'She would probably think it very romantic. I don't imagine the French are as prudish as we English.'

'Even so, I don't want what happened last night to come to Hester's attention. We'd never hear the last of it, and I couldn't live with that.'

'I'm hardly going to boast about it, Rosie. It wasn't my finest hour.'

She smiled reluctantly. 'Maybe it was in a way. You must have been in agony by the time you climbed all those stairs on your crutches. I suppose I should be flattered.'

'You are a wonderful woman. You would have made an amazing military wife – I just wish I'd carried you off when I had a chance.'

Rosalind shook her head. 'You must stop thinking like that. When we get home you are going to marry my sister. Patsy is very young, but she will learn to cope with any situation that arises when you are living in married quarters. She will charm all your fellow officers and you will be the proudest husband in the regiment.'

'Do you really believe that, Rosie?'

'I have to,' Rosalind said simply. 'Piers is on the mend and soon we will go home and resume our old lives. All this will seem like a dream.'

Alex glanced over her shoulder. 'Good morning, Hester. I hope you slept well.'

'I thought I heard voices coming from your room last night, Rosie. I suppose I was dreaming. It must have been that foreign cheese.'

'Yes, I think it must,' Rosalind said quickly. 'Would you like some coffee? I was just going to the kitchen to make a fresh pot.'

'I'd prefer a cup of tea, but I suppose coffee will do. My head is aching and I blame the colonel for that. It's just as well he's leaving today – he's a bad influence.' She stared at Alex's splinted leg. 'If I didn't know it was impossible I would have thought it was your voice I heard last night, Alexander.'

He smiled innocently. 'Well, as you see, I've made it this far from my bed, but I doubt if I could manage two flights of stairs. I've heard that cheese eaten before bedtime can give you nightmares.'

Rosalind escaped to the kitchen, taking the coffee pot with her. She knew that Hester was suspicious and that the situation between herself and Alex could easily get out of hand. They needed to get back to the family and familiar surroundings. As soon as the doctors discharged Piers from hospital she would do her utmost to find a vessel to take them home.

It took a month to get Piers well enough to travel and by this time Alex was able to move around reasonably well on crutches, but the doctor said it would be at least another couple of months before he returned to anything like normal. Piers, on that other hand, had recovered fully from the lung infection and the head injury, although he was still very weak and had been ordered to rest as much as possible. With this in mind Rosalind had chartered a vessel to take them direct to the quay at Rockwood, and she sent a message ahead advising her family of their expected date of arrival. Even so, it was a pleasant surprise to disembark late on a cold February afternoon to find Jim Gurney waiting for them with the landau. Half an hour later they were being greeted by Jarvis, who could not quite conceal his delight in seeing them safe and sound.

They had barely taken off their outdoor garments when Lady Pentelow bore down on them. 'Piers, my boy, and Alex. You poor things, we've been so worried about you.'

'I didn't think you would still be here, Lady Pentelow,' Rosalind said, frowning.

'I stayed because I was needed, Rosalind. Your mother and her new husband left for London immediately after the wedding, without stopping to consider what might happen to Patricia, who was distraught. It was my duty to remain here and supervise the running of the household.'

'It was good of you, Grandmama,' Piers said, kissing her on the cheek. 'Thank you.'

'You must be exhausted after that long voyage, Piers.' Lady Pentelow glanced at Alexander, shaking her head. 'You look a sorry state, Alex. Come into the drawing room and I'll send for refreshments.'

Hester bridled visibly. 'There's no need to trouble yourself, Lady Pentelow. I will take over now.'

'We'll all take tea in the drawing room, Hester,' Piers tucked his grandmother's hand in the crook of his arm. 'You'd better tell Cook that there will be four extra for dinner.'

'I'm sure that Hester is just as tired as the rest of us after that long journey,' Rosalind said hastily. 'There's no need to go to any trouble, Hester. Come and sit with us and I'll ring for Tilly.'

'It's all right, poppet.' Hester gave her a weary smile. 'I'll go to my room to rest before dinner, but I'll call in at the kitchen on my way. I want to make sure that Mrs Jackson knows who is in charge now.'

Rosalind met Hester's wry smile with a chuckle. 'Of course. We must get back to normal as soon as possible.'

Piers headed for the drawing room. Rosalind noticed that he was walking much slower than normal and he seemed to be leaning on his grandmother's arm for support. She felt a shiver run down her spine. The crossing from France had taken less than twenty-four hours, but now she worried that it might have been too much for him.

She looked round to see Alex standing at her side. 'Don't worry about him, Rosie. My brother is stronger than he looks.'

'Yes, of course. How are you, though, Alex? Is your leg very painful?'

He smiled. 'I can bear it. Anyway, it's good to be home. I feel more comfortable here than I do at Trevenor – don't ask me why.'

Rosalind gave him a vague smile. If she encouraged him they were in danger of lapsing into the relationship that had developed between them in France, and she was painfully aware that this must be avoided at all costs. 'Patricia will be waiting to see you. She must be so excited.'

They followed Piers and his grandmother into the drawing room where Patricia and Aurelia were seated at a table, playing a game of loo.

'Patsy,' Alexander said tentatively.

'We're home at last.' Rosalind made an effort to sound casual, but she could see that her sister was not going to let Alex off lightly.

'Patricia,' Lady Pentelow said sharply. 'Have you nothing to say to Alexander?'

Patricia looked up from the hand of cards she was clutching. 'What does one say in a situation like this?'

'Don't be mean, Patsy.' Aurelia jumped to her feet and hugged Alex and then Piers. 'Welcome, brothers. I'm so glad you are both on the mend.' She turned to Rosalind with a smile. 'Thank you for everything you did for them, Rosie. You are a heroine in my eyes.'

Lady Pentelow sat down with a regal nod of her head. 'I've told Rosalind she should have hired a nurse to take over the personal duties. It isn't done for a lady to soil her hands in such a way. That's why we have servants.'

'Perhaps my grandmother is right.' Piers drew Rosalind aside, lowering his voice, while Lady Pentelow continued in the same vein. 'I didn't think at the time, but we should have paid someone to look after both myself and Alex. It wasn't for you to do.'

Rosalind stared at him in amazement. 'I thought that was part of my marriage vows, Piers. You were sick and I was there to look after you.'

'But you weren't married to Alex. It's obvious that he's still very fond of you, despite being engaged to your sister, and that worries me.'

'Are you feeling all right, Piers?' Rosalind raised her hand to lay it on his forehead. 'I hope the boat trip hasn't brought on another bout of fever.'

'Of course it hasn't. I'm quite well now and we're home at Rockwood, although heaven knows what state the business is in. I'll need to travel to Cornwall at the first opportunity to check that Pedrick has been coping during my absence.'

'All in good time,' Rosalind said gently. 'But first you need to rest and recover from the journey. You know that the doctor said you were to take matters very easily for a while.' If she had thought that coming home would make things easier, she realised now that they still had a long way to go. Piers was jealous of his brother and he made that very clear. No matter how hard Rosalind tried to convince him that there was nothing between herself and Alex, she was aware that her husband sensed the change in their relationship.

'I was talking to you, Rosalind,' Lady Pentelow said peevishly. 'You'll have plenty of time to chat to Piers later.'

'I'm sorry, ma'am,' Rosalind said hastily. 'What did you say?'

'I asked you to speak to your sister. She's behaving like a child.'

Rosalind crossed the room to sit beside Patricia. 'I'm sorry it took so long to get home, Patsy, but it was unavoidable. We had to make sure that both Alex and Piers were fit to undertake the crossing.'

'That's no excuse.' Patricia shrugged and turned back to her hand of cards.

'Whatever you think, we're here now, Patsy. You

can plan your wedding and I promise you it will be twice as splendid as the one that Mama and Claude had.'

Patricia tossed her head. 'I'm not sure I want to marry Alex.'

'Why not?' Alexander stared at her in amazement. 'I couldn't help being injured when the ship ran aground.'

'You didn't even write to me. It was your leg you hurt, not your right hand. Even if you couldn't hold a pen you could have asked Rosie to note things down for you. I'm not sure I want to marry such a selfish, thoughtless person.'

'That's a bit unfair, Patsy,' Aurelia said, frowning. 'They were in a foreign country.'

'What do you know about it, Aurelia? You are hardly an expert in affairs of the heart. If you had shown more interest in Hugo Knighton he might not have married that ugly heiress.'

'Don't get into an argument with my sister because of me, Patsy. I admit that I should have tried harder to contact you, but I was in such terrible pain for so long that all I could think about was myself.' Alex sent a pleading look to Rosalind. 'Isn't that so, Rosie? I was a difficult patient and you are glad to be free from me.'

'No, Alex. I'm not going to lie because my sister has chosen to be difficult.' Rosalind looked from one expectant face to the other and she shook her head. 'As a matter of fact, Alex was a model patient. He charmed everyone, even our grumpy landlady, Madame Planche. Her drunkard of a brother, Delfosse, would do anything for Alex, as well as Agathe, the young maid who acted as our interpreter.'

'You're making matters worse.' Aurelia glanced anxiously at Patsy. 'Rosie is teasing you.'

'No, I am not.' Rosalind eyed them all defiantly. 'You can't imagine the difficulties we all faced in France. We were living in this creepy old château far from home. Piers nearly died and Alex couldn't do a thing for himself, at least not in the beginning. Hester and I worked really hard to look after them both.'

'What do you want me to say?' Patricia demanded crossly. 'It seems to me that I'm the one who has been badly treated. I had to stand by and watch my own mother take her marriage vows in front of all the guests who had come thinking they would see Alex marry me.'

Alexander eyed her, frowning. 'I was in hospital, Patsy.'

'They all thought I had been jilted.' Patricia tossed her head. 'Everyone pretended to be sympathetic, but I know what they were thinking. I was utterly humiliated.'

'I'm sorry,' Alexander said humbly. 'I don't know what else to say.'

'Perhaps it would be better if you two talked this over in private?' Rosalind suggested tentatively. 'We've had a long journey and we're all very tired.'

Patricia tossed her cards on the table. 'I don't want to play any more.' She stood up, facing Alexander with a defiant look. 'I'm releasing you from our engagement, Alex. I've had a taste of what it might be like to be married to a soldier and I don't think I want to live like that.'

'Perhaps you're right,' Alexander said slowly. 'But maybe we just need to get to know each other again. It's going to be a couple of months at least before I am considered fit enough to resume my duties. We could begin again, Patsy.'

She shook her head. 'Aurelia and your grand-mother are returning to Trevenor. I think it best if I go with them. Quite honestly I don't want to be stuck here with you hobbling around on crutches, trying to make me feel sorry for you.'

'Patsy, that's a horrible thing to say.' Rosalind could hardly believe her ears.

'I think, in the circumstances, that it is eminently sensible,' Lady Pentelow said bluntly. 'We were plan-ning to return home, but I wanted to make sure my grandsons were in good health before I left Rockwood. To be frank, I have had enough of this draughty old pile, and I long for the comforts of home.'

'If you give me a day or so to get over the journey from France, I'll accompany you, Grandmama.' Piers managed a smile. 'I need to see Pedrick and make sure the business has not suffered too much from my absence.'

'Of course, Piers, my dear. Anything you say.' Lady Pentelow smiled contentedly. 'It will be delightful having my dear grandson with me again.'

'I won't be joining you, Grandmama,' Alexander said firmly. 'I can't ride yet, and anyway, I have to return to my regiment as soon as my leg heals.'

'In that case I think Rosalind ought to accompany me to Trevenor.' Piers glared at his brother. 'My wife isn't your nurse, Alex. You'd do well to remember that.'

'I will stay here, Piers.' Rosalind met his angry gaze with a defiant lift of her chin. 'We agreed from the start that we would live at Rockwood until such time as I was no longer needed here. You can't go back on our agreement now.'

'I'm your husband and I say that your place is with me.'

'What's the matter with you, Piers?' Aurelia stared at him in disbelief. 'Why are you being so unreasonable?'

Piers sank down on a chair by the fireplace. 'I'm not the one who is in the wrong.'

'I'm glad I'm not marrying into your family.' Patricia twisted her engagement ring off her finger and threw it at Alexander. 'You are both as bad as each other. I can't think why I agreed to marry you in the first place.'

'I'm sorry, Patsy. That's all I can say.' Alexander limped out of the room.

'You saw that,' Patricia said angrily. 'Alex just

walked away. He doesn't love me. I don't think he ever did.'

'Patsy, you just threw your engagement ring at him.' Rosalind stared at her sister in disbelief. 'What did you expect him to do?'

'If he really cared for me he would have tried to persuade me to change my mind. Now I know it was a terrible mistake.' Patricia ran from the room, sobbing.

'Really, such displays of emotion are very vulgar.' Lady Pentelow rose from her seat and walked to the door. 'I'm going to my boudoir. Aurelia, come with me. I think we should instruct our maids to start packing.' She stormed out of the drawing room, almost bumping into Tilly, who was carrying a tray loaded with tea and cake.

'See what you've done, Piers. We were going along quite happily until you returned.' Aurelia cast him a withering look as she followed her grandmother from the room.

'This is some homecoming,' Piers said stonily. 'Aurelia is right in one thing. This is my brother's fault. We were happy until he came back on the scene.'

'Thank you, Tilly.' Rosalind waited until Tilly had left the room. 'Things haven't been good between us for a while, Piers. You spend so much time away on business that I rarely see you, and when you are at home you're too tired to pay much attention to me.'

'Are you saying I'm a bad husband?'

'I'm saying you're a good businessman, but where does that leave me?'

'I've done everything you asked of me. I've poured money into renovating Rockwood and I live here instead of my home in Cornwall, which in turn means that I have to spend time away in order to keep the business going. This old pile of stones doesn't even belong to us. Bertie will marry one day and he'll bring his wife here to run the household. Where will you be then?'

Rosalind poured the tea and took a cup to him. 'That's what I'm trying to say, Piers. We need time together and that doesn't entail living at Trevenor, with your grandmother organising every minute of our lives. I love Aurelia but she is very demanding. Moreover, you should heed what the French doctor told you, and that means rest and recuperation.'

'What exactly are you saying?' Piers eyed her coldly.

'I'm asking you not to go to Cornwall for a while. Send instructions to Pedrick, or even ask him to come here and report to you, but please be sensible.'

Piers stared into the teacup. 'Perhaps you're right. I'll stay here for a week or two, but only if Alex goes to Cornwall. If he stays here he will take up most of your time – I know my brother better than you do.'

'Of course, but he said he can't ride. It's a long journey.'

'He can ride in the carriage with Grandmama and Aurelia.'

'You're forgetting that Patsy wants to go with them.'

'She can choose to remain here if she doesn't wish to associate with Alex, but perhaps they would make up their differences if they spent time together.' Piers sipped his tea. 'Does that thought bother you?'

'No, of course not.' Rosalind hoped she sounded confident, although if she were to be honest she was not sure. A small part of her had felt relieved when Patsy threw the ring at Alex. She realised now that the weeks spent in the Château Gris had been like living in a fantasy world where romance was the key. She had allowed herself to fall in love with Alex all over again, even though they had parted two years ago. Now she was back in her old home and once again she would become Mrs Piers Blanchard and the rebellious, romantic young woman would be left behind in France to haunt the Château Gris along with the other unhappy souls.

'What are you thinking, Rosie?'

She met his challenging look with an attempt at a smile. 'I think you're right, Piers. We need to start again. It's up to Patsy and Alex how they approach the future, whether together or apart, but I think I should have a word with my sister before things get even more out of hand.'

Rosalind hurried upstairs to Patsy's room. She knocked and entered without waiting for an answer.

'What do you want?' Patsy was seated in front of the dressing-table mirror, brushing her hair. 'I've said all I have to say.'

Rosalind sat on the edge of the bed. 'I understand why you're upset, but it's not fair to blame Alex for everything.'

'You always take his side. I think you still have a soft spot for him.'

'I admit that I'm very fond of Alex, but he's my brother-in-law. I love Piers.'

Patricia turned to face her. 'Do you really? You don't seem to be on very good terms now.'

'We've had a long journey and we're tired. Piers isn't fully recovered from his illness. I want him to stay here until he's regained his strength.'

'Why do you want to live here, Rosie? You married Piers, and Trevenor is your rightful home.'

The direct question took Rosalind's breath away momentarily, but she managed a smile. 'Piers might be the owner but Lady Pentelow runs the household. Can you imagine anyone trying to take her place?'

'I think it's Rockwood Castle you love more than anything or anyone. This place has a strange effect on people.'

'What are you talking about, Patsy?'

'Aurelia and I believe that Marianne Carey's ghost still walks this castle. Farmer Greep's wife told us about the curse that Marianne is said to have put on Rockwood after the man she loved left her at the altar.'

'Dora Greep is a gossip and she loves to create a stir. I know the legend, and that's all it is.'

'Only it happened to me. I was left at the altar.'

'But not from choice. Alex couldn't get home in time.'

'It was Marianne's curse. The women of Rockwood are doomed to fall in love with the wrong man, and their marriages end in disaster.'

'Surely you don't believe that balderdash?'

'Look at Grandpapa – he adored our grandmother, but she died.'

'Everyone dies sooner or later. That is a fact of life.'

'I don't think it's funny, Rosie. Grandpa fell in love with Hester – now that's a strange match, you must agree – then he died.'

'He was an old man, and Hester looked after him devotedly.'

'Well, then, what about Mama? She had a miserable life with our father, and then she fell under the Rockwood spell and married Claude on what should have been my wedding day.'

'But they were going to get married anyway, Patsy.'

'Then there's you and Piers. You were so in love while you were living here, but you've come back from abroad acting like strangers. I'm afraid if I remain here Marianne's curse will make me fall in love with Alex all over again, and we'll end up hating each other. I need to go to Trevenor to get away from this place.'

Rosalind stared at her sister in amazement. 'I've never heard such nonsense. You've been reading too many Gothic novels.'

'You may laugh at me, but beware, because Rockwood has you firmly in its hold and you won't escape unless you leave.'

'I was going to try to persuade you to stay, but if you feel like this I think you should accompany Lady Pentelow and Aurelia to Trevenor.'

'I intend to, Rosie, and you will come too, if you know what's good for you.' Patricia turned away and began brushing her hair energetically.

Rosalind sighed and rose to her feet. The legend of Marianne Carey was that of a troubled young woman in the seventeenth century, who, having been jilted by her lover, threw herself off one of the towers on St Agnes' Eve. The actual curse was probably something added on later to embellish the story. The rest was simply coincidence.

Rosalind went in search of Hester, who could always be relied upon to give sound advice.

Two days later Lady Pentelow, Aurelia and their servants left for Trevenor. Patricia insisted on accompanying them, despite Alexander's attempt to appease her. Rosalind could understand her sister's reluctance to believe him when he said his feelings for her had not changed, as it was obvious to anyone who knew him well that he was not speaking from his heart.

Piers was also keen to return to Cornwall, purely

for business reasons, but Rosalind managed to persuade him to stay at Rockwood until he had regained his former strength and vitality. She gave him all her attention, making sure that he ate nourishing meals and had plenty of rest. At first their attempts at reconciliation in the bedroom were overshadowed by the jealousy that Piers admitted he felt for his brother, even though Rosalind did her best to convince him that nothing had changed. But gradually they returned to something like their former close relationship and Rosalind put her feelings for Alexander firmly behind her. Piers was her husband and she did her best to prove her love for him was just as strong as ever. She was careful not to pay too much attention to Alexander, especially when Piers was around. Alexander played his part and kept out of the way as much as possible, with Hester keeping a strict eye on him. Dr Bulmer advised him to build up his muscles with a set of exercises, which Alexander did every day, and the month of February came to an end without any upsets. However, as Piers grew stronger, he insisted that it was time for him to travel to Cornwall and make sure that Pedrick was running the business properly.

At the end of the second week in March Rosalind stood in the blustery courtyard, waving her husband off as the carriage rumbled over the cobblestones.

'I'm sorry, Rosie.'

She turned to see Alexander standing behind her.

'It's not your fault. Piers can be very stubborn and he's determined to make the business even more of a success.'

'I should have gone to Trevenor when we returned from France, and then Patsy would have stayed here.'

'You couldn't travel in the state you were in, and you did try to make things right with her.'

'Yes, and look how that turned out. She hates me and I can't say I blame her.'

'She'll come round in time.'

'I don't think so, and perhaps it's for the best. The life of an army wife isn't for every woman. I should have realised that from the outset. But it's you I worry about, Rosie. I tried to put things right with my brother, but he knew I was lying when I said I didn't have feelings for you.'

'I tried to convince him of that, too.' Rosalind watched until the carriage disappeared from view. 'Perhaps I should have gone with him today, but there is so much to do at Rockwood and it's my responsibility with Bertie away in the army.'

Alexander slipped his arm around her shoulders and guided her back into the comparative warmth of the entrance hall. 'There's one thing you love above any other, Rosie, and that is Rockwood. Neither Piers nor myself could compete with this old pile of stones.'

'That's not true.'

He met her worried look with a smile. 'Isn't it?'

'Why are you saying these things, Alex? Are you trying to upset me?'

His eyes darkened and he raised his hand to touch her cheek. 'No, I'd never do that. I'd die first.'

Rosalind held her breath. She knew that she had only to move closer and their lives would be changed in an instant, but the sound of approaching footsteps made them spring apart.

Chapter Ten

'Hester.' Rosalind knew instantly who it was, but she turned slowly, forcing her lips into a smile. 'What are we going to do with ourselves now? Rockwood is going to seem so quiet.'

Hester shot a sideways glance at Alexander. 'You'll be wanting to get back to your regiment as soon as possible, no doubt.'

'Most certainly,' Alexander said affably.

'I've checked the store cupboards. At least Mrs Jackson has had the decency to leave the jars of calf's-foot jelly untouched. As it's a fine day I thought I'd visit some of the older tenants. I think it's high time we took care of those who depend upon us, don't you, Rosie?'

Rosalind nodded. 'You're right. I'll fetch my bonnet and cape.'

'That's settled then. Tilly is filling two baskets and

she'll bring them to the door. I'll send young Molly to the stables to tell Gurney to bring the pony and trap round to the front entrance. It's too cold to walk far.' Hester walked away with a purposeful step.

'Do you get the feeling that she is intent on keeping us apart?' Alexander pulled a face. 'I feel like a schoolboy.'

'I know what you mean, but I have responsibilities to the tenants and I've put them aside recently. Things have to change.'

'I respect your wishes, Rosie, but my feelings will remain the same, no matter what.'

She had no answer for this and she hurried off to collect her outdoor garments. Hester was right. Rockwood was not simply an ancient castle and the ancestral home of the Carey family, it came with responsibilities and she was the only one in the family left to carry them out.

Rosalind and Hester visited Widow Madge and her brood of growing children. After that they went two doors along the cottages on the quay to call upon Jarvis's sister, Minnie. Years ago she had worked in the sewing room at the castle, but rheumaticky hands and old age prevented her from earning her living now. However, the cottage was bright and clean and she was obviously delighted to see them. She offered them tea, but Rosalind knew that it was an expensive commodity and she refused tactfully. Lastly they called on Jessie Wills, whose husband, Saul, and his brother Seth were in prison for smuggling.

As they left the house they met the vicar coming up the garden path.

'Good morning, Rosalind. It's good to see you and Lady Carey out and about again.'

'Thank you, Mr Shaw. We've been taking small gifts to the poor. I'm afraid we've neglected our duties recently,' Rosalind added hastily. 'But it was unintentional and I hope to make up for it now.'

The Reverend George Shaw acknowledged this with a gentle smile. 'I understand, of course. It's been a difficult time for your family.'

'How is Mrs Shaw? Well, I hope, and Louise, too.'

'My wife and daughter are very well indeed. You must visit us at the vicarage, and I trust we will see you in church this Sunday? You haven't been to matins for quite a while.'

'Of course you will,' Hester said before Rosalind had a chance to respond.

'We missed so much, being in France, and my husband has been recuperating since our return,' added Rosalind.

'But both Mr Blanchard and Captain Blanchard are fully recovered now, I hope.'

Rosalind sent a warning look in Hester's direction. 'My husband has gone to Cornwall to check on business matters. Captain Blanchard will return to his regiment as soon as the doctor says his leg is sufficiently healed.'

'A bad business, but the outcome could have been worse.' George Shaw tipped his hat. 'I'm just going to call on Jessie. Life is difficult for a young woman left to cope alone when her husband is in prison. My wife tells me that the gossips are spreading stories about her.' He shook his head. 'But that need not concern you. Don't forget to call on Mrs Shaw, Rosalind, and you too, Lady Carey.' He strode up the path and knocked on the door.

Hester sniffed and walked away. 'You see, he put me last. He may be a man of God, but he still sees me as a servant. His snobbish wife is even worse.'

'You don't like Tabitha Shaw anyway, Hester. You've said so often enough.'

'She's a hypocrite. I feel sorry for that spinster daughter of hers. Poor Louise can't help being plain.'

Rosalind laughed. 'Hester! That's not like you. You're usually very charitable. Louise is homely-looking but she has a very nice nature.'

Hester climbed into the trap, taking the reins in her hands. 'You may call upon the vicar's wife. I'll go to Hannaford's shop and get the provisions that Mrs Jackson neglected to put on the order. I'll pick you up in half an hour.'

'Don't worry, I'll walk home. It's cold but it isn't raining. I'd enjoy the exercise.'

'If you say so.' Hester nodded and flicked the reins. 'Walk on.'

Rosalind made her way to the vicarage. The maid who opened the door was very young and Rosalind suspected that she was yet another child plucked from the orphanage, who would most probably be replaced within the year if she did not learn quickly enough to satisfy a demanding mistress like Tabitha Shaw.

Rosalind took a visiting card from her reticule and handed it to the girl. 'Would you give this to Mrs Shaw?'

'Yes, miss.'

Rosalind found the door slammed in her face and she took a step backwards. She could hear small feet running down the tiled hallway and moments later the door opened and the girl eyed her tearfully.

'She says to come in.'

Rosalind noted the red mark on the side of the child's face. 'What happened?'

'I done wrong.' Tears spurted from the girl's eyes and she bowed her head.

Rosalind gave her a hug. 'It's all right. Don't cry.'

'What on earth is going on?' Tabitha Shaw emerged from the parlour, looking elegant in a morning gown of silvery grey linsey-woolsey. 'What has the little fool said?'

'Nothing, I assure you. She seems to have hurt herself, Mrs Shaw.'

'She's clumsy and terribly stupid. I don't know why we chose her out of all the girls who were shown to us at the orphanage. Stop snivelling, Nancy. The coal scuttle needs refilling and then you can help Cook prepare luncheon.'

'How did you hurt yourself, Nancy?' Rosalind

asked gently. 'You looked fine to me when you opened the door.'

'She walked into the wall,' Tabitha said sharply. 'The child is so stupid. I think she's only half there. We're going to take her back to the orphanage tomorrow and look for a replacement. It's so hard to find good servants these days.' Tabitha shook her finger at the trembling child. 'Go about your business, Nancy, and stop pestering Mrs Blanchard.'

Rosalind straightened up. 'I could do with some extra help at the castle, Mrs Shaw. I'll take Nancy off your hands.'

'Why would you want to burden yourself with a half-wit? She's so small and skinny that she can hardly lift a coal scuttle when it's empty. She's useless.'

'Nevertheless, I would like to have her at Rockwood. Hester is very good at training young people who come into service.'

Tabitha took a deep breath. 'Have it your own way, Mrs Blanchard. Do come into the parlour.' She shot an impatient glance in Nancy's direction. 'Pack your bag, girl. You'll be leaving with Mrs Blanchard.'

Rosalind followed Tabitha into the large room with its walls hung with paintings of fruit and flowers, scenes depicting highland cattle and sketches of angelic-looking children. Louise Shaw was seated by the fire, but she rose to her feet when she saw Rosalind.

'It's so nice of you to visit us, Rosalind. I haven't seen you since before Christmas.'

'That's why I came this morning.' Rosalind smiled.

'You'll know that I had to go to France after the terrible accident that involved my husband and his brother.'

'I heard that Captain Blanchard was injured when his ship went aground,' Louise said softly. 'Was he badly hurt?'

'It's none of our business, Louise. Go to the kitchen and instruct Cook to make up a tray of tea and biscuits, and box that child's ears,' Tabitha added in an undertone.

Louise cast an agonised glance in Rosalind's direction. 'I shan't do anything of the kind, Mama.'

'Just go, Louise.' Tabitha turned to Rosalind with a smile. 'Do take off your cape and gloves, and be seated. It's a pleasure to see you and I want to hear all about your time in France. Although, of course, you missed your mama's wedding. It was such a surprise to have the arrangements altered at the last moment, but my dear husband coped heroically. Your mama is a very handsome woman and Mr de Marney charmed us all.'

Rosalind took off her outer garments and sat down. She was obliged to listen to every detail of her mother's marriage to Claude. It was a relief when Louise entered carrying a tray of tea, and biscuits still hot from the oven.

'The child should have brought that, Louise,' Tabitha said angrily. 'It's her last task here and she can't even do something simple like that. Now you see what I mean, Mrs Blanchard.'

'Nancy is too small to carry such a heavy tray, Mama.' Louise set it on the table beside her mother's chair. 'Would you like me to pour?'

'Yes, of course. I feel quite faint with all the servant problems thrust upon me.'

'Perhaps if we hired an older and more experienced woman we wouldn't have such difficulties.' Louise filled a cup and handed it to Rosalind. 'Are you really going to take young Nancy to work for you?'

'I'm sure she will prove very useful, when she's a bit older,' Rosalind said carefully. 'What would happen to her if you returned her to the orphanage?'

'She would be sold on again to anyone who would be prepared to pay for her,' Louise said sadly. 'I've heard that mill owners from different parts of the country buy young children and make them work for long hours in appalling conditions, particularly in the cotton industry.'

'That's terrible. It makes me more determined to take the child back to Rockwood.'

Tabitha took a teacup and saucer from her daughter. 'You should not pass on gossip you've heard in the village, Louise. I'm sure that the orphans are well cared for and grow up to be decent citizens.' She turned to Rosalind with a sugary smile. 'But we're both dying to hear about your time in France. Was it terribly exciting?'

It was almost an hour before Rosalind could get away from the vicarage, but this time she was not on her own. With Nancy's small fingers clutching her hand Rosalind set off for Rockwood, carrying the small linen bag that contained all Nancy's worldly goods.

'How old are you, Nancy?'

'I don't know exactly, miss. I think I'm ten.'

Rosalind nodded. Nancy was so small and under-nourished that it was difficult to tell. Her pansy-brown eyes were huge in her pale face, and her mouse-brown hair was scraped back into a knot at the back of her head. 'Have you got another name, Nancy? What I mean is, do you know your parents' surname?'

'They found me on the doorstep on a Sunday morning, so they called me Nancy Sunday. That's all I knows. Am I going to be your servant, miss?'

'My name is Mrs Blanchard, and I'm thinking that what you need most is a good meal and some new clothes. What do you think about that?'

Nancy gazed up at her in astonishment. 'Cook says I was standing behind the door when God gave out brains, and I'm clumsy. I expect you'll take me back to the orphanage in a day or two.'

Rosalind squeezed Nancy's hand. 'That won't happen, and I think the vicar's cook was wrong and very unkind. At Rockwood you will never be asked to do anything that's too difficult for you to manage. That's a promise.'

Despite her young age, Nancy was exhausted by the time they reached the castle, and Rosalind carried her into the courtyard. She was met by Alexander, who was now walking with the aid of one crutch.

'Who is this little waif?' He lifted Nancy easily in one arm. 'She looks done in.'

'This is Nancy Sunday. She is the Shaws' idea of charity, taken on from the orphanage and about to be sent back because she couldn't lift a full coal scuttle.'

Alexander shook his head. 'Poor little mite. What would you like me to do with her?'

'Is Hester back yet? She'll know what to do to make Nancy comfortable. I think she might have a slight fever.'

'Yes, Hester returned about half an hour ago. I'll take this little one to her parlour, shall I?'

'That's a good idea. Hester knows far more about childish ailments than I do. She treated all of us as children, although her cures were often worse than the illness itself.' Rosalind shuddered dramatically, which made Alexander laugh.

She smiled back at him, enjoying the mutual understanding that had always been part of their relationship. More often than not she had to explain her feelings to Piers, whereas Alex understood without having to be told. She walked on quickly, leading the way to Hester's parlour.

Alexander laid Nancy on the sofa. She had fallen asleep, probably from exhaustion or maybe from the fever, which seemed to be getting worse.

'You stay here, Rosie. I'll go and find Hester.'

'No need. I'm here.' Hester walked into the room.

Rosalind sighed, wondering if it was simply a coincidence that Hester appeared suddenly whenever she was alone with Alex, or if she was keeping watch on their every movement.

'I'll leave you to it.' Alexander backed away, leaving Rosalind to explain Nancy's presence.

With her customary common-sense approach, Hester examined Nancy. 'I think it's just a chill, but we'd better put her to bed and keep her warm.' She shook her head. 'She needs good food and rest, poor little mite. I'm surprised at the vicar's wife. You'd think she would know better than to treat a little one like a work horse.'

'I'll get Tilly to make up a bed for her.'

'There's a truckle bed in my room. We'll put her in there while she's in this state, in case what she's suffering from passes to the other girls.'

'I knew you'd take care of her, Hester,' Rosalind said, smiling. 'I couldn't leave her at the vicarage. They were going to take her back to the orphanage because she couldn't cope with the hard work expected of her.'

Hester tut-tutted, shaking her head. 'And they are supposed to be pillars of the community. Shame on them. Leave the little one to me.'

Rosalind knew better than to argue with Hester and somewhat reluctantly, she left the parlour and went straight to the dining room, where Tilly and Molly had set out cold meats, bread and cheese and a large tureen of leek and potato soup. Alexander was waiting for her and he pulled out a chair.

'What did Hester say?'

'She thinks it's just a chill and she's going to look after Nancy. I had nothing to do so I thought I'd join you for luncheon.'

He took his seat at table and Rosalind filled two bowls with soup. She handed one to Alexander and he accepted it with a broad grin. 'How domesticated. We're getting to be like an old married couple, Rosie.'

'Don't say things like that, even in jest. You never know when someone is listening.'

He raised the spoon to his lips. 'This is very good. I'll limit my conversation to the trivial things. Does that suit you?'

'Don't make fun of me, Alex. It's all too painful.' She held up her hand as he was about to rise from his seat. 'That wasn't a plea for you to comfort me. I'm doing my best to live a normal life, even under such difficult circumstances.'

'I know and I'm sorry. As soon as my leg heals I'll return to my regiment. I expect to be sent to the Crimea, so I'll be far away from here.'

'That will be even worse.' Rosalind stared into the bowl of soup, her appetite suddenly deserting her. 'This isn't working, Alex. It's too difficult now that Piers has left for Cornwall.'

'I know. I feel the same, so maybe I ought to go to Trevenor, after all. I could hire a carriage and do the journey in easy stages. My leg is healing nicely now and I can manage with one crutch.'

'You're forgetting that Patsy is still there. Are you ready to face her again?'

'If I arrive unexpectedly at Trevenor I think Patsy will return home. Perhaps that would be the answer, Rosie. We can't go on like this. I'm only human and being so close to you is torture. I shouldn't even tell you that, but it's true.'

She bowed her head, overcome by the need to agree with him, but they were teetering on the brink of disaster and she knew she must say nothing to make things worse. 'I think perhaps that would be the best thing to do, Alex. It's been difficult these past few weeks, but now it seems even more so.'

'You really want me to leave Rockwood?'

'I think it would be for the best.' She pushed her plate away and stood up. 'I'm not hungry. I'll go and check on Nancy.'

'Rosie, come back. I'm sorry.'

She closed the door, shutting out the sound of his voice. There was only so much she could bear, but she had known all along that their time together would be short, and the sooner he left the better it would be for everyone.

Rosalind hardly slept at all that night, and she came down to breakfast prepared to say her last goodbye to Alexander, but he was nowhere to be seen and Hester was seated at the breakfast table.

'Have you seen Alex this morning, Hester? He said he was going to Trevenor today.'

'He left at dawn.' Hester concentrated on buttering a slice of toast. 'He said you would understand. Gurney took the barouche so that he could bring Patsy back with him if she decided to come home.'

Rosalind bowed her head. 'Yes, of course.'

'It was the right thing to do.'

'Yes, I know that, Hester. I look forward to seeing Patsy. I've missed her.'

'And what about your husband?'

'I still love him, Hester, but he's obsessed with the business and seems to think of nothing else these days.'

'Maybe he will change when he hears your news.'

Rosalind looked up, startled. 'What do you mean?'

'That he'll become a father in the autumn. That's right, isn't it?'

'How can you know that? I'm not sure myself.'

'I can always tell, and if you're wise you'll tell him as soon as possible. Don't allow any doubts to enter his head.'

'What do you mean?'

'Your husband was very ill and you were on your own with his brother, that's all I'm saying.'

'We were never alone in the château. Piers was there and so were you and Madame Planche and Delfosse.'

'Nevertheless, tongues will wag and you will have

187

to ignore the gossips. Now eat some breakfast. You need to look after yourself.'

'I can't be in the family way, not after all this time.' Rosalind took a plate to the sideboard and lifted the lid on a silver serving dish. Two fried eggs stared up at her and her stomach churned. The next thing she knew she was seated in her chair with Hester fanning her with a plate.

'What happened?'

'You fainted, poppet. I'll make sure that Mrs Jackson doesn't serve fried eggs for a while.' Hester replaced the plate on the table. 'Sip your tea and maybe you can manage some dry toast. You'll feel better as the weeks go by.'

Rosalind drank some tea and the mists began to clear from her brain. 'How do you know these things, Hester? You've never had children.'

Hester went back to her seat at the table. 'That's not true. I had a baby many years ago.'

'You never told me that.'

'It's not something I talk about. I was very young and I had only been in service for a few years.'

Rosalind sat forward in her chair. 'Was it the master of the house?'

'No, it was the butler. He was a bully and he liked to prey on young girls. Of course, I was sacked the moment the mistress of the house discovered my condition and I returned home to have the child.'

'What happened to the baby?'

'He was a beautiful baby boy, but I couldn't keep

him. My widowed mother took in washing and mending to pay the rent on our cottage and feed us, and I had to find another job. The vicar who christened my son knew of a childless couple who were desperate to adopt a baby. He took Tobias from my arms and I never saw him again.'

'How awful. You must have been devastated.'

'Poor people have few choices in life, Rosie. I started again as a scullery maid with another family and worked my way up, but I never forgot Tobias.'

'Wouldn't you like to find him? Even if it was just to make sure he was well and happy?'

'He will be well over thirty now. He will have been raised to think of the couple who adopted him as his parents. I have no place in his life.'

'That is very sad.' Rosalind flicked tears from her eyes. 'I am so sorry.'

A wry smile curved Hester's lip. 'If Tobias turned out to be like his father, I wouldn't want to know him.' She was suddenly serious. 'I lost my child because I had no choice. You need to be very careful how and when you give the good news to your husband.'

Rosalind nodded. 'It's a shock to me, too. I was beginning to think that I would be childless. I know Piers blamed me, and perhaps that was why he spent so much time away from home.'

'That may be so, but now you must concentrate on looking after yourself.'

'Yes, I will.' Rosalind reached for a slice of toast.

'I think I'll ask Mrs Jackson to make porridge for tomorrow's breakfast, or maybe you could do it for me, Hester.'

'Of course I will. You always loved my porridge.' Hester rose to her feet. 'Thinking of children reminds me of Nancy. I left her with Tilly, who seems to have taken a liking to the child.'

'She had a fever last night.'

'It had gone by morning. I think she was simply exhausted and overworked. You might like to spend time with her. You could teach her to read and write and I'll introduce her to kitchen work when she's a bit stronger.'

'You're right. I need something to occupy my mind and she seemed to be a bright little thing, no matter what Mrs Shaw says.'

Rosalind spent the next few days getting to know Nancy, who made a quick recovery and blossomed under the influence of kindness and good food. Meggie Brewer, the dressmaker, was sent for and she measured Nancy for new clothes, including a plain print work dress to wear when she started helping in the kitchen. It was not Rosalind's intention to have such a small girl working long hours, but if she was to have a future in service Nancy had to start somewhere. Rosalind ordered two more gowns for herself as well as a couple of skirts and several blouses. Already she could see a very slight difference in her figure and she had to confide in

Meggie, who was obviously thrilled with the news. Rosalind remembered keeping Meggie's daughter Eliza amused while Patsy had a fitting for a gown more than two years previously and clearly motherhood suited Meggie. Rosalind could only hope that she herself would fall into the role as easily.

Less than a week after Alexander's departure for Cornwall Tilly came rushing into the morning parlour where Rosalind was attempting to teach Nancy her letters.

'Mrs Blanchard, ma'am. The barouche has arrived. Gurney has driven it to the front door.'

Chapter Eleven

Rosalind hurried to the entrance hall, but as Jarvis opened the front door she came to a sudden halt as she saw Piers alight from the carriage, followed by Patsy, who rushed past him and flew into the hall as if carried by the mad March wind.

'Patsy, I wondered if you'd come home,' Rosalind said warily.

'What choice did I have when Alexander turned up unexpectedly? I could have died, Rosie. You should have kept him here until he was fit enough to return to his regiment.'

'Alex is a grown man. He does as he pleases and he wanted to return to Trevenor, which is his home, after all.' Rosalind turned slowly to face Piers. 'You look well. The Cornish air seems to have done you good.'

He kissed her briefly on the lips. 'You're very pale. Could it be that you've missed me?'

She managed a smile. 'Of course I have. Anyway, don't let's stand about in the draughty hall. Come to the morning parlour where it's nice and warm and I'll send for some refreshments.'

Patricia peeled off her fur-lined cape and handed it to Jarvis. 'For goodness' sake, Rosie. You sound as if you're speaking to a stranger. Surely you want to give Piers a proper welcome home.'

Rosalind met Piers' amused look and she laughed. 'All in good time, Patsy. Let's get you both settled and you can tell me everything that's been happening at Trevenor.'

'Well, I was having a splendid time with Aurelia until Alex arrived, and then it was very awkward. I can't imagine why I thought we were well suited.'

'My brother has a way with women,' Piers said drily. 'But I don't think he'll ever settle down to be a good husband.'

'Now you're being tedious, Piers,' Patricia said, tossing her head. 'We've talked about this all the way from Cornwall and I, for one, have had quite enough on that subject.'

Rosalind had no intention of getting involved in a conversation where Alex was the main topic and she hurried on ahead. She entered the morning parlour to find Nancy seated on the floor, studying the reading primer that Rosalind had come across in the old schoolroom. Nancy leaped to her feet when she saw Patricia.

'I'm sorry, missis. Shall I go now?'

Rosalind took her by the hand. 'No, it's quite all right, Nancy. This is my sister, Patricia, and the gentleman is my husband, Mr Blanchard.'

'Who is this?' Patricia demanded, eyeing Nancy up and down.

'Nancy has come to live with us,' Rosalind said firmly. 'She was far too young to be put to work at the vicarage and they were going to send her back to the orphanage.'

'So you stepped in and brought her here.' Piers smiled down at Nancy. 'You're very welcome. I'm sure my wife has great plans for you.'

'I'm going to be a scullery maid one day, sir.'

'A worthy ambition,' Piers said solemnly. 'I see you are learning to read.'

'Yes, sir. If I can read and write I might be a lady's maid when I'm older.'

'You're doing very well, Nancy,' Rosalind said, smiling. 'Can you remember how to get to the kitchen?'

'Yes, Mrs Blanchard.'

'Then I want you to find Tilly and ask her to bring coffee and cake to the morning parlour. There are three of us, and tell Cook I said you may have a glass of milk and a biscuit.'

Nancy puffed out her chest. 'I'll go now.' She raced to the door and let herself out into the hallway.

'I hope you know what you're doing, Rosie.' Piers stood with his back to the fire. 'You look as if you need a rest. I think you've been doing too much.'

'I don't know why Rosie should be tired,' Patricia said crossly. 'We've been on the road for the best part of three days. I'm exhausted, and now I'll have to unpack my clothes because I haven't got a lady's maid. Aurelia has Grainger to wait on her.'

'You can ask Tilly to help you, or I will.' Rosalind eyed her sister curiously. 'You can tell me what you've been doing at Trevenor. I don't suppose Piers wants to listen to gossip.'

'Leave all that until later.' Piers patted the chair nearest to him. 'Why don't you sit down, Rosie? Tell us what's been happening here. Is there anything I need to know?'

Rosalind did as he asked, but she could not bring herself to give him the good news while Patricia was in the room, and she launched into a detailed account of all the tenants she and Hester had visited.

Later that day Rosalind had changed for dinner and was seated at the dressing table putting the finishing touches to her coiffure when Piers emerged from his dressing room.

'You look lovely, Rosie.'

She turned to meet his gaze with a nervous smile. 'You asked me earlier if there was anything you needed to know.'

He nodded. 'Yes, I did and you assured me that everything was going well.'

'As I told you earlier, the tenants are taken care of and all the rents are paid.'

'I meant with you, not the tenants. We pay Lambert to manage the estate.'

'I'm well, Piers.'

He sat down on the edge of the bed. 'I wasn't my old self for a long time after the accident and my subsequent illness. I'm afraid I neglected you rather when we returned from France.'

'You were still recuperating, Piers. I understood.'

'I realise that I've concentrated too much on the business, and probably not enough on taking care of you. You know that I love you, don't you, Rosie?'

'Yes, of course I do.' Rosalind laid her silver-backed hairbrush on the dressing table. 'I do have some news for you, Piers. I just wasn't sure when to tell you.' She hesitated, choosing her words carefully. 'I think – no, I'm almost sure – that I'm . . . that we're going to have a baby in the autumn.' She waited, hardly daring to breathe as he remained silent for a moment, and then he leaped to his feet and lifted her from the stool, holding her in a close embrace.

'I thought it would never happen. I was afraid we would never have a child of our own, and when I saw young Nancy I was afraid you might want to adopt her.'

'No, that never occurred to me. You are pleased, aren't you?'

He kissed her soundly. 'Of course I'm delighted. What man doesn't want a son to carry on the family name?'

Rosalind could have cried with relief. 'Or daughter. It might be a girl.'

'Then I'll love her as I love her mother, and we'll have a boy next time.' He studied her face, with a crease between his brows. 'So that's why you look so pale. We must remedy that, my love. There'll be no more riding round the estate to visit tenants for you. You must trust Lambert to do everything necessary, and I will stay at home as much as possible.'

Rosalind smiled, shaking her head. 'It's a perfectly normal state to be in, Piers. I'm young and healthy and I don't need coddling.'

'You must allow me to be the judge of that,' Piers said firmly. 'I'll soon be a family man and I'll take care of you and our child. Pedrick has the mine under control and I will only go away in order to get new business. I am fortunate to have recovered so well from the head injury and the illness.'

Rosalind sank back on the dressing table stool. 'I haven't told Patsy yet.'

'I want everyone to share our good news. I suppose Hester knows already.'

'It was Hester who told me why I fainted at breakfast. There is no keeping anything secret from her.'

Piers nodded. 'Then you must tell Patsy this evening before we sit down to dinner. I'm sure she will be delighted to know she is soon to become an aunt.'

Patricia threw up her hands. 'I refuse to be called Aunt Patricia. It makes me sound middle-aged or, even worse, elderly.'

'We thought you would be pleased,' Piers said, smiling.

'I don't like children, especially babies.' Patricia tossed her head. 'I'm beginning to wish I'd stayed at Trevenor.'

'It won't affect you, Patsy.' Rosalind eyed her curiously. 'What would you have done had you married Alex? You would have wanted children, wouldn't you?'

'It was hardly a subject we would have discussed. I hadn't given it much thought, to be honest, so perhaps it's as well I broke off our engagement.'

'You'll change your mind if you find the right man for you.' Hester sipped her sherry. 'You'll eat your words one day, Patricia.'

Rosalind rose to her feet. 'I think it's time we went in for dinner. I'm suddenly very hungry.'

Piers smiled proudly. 'You're eating for two now, my love. Isn't that what they say, Hester?'

'It is indeed, Piers.' Hester raised her glass to him. 'I think you'll make a wonderful father.'

'I intend to do my very best,' Piers said, smiling

proudly. 'Now I have something to work for. I'll build up the business for my son to inherit.'

Patricia yawned. 'Are we going to suffer this until the baby is born? Anyway, Piers, he might take after his two uncles and want to join the army. Or it's possible you might have a daughter who will be just like me.'

Piers laughed good-naturedly. 'I could cope with that, Patsy. But every man wants a son to grow up in his image.'

'I really do need to eat soon.' Rosalind rose to her feet. 'I'm going to take Nancy to Exeter tomorrow, Patsy. Meggie Brewer has made some dresses for her. Would you like to come with us?'

'No, thank you. I can't think of anything more tedious than taking a small girl for a dress fitting. I think I'll call on Christina and Sylvia. They'll be dying to hear how I'm surviving with a broken heart.'

Piers drank the last of his sherry and stood up. 'I seem to remember Rosie and I chasing after you when you attempted to elope with Barnaby Yelland. You recovered from that quite quickly, as I recall.'

'That's not fair, Piers. I was very young then. I'm a woman now, and Alex was the love of my life – or so I thought.' Patricia jumped to her feet. 'Come on, Hester. Let's get dinner over and then I'll challenge you to a game of loo.'

'That was a bit unfair, Piers,' Rosalind said in a low voice as they walked hand in hand to the dining room. 'Patsy was only sixteen at the time.'

'It doesn't hurt to remind her that we're all fallible.' Piers squeezed her fingers. 'It wasn't all Alex's fault. They are both too alike to make a good match.'

'In what way, Piers?'

'They are both flirts. They enjoy the chase, but I doubt if either of them will ever settle down with one person. Thank goodness I'm not like that.' He leaned over to brush her cheek with a kiss. 'You and I will be together until death do us part.'

Next day, during the carriage ride to Exeter, Piers' words kept coming back to Rosalind as she sat beside an excited Nancy. She answered when Nancy asked her a question, but her mind was elsewhere. She could not help wondering what might have happened had she married Alex instead of his brother, but Piers was so excited at the prospect of becoming a father, and so attentive, that she knew she had made the right decision. He had even given her a purse full of money to pay for the clothes and anything she wanted to purchase for herself in town. She knew that this was his way of saying how pleased he was with the news that he was to become a father, and she struggled with feelings of guilt for even thinking of another man – but Alex was not someone who was easy to forget.

Gurney dropped them in the narrow street where Meggie Brewer lived.

'I'll drive round to the Cathedral Close, if that's all right with you, ma'am.'

'Yes, Gurney, of course. We don't want to block the road and I can't say how long we'll be. Nancy and I will come and find you when we're done here. I might even do a little shopping.'

'Very well, ma'am.' Gurney climbed back onto the box and drove off.

Rosalind took Nancy by the hand. 'Let's see what Mrs Brewer has made for you.'

Nancy was about to answer when a small, barefoot boy came running towards them pursued by a large and very angry man. The child's ragged clothes were badly singed and his hair and face blackened with soot.

'Stop that boy. He's a runaway,' the man bellowed, gasping for breath.

Rosalind caught the boy up in her arms. 'It's all right. Don't be frightened.'

He struggled but Nancy caught him by the hand. 'Mrs Blanchard is a good lady, boy.'

'You're safe with me,' Rosalind said firmly. She wrapped her arms around his skinny body and the man came to a halt, leaning against the wall of the terraced house while he caught his breath.

'You can give him back to me now, missis. That there boy belongs to me. I bought him fair and square.'

Rosalind faced him defiantly. 'You can't buy a child, sir. I take it from the state of him that he's a climbing boy and you must be the sweep.'

'It's a respectable trade, ma'am, and that boy is one of my apprentices.'

'Then shame on you, sir.' Rosalind tightened her hold on the trembling child. 'Just look at the state of him. He has burns on his feet and legs, and goodness knows what the soot has done to his lungs.'

'He's a lazy little good-for-nothing. I had to light the fire to make him climb higher. It's the only way to teach them.'

'You lit a fire while this child was in the chimney stack?'

'You don't know anything about the profession, ma'am. Give me the boy and we'll say nothing more about it.'

Rosalind looked down into a pair of imploring brown eyes and she shook her head. 'Certainly not. You've tortured this child and you aren't fit to have him.'

'I paid good money for the lad. He's my property.'

Nancy began to cry and she hugged the boy in spite of his filthy clothes. 'Don't let him take the boy, missis.'

At that moment Meggie Brewer opened her front door. 'Good heavens! What's going on? Are you all right, Mrs Blanchard?' She caught the hand of a small girl who attempted to escape into the street. 'Go inside, Eliza.'

'You'd best go indoors, too, Nancy,' Rosalind said hastily. 'Meggie will you take her, please? And this boy, too. I'm not letting him go back to this man.'

Meggie took Nancy by the hand. 'He's a climbing boy, ma'am.'

'I know very well what this man makes him do and I think it's appalling. Please take him inside.'

Meggie beckoned to the boy. 'Come on, my handsome. You'll be safe with us.' She ushered her daughter and Nancy into the house and the boy followed them.

'I own him, ma'am,' the sweep protested loudly. 'You've got no right to take him from me.'

'How much did you pay for him?'

A sly expression crossed his face. 'He's cost me money, missis. The snivelling brat eats too much and wears out his clothes. I reckon I've spent a fortune on him since I took him on.'

'I'm not interested in your problems, sir. Tell me how much.' Rosalind took the purse from her reticule.

'Five pounds would be what I need.'

'That's extortionate, sir.'

'Then give me back my boy.'

Rosalind opened her purse and took out three gold sovereigns. 'Take this and be grateful that I don't report you to the police for child cruelty.'

'This is robbery.'

'You would have given his poverty-stricken parents a pittance in return for their son. You are the one who should be ashamed.' Rosalind dropped the coins on the pavement in front of him. She had the satisfaction of seeing him grovel for the money as she entered Meggie's house. She slammed the door and leaned against it, trembling violently.

'Are you all right, Mrs Blanchard?' Meggie asked anxiously. 'You ought to sit down.'

Nancy rushed up to Rosalind and flung her arms around her. 'I'll help you, missis.'

'Thank you both, but it was just a slight dizzy spell. I'm fine now.' Rosalind smiled and made her way to Meggie's sofa, which she remembered of old. It was still as uncomfortable as ever, but she needed to sit for a while. She held her hand out to the boy, who was shivering in a corner. 'That man has gone. He won't bother you again.'

Nancy patted him on the shoulder. 'The missis is very kind. She took me in and look at me now. Maybe she'll keep you as well.'

'I don't know about that,' Meggie said hastily. 'Don't give the poor boy ideas, Nancy.'

'I won't go back to old Hodges.' The boy spoke for the first time, his large brown eyes filling with tears. 'I'll throw myself in the river first. That's where I was going.'

Rosalind jumped to her feet, forgetting everything other than the need to reassure the frightened child. She wrapped her arms around him, ignoring the sooty marks it left on her gown. 'You will come home with us, of course. I've no intention of abandoning you, but you could do with the application of some soap and hot water.' She glanced at Meggie. 'I'm sorry, I know I've put this upon you, but could you put the kettle on? I can't take him home in this state.'

'Of course, Mrs Blanchard.' Meggie beckoned to Nancy. 'Come into the kitchen and you can help me. We'll make a pot of tea while we're heating water to wash the climbing boy.'

Nancy followed her eagerly. 'I know how to make tea. Cook showed me.'

'Now then, boy,' Rosalind said gently. 'I can't keep calling you that. Will you tell me your name?'

'It's Tommy.'

'Have you another name, Tommy?'

'It's Trimble, missis.'

'Do you know how old you are?'

'I think I'm eight or nine. Am I going to work for you, missis?'

'No, Tommy. Well, maybe when you're fit enough you could help Gurney in the stables or something of the sort, but first of all we're going to get some of that soot off you, and put salve on those dreadful burns on your poor feet and legs.' She led him into the kitchen where Meggie was busy making tea and Nancy was attempting to entertain Meggie's little girls.

Meggie poured boiling water into the teapot. 'There's enough water left to wash off some of that dirt, Mrs Blanchard. I always keep the kettle simmering on the hob, but he'll need several hot baths to get the soot from his skin.' She emptied the contents of the kettle into an enamel bowl. 'There's soap in the dish and a jug of cold water on the windowsill.'

'I don't know what we can do about his clothes.' Rosalind brushed his filthy hair back from his forehead. 'You poor boy, these rags are so burned they're falling off you.'

Meggie frowned thoughtfully. 'My sister dropped off some of her boy's clothes for me to sell in the market. Maybe there's something there that would fit him.'

'Anything would do until we can get him home. Thank you, Meggie. I'm sorry to bring all this on you.'

Meggie smiled as she poured the tea. 'It's not every day I see Sweep Hodges bettered by a woman. I was watching out of the window. His face was a picture.' She reached for a tin and Eliza jumped up and down as her mother opened it and took out four biscuits. She gave one each to her daughters and another to Nancy. 'I expect you're hungry, Tommy. If you're anything like my sister's boy, he's always ready for food.' She handed the biscuit to him and he gobbled it in two bites. 'Maybe you ought to have another one.'

'If you take the girls into the parlour, I'll help Tommy to wash while Nancy tries on her new clothes. I'll take my gowns with me, Meggie. I know they'll fit perfectly, and if they don't I'll soon grow into them.'

Meggie poured milk for the girls and filled a glass for Tommy, which he downed in one long swallow. 'Poor child – he's starving. Hodges should be ashamed of himself.' She led Eliza into the parlour with Nancy dancing along with them.

'Now, Tommy. Let's see what I can do for you. It will be a lick and a promise, but when we get home to Rockwood, you can have a nice hot bath . . .'

When they arrived back at the castle Rosalind took both children to Hester's parlour, which was where she still headed whenever she needed advice.

'Hester, this is Tommy Trimble. I had to pay the sweep to release him, and now he's come to stay with us.'

Hester stared at Tommy, shaking her head. 'You didn't! Not another one, Rosie.'

'What would you have done?' Rosalind placed her hand protectively on Tommy's shoulder. 'He ran away after having a fire lit beneath him to make him work faster. I really believe he would have thrown himself in the river had I not intervened.'

'I would,' Tommy said firmly. 'That's where I was going, missis.'

'It's Lady Carey to you, boy.' Hester drew Rosalind aside. 'You can't go round the country taking in all the waifs and strays you come across. What will Piers say?'

'I'm sure he'll agree with me when he sees the state this poor boy is in. The most important thing is to get him bathed and treat his burns. He needs a good meal and a warm bed, and we'll worry about the details when he's settled in.'

Hester rolled her eyes. 'I know better than to argue when you're in this mood, Rosie.' She turned to Tommy, who was eyeing her warily. 'Now then, young man, you will come with me and we'll see what we can do to make you more comfortable.'

'Do as Lady Carey says, Tommy.' Rosalind gave him a reassuring smile. 'Nancy will tell you there's nothing to fear, won't you, Nancy?'

'Yes, boy. I've been here a while now. The castle isn't as scary as it looks when you first come here.'

'Come along, Tommy. Don't dawdle.' Hester marched off with Tommy following somewhat reluctantly.

Rosalind turned to Nancy. 'You'll be able to show Tommy round when he's feeling better. In the meantime I'll order tea and cake, and you can help by putting your new clothes away. Molly took them to your room and I'm sure she'll assist if you can't manage.'

'I can do it on my own, ma'am.' Nancy headed for the doorway, stepping aside as Piers entered the room. She smiled shyly and scurried off, leaving the door to swing shut.

'So was your trip to Exeter successful, my love?' Piers went to stand by the fire. 'I hope you didn't get too chilled. It's cold for the time of year.'

'I'm fine, Piers. Please don't fuss.'

He moved to the sofa and sat down beside her, placing his arm around her shoulders. 'You'll forgive me if I want to make sure that my wife and child are safe and well.'

'Of course, but I am perfectly healthy, Piers.' She twisted round to face him. 'But there's one thing I have to tell you. It's nothing to do with me or my condition, it's just that I saved a small climbing boy who was being badly treated by his master.'

'Are you telling me you've brought him home with you, Rosie?'

'He's only nine or ten and even then he's not sure how old he really is. You'll understand when you see him, Piers. He's being bathed as we speak, and Hester is treating his burns. The poor little fellow had run away from a terrible bully, and was intent on ending his life of misery in the river. What else could I do?'

Piers was silent for a moment, regarding her with a resigned expression. 'I hope this isn't going to happen every time you leave the house.'

She smiled reluctantly. 'No, of course not. It was just that he came racing towards us before I'd even knocked on Meggie's door. His master is a dreadful man.'

'I'm sure you're right, but we can't rescue all the poor little orphans and sweep's boys.'

'Of course not, but Tommy is special.'

Piers leaned over and kissed her on the lips. 'If you want him to stay then that's what will happen, Rosie. But you shouldn't have got into an altercation with the sweep, especially in your condition.'

'I'm not ill, Piers. Women have been having babies since the beginning of time.'

'Yes, maybe so, but I'm concerned for you and our child. From now on I want you to take Hester with you when you go out, or one of the maids, and I don't want you riding your horse either. You must take the chaise or, better still, Gurney should drive you in the barouche.'

'Piers, you're worrying unnecessarily. I'm young and healthy and I know how to look after myself and my baby.'

'We've hoped for this event for two years or more, my love. I can't wait to introduce my son to the world. He'll carry on the business and make it even more successful. The future of Blanchard Clay is assured.'

Rosalind shook her head. 'Oh, Piers. Do you never think of anything else?'

'Of course I do, Rosie. I'm thinking about you all the time. By the way, talking of the mine, I really will have to travel to Cornwall in the next day or so. I need to keep any eye on things. You don't mind, do you?'

Chapter Twelve

Piers left for Trevenor early next morning, and when Rosalind went down to breakfast she found Hester already at the table.

'You're up early, Hester.' Rosalind helped herself to a small portion of buttered eggs.

'I kept Tommy in my room last night, which was a mistake. That poor boy was moaning in his sleep and crying out for his mother. That man Hodges should be horsewhipped for treating children like that.'

'I'm afraid it will go on until the government enforce the Act making it illegal for young children to climb chimneys. I think I'll take it up with Sir Michael when I next see him – not that it will do any good.'

'You can but try. In the meantime what are we going to do with the young fellow? I've sent him to the kitchen to be fed, but he's neither a member of the family nor is he a servant. You need to decide which it's to be.'

'I've been thinking about it and I've decided to use the old schoolroom. I'm going to give Nancy and Tommy lessons myself.'

'They'll end up in service, Rosie. Be careful that you don't give them expectations that can never be fulfilled.'

'I'm going to teach them to read and write, and basic arithmetic. Just because they were born into poverty doesn't mean they have to spend the rest of their lives in that situation. As to going into service, they could do worse, but they could also do better. The Lent Term ends soon and Walter will be home for Easter. He can help me to work out a syllabus. He'll love doing that.'

'So you are going to treat those orphans as if they were your own?'

'I've taken responsibility for them, so of course I will. They deserve a better start in life than they've had up until now.' Rosalind turned her head as the door opened and Patricia burst into the room.

'Who is that grubby urchin I found in my dressing room?'

'You arrived home too late from Greystone Park for me to tell you,' Rosalind said reasonably. 'Do sit down and have some breakfast.'

'So who is he? I asked him and he began to snivel.'

'I hope you didn't scare him, Patsy. He's suffered

enough for one so young.' Rosalind leaped to her feet. 'Where is he now?'

'How should I know?' Patricia stormed over to the sideboard and helped herself from the silver serving dishes. 'I go out for the day and come back to an orphanage.'

'Sit down, Rosie.' Hester rose slowly to her feet. 'I'll go and find the little fellow. I told him to go to my parlour when he'd finished breakfast as I need to dress his burns. I expect he got lost and wandered into your room by mistake, Patricia.'

'Where's Piers?' Patricia took her seat at the table. 'What has he got to say about you taking in these strays?'

'Piers is happy to leave matters to me. Anyway, he's gone to Trevenor to check that Pedrick is doing as he asked.'

'Piers loves the china clay business more than he does his family.' Patricia reached for the toast rack. 'I don't blame him for getting out of this madhouse. To tell you the truth I'm thinking of doing the same.'

'You're going back to Trevenor? What about Alex?'

'No, of course I'm not going there. I thought I'd go to London and stay with Mama and Claude for a while. Rockwood is deadly dull and Christina thinks she's in love with Oscar Cottingham. She can't talk about anything other than what they will do together when he comes home for Easter, and Sylvia is still a child. We have very little in common now.'

'Are you jealous, Patsy? I seem to recall that Oscar was one of your conquests not so long ago.'

'Don't be ridiculous, Rosie. He's going to take holy orders when he finishes at Oxford. Can you imagine me as a vicar's wife? I think not.'

'I'm sure you'd get on well with his mother. Glorina lives up to her Romany ancestry. She's always causing a stir in the village.'

'That's true, but the squire simply adores her, according to Christina. Anyway, she is welcome to have Glorina Cottingham as a mother-in-law. I intend to aim higher than a squire's son. I want to marry a really wealthy man who will take me touring on the Continent, and lavish expensive presents on me. I don't fancy standing in church handing out musty prayer books like Mrs Shaw and poor Louise, who is definitely on the shelf.'

'So you think you'll meet this person in London?'

'Of course. At least I'll have a much better chance there than here at Rockwood, and you know what I told you about the curse on this place. All the Rockwood brides have been deserted or widowed, or have had unhappy unions. Alex might have married me, but for the Rockwood curse.'

'*You* broke off your engagement, Patsy.'

'Only because I knew his heart wasn't in it. Aurelia agrees with me. She said it was the right thing to do.'

'I see.' Rosalind eyed her thoughtfully. 'Does Mama know you plan to join them?'

'She invited me after the wedding. Claude had booked her for a whole season at the Royal Opera House, and they're renting a residence not too far from the theatre. I'm leaving tomorrow, Rosie.'

'So soon?'

'Yes, but I need someone to chaperone me on the journey.'

'I don't think Hester would be very keen. She doesn't like London.'

'I wasn't thinking of Hester. I thought you might be ready for a break from Rockwood for a few days.'

'Me? But I have too much to do here, and I need to make sure that Nancy and Tommy are looked after.'

'That's just an excuse. Surely your sister's well-being is more important? What would Mama say if I travelled on my own?'

'But it would mean I'd have to return to Devon without anyone to accompany me.'

'You're a married woman, Rosie. You can do what you like.'

'Really?' Rosalind laughed. 'If that's what you think you'll find the married state quite a disappointment.'

'You like saying these things, but seriously, Rosie, please will you come with me? I'll get lost in London on my own. You can return to your precious Rockwood the day after we get there if you're homesick. I just thought it would do you good to get away for a while.'

'Let me think it over, but I know Piers wouldn't want me to go. He was very particular about what I should and shouldn't do while I'm in this state.'

'All the more reason for you to assert yourself, Rosie. I never knew you to bow down to anyone, least of all Piers. You were always so independent.'

'He worries for the baby. You know how much he wants a son.'

'Then your child is almost certain to be a girl. Please say yes, Rosie. I can't stay here and dwindle into an old maid.'

'That will never happen, Patsy.' Rosalind gazed out of the window. The sun was shining and when she had opened her bedroom window that morning there was a hint of spring in the air. For the next few months she would have to curtail her activities to please her husband and to protect her unborn child – this might be her last chance of doing something out of the ordinary before her confinement. 'All right Patsy. I'll accompany you, but that means I have a lot to do today. You may order the carriage to take us to Exeter station tomorrow morning, first thing.'

Patsy dropped her knife and fork on her plate and jumped to her feet. She hurried to Rosie's side and hugged her. 'You are the best sister in the world. You won't be sorry. I'll make sure that Mama and Claude look after you as if you were made of glass. We'll have a lovely time in London.'

'You do realise that I can't stay for long. I'll have

to travel back to Devon in a day or two. Piers would be furious if he came home and I wasn't here.'

'Oh, him!' Patricia dismissed the idea with a wave of her hand. 'He's a stuffy husband. You could have done better.'

'Rockwood might have ended up a ruin if Piers hadn't poured money into the renovations. He's a good man and I love him.'

'Of course you do, but he's obsessed with making money from that wretched clay mine. Aurelia hates it as much as I hate this place. You might enjoy being buried in a historic ruin but I want some fun in my life. At least Alex was never boring. Please say you'll come with me.'

Rosalind sighed, knowing she had lost the argument. 'If we're going to London tomorrow, I'd better start making arrangements. Somehow I'll have to persuade Hester that you need me as your chaperone, and that's not going to be easy.'

Patricia smiled triumphantly. 'You want to go to London as much as I do. Admit it, Rosie.'

It was late in the afternoon next day when Rosalind and Patricia arrived at the address in Bedford Street. The elegant, four-storey terraced house was in an area that was well-to-do, but too close to Seven Dials to be fashionable. However, the maid who showed them to the drawing room on the first floor was polite and well trained.

Felicia was seated in a comfortable armchair by

the fire, but she rose to her feet and advanced on her daughters with her arms outstretched. 'My darling girls, how lovely to see you. Come and sit by the fire and tell me all your news. Dawson will bring us tea and pastries.' She dismissed Dawson with a wave of her hand. 'Did you have a good journey?'

'It was tedious, Mama.' Patricia arranged herself on the sofa, spreading her skirts so that there was little room for Rosalind.

'So you managed to persuade your sister to leave Rockwood for a while.' Felicia returned to her chair by the fire. 'How did you do that, Patsy?'

'I just came to chaperone her on the journey, Mama.' Rosalind perched on the arm of the sofa. 'I'll return to Devon tomorrow or the next day.'

'Don't be ridiculous, Rosalind.' Felicia shook her head. 'You can't come all this way for such a short stay. You'll want to see my performance at the theatre. Besides which, there's someone in town who I know you'll want to see.' Felicia paused, looking from one to the other. 'It's Bertie. He accompanied his commanding officer to London, which is so fortunate for us.'

Rosalind breathed a sigh of relief. 'I thought he was fighting in the Crimea. How wonderful.'

'I suppose it will be fun to meet him and his fellow officers,' Patricia said thoughtfully. 'They can be quite dashing in their uniforms.'

'You look well, Mama.' Rosalind steered the

conversation away from the topic of army officers. The last thing she wanted was for her mother and sister to dwell on Patricia's involvement with Alex. Just the mention of his name made the colour rush to her cheeks and Mama was no fool when it came to relationships. 'And how is Claude? I hope he's treating you well.'

'Claude is a darling and if I look blooming it's because I am happy.' Felicia narrowed her eyes as she gazed at Rosalind. 'You, on the other hand, look decidedly peaky. Are you unwell, dear?'

'Of course, you don't know, Mama. Rosie is in the family way. This will probably be her last trip without the burden of crying babies and all that goes with them. You're going to be a grandmother.'

Felicia's smile froze. 'Don't say that where anyone might hear you. I doubt if my huge following of admirers would believe it anyway, but my rivals would broadcast it to the world. How could you do this to me, Rosie? I'm far too young to be a grandparent.'

'I won't be here long enough to embarrass you, Mama,' Rosalind said calmly. Her mother's reaction was exactly as she had expected, but it still hurt.

'Don't worry, Mama.' Patricia leaned over to pat her mother's hand. 'No one will believe it, and those who do will imagine that you must have been a child bride.'

'Thank you, darling. You always say the right thing.' Felicia turned to Rosalind with a half-smile.

'Congratulations, of course. I'm sure that Piers is delighted, especially after waiting so long for a son and heir.'

Rosalind was trying to think of a suitable response when the door opened and Claude breezed into the room, followed by Dawson, carrying a laden tea tray.

'Rosalind, my dear. How lovely you look.' Claude kissed her on the cheek. 'And Patsy, how are you? Have you forgiven us for stealing your wedding day?'

'That's not funny, Claude.' Felicia turned to Dawson. 'Put the small tea table in front of Miss Rosalind, or should I say Mrs Blanchard, especially now.'

Dawson did as she was asked and left the room quietly.

'You did me a favour, Claude,' Patricia said airily. 'I was never meant to marry Alexander. I hope to meet someone far more suited to my taste and temperament, maybe while I'm in London. I hope you know plenty of eligible bachelors.'

'I'm sure I can find one or two.' Claude eyed Rosalind curiously. 'Piers didn't accompany you to London?'

'He is away in Cornwall.' Rosalind filled a cup with tea and handed it to him. 'I'm only staying for a day or two, Claude. I have so much to do at home.'

'Rosie has taken it into her head to adopt orphans,' Patricia said, smiling.

'Don't exaggerate, Patsy. I haven't adopted them.

Nancy is a small girl who was working as a servant in the village and about to be handed back to the orphanage like an unwanted parcel. The other is a young climbing boy who was being ill-treated by his master.'

'Well done, I say.' Claude beamed at her. 'You always were a kind-hearted young woman, my dear. Piers is a lucky man to have snapped you up.'

'My sister is keen to fill the nursery, Claude,' Patricia added. 'Soon the castle will be filled with little replicas of Piers.'

'I think we've exhausted that topic of conversation,' Felicia said before Claude had a chance to speak. 'I have to be in the theatre in half an hour. Claude and I have a later supper after the performance, but you girls might like to eat earlier.'

'We don't want to put you out, Mama,' Rosalind said hastily.

'As it's your first night in London I'll take you both to Rules for dinner.' Claude gave his wife an apologetic smile. 'And I'll have supper later with you, my love.'

'Very well, Claude. If you feel it's necessary.'

'We don't want you to go to any extra trouble on our behalf,' Rosalind said quickly. She could see that her mother did not like the idea.

'No, it's no trouble.' Claude rose to his feet. 'I'll send Dawson to the restaurant to make a reservation. We'll dine early so that I can be back in the theatre before the interval,' he added, eyeing his wife warily.

'Don't fret, my love. I'll be there when you need me.'

Claude was an excellent host and he entertained them at dinner with amusing stories of his past when he represented several well-known performers. They dined well and were about to leave when Rosalind heard a familiar voice. Claude was on his feet already.

'Bertie, if I'd known you were dining here we could have shared a table.'

'Bertie.' Patricia pushed past Claude to throw her arms around her brother's neck.

'Patsy. How much wine have you had?' Bertie held her at arm's length. 'What are you doing in town?' He glanced over her shoulder and his smile widened. 'And Rosie is here, too. It's fortunate we chose to come here instead of Simpson's.'

Rosalind's smile of welcome faded as she looked past Bertie and saw that his companion was Alex. The shock of seeing him so unexpectedly combined with exhaustion after the long journey, and for a moment she thought she was going to faint, but she managed to remain on her feet. 'Bertie, this is a lovely surprise.' She forced herself to remain calm. 'And you, too, Alex.'

'I wouldn't call it that,' Patricia said icily. 'You'll excuse us, Bertie. But we're both tired after our long journey. I'm staying in Bedford Street for a while, so perhaps I'll see you again soon.' She walked past Alex without acknowledging him.

'Well, I'm blowed.' Bertie stared after her. 'I thought she'd have got over it by now, Alex. I'm sorry, old chap. I really didn't know she would be here.'

Alex shrugged. 'Don't worry about it, Bertie.'

'Well, I must see the young ladies safely back to Bedford Street,' Claude said gruffly. 'Call on us at any time, Bertie.' He gave Alex an apologetic smile as he walked past him.

'I'll call on you tomorrow, Rosie,' Bertie said hurriedly. 'It's good to see you, but we'd better take our table before the waiter gives it to someone else.' He followed the waiter, leaving Rosalind and Alex facing each other.

'I thought you were in Cornwall, Alex.'

'Colonel Munday sent me an appointment to attend the War Office tomorrow. I've no idea why.'

'I should go.' Rosalind made an attempt to leave but Alex caught her by the hand. 'It's so good to see you again. I can't tell you how much I've missed you, Rosie.'

She stared down at their entwined fingers. 'Please don't say any more.'

'How long will you be in London? I have to see you again.'

'I don't know. I only came to chaperone Patsy because she was desperate to get away. You must understand why it's best that we don't meet, Alex.'

'Rosie, are you coming?' Claude's voice shattered the moment.

Rosalind snatched her hand free. 'Goodbye, Alex. I have to go now.' She edged past, dizzy with the scent of him that filled her nostrils, bringing back memories of their time together in the Château Gris. But that was in the past and must remain there. She hurried after Claude and Patricia without looking back, even though the temptation was overwhelming.

'I hope you were giving Alex a good telling-off,' Patricia said angrily. 'I don't know how he has the nerve to turn up like that. Bertie should be ashamed of himself for befriending the man who jilted me at the altar.'

Claude slipped Rosalind's hand through the crook of his arm. 'Patsy is so like her mother, I could almost believe that it was Felicia speaking.'

'He wasn't to know you would be there, Patsy,' Rosalind said lightly. 'But it was good to see Bertie. I've been so worried thinking he'd been sent off to the Crimea, and it seems he's been in London all the time.'

'Yes, he's a likeable fellow. We get on well.' Claude quickened his pace. 'I'd better get you home so that I can hurry to the theatre. Your dear mama relies on me completely, and I don't want her going back on stage after the interval in a state.'

'I'm tired anyway,' Rosalind said, stifling a yawn. 'I think I'll go straight to bed.'

'You are so tedious now you're in the family way. Might I go to the theatre with you, Claude?'

He nodded. 'Of course you may. I'd be delighted to have your company. We'll see Rosie settled first and then we'll go to the theatre.'

Next morning Rosalind was up early, partly from force of habit but also because she had slept badly. Alexander was the last person she had expected to meet in London, and seeing him so unexpectedly had unsettled her more than she would have imagined. She went downstairs to the dining room and met Dawson in the doorway.

'I beg your pardon, ma'am. I didn't think anyone would be up this early.'

'I'd be quite happy with a pot of coffee and some toast, Dawson. Don't go to any trouble on my behalf.'

'It's no trouble, ma'am.' Dawson gave her a sideways glance. 'Would a boiled egg be acceptable?'

'It would, thank you.'

Dawson nodded and hurried off in the direction of the green baize door that separated the servants' quarters from the residents above stairs.

When she had finished breakfast, Rosalind went to the morning parlour. There was still no sign of her mother and Claude, and she suspected that Patsy would sleep until midday. As Dawson had said, there was a fire blazing away in the grate and the morning room was awash with spring sunshine. Rosalind tried to settle down to read a copy of *The Times,* but she could not concentrate, and in the end she rose to her feet and crossed the floor to stand by one of the tall windows. People were hurrying about their business, and horse-drawn vehicles jostled for position in the crowded street. It was all so different from the peace and solitude of Rockwood that it took her breath away. It would have been wonderful to spend a few days in London, visiting the art galleries and museums, or simply walking down to the river to watch the ships unloading at the wharfs. She would have loved to spend time with Bertie, but after meeting Alex the previous evening she knew that the sensible thing to do would be to return to Devon as quickly as possible. Mama would expect them both to attend the opera that evening, but Rosalind made up her mind to leave for home first thing in the morning. She turned with a start at the sound of a faint knock on the door.

'Come in.'

Dawson opened the door but Alexander strode into the room before she had a chance to announce him.

'I'm sorry, ma'am – the gentleman—'

'My apologies.' Alex treated her to a disarming smile. 'I'm an old friend. Aren't I, Rosie?'

Rosalind clutched the back of a chair as the familiar faintness threatened to overcome her, but she forced herself to sound casual. 'Thank you, Dawson. Captain Blanchard is my brother-in-law. That will be all.'

'Yes, ma'am.' Dawson fluttered her eyelashes as she shot a coy look in Alexander's direction and she closed the door.

'You shouldn't be here, Alex,' Rosalind said breathlessly.

'I doubt if anyone could find fault with your brother-in-law calling on you, even if it is a trifle early in the morning.'

'Why did you come when I expressly asked you to stay away?'

He crossed the floor, leaning heavily on his stick. 'I thought I could control my feelings for you, Rosie, but I can't get you out of my head or my heart. I expected to be posted to the Crimea, but Colonel Munday thinks I'll be given a desk job in the War Office, at least until my leg is properly healed. A lame soldier is not much use when it comes to a fight.'

'You know there can never be anything between us, Alex. Anyway, if you get the job you'll be in London, miles away from Rockwood.'

'My interview is later this morning, but I wanted to come and tell you about it first. I was afraid you might make a bolt for it, and catch the first train to Devon.'

'I was tempted, but Mama wants Patsy and me to see her performance tonight.'

'You could stay for a few days. It would be quite proper for you to meet Bertie for luncheon or a trip to the Zoological Gardens.' He reached out to take her hand in his. 'I promise not to say anything that will make you unhappy. It will be enough just to be with you one last time, because I will get posted eventually, and we might never see each other again.'

'Alex, you're making this so hard for me.'

He smiled and squeezed her fingers. 'I know, and I'm pressing home my advantage because I think you want to be with me, too.'

'You haven't said anything to Bertie, have you?'

'No, of course not. I know there's no chance for me, Rosie. I know I've said it before, but I should have carried you off before my brother snapped you up. I made the biggest mistake of my life then and I will pay for it for as long as I have left on this earth.'

She raised his hand to her cheek. 'Don't say things like that. You'll break my heart.'

'Never! I'd die first, Rosie. I'm not a cad. All I want is a few days in your company, as we had in France. I think those were the happiest days of my life.'

'If I say I'll stay until tomorrow at least, will you go now? I don't want Patsy to find you here.'

'All right. I'll leave, but if Bertie invites you to join him for any reason, please accept. I promise to behave like an officer and a gentleman.' He kissed her hand and released it with obvious reluctance.

Rosalind nodded, biting back the tears that threatened to overcome her. 'All right, I will. Now go, please.'

Alex left and she gazed out of the window,

watching him as he made his way along the street and then he stopped to hail a passing hansom. Almost immediately another cab pulled up outside the house and Bertie stepped onto the pavement. Rosalind rushed to the nearest wall mirror to check her appearance. She took several deep breaths and went to sit by the fire, forcing herself to be calm when Dawson showed Bertie into the parlour.

'I might have guessed that the others would still be in bed,' he said, chuckling. 'How are you, Rosie? I thought you looked a bit peaky last evening?'

'I was just tired after the journey, but I'm fine now, and it's lovely to see you safe and sound. I thought you had been sent to the Crimea.'

'My regiment will be sent there soon. I'm not sure when, but I was planning on visiting you at Rockwood if I had a chance. Is Piers well? And what about Hester?'

'Both well, although Piers has gone to Cornwall again to check on the business.'

'You could leave Rockwood and move to Trevenor.'

'Do you want me to?'

'Heavens, no. Rockwood is yours for as long as you want it. To be honest I can't see myself living there permanently, and the title means very little to me. I suppose the old place will always be home in a way, but I like army life. It suits me well.'

'What about if you marry? Your wife may feel differently.'

'If I meet a girl who will put up with being an

army wife she won't want to be tied to an old castle either.'

'It's ours to pass on to future generations, Bertie. Curse or no curse.'

He grinned. 'Yes, I've heard all about Marianne's famous curse. Not that I believe it. Look at you and Piers, for instance. You're so well suited that I can't imagine anything coming between you two.'

'The legend is just a myth,' Rosalind said carefully.

'Let's forget all about that. While you're here let's make the most of it. I suggest we go out to luncheon. Alex is very keen to join us. You don't mind, do you?'

Chapter Thirteen

'Are you sure you don't want to come with us, Patsy?' Rosalind asked, hoping desperately that her sister would refuse the invitation to luncheon.

'I have better things to do than sit through a boring luncheon with Bertie and his colonel. They'll talk about military matters and I would want to run away. Besides which, Alex might be with them and that would be even worse.'

'If you're sure . . .'

'I'm going to the theatre anyway. The intendant thinks I have good stage presence and he asked if I would be interested in joining the company.'

'Really?' Rosalind stared at her in astonishment. 'I didn't know you could sing.'

Patricia smiled modestly. 'Apparently my looks count for a great deal and I have a sweet voice, so I was told.'

'What did Mama say to that?'

'I think she was pleased. It's so hard to tell, but she said of course it was natural that one of her daughters should have inherited some of her talent.'

'Then perhaps that's what you should do. You won't know if the life suits you until you try.'

'Yes, I agree. I'm going to the rehearsal this morning, so I won't be able to come with you anyway.'

'I'll tell Bertie. I'm sure he'll be pleased to think you've found your niche.'

Patricia rolled her eyes. 'No, he won't. He'll tease me endlessly, but I don't care. Perhaps I'll be the next star of the opera world.'

'Mama definitely won't like that.' Rosalind glanced at the ormolu clock on the mantelshelf. 'Shouldn't you be at the theatre? If you're going to take part in the morning rehearsal, that is.'

'You're right. I must dash.' Patricia seized her bonnet and shawl. She left the drawing room in a flurry of lace petticoats.

Minutes later a hackney carriage drew up outside the house and Rosalind took a deep breath. She tried desperately to supress the feeling, but the butterflies in her stomach and the thudding of her heart against her stays made it impossible. She knew it was ridiculous, she was a happily married woman who would soon become a mother, and yet she was as excited as a young girl about to attend her first ball. However, she managed to maintain a calm exterior as she stepped out onto the pavement.

Bertie leaped out of the cab. 'You look blooming today, Rosie. It must be the hint of spring in the air that's brought the colour to your cheeks.' He helped her into the cab, but it was Colonel Munday who was seated opposite her, not Alex.

'Good morning, Mrs Blanchard.' He tipped his hat. 'You'll excuse me if I don't stand. I'm afraid I would go straight through the roof.'

She relaxed instantly. 'Please don't do that, Colonel. I don't think the cabby would be amused.'

Bertie climbed in and sat down beside her. He thumped on the roof and the cab moved off into the traffic. 'We're meeting Alex at Wiltons in Jermyn Street. I have a fancy for a dozen oysters for luncheon. What about you, Colonel?'

'I can't think of anything I'd like more. What about you, Mrs Blanchard? Do you like shellfish?'

Rosalind experienced a sudden bitter taste in her mouth and she shook her head. 'Not really.' She had not the heart to tell them that she disliked oysters, and she had to fight down a feeling of sickness. She sat quietly for the rest of the journey while Bertie and the colonel chatted about mundane things, occasionally asking her opinion, which she answered with a smile and a nod.

Eventually the cab drew up outside the restaurant and she saw Alexander, who was pacing up and down.

Bertie chuckled. 'You would think he was waiting for his sweetheart.'

'Probably just hungry, old chap,' Colonel Munday said jovially. 'I get the same way when I'm kept waiting for my food.'

Rosalind said nothing. She allowed Bertie to hand her down from the cab and she greeted Alexander with a bright smile. 'Have you been waiting long?'

He took her hand and raised it to his lips. 'I was rather early, and it's quite chilly for the time of year.'

'Never mind the weather,' Bertie said impatiently. 'Let's go inside. I booked a table because the colonel and I have to leave no later than half past one. We have a meeting to attend.'

The doorman jumped to attention and Bertie ushered Rosalind into the restaurant. When they were seated and had given the waiter their orders, Bertie turned to Alexander with a wide grin. 'So why were you so agitated outside the restaurant, Alex? A strong fellow like you doesn't feel the cold.'

'To tell the truth I was worried that Patricia might have decided to join us.' Alex met Bertie's gaze with an apologetic smile.

'Is that the young lady you left standing at the altar, Alexander?' Colonel Munday said chuckling.

'Not from choice, Colonel.'

'My sister is very dramatic.' Rosalind picked her words carefully. She did not want to appear to be jumping to Alexander's defence. 'Patsy has decided that she wants to go on the stage, like our mother. In fact, she's at a rehearsal as we speak.'

'No!' Bertie turned his attention to her, open-mouthed. 'I thought Patsy was after a rich husband.'

'I couldn't have lived up to that, I'm afraid.' Alexander sat back in his seat as waiters arrived carrying platters of oysters, which they set on the table.

'Excellent.' Colonel Munday tucked a table napkin into his shirt collar. 'There's nothing I like better than a nice plump oyster.' He took one and swallowed it with obvious enjoyment.

Rosalind toyed with the bowl of soup that had been put before her, but the sight of the shellfish brought back the nauseous feeling and she half rose from her seat.

Alex leaped to his feet and was at her side before anyone could move. 'Are you all right, Rosie?'

She shook her head. 'I'm sorry – it's the oysters . . .'

'It's all right, Bertie,' Alex said firmly. 'I feel the same when it comes to rice pudding. A breath of fresh air is all she needs.' He placed his arm around her waist and guided her out into the street. 'Take deep breaths. You'll feel better in a moment or two.'

She inhaled and exhaled slowly. 'I'm all right now, thank you, Alex.'

'Are you sure?' He was standing so close that the familiar scent of him filled her whole being. She leaned against him, revelling dangerously in the feeling of security that his nearness always brought, even though she knew it was false and she was in dangerous territory.

'I hate oysters,' she said in a whisper.

'Are you certain that's all this is?'

'Yes, of course.' Rosalind straightened up, taking a deep breath. 'I'm quite all right now, Alex. We'd better go back inside.'

'I can take you home, if you prefer.'

'No. I'm sure they will have eaten their fill by now. I'll apologise to the colonel.'

'You'll do no such thing. You said you didn't like the wretched shellfish, but we chose to order them anyway. It's we who should apologise to you, Rosie.'

'Don't make a fuss, Alex. I'm perfectly fine now.' Rosalind slipped her hand in his and their eyes met. She knew at that moment she would remember the look of concern in his hazel eyes for the rest of her life, even if they were to part now and never see each other again.

'There's something you're not telling me. I know you so well, Rosie. You can't keep things from me.'

'Alex, the time we spent together in France was wonderful, but it wasn't real. There can never be anything between us. You know that and so do I.'

'But you came today. You knew I would be here.'

She bowed her head. 'We'd better go back to our table.'

'This conversation isn't over, Rosie. I'm not going to let you walk away again.'

'Alex, we don't have a choice.'

'My brother is married to the clay mine. Come away with me, Rosie. We might not be able to be married but we could live abroad.'

'You know that's impossible,' Rosalind said gently. 'You are a soldier, Alex. It's all you know, and when your leg heals completely you'll go back on active duty.'

'I'd willingly give up my career for you. Could you bear to leave Rockwood?'

'It's not about Rockwood or even Piers. The truth is that I'm in the family way. Piers is so happy and he's convinced that it will be a boy.'

Alexander took a step away from her. 'It can't be true. Not after all this time.'

'I'm sorry. I didn't want to tell you like this, but you wouldn't listen to me.'

'Where is my brother? Why did he allow you to travel to London in your condition? If you were my wife I wouldn't let you out of my sight if you were carrying our child.'

'It's not his fault. Patsy wanted a chaperone and I agreed to come with her. Piers is in Cornwall.'

Alex grasped both her hands in his. 'He should be taking care of you. Leave him. Come with me and I'll bring up the child as if it were my own. I mean, we shared a bed once in the château . . .'

Rosalind held up her hand. 'Don't, Alex. You know nothing happened between us. Don't ruin my marriage because of hurt pride.'

'As if I would. But you know you feel the same as I do.'

'Alex, please . . .'

'No, I won't just give in and go away so that we can conform to the standards set by others. Tell me you love me.'

Rosalind glanced over his shoulder. 'Bertie has come looking for us. Don't say anything more, please.'

'Are you all right, Rosie?' Bertie hurried up to them, his face creased into lines of concern. 'Do you want to go back to Bedford Street?'

'I'll take you if you do,' Alexander said hastily.

'No, thank you both, but I feel all right now. I expect my soup will be cold,' she added in an attempt to lighten the mood.

'They'll have plenty more in the kitchen.' Bertie proffered his arm. 'I was getting worried. Are you sure you aren't sickening for something?'

Rosalind managed a smile as she tucked her hand in the crook of her brother's arm. 'It's normal in my condition, Bertie. You're going to be an uncle in the autumn.'

'No! Really?' Bertie kissed her on the cheek. 'Why didn't you tell us before? This is wonderful news, isn't it, Alex?'

'Yes, of course.' Alex hesitated. 'You two go on in. I've just remembered that I have to see someone at the War Office. It's about my appointment so I should hurry. I'm sorry, I'll have to leave right away.'

He stepped into the road to hail a cab and leaped on board, barely waiting for the cabby to draw his horse to a standstill.

'He's forgotten his hat and cane,' Bertie said drily. 'That's so typical. I know for a fact that he had his interview this morning. You may depend there's a woman involved, Rosie.'

'Why do you say that?'

'There always is. Alex has a reputation in the regiment for being a ladies' man. I think Patsy had a lucky escape.' Bertie gave her a searching look. 'You're shivering, Rosie. Let's get you inside. A hot meal is what you need and then I'll see you safely back to Bedford Street.'

The rest of the day passed in a haze. Rosalind was exhausted by the tumultuous emotions that her meeting with Alex had created, and her one desire was to leave London and return to the security of Rockwood Castle. Bertie had said that Alex was a flirt, and that was true, but she knew that what they shared had been real. Their brief time in the Château Gris was theirs for ever and no one could take that away from them. Her feelings for him would have to be buried deep within her soul, never to resurface, and she would devote herself to her husband and her child.

It was fortunate that Patricia had enjoyed a triumphant first day at the rehearsal and had been offered a part in the chorus. She was bubbling over with excitement and Felicia seemed delighted, although Rosalind detected a hint of resentment. Neither of her daughters must be allowed to outshine the leading lady, and as usual, Rosalind found herself pushed firmly into the background. Felicia de Marney was not going to broadcast the fact that she would soon become a grandmother, and Patricia was living in a romantic dream all her own. The only person who took notice of the fact that Rosalind announced she would be leaving next morning for Devon was Bertie.

'You can't travel on your own, Rosie. What would you do if you felt faint during the train journey? I'll come with you. I suppose I should put in an appearance at the old ruin now and again.'

'It is your home, Bertie.'

He shrugged. 'It's yours for as long as it pleases you to stay. Colonel Munday told me in confidence that we will be embarking for the Crimea very soon. Heaven alone knows when I'll return.'

'Then we'll leave tomorrow morning, if that's all right with you, Bertie.'

'What are you two talking about?' Patricia demanded crossly. 'We're off to the theatre to get ready for tonight's performance. I'm just walking on to start with, but when I've mastered the libretto I will join the rest of the cast. Isn't it exciting?'

'Yes, I'm thrilled for you, Patsy,' Rosalind said earnestly. 'We'll watch you from the stalls. Good luck.'

'I won't need it. The intendant says I have great talent, just like Mama. Although to tell the truth,' Patricia lowered her voice, glancing surreptitiously over her shoulder, 'I think she is a bit worried that I might one day steal the limelight. Isn't that amusing?'

'Very,' Bertie said drily. 'I wouldn't care to be in your shoes then, Patsy.'

'I can take care of myself. When I'm famous and Alexander wants to associate with me I'll snap my fingers in his face and walk away. Make certain you don't include him in any of the festivities at Rockwood that I might attend, Rosie. Now I must fly.'

Rosalind followed her into the hallway to find her mother and Claude were there before them. A maidservant stood patiently holding Patricia's cloak and gloves.

'Do hurry up, Patricia,' Felicia said impatiently. 'I don't want to be late.'

'Coming, Mama.'

Rosalind tapped her mother on the shoulder. 'I'll be leaving first thing in the morning.'

'Have a good journey, dear. Open the door, Claude. I can't wait any longer.'

Claude gave Rosalind an apologetic smile. 'Goodbye, Rosie. I hope you have a good journey back to Devon.' He hesitated with his hand on the latch. 'You're not travelling alone, are you?'

'No, Claude. Bertie has decided he wants to see Rockwood again before he embarks for the Crimea. He's coming with me.'

241

'My boy will be a hero. Just like his forebears.' Felicia swept out of the house with Claude and Patricia hurrying after her.

Bertie emerged from the morning parlour. 'Is it safe to come out now?'

'Yes, they've left for the theatre.'

'I suppose we can't get out of watching the performance, although I have to admit I dislike opera intensely.' Bertie pulled a face. 'I was hoping that Alex would join us, but he sent a message to say he was otherwise engaged, which fuels my theory that there's a woman involved.'

'Who knows?' Rosalind sighed. 'I can't wait to get back to Rockwood.'

'It is good to be home again,' Bertie said as the hired carriage drove them into the bailey of Rockwood Castle, coming to a halt outside the main entrance.

Rosalind was about to reply when the front door opened and Walter stepped outside to greet them, followed by Piers. Walter opened the carriage door and helped her to alight.

'Piers has just told me your good news, Rosie.' He kissed her on the cheek. 'It's wonderful. I can't wait to be an uncle.'

Piers edged him out of the way to take Rosalind in a warm embrace. 'Hester told me that you'd gone to London. You really shouldn't do long journeys now, my love.' He kissed her firmly on the lips. 'At least Bertie has had the decency to see that you arrived home safely. Thank you, old chap. I'm much obliged.'

'That's all right, Piers.' Bertie paid the driver, who lifted their luggage from the roof. 'It was my pleasure. It's time I came home, although I won't be here for long.'

'It's good to see you, Bertie,' Walter said eagerly. 'How's army life?'

'Excellent, as far as I'm concerned. I'm just waiting for orders to join the ship that will take us to the Crimea. However, I'll enjoy some time with my family before I go.'

Rosalind smiled to see her brothers reunited, if briefly. 'It's lovely to come home to such a welcome, Piers. I thought you would still be in Cornwall.'

'Pedrick had matters in hand. It was just a case of checking the books and going over a few things with him. I missed you too much to stay away for long, sweetheart.'

'That's so nice, Piers. Sometimes I think I come second to that wretched clay mine.'

'We must remedy that.'

They walked side by side into the entrance hall where Rosalind took off her cape and handed it to Jarvis.

'Welcome home, ma'am.'

'Thank you, Jarvis, but I've only been away for a few days.'

He stood stiffly to attention. 'You were missed, ma'am.'

'Oh dear,' Rosalind said, laughing. 'That sounds ominous. I hope the children weren't naughty.'

Jarvis rolled his eyes. 'Not exactly, ma'am.'

'I'll ask Hester. She'll tell me everything.' Rosalind smiled up at Piers. 'I'm glad you're here.'

'Where else would I be? I realise that I've neglected you, Rosie. All that will change from now on. We'll be a proper family and I'll be here to see that my son grows up to be the sort of man I wish him to be.' Piers came to a sudden halt. 'I was hoping that Alex might have accompanied you. Aurelia told me that he was thinking of taking a position at the War Office until his leg heals well enough for him to rejoin his regiment.'

'Does he write to Aurelia?'

'I think she corresponds with Alex on a fairly regular basis, and occasionally he replies. Did you see him in London?'

'Briefly. I think he's very busy now.' Rosalind turned away. 'Where's Hester? I need to see her and find out what's been happening in my absence.'

'Yes, I've met your latest protégé. Poor boy, he's certainly been through a hard time. I hope he's the last of your charity cases, Rosie. You have enough to do with everything else, and you should rest as much as possible. In fact I'm going to make sure that you don't overdo things. I'll be a model husband from now on.'

Bertie came up behind them. 'That's what I like to hear. My sister deserves the best.'

'And I will make sure that she doesn't work herself to the bone for the people who depend upon her.'

Rosalind met his fond gaze with a worried glance. 'Perhaps I have put Rockwood first. If you really wish it I will make Trevenor my home.'

Piers kissed her gently on the lips. 'I wouldn't want to tear you away from the place you love most in the world. Besides which, I can't imagine Grandmama taking kindly to having another woman taking charge. I couldn't cope with two unhappy women in my life.'

'Sensible fellow,' Bertie said, chuckling. 'How do you feel about a day's fishing, Piers? We could hire one of the fishermen to take us out into the bay.'

'I might just take you up on that.' Piers glanced at Rosalind with raised eyebrows. 'Would you mind if we deserted you for a whole day?'

She laughed. 'I think I can manage to fill my time. Go with Bertie and enjoy a day on the water.'

'That's settled then.' Bertie turned to Walter. 'What about you, brother? Would you like to come fishing with us?'

Walter shook his head. 'I have some studying to do. Anyway, you know I'm not much of a fisherman. I don't like killing the poor creatures.'

'But you don't mind eating what I catch.' Bertie slapped him on the back. 'It's all right, Walter. You do whatever makes you happy. One day you'll eclipse us all.'

'I'm going to find Hester.' Rosalind left her brothers and Piers chatting amicably as they made their way to the drawing room, and she headed for Hester's parlour.

'Nancy told me you'd arrived,' Hester said, smiling. 'Come and sit down and tell me all about London.'

'When did Piers come home? I wasn't expecting him so soon.'

'He's concerned for your welfare, Rosie. That man really loves you, even if he doesn't always show it.' Hester gave her a long look.

'Yes, I know he does and I love him, too. Everything will be different now.'

'You've seen Alexander?'

There was no hiding anything from Hester, and Rosalind nodded. It was a relief to talk to someone who knew everything, even if she could be rather judgemental at times. 'Yes, I did, but I'm putting all that behind me now.'

'Did you tell him about the baby?'

'Yes, he knows. He also knows that I love Piers. It's hard because I love them both, but that's as far as it goes. Alex understands that now, even if it hurts.'

'You're bound to meet from time to time, Rosie.'

'I hope it will get easier. It has to.' Rosalind went to sit beside Hester on the sofa and laid her head on Hester's ample shoulder. 'I knew you'd understand.'

'I do, of course. I've practically raised you, Rosie, and I don't want to see you get hurt any more than you are now. You've done the right thing.'

'Yes, I know, but that doesn't make it any easier.'

'I'm here to help you, and you won't have time to brood over what might have been after the little one arrives. There are so many people who depend upon you, poppet. You are the heart of Rockwood. Never forget that.'

Chapter Fourteen

The day after her return home, Rosalind sent two of the cleaning women to the old schoolroom to give it a good airing. They were instructed to take the carpets outside into the stable yard and beat them until every trace of dust had blown away. The floors were scrubbed and the windows cleaned, the furniture was polished with beeswax and it was only then that Rosalind deemed the room fit for use. Every morning, after breakfast, Nancy Sunday and Tommy Trimble began an hour of lessons in reading, writing and basic arithmetic. Rosalind taught them herself, but as the weeks went and spring warmed into summer, she found that her other duties became more pressing, and she enlisted the help of Louise Shaw.

Louise looked round the schoolroom with a nod of approval. 'This is wonderful. You are giving those poor children a start in life that they could only imagine.'

'I would take others in, but children of their age are invariably sent out to work in order to support their families. I hope the day will come when schools are provided for all youngsters over the age of five, but I'm afraid that is some way off.'

Louise nodded. 'I agree entirely. I'm only too happy to take over from you. I've been longing to find something worthwhile to do, apart from the charitable work that Mama undertakes. It's very worthy, of course, but we see the same people week after week and I sometimes wonder if we're doing any good at all.'

'I'm sure you do, but this is even more worthwhile. Perhaps Tilly and Molly could join in the reading classes? I'm sure we can spare them for an hour a day and it would improve their chances later in life if they had at least some education.'

'Yes, indeed. I think it's a very exciting idea.' Louise picked up a reading primer and leafed through the pages. 'I always wanted to be a teacher, but my parents wouldn't hear of it. They wanted me to stay at home until I married.'

'I'm sure you've been a great help to both of them,' Rosalind said hastily.

Louise sighed and shook her head. 'I'm twenty-seven, Rosalind. I would love to be pretty like you and Patsy, but I know that will never be the case, and soon I'll be officially on the shelf. I think

Mama is ashamed of me, although she won't admit it.'

'Surely not.' Rosalind could not bring herself to agree with Louise, even though she thought it highly likely.

'Well, I would like to be married, but only if I truly love that person.'

'I agree entirely.'

'I was so sorry for Patricia when her wedding was cancelled at the last moment. I hope she's recovered from the disappointment.'

'My sister is going to be an operatic singer, or so she hopes. She's been taken on by the intendant at the Royal Opera House, so it's a promising start. I think it would have been a mistake for her to marry Alexander.'

'He is very handsome,' Louise said, blushing. 'I danced with him once at a ball you held here. He was so amusing and quite charming. He made me feel important.'

'That sounds like my brother-in-law.' Rosalind smiled, but the old familiar ache in her heart reminded her that she was on dangerous ground. 'So when can you start, Louise?'

'Would tomorrow be too soon?'

'Not at all. That would suit me very well.'

'Might I just ask one question?'

Rosalind had been about to leave the schoolroom, but she hesitated in the doorway. 'Of course.'

'It's really none of my business, and I think it's a

wonderful thing, but what do you hope to accomplish by educating those poor orphans?'

'Surely everyone ought to be able to read and write?'

'I agree, but are they to be treated like servants or members of the family?'

'Nancy and Tommy are just children. I don't consider them as servants.'

'That's what I mean, Rosalind. Isn't there a danger of educating them above their station in life?'

'That sounds like something your papa might say, even though he preaches that we are all equal under the eyes of God.'

'I agree. There is a certain amount of hypocrisy in teaching equality and then treating others like inferior beings. I was bitterly ashamed of the way my parents treated Nancy. She is a dear child and I care what happens to her.'

'As do I,' Rosalind said quickly. 'You're right, Louise. I haven't given it enough thought. All I wanted was for them to grow up to have decent lives, but perhaps that was naïve of me. I can't change society, but it occurred to me that if Tommy and Nancy were my wards, I might be able to do more for them. After all, I took responsibility for them.'

Louise smiled. 'Most people would consider it enough just putting a roof over their heads and food in their mouths.'

'I'll speak to my husband. I'm sure he'll support me in this.'

* * *

Piers' reaction when Rosalind told him and Hester of her plan was not quite what she had expected.

'You haven't thought this through, Rosie. I can see why you want to do this, but you don't know what sort of family those children came from. They could be felons or madmen or simply just wrongdoers. To take them into our family like that could prove a disaster.'

Rosalind stared at him in astonishment. 'Even if that were so, you can't blame those innocent children for the faults of their parents. It will be up to us to see that they take the right path.'

'I know you are doing this out of the goodness of your heart, but I draw the line at becoming their guardian, and the law prohibits you as a woman from acting as a guardian, and that includes our own child.'

Rosalind faced him mutinously. 'Even so, I will see that they receive an education, and when they are older they can choose what they want to do.'

'I thought that Nancy's ambition was to become a lady's maid,' Piers said, smiling. 'Educate them, by all means, but I think Louise was right. They will have to find their place in the world one day, and if you give them too many grand ideas they will face rejection from many quarters.'

'What do you think, Hester?' Rosalind turned to her eagerly. 'Am I wrong to want the best for the two children we've taken into our household?'

'Of course not, poppet, but Piers is right and I

suspect that Louise Shaw put it better than either of us. Teach them to read and write and add up, but allow them to find their own way. I've seen young Tommy's face when he's in the stables with Gurney. Nancy enjoys sewing and anything to do with keeping your gowns in perfect condition. Your room has never been so tidy and your hankies, stockings and undergarments are all folded and put away neatly. She does all this without being asked because she loves you and she enjoys doing things like that. It isn't work to her.'

Rosalind smiled reluctantly. 'All right. I've listened to everyone and I have to admit you're right. They will receive a basic education, and they can do what they like with their free time. In fact I'll go and find them now and have a word.'

'I still think you're doing too much,' Piers said stubbornly. 'You should get more rest in your condition.'

'Nonsense, I've given the teaching to Louise, and Hester is virtually running the household. I'm just not the sort of person who can sit and do nothing, Piers. You ought to know that by now.'

'Yes, of course I do.' Piers and Hester exchanged resigned looks but Rosalind ignored them. She left the room and made her way to the stables where she was greeted ecstatically by Bob her devoted Labrador. 'Down, boy,' she said laughing. 'You can come with me and help me find those children.'

Gurney popped his head out of one of the stalls.

'I think you'll find them in that there tree house, ma'am. They've took to playing with some of the local young 'uns.'

'Thank you, Gurney.' Rosalind hesitated with her hand on Bob's collar. 'Is Tommy proving to be a help to you in the stables?'

'Aye, ma'am. He's a good lad and when he's older he'll make a fine groom. He has no fear of horses and he has a way with them.'

'Thank you, Gurney. That's all I wanted to know.' Rosalind walked off in the direction of the home woods with Bob on her heels. She found Nancy and Tommy, as Gurney had suggested, in the tree house. Their laughter echoed round the clearing in the tall trees and it had such a joyful sound that Rosalind could have cried with relief. They scrambled down the ladder in answer to her call and Bob made such a fuss of them that Rosalind was almost jealous.

'Have we done wrong, ma'am?' Nancy asked anxiously. 'Was I supposed to be helping in the kitchen?'

'I done me bit in the stables, miss,' Tommy added. 'Mr Gurney said I done well.'

'I'm glad to see you using the old tree house,' Rosalind said, smiling. 'My brothers and I used to play here often when we were your age. Just be careful you don't fall out of it and break an arm or a leg. That would be very painful.'

Nancy eyed her warily. 'We'll be careful, ma'am.'

'I'm taking Bob for a walk to the backwater. Come with me.'

The children fell into step with Rosalind, and Bob raced on ahead. Gradually and without alarming them, Rosalind encouraged them to talk about their hopes for the future and their feelings about their new home. By the time they ended their walk she was satisfied that they were both happy and had adjusted to their new way of life without any damage to their wellbeing. Tommy was gradually putting the horrors of his short career as a climbing boy behind him and he spoke enthusiastically about helping Gurney with the horses. He had developed a bond with Bob and it was obvious that he had a way with animals. On the walk home Tommy shyly slipped his small hand into Rosalind's, smiling up at her with genuine affection. Rosalind felt an almost overwhelming desire to protect the little boy and she squeezed his fingers. No matter what the rest of the family said, she would make sure that Tommy had a decent start in life, and was given the affection that he obviously craved. There was a refinement about Tommy, both in looks and manners, that set him in a category of his own, and something vaguely familiar about the way his soft dark blond hair waved back from his forehead and the golden lights in his brown eyes. The more she grew to know him the more determined Rosalind became to see the child develop to his full potential. She felt the same for Nancy, but to a lesser degree. There was a streak of independence in Nancy that Rosalind admired and would nurture but, if she were to admit it, Tommy had a special place in her heart.

Despite his promises, Piers spent at least one week every month in Cornwall, or else he was travelling to different parts of the country promoting the china clay business. Rosalind was kept busy with matters concerning the tenant farmers, although she allowed Ralph Lambert, the steward, to take over much of the work that she had done herself in the old days when she used to ride from farm to farm collecting the rents. It had brought her closer to the tenants, and if there had been a poor harvest or if disease had struck their livestock she had often let them off their payments. She suspected that Lambert was not so generous, but Piers was pleased with his work, and by midsummer Rosalind was beginning to slow down as her pregnancy progressed. However, that did not prevent her from taking the pony and trap and driving herself to visit friends and neighbours and call upon the poorer tenants who might need help.

It was the end of July and Piers had travelled to London the previous day for a business meeting. Rosalind was on her way to the stables when she heard someone sobbing. She opened the door to the feed store and found Tilly Madge curled up on a pile of empty sacks, crying as if her heart would break. Rosalind bent down to pat her on the shoulder.

'Tilly, what's the matter?'

Tilly scrambled to her feet, wiping her eyes on her sleeve. 'Sorry, ma'am. I didn't mean to disturb you.'

'Don't apologise. You're obviously very upset about something. What is it?'

'It's Ma and the young 'uns. They're being evicted from our cottage today.' A fresh bout of sobbing rendered her incapable of speaking.

'Why are they being evicted? This is the first I've heard of it.'

'Ma couldn't pay the rent,' Tilly sobbed.

Rosalind took her by the hand. 'Come with me, Tilly. I'll soon put a stop to this.' She marched to the stables where Gurney had the pony and trap ready for her. He stared curiously at Tilly, but Rosalind was not in a mood for explanations. 'Get in, Tilly.'

'Should you be driving on a day like this, ma'am?' Gurney asked tentatively.

'I have something important to do, Gurney. Stand aside, please.' Rosalind flicked the reins and clicked her tongue against her teeth. 'Walk on, Ajax.'

The ageing Dartmoor pony was still eager to oblige, and Bob ran along beside the trap as it gathered speed. The cottages on the quay belonged to the Rockwood estate, and Widow Madge had paid a reduced rent since her husband was lost at sea. They arrived to find Tilly's four sisters lined up on the quay wall, while bailiffs dragged furniture from the tiny cottage. Rosalind had never understood how the family managed to exist with only one room on the ground floor and one bedroom above it, but somehow Widow Madge had raised six children. Her son had followed his father's footsteps and become a fisherman at the age of eleven, but tragically both father and son had drowned during a sudden storm. Tilly had gone into service at the castle a few months later. However, the younger children still depended upon their mother to support them and she did this by taking in washing and mending.

Rosalind handed the reins to Tilly and she alighted slowly and carefully. 'What's going on, Mrs Madge?'

'Oh, ma'am, I am so sorry. I tried so hard to raise the rent money but young Jennet was poorly and I had to send for the doctor. Then I had to buy medicine and it's cost me dear.'

'Don't cry, Mrs Madge.' Rosalind stepped in front of the burly bailiff. 'You can put all that furniture back in the cottage where you found it.'

'I got orders, missis.'

'Who gave you the order to evict this poor woman and her children?'

'I did.' Ralph Lambert strode out of the cottage, clutching his riding whip in his hand. 'I should have told you, Mrs Blanchard. But this woman is more often than not a late payer. This time she owes two months' rent.'

'You should have checked with me first, Mr

Lambert,' Rosalind said icily. 'You gave the order and now you can cancel it. Tell that man to put everything back as it was.'

'I can't do that, ma'am. An official order has gone out. Mrs Madge is no longer your tenant.'

'Tell your man to replace everything, Lambert. I won't say it again. Mrs Madge will pay as and when she is able. You will not evict anyone in future without consulting me.'

'With all due respect, ma'am, it was Mr Blanchard who hired me. I answer to him.'

'Rockwood Castle belongs to the Carey family, Mr Lambert. I was a Carey before I married Mr Blanchard, and I am my brother's representative when it comes to matters concerning the estate. You will do as I say or you will be looking for another position.'

Eliza Madge hurried to Rosalind's side. 'Don't get yourself upset over us, ma'am. I've been in your condition eight times in all and it don't do to get in a state. That's how I lost two of my babies.'

'I am quite all right, thank you, Mrs Madge.' Rosalind gave her a reassuring smile. 'Mr Lambert, you will do as I say immediately or suffer the consequences.'

He slapped his riding crop against his leg and a muscle in his jaw twitched, but he nodded to the bailiff. 'You heard what the lady said. Put everything back where you found it.' He strode over to Rosalind, towering over her, his handsome features controlled with an obvious effort.

'I will do as you say, Mrs Blanchard, but I will write a full report for your husband.'

'I wouldn't do that if I were you, Mr Lambert. My husband will stand by what I've just said. If you don't wish to take orders from a woman I suggest you hand in your notice and find another job.'

His nostrils flared but he said nothing and turned away. 'Hurry, man. Do as I say.'

Rosalind knew she had made an enemy, but she did not care. Lambert would find that she was not the soft little woman he had taken her to be. She could give orders just like her late grandfather, Vice-Admiral Sir Lucius Carey, baronet. She might not have inherited the land and title, but centuries of ownership of Rockwood were in her blood.

She turned to Tilly and hugged her. 'You can have the rest of the day off to help your ma get everything straight.'

'I don't know how to thank you, ma'am,' Eliza said tearfully.

'You have rights like anyone else, Mrs Madge. If you have problems I want you to come to me.' Rosalind glanced at the eldest of the children still at home with their mother. 'How old are you, Jennet?'

'I'm nine, missis.'

'Manners, Jennet.' Eliza frowned at her daughter. 'It's "ma'am" or "Mrs Blanchard".'

'That's all right, Mrs Madge,' Rosalind said, smiling. 'If Jennet is interested there is always work in the grounds at Rockwood Castle. I'll tell Abe Coaker to be on the lookout for her. I'm sure he can find work for Jennet. The wage isn't huge, but it would be the same wherever she went to work.'

'I'm more than grateful, ma'am.'

'We'll say no more about it, Mrs Madge. Consider yourself debt free and we'll start afresh next month. I know exactly how hard it is to get by when money is tight.'

'I don't know what to say, ma'am.'

Rosalind turned to Ralph Lambert, who was standing just a few feet away, scowling. 'I expect you heard that, Mr Lambert. Mrs Madge owes nothing. I hope we understand each other.'

He tipped his hat. 'Perfectly, ma'am.' He strode away, swishing his riding crop as if cutting down a field of ripened corn.

Rosalind said her goodbyes to the family and climbed into the trap. She urged Ajax to a walk and they set off, but as she drove past the home wood she heard the sound of a horse's hoofs. Lambert drew up alongside the trap.

'Mrs Blanchard, I would ask you respectfully not to countermand my orders in future.'

'I thought I had made it clear that your powers are limited, Mr Lambert. I speak for my brother when it comes to managing Rockwood. You are hired to collect rents and deal with tenants' problems. I do not expect you to send the bailiffs in to a poor widow who is struggling to bring up her family.'

'Nevertheless, ma'am. I don't take kindly to my authority being challenged in that manner.'

'Mr Lambert, I've been very patient, but you are trying me too far. One more word from you and you may consider your employment at Rockwood terminated.'

'Mr Blanchard is my employer. If he wants me to leave then he must tell me in person. In the meantime I have work to do.' Lambert dug his heels into his horse's flanks, controlling it easily as it reared and then sped off.

Shaken but more angry than upset, Rosalind allowed Ajax to have his head and he ambled homeward, giving her time to recover before she arrived back at the stables. When Piers returned from London she would insist that he dismiss Lambert personally, since the wretched man would not take it from a woman. She left Ajax with Gurney and made her way into the house, still seething with anger.

She was on her way to her room to change when she met Louise coming downstairs.

'Are you all right, Rosalind?' Louise asked anxiously. 'You look very flushed.'

'It's rather hot today and I've just had an unpleasant encounter with Ralph Lambert. He really is an impossible man.'

'Oh dear! What has he done to upset you?'

'He's a bully and he's arrogant.' Rosalind eyed Louise curiously. 'Don't tell me that you find him charming.'

'He is a fine figure on horseback and I can see that women might find him quite good-looking.'

'Handsome is as handsome does, as Hester would say. That man sent the bailiffs in to evict Widow Madge and her children. I only got there just in time to prevent them snatching everything the poor woman owns. Heaven knows, it's very little, and all of it old and well used.'

'He should be ashamed of himself.' Louise laid her hand on Rosalind's arm. 'Why don't you go to your room and rest for a while? I'll bring you a cool drink or a cup of tea, whichever you prefer.'

'Thank you, Louise, but I'll be all right once I've cooled down. Have you finished the morning lessons?'

'Yes, and the children have done very well. Tommy, in particular, has come on so quickly I can hardly credit it. For a child of the slums he's very bright and far too intelligent to be a climbing boy.'

'I sensed that he's special,' Rosalind said, smiling proudly. 'And what about Nancy? Is she doing well?'

'Nancy is a dear child and she's very eager to please. She works hard whereas Tommy seems to absorb learning without making much of an effort. It's wonderful to see them develop. Anyway, I mustn't keep you from your rest. I'll see you tomorrow.'

Rosalind negotiated the stairs easily enough but she was hot and even more tired by the time she reached her room. She took off her outer garments and undid her stays before lying down on her bed.

With a cool sea breeze wafting in from the open window, made fragrant by the blooms in the rose garden, she fell into a deep and dreamless sleep.

Someone was calling her name and a small hand was clutching her arm. Rosalind opened her eyes and sat bolt upright. 'What's the matter, Nancy?'

'You'd better come, ma'am. Hester said not to wake you, but there's a nasty man downstairs and he's shouting at Hester. He says he won't go until he's spoken to you in person.'

Rosalind stifled a yawn. 'Did this person have a name?' She half expected Nancy to say it was Ralph Lambert. She was ready to do battle if he had come to make trouble.

'He said his name is Trimble – like Tommy.'

Icy fingers of fear ran down Rosalind's spine. 'Are you sure it wasn't Hodge, the chimney sweep?'

Nancy shook her head. 'No, ma'am. It was Trimble and I think he wants to take Tommy away from us.'

'Help me with my stays, Nancy, and pass me my print gown. No one is going to take Tommy from us. Where is he?'

'Hester told Molly to take him to the kitchen. Cook has lots of knives – she won't let anyone hurt Tommy.'

Rosalind struggled into her clothes with Nancy's help and she hurried downstairs to Hester's parlour. She stopped outside the door. 'Go to the kitchen and ask Cook to give you and Tommy something to eat. Keep him there and don't come above stairs until I send for you. Do you understand?'

'Yes, ma'am.'

Rosalind brushed a stray curl back from her forehead and took a deep breath before entering the room. She was instantly aware of a large and very irate man who stood in the middle of the floor, glowering at Hester.

'What is going on?' Rosalind demanded coldly. 'Who are you, sir?'

He turned on her, his face flushed and glistening with drops of perspiration. 'I've come for me son. The one you took from his master, the sweep.'

'Hodges sold Tommy to me for three guineas,' Rosalind said calmly. 'I believe you sold the boy to him.'

'I never sold the brat. I paid his indenture. He was going to learn the trade.'

'He was being beaten and burned by a sadistic man who should never be allowed to have young children under his control.'

'I am the boy's father. I want me son back. You can't keep him.'

'How do I know that he's your son, sir? You were happy enough to sell him into a life of pain and suffering. I don't think you are a fit parent.'

'I'll take you to court if I has to.'

'Then prove to me that Tommy is your son. Maybe we can come to some arrangement that would suit us both.'

'You live in a castle – you can afford to compensate me for losing a wage-earner.'

'I'm not giving you a penny. I don't believe that Tommy is your son.'

'You want proof. I'll get you it. Just you see.' Trimble stormed out of the room, slamming the door behind him.

Rosalind sank down on the sofa. 'I'm not giving in to that brute. I don't care what Trimble says, I'm not giving Tommy into his care.'

Chapter Fifteen

Tommy was obviously terrified of Trimble and it took Rosalind an hour or more to comfort him. She promised that she would never allow anyone to take him away from them, but he was still tearful. Even a large slice of Mrs Jackson's feathery light sponge cake could not completely convince him that he was safe from the man who had made his young life a misery. Rosalind gave orders for everyone to be on the lookout for Trimble and they were instructed to refuse him entry should he return, although she knew that she had not seen the last of him. Trimble had sensed money and he was unlikely to give up easily.

Next morning Rosalind reassured Tommy yet again, but she made him promise not to venture far from the castle, and the woods were definitely out of bounds for the foreseeable future. She repeated this to Nancy, who gave her word that she would keep Tommy out of trouble, but Rosalind knew that it was not going to be so easy. It was only a matter of time before Trimble turned up again.

The following day she happened to be looking out of the oriel window above the front entrance when she saw two people riding a cart horse. The poor animal looked as though it should have been pensioned off years ago, and it was no surprise to see Trimble holding the reins. She could only assume that the woman must be Tommy's mother, and her heart sank. It would be hard for the child to go against both parents, and if his mother became distraught Tommy might be persuaded to return home. Rosalind had just come from the schoolroom where Nancy and Tommy were busy with their lessons, so she knew they were safe for at least another hour, and she was more determined than ever to stand up to Trimble's bullying tactics. She hurried downstairs and went outside where she was met by an enthusiastic Bob, who seemed to think she had come to take him for a walk. 'Down, boy,' Rosalind said firmly. She came to a standstill with Jarvis hovering anxiously in the background.

'Shall I send for Gurney and one of the grooms, ma'am?'

'Not yet, Jarvis. I'll see if I can reason with the fellow first, and it looks as if he's brought his wife with him. Let's hope she's more reasonable than he is.'

Rosalind waited until Trimble had dismounted, leaving his wife to slither to the cobbled yard without any assistance. 'Well, what is it today, Mr Trimble? I can save you time by telling you that I haven't changed my mind. Tommy stays here.'

Trimble advanced on her but she held her ground. He was a big man, tall and burly with hands like hams and muscular forearms exposed by his rolled-up sleeves. His expression was grim. Bob growled and moved closer to Rosalind. She placed her hand on his collar in an attempt to reassure him.

'I've brought the missis. You won't deny a poor woman the comfort of seeing her only child, will you, ma'am?' Trimble's wheedling tone was at odds with his scowl, and his fists were clenched at his sides as he eyed Jarvis suspiciously.

'You sold your boy to Hodges,' Rosalind said firmly. 'You gave him up, so why do you want him back now?'

Trimble grabbed his wife by the arm and thrust her forward. 'You tell her, Emmie. Tell the lady how you cries yourself to sleep because you miss the lad.'

Emmie cringed, keeping her eyes downcast. She muttered something inaudible and received a sharp slap for her pains. 'Speak up, woman.'

'I misses him, ma'am.'

Trimble twisted her arm. 'Say it with more feeling, you silly slut.'

'That's enough, Mr Trimble,' Rosalind said angrily. 'If you treat your wife so cruelly, why should I allow a young child to return to your household?'

'Because he's my flesh and blood.' Trimble's eyes narrowed and he bared his teeth. 'How many times do I have to say it?'

'I believe you only want Tommy back because you intend to sell him again. Or perhaps you hope that I will give you money for him?'

'I dare say we could come to an arrangement,' Trimble lowered his voice. 'Something that would make up for the pain of losing a dear one.'

Rosalind turned to Jarvis. 'Mr Trimble looks as if he is in need of refreshment, Jarvis. Please take him to the still room. I'm sure a glass of ale will go down well on such a warm day, and I'll look after Mrs Trimble.'

'She comes with me,' Trimble said hastily.

'No, Ezra. I'll stay here and wait for you.' Emmie Trimble faced him defiantly. 'I knows what to say.'

'Come with me, my man.' Jarvis folded his arms. 'You've been offered a glass of ale. It would be unwise to refuse such hospitality.'

Rosalind waited for Trimble to make an excuse, but to her surprise he followed Jarvis without any further argument. She turned to the frail woman, who looked as if a puff of wind would blow her away. 'Come with me, Mrs Trimble. I'm sure a cup of tea and something to eat would be welcome.'

Emmie nodded. 'Thank you, ma'am.'

Rosalind took her to the morning parlour, having sent Molly to fetch a tray of tea and biscuits. Bob had bounded on ahead and he flopped down in front of the empty grate, but Rosalind knew that he was far from relaxed.

'Now then, do take a seat and tell me why you want to take the boy away from us. You must realise that he's better off here than climbing chimneys for a sadistic master sweep.'

'I daren't tell you anything, ma'am. Trimble will kill me for sure.'

'I won't let that happen.'

Emmie snorted with hollow laughter. 'You wouldn't be able to stop him. I got two kids of me own, and I don't want to risk them being sold to the highest bidder.'

'Are you telling me that Tommy isn't your child?'

Emmie bit her lip. 'I shouldn't have said nothing.'

'You can trust me, Emmie. I won't say anything to your husband.'

Emmie hesitated before answering. 'I had a younger sister. She was in service at Greystone Park.'

'Really? I know the family well. I might have seen your sister there.'

'I doubt if you'd have noticed her, ma'am. No one above stairs looks a servant in the face. Sally was the prettiest of us sisters, and lively, too. She could make anyone smile with her winning ways.'

There was a pause as Molly entered and set a tea tray on the table near Rosalind's chair.

'Thank you, Molly,' Rosalind said, smiling. 'That will be all for now.'

Molly bobbed a curtsey and left the room, but she hesitated, glancing over her shoulder as she closed the door.

'Don't worry about her,' Rosalind said hastily. 'Molly won't say anything.' She poured tea into two cups and handed one to Emmie. 'Do help yourself to biscuits.'

'Ta.' Emmie crammed a piece of shortbread into her mouth.

'You were telling me about your sister.'

Emmie swallowed a mouthful and washed it down with a gulp of tea. 'She met a young man who wasn't from our class, if you know what I mean. They fell in love and the usual happened.'

'She had a child?'

'She was only sixteen.'

'Did the young man stand by her?'

'He was away at boarding school most of the time. He weren't much older than Sal.'

'But she told him about Tommy?'

Emmie shook her head. 'She said it would get him into trouble with his family. I think she really loved Bertie.'

Rosalind leaned forward, knocking her cup over and spilling her tea on the carpet. 'What did you say his name was?'

'Let me mop up the tea, ma'am. It will ruin the carpet.'

'Not until you tell me everything. Never mind the carpet. What was the father's name?'

'Bertie Carey. That's why I needed to tell you in private, ma'am. Trimble don't know and I don't want him to find out. I promised Sal on her deathbed that I'd do me best for Tommy, but I'd never ask Bertie's family for help. I've failed so far because I couldn't stop Trimble selling him to the sweep. I don't want to make things worse.' Emmie seized a dainty table napkin and went down on her knees to scrub at the spreading tea stain.

'Get up, please, Mrs Trimble. You really don't have to do this.'

'I only married Trimble to put a roof over me head. I thought it would be best for Tommy, but I was wrong.' Emmie resumed her seat.

'You said your sister died – I'm so sorry to hear that.'

'She caught a fever. Tommy was only two. Trimble thinks he's my kid and I want it to stay that way. If he knew the truth he'd be demanding money from your family and he'd come back again and again. I got two little ones now and another on the way. If Ezra ends up in prison it will be the workhouse for me and the children.'

'I'm sorry, Mrs Trimble, but are you sure it was my brother who fathered Tommy? I don't think Bertie would have kept his relationship with your sister a secret.'

'His grandfather knew about it. Bertie wanted to

273

marry Sal, but Sir Lucius put a stop to it. He gave Sal money on condition that she moved to another town, which is how we ended up in Exeter. You'd never have known about Tommy if he hadn't run away from the sweep.'

Rosalind rose to her feet and went to stand by the window. She wanted to believe Emmie, but it could all be a ruse instigated by Trimble to blackmail the family into buying his silence. She turned slowly to face Emmie, who was stuffing biscuits into her mouth, barely giving herself time to swallow.

'Mrs Trimble, I want to believe you, but I would need proof. Is there a birth certificate for Tommy?'

Emmie shook her head. 'No, ma'am. We was struggling to survive day by day. It didn't seem important at the time.'

'Was he baptised?'

'Yes, ma'am. Sally was very particular about that. She didn't want him to be taken by the devil, should he fall sick and die.'

'Then there must be a record in the church register. Can you remember where the baptism took place?'

Emmie frowned. 'I think it was St Pancras Church, if I remember rightly.'

'What was your sister's maiden name? I'll need to know.'

'Farthing, ma'am. She was Sarah Farthing, only we called her Sally or Sal.' Emmie glanced nervously over her shoulder. 'What are you going to do, ma'am?

Trimble will be furious if he finds out I told you all this.'

'Tommy stays here, no matter what. I don't care if he is my nephew or not, he is still a dear child who needs a good home. I'm fond of him already and I have no intention of allowing Mr Trimble to take him away from us.'

'Will you tell his father?'

'I will, when I'm certain that Tommy is his child. My brother is in the Crimea as we speak, so I don't know when I'll see him again, but I hope it won't be too long.'

Emmie's pale grey eyes filled with tears. 'I'm so grateful to you for looking after the boy. I can't protect him from Trimble. He just sees Tommy as a way of making money. Poor Sal would be turning in her grave if she knew.' She turned with a start as the door opened and Trimble marched into the room, followed by Jarvis.

Bob was instantly alert and he sat up straight, eyeing Trimble warily.

'I'm sorry, Mrs Blanchard,' Jarvis said stiffly. 'This person insisted that he wanted to speak to you.'

'Just look at you, Emmie Trimble! Sitting there like you was a lady, which you ain't.' Trimble dragged her to her feet. 'Go outside and stay with the horse. I want a word with madam.'

'There's no need for that, Mr Trimble.' Rosalind said icily. 'Mrs Trimble is entitled to a little civility, and I have nothing to say to you.'

'We want our son back, or else some recompense for his loss.'

'You won't get a penny piece from me.' Rosalind faced him angrily.

'Then I'll inform the police that you've kidnapped our boy.'

'Trimble, please don't do that.' Emmie clutched his sleeve. 'Can't you see that he's better off here? We need to go home. I can't leave Ma in charge of the babes for long. You know what she's like when she starts on the gin.'

He threw her to the floor with a casual flick of his wrist. 'Shut up, woman.'

Bob rushed at him, barking and baring his teeth.

'You, sir, are a bully and a rogue.' Rosalind helped Emmie to her feet. 'Are you all right?'

'Yes, ma'am. I tripped and fell.'

'That's not what I saw.' Rosalind grabbed Bob by the collar. 'I'm asking you to leave, Mr Trimble. If your wife chooses to remain here I wouldn't blame her.'

Emmie hurried to her husband's side. 'No, ma'am. I thank you for the tea and biscuits, but we'd best be on our way.'

'Where's the boy?' Trimble pushed her aside. 'I ain't leaving without him.'

Jarvis stepped forward. 'You heard Mrs Blanchard, sir. I'd advise you to go now or I'll send for some of the groundsmen to help you on your way.'

'I ain't afraid of an old man like you.' Trimble

raised his hand as if to strike Jarvis, but Bob leaped up and grabbed him by the arm, growling ferociously.

'Get your dog off me or I'll strangle the brute.'

Rosalind rushed forward and pulled Bob away. Her normally gentle friend was clearly disturbed and she had no doubt that he would defend her to the death if required, but she was not going to allow Trimble or anyone to hurt him.

'I've asked you politely and now I'm telling you to leave my property, Mr Trimble. If you return you will not be admitted under any circumstances.'

'I want the boy,' Trimble said stubbornly.

Rosalind released Bob, giving him a command to sit, which to her surprise he obeyed. 'As I told you before, I paid the sweep three guineas for Tommy, so he's legally mine.'

'Let's go home, Ezra. We can't do any more here.' Emmie patted him on the arm. 'Leave the boy.'

Trimble shook her off as if she were an irritating fly. 'I told you to go outside and wait with the horse.'

Emmie shook her head. 'No, I'm not going anywhere without you. I know what you're like when you get angry. You'll only make trouble for yourself.'

Trimble glanced at Bob, who was still growling softly in the back of his throat. 'All right, I'm coming. But I will be back and if necessary I'll bring a constable with me. I will have what's rightfully mine.'

'You can't do that, Ezra. You aren't his pa.'

Trimble raised his hand and brought it down hard on the side of his wife's head, sending her sprawling to the floor. Jarvis stepped forward and before Trimble had a chance to argue Jarvis twisted the man's arm behind his back.

'I won't stand by and see a woman treated like that. You're leaving now, cully. Walk.'

Rosalind watched in awe as Jarvis seemed to shrug off his years and he marched Trimble out of the parlour. She bent down to help Emmie to her feet.

'Are you all right?'

Emmie nodded. 'I'm used to his ways, ma'am. He'll be sorry later and I'll forgive him. That's how it goes with us.'

'If you ever decide to leave him, I could find you somewhere to live on the estate. You don't have to stay with a man who treats you worse than a dog.'

'I'm glad you've taken Tommy in. I know he'll be all right with you. Now I have to go or Ezra will get suspicious.' Emmie hobbled from the room, passing Hester in the doorway.

'What's going on?' Hester demanded. 'I've been helping Mrs Jackson to check through the contents of the storeroom. I could hear the shouting from below stairs.'

Rosalind sank down on the sofa. 'Hester, does the name Sarah or Sally Farthing mean anything to you?'

'How do you know about her?'

'So you are familiar with the name?'

'It was years ago, Rosie. You were only twelve or thirteen at the time.'

'And Bertie was seventeen or eighteen. Did Grandpapa tell you what was going on between Bertie and that girl?'

'I knew.' Hester subsided onto an upright chair. 'It was just an infatuation. Bertie thought he was in love with one of the servants from Greystone Park. Your grandpapa put an end to such nonsense.'

'But it wasn't nonsense, apparently.'

'What do you mean by that?'

'Sarah Farthing gave birth to a baby boy. She named him Tommy.'

'Were those people claiming that the sweep's boy is Bertie's son?'

'Not Trimble. He tried to convince me that Tommy is his child, but I had a chat with his wife. Emmie Trimble is Sarah Farthing's sister. She says that Tommy is Bertie's son.'

'Let the mother come forward then, and we'll ask her.'

'She died of a fever five years ago, Hester.'

'Then there's no proof.'

'Tommy was baptised in St Pancras Church in Exeter.'

Hester exhaled sharply. 'Did the woman say that Bertie knew about the child?'

'Apparently Sarah didn't tell him because she knew he would be in trouble with Grandpapa, who

279

incidentally paid her to move to Exeter. Did you know about that?'

'He might have mentioned it, but your grandfather was very concerned for Bertie. He was little more than a boy – such a liaison would have ruined him.'

Rosalind stared at her, shaking her head. 'You knew all this and you never told us?'

'It wasn't my place to speak about it. Your grandfather trusted me and I would have died rather than betray him.'

'You really did love him, didn't you?'

'Believe me, Rosie. I know exactly how it feels to love someone who is unattainable. I felt for Sarah Farthing, but she would never have been accepted socially. Neither she nor Bertie deserved a fate like that.'

'But you married Grandpapa.'

'Yes, in the end I did, but only after years of keeping in the background and being treated like a servant. You'll never know how that feels.'

'We've always loved you, Hester.'

'I know, poppet, and that made everything worthwhile.'

'Despite the problems it might cause, Bertie will have to be told.'

'Yes, I agree.'

'But maybe I'll wait until he comes home. I don't think it's the sort of news that I could put in a letter, and I do want to make sure that Tommy is his child before I tell him.'

'What will you do? Will you tell Piers?'

'I don't know, Hester. I haven't had time to think it through. For the moment it's probably best that we continue as we have been doing, but I'll go to Exeter to check the baptismal records when I have a chance.'

Hester sighed. 'It's a secret I've kept for so long. However, I should tell you that Tommy looks just like Bertie did at that age. I saw it when you brought him home, but some things are better left in the past and so I didn't like to say anything.'

'If Tommy really is Bertie's son then he's part of the family and that is very important. I'm not allowing Trimble anywhere near him.'

'When you go to Exeter I'm coming with you,' Hester said firmly. 'You need to keep away from Trimble, especially in your condition.'

'You're right, of course. We'll go next week. I hope Piers will be home by then.'

'But you're not going to tell him?'

'Not until I have proof. But first I'm going to visit Greystone Park and I'll do that tomorrow morning. I want to find out everything I can about Sarah Farthing and her family. Maybe Tommy has relations here in Rockwood.'

'All right, Rosie, but I want you to promise that you'll get Gurney or Hudson to drive you. You shouldn't be handling the reins now.'

Rosalind smiled. 'You worry too much, but,' she added hastily, 'I will do as you wish if it makes you happy.'

Foster, Sir Michael's butler, showed Rosalind into the drawing room where Sir Michael and his younger daughter, Sylvia, were facing each other with expressions on their faces that suggested they had been having a heated argument.

Sir Michael's frown was replaced by a wide smile. 'My dear Mrs Blanchard, this is a pleasant surprise.'

Sylvia slumped down on the sofa. 'I don't suppose you've heard from Patsy, have you, Rosie? She's forgotten all about us since she decided to be an opera singer.'

'I'm sure she hasn't.' Rosalind peeled off her lace gloves. 'It's very hot today. I'm glad I came early.'

'Won't you sit down,' Sir Michael said anxiously. 'Would you like some refreshment? Perhaps some lemonade?'

'That would be lovely.' Rosalind took a seat opposite Sylvia. 'I expect Patsy will come home at the end of the season. She'll be able to tell you all the gossip from the theatre.'

Sylvia's pretty mouth pursed into a pout. 'She'll have forgotten all about her country friends.'

'I'm sure that's not true, Sylvia.' Sir Michael strolled over to the elegant Adam fireplace and tugged at the bell pull. 'It's a pleasure to see you,

Mrs Blanchard, but might I ask if there's a reason for your visit?'

Rosalind smiled. 'Sir Michael, we've known each other for many years. There's no need for formality, please call me Rosalind.'

'Of course, but you haven't answered my question, or is this a purely social call?'

'It is, but there is also a reason for my coming here today. You might know that I have taken in two orphans.'

'Yes, I have heard something of the sort.'

'Well, one of them, who was being sent up chimneys and in danger of being burned alive or suffocated, or worse, is apparently the son of a woman who used to work here as a chambermaid.'

Sylvia sat on the edge of her seat, her eyes wide with interest. 'Really? Would I know her?'

'Sarah or Sally Farthing. She was here ten or eleven years ago.'

'I would have been seven or eight then. I don't think I remember her.'

'The name is vaguely familiar,' Sir Michael said slowly. 'Is there a reason for this sudden interest?'

'I'm wondering if Tommy has any family left in the area. He's settling in nicely at Rockwood, but he might have relatives who would want to adopt him. What sort of girl was Sally?'

Sir Michael frowned. 'If I recall rightly she was very young. A pleasant enough girl, eager to learn and to do her job well. But my housekeeper, Mrs

Hardwick, would know more about her.' He turned his head at the sound of a knock on the door and a maid entered. 'Ivy, please bring a jug of lemonade and two glasses. I'll have coffee and perhaps Cook has made cake.'

'Yes, sir.' Ivy bobbed a curtsey.

'And send Mrs Hardwick to me. Thank you, Ivy.'

'Yes, sir.' Ivy curtsied again and left the room.

'I haven't seen Christina for a while,' Rosalind said conversationally. 'Is she well?'

'She's always out with Oscar Cottingham.' Sylvia tossed her head. 'I'm sure she could do better. He's finished university but he shows no sign of trying to find a parish. Somehow I can't imagine him as a clergyman.'

'He has the Cottingham fortune behind him,' Sir Michael said smugly. 'They're a respectable family, even if Glorina is a little unconventional. Christina could do worse.'

'The squire's wife smokes cigarillos in public.' Sylvia pulled a face. 'And I think she dyes her hair. No one has hair that red naturally. The servants say she dances naked on the lawn when there's a full moon.'

Rosalind laughed. 'I don't imagine she's doing any harm by that. She's a charming woman when you meet her.'

'She can tell fortunes,' Sylvia added. 'She probably has a crystal ball in her possession.'

'Sylvia, that's enough tittle-tattle,' Sir Michael said

firmly. 'These rumours are spread, whether or not there is any truth in them, simply because Mrs Cottingham has Romany blood somewhere along the line. The world would be a dull place if we were all the same.'

'Might I speak to Mrs Hardwick in private, Sir Michael?' Rosalind chose her words carefully. 'It might seem an unusual request, but there are things that the Farthing family might not wish to be known.'

'Of course. I was just going to my study and Sylvia has to practise the pianoforte before her next lesson.'

'Really? Do I have to, Papa? You know I have no talent for music.'

'It's an accomplishment you might value one day, Sylvia. Now, please do as I ask.' Sir Michael walked to the door and opened it, ushering Sylvia out into the hallway. 'Ah, here is Mrs Hardwick and the refreshments as well. I'll leave you to talk in private, Rosalind.'

Chapter Sixteen

All the information that Rosalind was able to gather convinced her that Tommy was Bertie's son. Mrs Hardwick had given a glowing account of Sally Farthing's character and her sweet nature. The Farthing family, she said, had refused to have anything to do with their daughter in her time of need, but her elder sister, Emily, had stood by her. Rosalind gathered from her chat with Mrs Hardwick that Sally had been well-liked and everyone at Greystone Park was sorry to see her leave. A trip to Exeter with Hester had also confirmed that it was Bertie who had been named as Tommy's father, even so far as giving his address as Rockwood Castle. Rosalind could only hope that Trimble would not think of checking the parish register, but if Emmie had not mentioned it to him before she was highly unlikely to do so now.

*   *   *

Rosalind finally explained the situation to Piers some weeks later when he came home after an extended business trip to Trevenor. He listened attentively, but to her surprise he did not seem shocked.

'These things happen, my love,' he said seriously. 'Look at Patsy and that Yelland fellow. We had to chase halfway to Gretna Green to bring them back when they attempted to elope.'

Rosalind laughed. 'Not quite that far, but I see what you mean.'

'Bertie was a hot-blooded young fellow and it sounds as if Sally was a nice girl. You only have to look at Tommy to tell that he's a cut above Trimble, and I haven't even met the man.'

'He's a brute and a bully, Piers. He's tried twice to get into the castle but Gurney and Hudson saw him off. If he discovers that Tommy is Bertie's son, who knows what he'll do?'

'Let him try. I'm not going far until after our baby is born. I'll have a word with Constable Burton and I'll ask him to keep an eye out for our friend Trimble. He won't bother you again, Rosie. I'll make sure of that.'

'I wonder if I ought to write to Bertie and tell him about Tommy.'

'I think you should, Rosie. Just in case anything happens to him. Not that it will,' he added hastily. 'Bertie knows how to take care of himself. If you write to him we'll get Alex to send it through official channels.'

'You've heard from your brother?' Rosalind made an effort to sound casual. She had not seen or heard from Alexander for what seemed like an eternity. She knew that there was no possibility of any meaningful relationship with him, but she missed his company. He had always had a way of making her laugh, and they shared a similar sense of humour. She loved Piers, of course, but he was always so serious these days, and despite his promises to the contrary he was still spending most of his time away from home. Building up the business was beginning to seem like an obsession, which Piers strongly denied.

He looked up from a document he had been studying. 'Didn't I tell you? Alex wrote to me last week. He's been discharged from the army on medical grounds. They say his leg will never heal well enough for him to go on active service, and he couldn't settle to an office job at the War Office.'

'What will he do, Piers? The army has been his whole life.'

'I've offered him a partnership in the business. He'll be based at Trevenor, but I've invited him here for a while so that I can give him a thorough grounding in the business. You don't mind, do you?'

'No, of course not.' Rosalind turned away to pat Bob on the head. It was a hot sultry day outside, but the rush of colour to her cheeks could not be explained by the cool temperature in the drawing room.

'Walter is here until he returns to university in October,' Piers said casually. 'It will be good for him to have some company. Maybe Alex can get him away from those damned books for a while.'

'That's not fair. Walter is working hard on his latest literary effort. He won't tell me what it is but I have a feeling he's writing a novel. The only person he'll take into his confidence is Louise.'

'Don't tell me that Walter is taking an interest in a young woman at last?'

'She's a good listener and very well read. Louise is a very nice person and extremely intelligent.'

'She must be at least five years his senior.'

'Oh, Piers. You are so old-fashioned. Mr Disraeli's wife is twelve years older than him and they are a devoted couple. If it were the reverse no one would comment.'

'You're right, of course. I give in.' Piers leaned over and kissed her on the cheek. 'I would be delighted to see Walter with a wife, however much difference there might be in their ages. Walter is a thoroughly decent fellow, even if he does live in another world from the rest of us. Which reminds me, will you ask Hester to see that a room is made ready for Alex? He'll be here tomorrow.'

'So soon?'

'Is that going to prove difficult?'

Rosalind managed a smile. 'Of course not. I'll make sure we're ready to welcome him. I'll go and find Hester and then I'll write that letter to Bertie.' She left Piers to read his newspaper in peace while she went in search of Hester, and having done that she made her way to the library. As she had expected, Walter was seated at the table in the centre of the room with papers spread around him and a pile of reference books to hand. He looked up and smiled.

'Are you all right, Rosie? You look flushed.'

She sat down by the open window and Bob flopped down at her feet. 'It's hot today and I had to go looking for Hester. Piers has only just told me that Alex will be arriving tomorrow. He's staying for a while.'

'That's good. I like Alex.'

'Walter, there's something I haven't told you.'

He put his pen back on the inkstand. 'I'm listening.'

'It's about Tommy.'

'Yes, he's a fine little fellow. He's very keen to learn, so Louise says.'

'I couldn't tell you until I'd told Piers . . .'

Walter put down his pen. 'Go on.'

'Tommy is the illegitimate child of a girl who used to be in service at Greystone Park. I've only just had the proof, but he's Bertie's son.'

Walter pushed his chair back from the desk. 'How on earth did you come to that conclusion?'

'You know, of course, that I rescued him from the sweep. Well, shortly afterwards this man called Ezra Trimble turned up, claiming to be Tommy's father. His poor little wife was obviously terrified of him, but she told me that Tommy was her late sister's child. Sally Farthing who was a maid at Greystone Park.'

'Yes, I remember her. Bertie used to sneak out at night to meet her and I was their lookout.'

'Really? You never said anything about that.'

Walter chuckled. 'I wouldn't, would I? I was sworn to secrecy and Bertie paid me with bags of toffee from Hannaford's shop. I never thought anything of it, and I didn't know that Sally was in the family way.'

'Neither did Bertie, or so Trimble's wife says, but Grandpapa knew and so did Hester. Grandpapa sent Sally away to have her baby and her sister Emily went with her. Bertie doesn't know that he's a father.'

'Well, I'll be jiggered! It will come as a shock to him, but from what I've seen of young Tommy he's a credit to the family. Louise has told me what the poor kid suffered when he was a climbing boy. It's all wrong using children that way. In fact I'm incorporating that in my novel. Maybe it will make the government sit up and think, if I manage to get it published.'

'That's wonderful, Walter. I knew you'd be a success at writing one day. You've never been interested in anything but literature and poetry.'

'I might have a leg up when it comes to publishing. My friend's father is a publisher and I've been helping Timothy when he's stuck for words. He's promised to put a good word in for me.'

Rosalind rose from the window seat. 'I'm sure

you'll get published on your own merit, Walter. Just keep at it.'

'That's what Louise says.'

'She's a very sensible lady. You should listen to her. Now I must write that letter to Bertie. I'll be in the study if you need me.'

Rosalind barely slept that night. Piers' even breathing in the bed beside her made lying wakeful in the small hours even more frustrating, and she envied him his peaceful slumber. She rose early, washed, dressed and went downstairs to the kitchen to discuss the day's menus with the surprised cook.

'Should I make you some breakfast, ma'am?' Mrs Jackson gave her a searching look. 'I was like you when I had my first baby. Up all hours and very little sleep.'

'I didn't know you had a family, Mrs Jackson.'

'They're all grown up and married, or gone to sea in the case of my sons. I had six babies and all survived, I'm pleased to say.'

'But you're still working, Mrs Jackson.' Rosalind did not like to ask why Cook's children allowed their mother to work hard for her living after bringing them all into the world and raising them to stand on their own two feet.

'I could reside with any one of them, ma'am, apart from the boys, who are at sea. But I like my independence, and I enjoy working here.'

'I'm very glad of that,' Rosalind said, smiling. 'You

are an excellent cook and we all appreciate your efforts. As to myself, I'll have breakfast when my husband wakes up. My brother-in-law arrives today, so I think I'll just check that everything is ready for him.'

'I know that Annie had the cleaning women go over everything twice yesterday, ma'am. I don't think you'll find anything lacking.'

'I'm sure I won't. Anyway, the menu sounds perfect, Mrs Jackson. By the way, Captain Blanchard has a fondness for oysters. I believe the season is due to start in a week or so, perhaps you could make sure they are on the menu?'

'Of course, ma'am. I'll put an order in for some.'

'Thank you.'

Rosalind was about to leave when Mrs Jackson called her back. 'Excuse me for asking, ma'am, but with regard to Miss Nancy and Master Tommy. Are they still to take their meals in the nursery?'

Rosalind nodded. 'Yes, there's no change there. Why do you ask?'

'You'll forgive my saying so, ma'am, but the servants are finding it rather confusing. Are the children part of the family or are we supposed to train them for service?'

'They are to be treated like members of the family, for now at least. I haven't quite decided which the best course is for Nancy, as she is so interested in learning how to cook. If you would let her help you when you're not too busy that would be excellent.'

'And Master Tommy?'

'He is still very young. We'll allow him to be a child for a while longer, if only to make up for the terrible time he had as a climbing boy. Does that answer your question?'

'Yes, thank you, ma'am.'

Rosalind hurried from the kitchen. She had known there would be difficult questions to answer about the children, but Mrs Jackson had caught her off guard. She slowed down as soon as she reached the main entrance and ascended the stairs to the east tower, despite Mrs Jackson's assertion that the room set aside for Alex was completely ready. She knew she was fussing, but keeping busy kept her mind off their imminent reunion. The arched window was open and the chintz curtain fluttered in a slight breeze that rustled the leaves on the trees in the deer park, and created white crests on the waves in the bay. The scent of late roses and lavender from the gardens wafted around the sunny room, and Rosalind automatically straightened the pillows on the four-poster bed, and smoothed the coverlet. Tilly had done her work well and the room was ready for a guest who would find everything had been done to make him comfortable.

Rosalind smiled as she recalled the state of the Château Gris when they had first arrived, and the bed that Delfosse had dragged down to the drawing room for Alex, when his broken bones made it impossible to cope with the stairs. Their relationship had changed subtly as the days and weeks went by, and the memory of New Year's Eve, which she had suppressed until now, came back with such force that it took her breath away. No one would believe that they had spent the night sharing a bed as innocently as two children, but the colour flooded her cheeks at the memory of his head on the pillow next to hers when she had awakened next morning. His tumbled hair had flopped across his brow, and his long eyelashes had formed dark crescents on his tanned cheeks. She would never forget the smile that lit his hazel eyes when he opened them and saw her, or the touch of his long slim fingers as he caressed her cheek. Asleep he had looked like an innocent child, but it was a man who had drawn her gently to him and claimed her lips in a kiss that she would remember for the rest of her days. She came back to earth with a start. That was dangerous ground and she must not go there again. She left the room quickly and made her way downstairs.

Her restless mood continued all morning. She had managed to eat enough at breakfast to keep Hester and Piers from commenting on her lack of appetite, and for once she was grateful for the fact that Piers went straight to the study to work on some business papers. Walter never took breakfast with them, preferring to have coffee in the library when he started writing. Louise had arrived on time as usual and the children had begun lessons, leaving Rosalind little to do. She decided to go for a walk with Bob while it was reasonably cool, but she had only just reached the end of the drive when a cloud of dust and the thudding of horses' hoofs announced the arrival of not one carriage, but two. Rosalind turned on her heel and hurried back to the house with Bob prancing along ahead of her.

She was hot and breathless by the time she entered the cool entrance hall and her hair was escaping from the carefully arranged snood at the back of her neck. It was not so easy to move fast these days, even though Hester assured her that she was small considering her advancing pregnancy.

'We have visitors, Jarvis.' Rosalind fanned herself with her hands. 'There are two carriages but I was only expecting Captain Blanchard.'

Jarvis stepped outside. 'I think that's Heslop driving the barouche, ma'am.'

Rosalind stifled a cry of dismay. 'He's Mama's coachman. Oh, no. Do you recognise the other driver, Jarvis?'

'No, ma'am. It's a growler, probably for the servants.'

'But I wasn't expecting them.' Rosalind took a deep breath. How like Mama to turn up without bothering to find out if it was convenient or not. She patted her hair in place and followed Jarvis out into the castle bailey.

Heslop drew the pair of bay horses to a halt before climbing down, somewhat stiffly, to open the carriage door and put the steps down. Felicia was the first to alight, following by Patricia and then Claude. In the meantime the other carriage had driven to the side of the house and the servants' entrance.

Felicia ran towards Rosalind with open arms. 'Just look at you, the little mother-to-be. How splendid you look, Rosie. Although perhaps you should eat more. You're much too thin. I was absolutely huge when I had Bertie.'

Rosalind suffered a hug and a kiss that just missed touching her cheek, and she almost choked on a waft of her mother's expensive perfume. 'It's always lovely to see you, Mama. But why didn't you let me know you were coming?'

'It's not a problem is it, darling? I mean, you have this enormous castle and more rooms than you could fill with the whole village, so I don't see the difficulty.'

'Of course, you're very welcome,' Rosalind said hastily.

'The truth is that the season is well and truly over and we haven't another engagement for months.' Patricia sailed past them and disappeared into the cool darkness of the entrance hall.

'We are between engagements, that's true,' Felicia said sweetly. 'But that gives us the opportunity of seeing you and Piers and getting some lovely fresh Devonshire air.'

'It's good to see you again, Rosie.' Claude raised her hand to his lips. 'You look very well, my dear. I hope we are not intruding.'

'Of course I'm delighted to see you all,' Rosalind said warily. 'But Alexander is due to arrive at any time today. I don't imagine Patsy will be very pleased about that.'

'Really! Does that man have to stay here, darling?' Felicia frowned ominously.

'He is Piers' only brother, Mama. He's coming here to learn about the clay mining business so that he can join the firm.'

'I suppose he wants an excuse to get out of the war in the Crimea.'

'No, Mama. I'm sure he is devastated that the army has refused to take him back because of his leg injury. They said he wasn't fit for active service.'

Claude slipped his arm around his wife's shoulders. 'Let's go indoors, my love. It's too hot for Rosie to be standing out here.'

'I'm delicate, too,' Felicia insisted. 'I have to look after my voice and this heat does it no good at all. Rosalind, I need a glass of Madeira to soothe my throat. And you'd better warn Patricia that her former fiancé is coming to stay. I don't think she'll be very happy about that. And take that wretched dog away. He's covering my skirt with hairs.'

Rosalind beckoned to Hudson's young son, Pip, who had just started helping in the stables. 'Pip, will you take Bob, please? You can take him for a nice long walk and I'll collect him later.' She followed her mother and Claude into the house.

'Where did Miss Patricia go, Jarvis?' Felicia demanded sharply.

'I believe she was heading for the drawing room, ma'am.'

'I leave it to you to direct my maid to our usual rooms, Jarvis.' Felicia marched past him and walked off in the direction of the drawing room.

Jarvis gave Rosalind an enquiring look. She shrugged. 'I'll have the rooms made ready as soon as possible. Miss Smithers knows where everything is, which is fortunate. Will you see that she gets help with the luggage, please, Jarvis?'

'Of course, ma'am.'

Rosalind reached the drawing room in time to hear her sister utter a shriek of either rage or dismay, or a mixture of both.

'Do calm down, Patricia,' Felicia said crossly. 'Alexander will have to stay at the village inn. That's all there is to it.'

'Alexander will stay here, Mama.' Rosalind faced them all with a defiant stare. 'Alex is Piers' brother and he has just as much right to be here as anyone. You will just have to put up with it, Patsy.'

'He jilted me, or have you forgotten?'

'You know that's not true. Alex was injured and we were all stuck in France until Piers was well enough to undertake the voyage home. You broke off your engagement, if I remember rightly.'

'I don't care. I won't stay in the same house.'

'Where will you go?' Rosalind asked wearily. 'Isn't it time you put all that behind you, Patsy? After all, you are a rising star in the opera world now. What does Alex matter to you?'

'It's true, isn't it Mama?' Patricia sniffed and looked to her mother for confirmation. 'I am in the chorus, but the intendant has promised me a small part in next season's work.'

'If you're going to be difficult, why don't you go and stay with the Greystones with your friend Christina?' Felicia said impatiently. 'Have you sent for the refreshments, Rosalind? My throat is so dry I can hardly speak.'

'I'm about to ring for Tilly.' Rosalind walked over to the mantelshelf and tugged at the bell pull. 'That might be the best plan, Patsy. After all, you haven't seen much of the girls since you became an operatic singer. I'm sure they will hang off your every word, as will Sir Michael.'

Patricia shrugged. 'Anything would be better than staying under the same roof as Alexander Blanchard.'

'What on earth is going on?' Piers strode into the room. 'I could hear raised voices from my study.' He smiled when he saw Claude and held out his hand. 'It's good to see you, Claude. We weren't expecting you, though.'

Claude pumped his hand. 'I'm sorry, old chap. I did tell Felicia that we ought to check first, but she was certain of a warm welcome.'

'And of course we are very pleased to see you,' Piers added, bowing to Felicia. 'Do you have a problem with anything, Patsy?'

'I hear that your wretched brother is due to arrive. I've decided to visit Greystone Park. At least I can be sure of a warm welcome and no embarrassing situations.'

'Then you must tell Smithers not to unpack your things, Patsy. Send a message to Greystones and ask if it's convenient for you to stay.'

Patricia frowned. 'There's no need. I'm always welcome there, but I can't go without a personal maid. What would Sir Michael think?'

'I don't suppose you could spare Smithers, Mama?' Rosalind said tentatively.

'Certainly not. She has been my maid and dresser since I found my place in opera history. Haven't you got a maid you could spare, Rosie?'

Rosalind thought quickly. 'Molly Greep has a talent at arranging hair. She's training to be a housemaid but I'm sure she'd be delighted to have promotion to lady's maid. You must be patient with her, though, Patsy. No shouting and storming at her if she makes a mistake or two.'

'As if I would.' Patsy tossed her head. 'All right. You can organise it for me, Rosie. I won't even bother to take off my bonnet, so you can tell Heslop to bring the carriage round. I'll go immediately.'

'Really, Patricia, there's no need to be so theatrical,' Felicia said crossly. 'You could at least stay for luncheon and wait for a reply from Greystones. In fact, I insist upon it. I don't want everyone to think you're running away from Alexander. He's not worth it.'

'Leave it to me, Mama.' Rosalind shot a resigned glance in her sister's direction. 'Sit down, everyone, and I'll arrange everything. You will stay for luncheon as Mama suggests, Patsy. I'll send Gurney to Greystone to make sure that Christina is at home in the first place, and I'll ask Molly if she's willing to accompany you as your maid.'

'I confess I'm exhausted already.' Felicia fanned herself vigorously. 'Do as you think best, Rosie. You were always the practical one.'

Rosalind paid her second visit that day to the kitchen to tell Mrs Jackson about their unexpected guests, and she found Hester in the still room preparing rose petal face cream. Hester rolled her eyes.

'Trust your mama to turn up at the worst possible moment. If I didn't know better I'd swear that she does it on purpose.'

Rosalind laughed. 'Well, it's Patsy who's causing the problem. She refuses to stay here because Alexander is due at any moment.'

'There's always the village inn,' Hester said drily. 'Maybe she'd like to put up there for a while.'

'Not my sister, as you very well know. She wants to go to Greystone Park so I've sent a note with Gurney to make sure it's convenient. She also insists on having a personal maid, so I've asked Molly if she would like the position, and she said yes.'

'She hasn't had any experience of Miss Patricia Carey.' Hester sighed. 'I suppose that means we have to train a new housemaid. I'll ask Tilly if she thinks her sister Jennet would be willing.'

'Isn't she rather young?'

'I think she must be eleven or so. That's only a little younger than Tilly was when she started here. They're bright girls and they're trustworthy.'

'All right, Hester. Can I leave that to you?'

'Of course you can, poppet. I'm glad to help, seeing as how your mama has put upon you yet again.'

Rosalind kissed her on the cheek. 'At least I know I can depend upon you, Hester.'

'You can, my dear. Always.'

Rosalind left Hester's parlour and was heading for the drawing room to let Patsy know that arrangements were being made, when Jarvis called out to her.

'There's a chaise coming through the gates, ma'am. I think it might be Captain Blanchard. He's driving himself.'

Rosalind felt her heart miss a beat and for a moment she thought she was going to faint, but she took several deep breaths and the sensation passed. She would have to face Alex sooner or later, and it would be easier to do so without the rest of the family clamouring for attention. She walked slowly to the main entrance and was in time to see Alex climb down from the chaise and hand the reins to Hudson.

She held out her hand, forcing her lips into a smile. 'Alex, welcome to Rockwood.'

Chapter Seventeen

Alexander grasped her hand and raised it to his lips. 'It's good to see you, Rosie. You look beautiful.'

His smile wrapped her in a warm glow and she felt the weeks of separation falling away. Nothing had changed, but that was dangerous. She withdrew her hand quickly.

'Thank you, Alex. You always say the right thing. Do come in. Jarvis will see to your luggage.' She walked away quickly, heading towards the study where she hoped to find Piers, but just as they passed the drawing room the door opened and Patricia flounced into the hallway. She came to an abrupt halt.

'You! You're the last person I wanted to meet.'

Alexander acknowledged her with a brief nod. 'Patricia.'

'Is that all you have to say to me?'

'Patsy, is this absolutely necessary?' Rosalind demanded angrily. 'I think you've made your feelings perfectly clear. Now please let us pass. I was taking Alex to the study to see Piers.'

'Well, don't expect me to stay for luncheon. I told you to send for Heslop so that I can leave immediately.'

'There's no need to speak to Rosie like that,' Alexander said curtly. 'This is between us, Patsy. I'm sorry you still feel like this, but I was willing to marry you when I returned from France. You are the one who ended our engagement.'

'And can you blame me? I think you were relieved to be let off so easily. Because of you I was humiliated and left at the altar through no fault of my own.'

'There's no talking to you when you're in this mood,' Alexander said wearily. 'I know my way to the study, Rosie.' He walked off, leaving Rosalind to deal with her sister.

'I hate you, Alexander Blanchard!' Patricia pulled a face.

'You're being silly now.' Rosalind grabbed her by the arm and propelled her into the drawing room. 'You're behaving like a child.'

'Let me go.'

Rosalind closed the door behind them. 'Please sit down and stop making a scene. I've sent a message to Greystones and Gurney should be back within the hour. Hester is going to ask Molly if she's willing

305

to act as your maid, and luncheon will be ready in half an hour.'

'I don't want to eat, not if he's going to be at the table.'

'Darling, you are being over-dramatic,' Felicia said, yawning. 'Save the histrionics for the theatre. Surely you can put up with Alexander for as long as it takes to swallow a few mouthfuls of food.'

'I can't bear the sight of him.'

Claude rose from his chair by the window. 'I think I'll take a walk before luncheon. I need to stretch my legs after sitting in the carriage for hours.' He leaned over to kiss his wife on the forehead. 'I won't be long, my dear.'

Felicity shrugged. 'Do as you wish, Claude. Where is the Madeira, Rosie? I'm in need of sustenance, and as for you, Patricia, you are not helping. Stop acting like a prima donna; that's my prerogative. You will join us for luncheon, or you will go hungry.'

Patricia inhaled sharply and sank down on the sofa. 'Nobody understands how I feel.'

'Yes, we do, Patsy.' Rosalind sat down beside her. 'But don't take it out on Alex. If you want my honest opinion I don't think you would have been happy as an army wife. Maybe this is a chance for you to find the perfect husband who will treat you as you would wish.'

Felicia sighed. 'If such a person exists. There are several up-and-coming members of the chorus who would love to get to know her better, but she's rebuffed all their advances.'

Patricia shrugged. 'I'm not interested in members of the chorus, Mama. I have my sights set a little higher than that.'

'They might rise to become stars of the opera world with the right woman behind them.'

'I'm not interested in promoting someone else. I want a husband who will spoil me and pamper me, and buy me expensive jewels.'

'That sounds more like a rich lover than a husband,' Felicia said, curling her lip. 'One day you'll come down to earth, my girl. In the meantime I want you to be civil to Alexander, and then you may go to Greystone Park with my blessing. Perhaps Christina can find you a wealthy beau.'

'I don't need her help. I can get any man I want, should I choose to do so.'

Felicia opened her mouth to reply but a tap on the door announced the arrival of Tilly. She placed a tray set with a decanter of Madeira and several glasses on a table beside Felicia's chair.

'At last!' Felicia poured a generous amount of the wine into a glass. 'Would you like some, Rosie?'

'No, thank you, Mama. I find that any wine or spirits make me feel ill at the moment.'

'That's one thing I never intend to suffer,' Patricia said with feeling. 'Whoever marries me must be prepared to forgo being a parent. I never want to lose my figure or suffer the pain of childbirth.'

'Then you'd better look for a rich widower,' Felicia said, sipping her drink. 'If you smile nicely at Sir Michael, maybe he will oblige.'

'He is rather old, but he's very wealthy.' Patricia's sulky scowl was replaced with a mischievous smile. 'How droll it would be if I became Christina and Sylvia's stepmother.'

Patricia left soon after luncheon, having behaved reasonably well during the meal, in that she remained stubbornly silent. This might have made things awkward but Alexander and Claude kept everyone entertained with anecdotes about their widely varying experiences. Alexander talked about near disasters on the military field that had ended surprisingly well. Claude's tales were slightly more scandalous, involving gossip concerning the lives and loves of well-known theatrical personalities. Felicia had drunk two glasses of Madeira as well as claret with her meal, and she was pleasantly tipsy. She kissed Patricia warmly when it was time for her to leave, ignoring her daughter's sullen expression. Claude tucked Felicia's hand in the crook of his arm and led her upstairs to take an afternoon nap.

Piers excused himself on account of some work he was preparing and he retired swiftly to his study. Walter, who had left his books for long enough to eat luncheon, returned to the library with Louise, having asked for her opinion on his latest efforts. Rosalind had invited Louise to stay for the meal in the vain hope that her quiet charm might set a good example to Patricia, although in fact it had had the opposite effect. Patricia seemed determined to make her presence felt, even in silence. It was a relief to wave goodbye to her as the carriage drove off laden with her luggage.

Rosalind turned to Alexander, who was standing quietly behind her. 'I'm so sorry that Patsy behaved like that. It was inexcusable.'

He shrugged. 'Nothing more or less than I would have expected. I might have refused Piers' kind offer had I known that she would be here.'

'None of us knew they were coming, Alex. That's what my mother does every time – she just descends upon us, only this time she had Patsy with her.'

'If my being here is upsetting you, I'll leave immediately.'

'No, no, of course not. Piers told me that you've been discharged from the army on medical grounds – it must be terrible for you.'

'It was a blow, I must admit, but I'm coming to terms with it, Rosie. I was wondering what I would do with myself when Piers offered to make me a partner in the clay mining business. It would be madness to refuse, but I won't take him up on it if it's going to make you unhappy in any way. I'll be based at Trevenor, anyway.'

'Of course.' Rosalind eyed him curiously. 'But won't you find that dull? I mean you've been used to living such a different way of life.'

He gave her a wry smile. 'I've been playing toy soldiers for long enough.'

'You don't mean that, Alex. I know you love army life.'

'Fate has decided it for me. I was offered a position in the War Office, but I'm not the sort of man who can sit behind a desk all day, telling others what to do. You know me, Rosie.'

'Yes, I do.' Rosalind turned her head at the sound of footsteps.

'Alex,' Piers said cheerfully. 'I was just going over the accounts for last month, then I realised it would be a good place for you to start. Unless you're tired after your journey, of course.'

'No, I'm fine. I have to begin somewhere. If you'll excuse me, Rosie, I'll allow my brother to start educating me into the fascinating world of china clay.'

'You should rest, Rosie,' Piers said firmly. 'You do too much as it is. You must let Hester take over the running of the household from now on.'

'Really, Piers, I'm not an invalid.'

'No, but you're carrying the heir to Rockwood and Trevenor. He's going to be a very influential person when he grows up.'

Rosalind sighed. 'Bertie inherited the baronetcy and the property, Piers. If anyone is to be his heir it should be Tommy.'

'Tommy?' Alexander looked from one to the other. 'Who is this person?'

'He's a child,' Rosalind said hastily. 'A poor little boy who had been sold to work for a ruthless chimney sweep.'

'It seems that he's Bertie's love child,' Piers said with a dry smile. 'No doubt Rosie will tell you all about it later, but for now I want you to come with me and start learning the business.'

During the next few days Rosalind saw very little of Alexander, as he spent most of the time with Piers, going over what she imagined would be deadly dull accounts and the workings of a successful mining business. They met up in the formal atmosphere of the dining room for meals, but Rosalind rarely managed to get a word in edgeways as her mother monopolised the conversation. She had a captive audience and she was obviously making the most of being the centre of attention. Claude looked on fondly and Rosalind could only admire his devotion to her mother.

At the end of the first week after Alexander's arrival Felicia announced that she was missing Patricia and she intended to visit Greystone Park. As Rosalind had feared, that outing included her, and as she could not think of a plausible excuse to remain at home, she dutifully accompanied her mother.

Sir Michael received them in the Chinese room, where the walls were covered in hand-painted paper depicting exotic birds and flowers. The furniture and porcelain vases reflected the same theme, as did the oriental rugs and framed oil paintings.

'How kind of you to call on us, Mrs de Marney,' Sir Michael said, smiling. 'Won't you take a seat? I expect you want to see Patricia.'

'I wanted to thank you for offering her your hospitality, Sir Michael.' Felicia settled gracefully on a small sofa. 'My daughter probably explained the reason for leaving Rockwood so abruptly.'

He nodded. 'She did, of course, and I understand completely. Patricia is a young lady of great sensibility.'

Rosalind subsided onto the nearest chair. It was elegant but not very comfortable. She gave Sir Michael a searching look, wondering if he was being sarcastic, but he seemed to be sincere. 'Sensibility' was not a word she might have used when describing her sister, but Patsy was a good actress.

'I wouldn't have my daughters behave in any other way,' Felicia said graciously. 'And how are your girls, Sir Michael? They are such charming young ladies.'

'Christina is twenty-three now and about to become engaged to Oscar Cottingham, or so I've been informed. As a matter of fact I'm planning a ball to announce the event at the end of September. Your invitations are being written as we speak.'

'How delightful.' Felicia shot a sideways glance at Rosalind. 'What a pity you won't be able to attend, my dear.'

'I don't see why that should be,' Rosalind said sharply.

'It's not done for a woman so close to her time to attend social functions, Rosalind. Surely you know that, even here in the wilds of Devonshire.'

'I see no reason why that should prevent Rosalind from coming. We are very modern in our outlook here, Mrs de Marney. We might not be up to London standards but we are not behind the times, I promise you.' Sir Michael reached for the bell pull. 'Perhaps you would like to see Patricia. I'll send a servant to find her. In the meantime perhaps I can offer you both some refreshment.'

'That would be most acceptable. It's unseasonably hot, and the roads are very dusty. I have quite a thirst. A glass of Madeira would be most welcome.'

Rosalind was beginning to wish that she had stayed at home, but she wanted to see Patsy, if only to make sure that she was happy to remain at Greystone Park. It was a relief when Ivy, the parlour maid, was sent to find Patricia and she appeared eventually with Sylvia.

'You didn't need to check on me, Mama,' Patricia said in a low voice. 'I am not a child.'

'We've missed you, darling.' Felicia's smile was stretched to its limits. 'Also, Claude is making arrangements for us to travel to Italy for the new opera season. I'm booked to appear in Rome, and you might get a part, too.'

'How exciting.' Sylvia clapped her hands. 'I wish

I could sing or dance instead of being stuck here at Greystone Park. I won't know what to do with myself when Christina marries and moves to Cottingham Manor.'

'I wouldn't want to live with my mother-in-law.' Patricia tossed her head. 'I would insist on having a home of my own. I told Oscar so many times when we were together.'

'Don't say that in front of Chrissie,' Sylvia pleaded. 'You know it upsets her.'

'I was Oscar's first love. Christina knows that very well, but she chooses to ignore it.'

'Even so, it's not the kindest thing to say to a young woman who is about to become engaged,' Sir Michael said, chuckling.

'Just because you were left at the altar there's no need to be spiteful, Patricia.' Sylvia stamped her foot and stormed out of the room.

'I think you ought to apologise,' Rosalind said hastily. 'You know how much Sylvia loves her sister.'

'I'm not apologising for speaking the truth.' Patricia reached for a glass of lemonade. 'I was Oscar's first love and there's no denying it. I could have him back with a click of my fingers.'

'Patricia, that's enough.' Felicia swallowed a mouthful of wine. 'Say you're sorry immediately.'

'You need a firm hand, young lady.' Sir Michael rose to his feet. 'It takes a strong man to handle a young filly.'

Patricia faced him with a defiant glare. 'Are you offering, sir?'

Felicia downed the last of her drink. 'I feel faint. I think it's time we returned to Rockwood, Rosalind. Send for Gurney, and you, Patricia, are coming with us.'

Patricia's eyes widened and she turned to Sir Michael with an engaging smile. 'I do apologise, Sir Michael. I know I went too far, and you have been such a generous host.'

'You need to save your apologies for Sylvia. You've upset her greatly.' Sir Michael's eyes narrowed. 'Give me one good reason why I shouldn't send you home.'

'Christina needs me to help with organising the ball. It would be different if you had a wife to do such things for you, sir.'

'I might be of some assistance,' Rosalind said slowly. 'I'd be more than willing to assist in any way I could.'

'But you have such a lot do with your waifs and strays, as well as being in a delicate condition.' Patricia smiled sweetly. 'You do too much already, Rosie.'

Sir Michael turned to Rosalind with a look of concern. 'Your sister is right, Rosalind. She's told us about the climbing boy you took in, and the orphan girl. I'm surprised that your husband allows you to overexert yourself in such a way.'

'Piers is very attentive,' Felicia said hastily. 'But my daughters both have minds of their own, as you will have discovered.'

Sir Michael smiled. 'Indeed I have, and I admire spirit in a woman.'

'I think I should go and find Sylvia.' Patricia bowed her head. 'I shouldn't have said what I did. I hope she will forgive me.'

'You really should come home with us, Patricia.' Felicia placed her empty glass on the tray. 'You will just have to try to be civil to Alexander and that's an end to it.'

'You won't see much of Alex,' Rosalind added. 'He spends most of his time with Piers, going over account books and order forms.'

Patricia cast a helpless look in Sir Michael's direction. 'I am sorry, Sir Michael. I know I was in the wrong.'

'Go and find her then, you little minx.'

'Really, Sir Michael,' Felicia said sharply. 'That's no way to talk to my daughter.'

'I'm sorry if I've offended you, Mrs de Marney. I meant it in the most affectionate way. Patricia is like a daughter to me.'

Rosalind could see that her mother believed him, or rather that she chose to think the best of Sir Michael, but Rosalind remembered how he had pursued her before her marriage and Patricia was now a similar age. Perhaps Patricia would get her wish for a wealthy husband after all, and maybe that was her reason for staying at Greystone Park in the first place.

'I think we should send for the carriage, Mama,'

Rosalind said quietly. 'It's obvious that Patricia is very much at home here.'

'Yes, although I'm not sure she deserves such special treatment,' Felicia sighed. 'You are a patient man, Sir Michael. As to the ball, as I said before, my husband and I are planning to leave for Italy at the end of the month. I hope that Patricia will accompany us.'

'I see.' Sir Michael frowned thoughtfully. 'That doesn't give me much time.'

'For what, exactly?' Rosalind eyed him warily.

'To organise the ball, of course,' Sir Michael said with a smug smile. 'I had decided on the last week in September so we can bring it forward a couple of days to make certain you are able to attend, Mrs de Marney.'

'That's very kind of you.' Felicia treated him to one of her special smiles.

'I'll send for your carriage.' Sir Michael rose to his feet and left the room.

Rosalind would have liked to help organise the ball at Greystone Park, but she had little time to devote to anything other than her immediate concerns at home. To her surprise Patricia threw herself into helping Christina with the arrangements, which she described in detail on her infrequent visits to Rockwood, and Rosalind was impressed. Maybe her little sister would find her true niche in the world as the wife of a Member of Parliament, and as such

Patricia would be very much in the limelight. Rosalind confided in Hester, although she kept her thoughts from her mother, whose reaction was unpredictable. In any case, Felicia was too busy supervising the packing of the clothes and accessories she intended to take to Italy to show much interest in Christina Greystone's engagement ball.

After a great deal of persuasion, Hester agreed to accept her invitation to the ball, but she refused to purchase a new outfit. The gown she had worn for her wedding to Sir Lucius was taken out of storage, smelling strongly of lavender and mothballs. It was only after several days of being hung outside in the sunshine that the odours faded, and a few dabs of Felicia's expensive perfume made it wearable. Rosalind was in the last stage of her pregnancy and when she tried on her favourite ball gown, she simply moved the hoops of her crinoline cage a little higher, adding a strategically draped shawl. She knew that Piers was worried about her attending a public function so close to her time, but she assured him that she would sit with Hester and the dowagers and enjoy the atmosphere. Alex said nothing, but she sensed that he was always watching her closely and somehow that was comforting rather than disturbing.

On the evening of the ball, Felicia and Claude had left earlier in their own vehicle and the others were about to leave for Greystone Park when a messenger rode into the bailey. He leaped off his horse.

318

'I have an important message for Mr Blanchard.'
Piers stepped forward. 'I am he.'

The messenger handed him a sealed document.
'Shall I wait to take an answer, sir?'

Piers glanced at the seal and frowned. 'No. I'll
deal with it.' He took a coin from his pocket and
handed it to the messenger. 'Thank you.'

The man nodded and vaulted nimbly onto his
horse, urging it into a brisk trot.

'I'll have to read this.' Piers broke the seal and
unfolded the document. 'You'd better go on without
me. I'll follow you in a while.'

'We can wait for you, Piers.' Rosalind eyed him
anxiously. 'Is anything wrong?'

He shook his head. 'Nothing I can't deal with.'

'Do you want me to stay?' Alexander handed
Hester into the waiting carriage.

'No, it's business, Alex. You take Rosie and Hester
to the ball. I'll come when I can.' Piers strode back
into the house.

'That's very odd. Do you know what might be
so urgent to do with the business, Alex?' Rosalind
hesitated as she was about to climb into the
carriage.

'No, but I'm sure Piers will tell us later. Let's go
and get this over, Rosie. I hope Patricia behaves
herself.'

'She won't make a scene at the ball.' Rosalind
squeezed in beside Hester. 'Aren't you travelling with
us, Alex?'

319

'I'll be riding alongside the carriage, don't worry. I won't let you out of my sight.'

'All the more room for us.' Hester stretched out her feet with a sigh of relief. 'I'll be with you all evening, Rosie. If you feel at all unwell we'll come home immediately.'

When they arrived at Greystone Park the huge gates were thrown open. The driveway was illuminated by flaming torches, creating a path of flickering light to guide the carriages to the front of the mansion. Footmen stood on either side of the entrance and grooms were on hand to guide the vehicles to the coach house and stable block. Alexander was there to assist Rosalind to alight and when she hesitated he lifted her gently to the ground.

'Are you all right, Rosie?'

She nodded. 'Yes, I'm fine. I just felt a bit dizzy, but I'm fine now.'

He assisted Hester to alight before taking Rosalind firmly by the arm. The entrance hall was lit by chandeliers and wall sconces, and the scent of expensive candlewax mingled with the equally costly fragrance of French perfumes and the more mundane bay rum. Rosalind knew most of the guests who thronged together, waiting to be announced as they entered the ballroom, but there were a few new faces and she assumed that they must be Sir Michael's political allies. The gentlemen had a certain bearing and their ladies were elegant with diamond jewellery flashing in the candlelight. They gathered together, gazing round at the assembled company with barely disguised disdain. These were the people who would have been part of her life had she accepted Sir Michael's advances.

When they reached Sir Michael he greeted them warmly, as did Christina and Sylvia, and to Rosalind's surprise, Patricia was included in the family group. For a moment Rosalind was afraid that her sister might snub Alex, but she merely extended her hand with a polite smile and then turned to welcome the next guest.

'What does she think she's up to?' Hester whispered as they followed the rest of the guests into the ballroom.

'One thing that Patsy is good at is doing exactly the opposite of what is expected of her.' Rosalind sighed as she tucked her hand in the crook of Alexander's arm. 'Let's find a table where we can sit and watch the proceedings without getting in anyone's way.'

'If you're referring to your condition,' Alexander said in a low voice, 'you've never looked lovelier, Rosie. Piers should be here to look after you.'

'It must be something quite urgent or he would have accompanied us. I can't think what it could be.'

Alexander guided her to a table as far away from the dance floor as possible and he pulled up a chair for Hester, who sank down on it with a grateful smile. 'Thank you, Alexander. I've crammed my feet into my old dancing slippers and they're agony. I wish I'd worn my boots.'

'Pride feels no pain – that's what you used to say to me, Hester,' Rosalind said, laughing. 'Now I can say it to you.'

'It's true, but I'm too old to bother with pride. I leave that to you young ones.'

Alexander held on to Rosalind's arm as she lowered herself onto a spindly gilt chair. 'You're not old, Hester. You are a woman in your prime. I expect to be warding off your gentlemen admirers all evening.'

Hester raised her fan to cover her face and giggled. 'You are a dreadful liar, Alexander.'

He smiled. 'Not at all. You're a very handsome woman, Lady Carey.'

'Well, you can start by getting me a glass of fruit punch.' Hester's tone was severe but there was a twinkle in her eye.

'I'd like some too, please,' Rosalind added. 'It's very hot in here. There must be a hundred candles, at the very least. Sir Michael really is showing off his wealth tonight.'

'I'll be back in a couple of minutes.' Alexander headed for the refreshment room.

'It's high time he went to Trevenor,' Hester said in a low voice. 'I know you're both trying to act as if there's nothing between you, but it's clear to anyone with eyes that he's in love with you, Rosie.'

Rosalind glanced round anxiously. 'Don't say things like that. We're very fond of each other and that's how it is. We know the boundaries and neither of us will do anything to hurt Piers or the family.'

'I hope so, poppet. But sometimes these things get out of hand. Piers is still away too often and he's behaving as if there is something preying on his mind.'

'It's just business, Hester. He takes it very seriously.'

Rosalind looked round at the sound of a female voice calling her name, and she saw Glorina Cottingham making her way between the tables, followed by the squire.

'My dear Rosalind, how well you look, considering your condition, of course.' Glorina pulled up a chair and sat down. She turned to her husband. 'Gervase, I am dying of thirst. A cup of fruit punch would be very welcome, and an added tot of brandy would make the evening a little more bearable.' She watched him as he walked away. 'He's a darling, but I have to prompt him all the time.'

'It's nice to see you, Glorina. You must be very proud of your son. Christina is a lovely young woman.'

'And she'll inherit a large fortune one day,' Hester added in a low voice.

Glorina brushed back a lock of hennaed hair, eyeing Hester with a calculating look. 'Some people marry for money and position. You would know all about that, Hester Dodridge.'

'As would you, Glorina Beaney. People round here have long memories.'

Glorina leaned towards Rosalind. 'I take no notice of people like her. I'm used to having my gypsy blood thrown back at me, but you, dear, you have trouble ahead, and I don't just mean giving birth.'

'What do you mean, Glorina?'

'You are a good person, but there is someone close to you who is deceiving you. They have been doing so for a long time.'

'What are you saying?' Rosalind clutched her hands to her belly, instinctively protecting her unborn child. 'Why are you telling me this?'

'For your own good. There is a person who pretends to have your best interests at heart but that is to cover his misdeeds. You must be careful, Rosalind.' Glorina looked up as Alexander approached carrying two cut-glass cups of fruit punch, closely followed by the squire. She rose to her feet. 'Enjoy the evening, but it will end too soon for you, my dear.'

'What did she say to you, Rosie?' Alexander demanded as Glorina walked away with her husband, talking volubly. 'You're white as a ghost.'

'Nothing, Alex. She always talks a lot of nonsense.'

Alexander handed a cut-glass punch cup to her and one to Hester. 'What did Glorina Cottingham say to Rosie? You must have heard, Hester.'

'I tried to listen but my hearing isn't as good as it used to be, Alexander. That woman is poison.'

'That's not fair, Hester,' Rosalind protested. 'Glorina tells the truth and she doesn't care if people like it or not. Everything she's said in the past has come true. I know that from other people.'

'So what did she say that scared you so much?' Alexander sat down beside her and took her hand in his. 'Tell me and I'll have it out with her.'

324

She smiled, withdrawing her hand gently. 'Nothing untoward, Alex. Let's enjoy the evening, please.' She glanced over his shoulder. 'I think Sir Michael is going to make the announcement now before the dancing starts.'

Sir Michael strolled into the centre of the highly polished floor, holding up one hand. 'My lords, ladies and gentlemen. Before we begin the proceedings I have an announcement to make, or to be exact I have two announcements of a very happy nature. The first concerns my daughter Christina, who has just become engaged to Oscar Cottingham.' He beckoned to them and they joined him, smiling and acknowledging polite applause from the guests. He waited until the clapping ceased and cleared his throat. 'My second, and perhaps more important announcement is that I have been fortunate enough to win the affection of a beautiful and talented young woman, who has agreed to become my wife.' He held his hand out to Patricia, who made an entrance worthy of her mother. 'My bride-to-be,' Sir Michael continued proudly, 'Miss Patricia Carey.'

There was a moment of stunned silence broken by a cry of distress from Christina, who flew at her father with her fingers clawed. 'How could you, Papa? You've ruined my big day and you're going to marry a girl young enough to be your daughter.'

She turned furiously on Patricia. 'You snake! You viper! You planned this all along – I hate you.' She collapsed into Oscar's arms.

Chapter Eighteen

Felicia was about to rush into the fray but Claude caught her by the wrist. She struggled furiously. 'Let me go. I will have my say.'

'Mama, this isn't the time or place,' Rosalind said in a low voice.

'He can't marry her without my permission.'

'Now isn't the time to discuss this, my dear.' Claude pressed her down onto her seat. 'I'll get you a glass of brandy. Don't move, Felicia.'

Sir Michael said something in a low voice to Oscar, who was struggling valiantly to keep Christina from attacking her father's new fiancée.

'You've ruined everything, you conniving cow,' Christina sobbed.

'Take her somewhere quiet, Oscar,' Sir Michael said angrily. He clapped his hands. 'Please enjoy the rest of the evening. The dancing will commence immediately.' He signalled to the conductor who tapped his baton on his music stand and the orchestra struck up the grand march.

Rosalind shook off Alexander's restraining hand and she edged her way towards Patricia, who was white with shock and trembling.

'She wants to kill me,' Patricia sobbed. 'She hates me now, Rosie.'

'What were you thinking of, Sir Michael?' Rosalind said angrily. 'You must have known how Christina would react. You ruined her engagement ball.'

'I'm marrying your sister, Rosalind. I thought you would be grateful.'

'You might be genuinely fond of her but you've humiliated both Patsy and Christina.'

'It was your sister who wanted me to announce our engagement this evening.'

Rosalind faced him angrily. 'And you're old enough to know better. Patsy, I suggest you come home with us.'

'What?' Patricia wiped her eyes on a scrap of lace handkerchief. 'Don't be silly. I'm going to be the mistress of Greystone Park. This is my home now.'

Felicia hurried up to them, followed by Hester, with Claude and Alexander following at a safe distance.

'My poor girl.' Felicia wrapped her arms around Patricia, who pushed her away.

'I am soon to be a married woman, Mama. I will

be Lady Greystone, and I will take precedence over you. Isn't that amusing?'

Felicia turned to Sir Michael, her eyes narrowed. 'You have taken advantage of a young girl, sir.'

Sir Michael's lip curled. 'You obviously don't know your daughter very well, Mrs de Marney. I have known Patricia since she was a child and I can assure you that she is perfectly capable of making her own decisions.'

'I will oppose the marriage, Sir Michael.'

'I don't think you will, ma'am. Just imagine what a scandal would do to your career.'

'It would not help your political ambitions either, Sir Michael.'

Rosalind laid her hand on her mother's arm. 'Mama, this should be conducted in private.'

'Quite so.' Claude came up behind them. 'We'll be leaving for Italy tomorrow, my love. Surely you don't want to part from Patricia like this?'

Felicia held her hands out to her younger daughter. 'Patricia, my dear, I'm only thinking of you.'

'Don't worry about me, Mama,' Patricia said airily. 'I know exactly what I'm doing. Michael and I have come to an agreement that suits us both, and everyone else will have to get used to the idea.'

Rosalind could see that Patricia had made up her mind and she knew that nothing would stop her now. She held out her hand. 'If you are certain you're doing the right thing, I won't stand in your way, Patsy.'

'Then you'll come to my wedding?'

Rosalind smiled reluctantly. 'Yes, of course.'

Alexander slipped his arm around Rosalind's shoulders. 'Would you like me to send for the carriage, Rosie? It seems that we're done here.'

'I'll send for our carriage, too,' Claude added in a low voice. He glanced anxiously at Felicia, who was fanning herself vigorously. 'I think we've all had enough for one night.'

'I always knew you would get your own way, Patricia,' Hester said with a heavy sigh. 'You are single-minded, just like your dear grandpapa. But be careful, my girl, you might have taken on something that will be too much, even for you. I think you ought to return to the castle with us until you're married.'

'You are not my grandmother.' Patricia tossed her head. 'I am staying here. I don't care what the gossips say.' She linked her hand through the crook of Sir Michael's arm. 'I want to dance, Greystone. We'll show everyone that we are serious.'

He smiled indulgently. 'Of course, my love. I've already spoken to the vicar about posting the banns. We'll be married within weeks.' He shot a glance at Felicia. 'With your permission, I hope, or at least without your opposition.'

'It seems I have little choice,' Felicia said bitterly. 'But I was headstrong like Patsy, so I can hardly criticise her for knowing her own mind.'

Hester glanced anxiously at Rosalind. 'Alexander

was right to send for the carriage. You're white as a sheet.'

'I'm a little tired, but the truth is I'm worried about Piers. He said he would join us, but he hasn't arrived. I wish I knew what was so important that it kept him at home.'

'We'll be home within the hour and you can ask him then. You know how he forgets everything when business is concerned.'

'Yes, of course.' Rosalind realised suddenly that she had left her shawl draped over the back of her chair. 'I won't be a moment.'

She made her way back to their table, but she stopped when she saw Glorina sitting on her own. 'I'm sorry that my sister spoiled your son's engagement announcement.'

Glorina shrugged and stubbed out the cigarillo she had been smoking. 'Don't be. I warned Oscar, but he's so besotted with Christina that he didn't care.'

'Even so, it wasn't the thing to do.'

'If you're worried about Patricia I would say that she can take care of herself. Sir Michael might think he is marrying a sweet and innocent young girl, but I would place my money on Patricia. She knows exactly what she wants, and he doesn't know what he's letting himself in for.' Glorina chuckled and drained her glass of brandy. 'Go home, Rosalind. You are the one who will face trouble. Be brave, my dear.'

Hester hurried to Rosalind's side. 'What is that woman saying to you, Rosie?'

'Mind your own business, Hester Dodridge,' Glorina said with a sarcastic smile. 'You'll find out soon enough, but beware, that's all I'm saying.'

'Come away, Rosie. Don't take any notice of her. She's drunk.' Hester tugged at Rosalind's arm.

'I hope you're wrong, Mrs Cottingham,' Rosalind said wearily. 'And I am truly sorry that your son's evening was ruined by my sister.'

Glorina shrugged. 'He's marrying into a fortune, which will make life as a humble clergyman much more bearable. Being poor isn't much fun, as you will remember, my dear. What is worse is to have wealth and then lose it all, so as I said, beware.'

'Keep your gypsy warnings to yourself, Glorina,' Hester said angrily. 'You belong in a fairground, not here.'

Rosalind left them and retrieved her shawl, which she wrapped around her shoulders. She realised that she was trembling from head to foot and although she tried to ignore Glorina's warning as the words of a drunken woman, she could not put them out of her mind.

When they arrived back at the castle Rosalind went in search of Piers, but he was nowhere to be found. She saw a sliver of light beneath the library door but when she went inside she found Walter, half asleep at the desk in the centre of the room.

'Have you seen Piers?' Rosalind demanded anxiously.

He blinked and yawned. 'No. I thought he was with you. How did the evening go?'

'Terribly, if you must know, but that's another story. Piers didn't come with us because a messenger brought him a document that he insisted he needed to read. He promised that he would join us but he didn't arrive.'

'I haven't seen him, Rosie. I had dinner in the nursery with the two young scamps because I didn't fancy eating alone, and then I came down here. I haven't seen anyone all evening.'

'I can't find him anywhere.'

'Maybe he passed you on the road. You're home early.' Walter eyed her curiously. 'Why was it a terrible evening?'

'Sir Michael announced Christina's engagement to Oscar, and then he told everyone that he was going to marry Patsy.'

Walter stared at her open-mouthed. 'No! Surely he was jesting?'

'Oh, no, he wasn't, Walter. He was deadly serious. Then Christina flew at Patsy and there was a dreadful row.'

Walter ran his hand through his already tousled hair. 'But surely Mama won't allow that to happen? Patsy hasn't reached her majority.'

'Mama and Claude are leaving tomorrow, in case you've forgotten. Sir Michael warned Mama that to oppose the match in any way might reflect badly on her career. That man is very clever.'

'So where is Patsy now?'

'She insisted on remaining at Greystone Park. There was nothing we could do, apart from kidnapping her.'

'I'm beginning to wish that I'd come with you.'

'Louise was there with her parents. She looked lonely, Walter.'

'I'm going to miss her when I return to university. It's my last year.'

Rosalind walked to the window and peered out into the bleak night. The moon was hidden beneath a mass of clouds and nothing but darkness met her anxious gaze. 'I wish I knew where Piers has gone. Why hasn't he left me a note?'

'Are you sure about that?' Walter rose from his seat and stretched. 'I'll help you look.'

'No, it's all right, Walter. I'm probably worrying about nothing. Piers might have gone out for a walk to clear his head, or something of the sort. I'll wait up for him, but you can't do anything so get back to your book.'

'If you're sure.' Walter sat down again and opened the book in front of him. 'But let me know if I can be of help.'

Rosalind left him in the library. She knew that she ought to go straight to bed after such a traumatic evening but she went to the kitchen instead, where she found Hester and Alexander drinking tea. They both leaped to their feet when she walked into the otherwise empty room.

'Have you found a note?' Alexander gave her a searching look. 'I can tell by your face that you haven't. I wasn't going to tell you until you've had some rest, but Gurney told me that Piers had his horse saddled up and he went out soon after we left for Greystone Park.'

'Did he tell Gurney where he was going?'

'No, he just said he wanted to go for a ride.'

Hester filled a cup with tea from the pot and handed it to Rosalind. 'Sit down, poppet, and drink your tea. I'm sure there's a reasonable explanation.'

'There's something you're not telling me, Alex.' Rosalind held his gaze. 'I know by your face that you're keeping something from me.'

'Gurney said that Piers had packed two saddle-bags. It looks as if he expected to be away for some time. I'm sorry, Rosie.'

'That's not all, is it? You're a poor liar, Alex.'

'It's probably village gossip, but Gurney said that Ralph Lambert had been seen drinking in the village inn last evening, and Lambert was boasting about getting even with the Blanchards. It may be nothing, which is why I didn't choose to tell you.'

'Piers had to dismiss Lambert because he was treating the tenants so badly. Anyway, I don't think Piers would be intimidated by a man like him. There must be something much more important to drag him away, particularly now.'

Alex laid his hand on hers as it rested on the table. 'There must be a logical explanation, Rosie. You should try to get some rest.'

Rosalind nodded tiredly. 'I know, but I won't sleep a wink. Something is wrong – I can feel it.'

Piers did not return that night nor the next day. Felicia and Claude were sympathetic but they had to leave for Italy and Rosalind assured them that there was nothing they could do, even if they postponed their departure for a day or two. Alexander and Walter rode round the area making tactful enquiries but no one had seen Piers, and Ralph Lambert had left the inn. Rosalind sent a messenger to Trevenor with a note for Piers and another for Lady Pentelow, but he returned with a brief letter from her ladyship saying that she had not seen Piers since his last business trip. She also added that Pedrick had been asking when Mr Blanchard would next visit the mine as he had urgent matters to discuss.

Walter was due to return to university, although he offered to stay until Piers chose to return home, but Rosalind insisted that he should continue his studies, and somewhat reluctantly he left the next day. Rosalind and Louise waved him off before making their way to the schoolroom.

Rosalind had formed a strong attachment to Tommy, especially in the knowledge that he was her nephew, and, as the days went by she was growing fonder of Nancy. Rosalind had taken to visiting the schoolroom in the morning and she was able to help Louise by listening to Tommy's attempts to read while Louise took Nancy through her multiplication tables. These quiet periods helped to lessen Rosalind's immediate fears for Piers' safety for a while, but not for long. There was no escaping the fact after a week had passed that Piers had disappeared, whether by intent or by mischance. If he had suffered an accident Rosalind was certain that they would have been notified, and this added to the suspicion that foul play had been committed. Although why anyone would want to harm Piers was a mystery. He had confessed and explained his involvement with the smuggling gang when he was younger, and he had atoned for his misdeeds. As far as Rosalind was aware he had led a blameless existence since they married three years ago, although now there was a nagging doubt in her mind. However, to voice such worries to either Hester or Alex might seem disloyal and she bore the anxiety in silence.

It was two weeks since Piers had left so abruptly and still no news of his whereabouts. The mild September weather had been overtaken by a cold start to October with rain and gales, but Rosalind was determined to carry on as usual. Without a steward she had undertaken to collect the rents herself, and visiting the tenants took her mind off her worries. She had known them all since she was a child and it was more like dealing with members of an extended family. Alex had tried to dissuade her, pressing home the point that she was getting very close to her time, but Rosalind needed something to do and she laughed off his worries. Hester knew better than to try to stop her doing something she had set her heart on, and Rosalind drove the sturdy governess cart with Ajax in the shafts. He was old and reliable, and he could find his way home on his own if absolutely necessary. She spent some time chatting to Dora Greep, who presented her with a beautiful knitted shawl for the baby. Rosalind went on to visit the other tenant farms, ending up late in the afternoon at the fishermen's cottages on the quay.

She had not meant to stay out after dark but the days were getting shorter and the clouds had come tumbling in from the west. Strong winds lashed the sea into a frenzy of white-tipped waves and gulls whirled overhead mewing and wailing like souls in distress. Widow Madge was the last of Rosalind's calls, but as she entered the tiny cottage a sharp pain made her double up, gasping for breath.

'You shouldn't be here, ma'am,' Widow Madge said anxiously. 'Not so close to your time, and it's going to be a wild night.'

Rosalind straightened up with a sigh. 'It's passed now, Mrs Madge. I'll just sit for a while, if I may, and then I'll set off for home.'

Eliza Madge shook her head. 'I've been through

this six times in all, ma'am. I don't think you're in a condition to drive yourself, not in this weather, anyway.'

Rosalind nodded breathlessly as another spasm shook her whole body. 'I think I'd better get home quickly, Mrs Madge.'

'When did you start having pains, ma'am?' Eliza leaned closer.

The small room was lit by the glow of a driftwood fire and a single tallow candle. The acrid smell of burning fat made Rosalind feel faint, but she took a deep breath. 'I've had them off and on since earlier this afternoon, but I've had something similar before, so I ignored them.'

'Tilly.' Eliza opened the door to the tiny kitchen at the back of the cottage. 'Never mind cleaning your boots, child. I want you to run to the castle and get help. Tell them that Mrs Blanchard's time has come.'

Tilly edged into the room, glancing warily at Rosalind. 'I could take the cart, Ma. I can handle the reins.'

'The wind is getting stronger by the minute and it's pouring with rain. The lane will be awash with mud. You'll get there quicker if you cut through the woods. Go now, quickly. Don't make me tell you again.'

'All right, Ma. I'm going.' Tilly grabbed a shawl and wrapped it around her head as she opened the door. She had a battle to close it again as the wind battered the front of the cottage. Eliza rushed to help her, scooping up two small girls as she went.

'Flossie, come down here now. I want you to look after the twins. Give them some bread and milk.'

Flossie thudded down the stairs. 'Why do I have to do it, Ma? Why is it always me?'

'You're a big girl now. Some little children are out on the street selling matches at your age, so do as I tell you. Mrs Blanchard isn't well.'

Rosalind stifled a groan. 'I'm sorry to put you to so much trouble, Eliza.'

'Never mind that. You concentrate on getting that baby born, ma'am.' Eliza thrust the three-year-old twins into their older sister's arms. 'Go into the kitchen and shut the door, there's a good girl.'

Rosalind lay back on the saggy couch and closed her eyes as another even stronger contraction engulfed her whole body. She bit her lip to prevent herself from crying out and scaring the young children.

'Don't worry, ma'am,' Eliza said soothingly. 'I've delivered so many babies I've lost count. You'll soon have a little one in your arms. Just listen to what I say.'

Rosalind could do nothing but obey Eliza's firm instructions. Time seemed to stand still and her whole body felt as though it was tearing itself apart. Then through a mist of pain she heard the door crash against the wall and the sound of footsteps.

'I came as quickly as I could, Mrs Madge.'

'She's here, as you can see, sir.'

'Alex?' Rosalind held out her hand. 'Alex.'

He clasped her cold fingers in a firm grip. 'I'm here, Rosie.'

'Don't leave me.'

'I won't. You're doing very well, my brave girl.'

'Move away a little, sir.' Eliza's voice was firm.

'Don't go, Alex.' Rosalind gripped his hand so hard that she felt his bones creak. 'I'm sorry.'

'Don't be. You squeeze as hard as you can. I can take it.'

'You're nearly there,' Eliza added triumphantly. 'Take deep breaths, ma'am. Don't push until I tell you to.'

Suddenly it was over and the pain ceased. Rosalind attempted to sit up. 'My baby?'

'You have a beautiful baby girl,' Eliza said, smiling. She wrapped the naked infant in a clean cloth and laid her in Rosalind's arms. 'Hold her while I go and make a pot of tea.' She backed away and stepped into the kitchen.

Through tears of joy Rosalind gazed at the mewling, red-faced scrap of humanity. 'She is a little angel.'

'She's beautiful, Rosie,' Alex said, gently caressing the baby's cheek with the tip of his finger. 'What will you call her?'

'I like Adela.' Rosie's lips trembled. 'But Piers wanted a boy. He'll be so disappointed.'

'Nonsense,' Alex said sharply. 'She's like a little

doll. He'll take one look at Dolly and he'll fall in love with her, as I have.'

'Really? Do you think so?'

'I know so, Rosie. Put any thoughts like that out of your head and rest. I'll take you home when Mrs Madge thinks you're ready.'

Rosalind sighed and closed her eyes. 'I am so tired, Alex.'

It was close to midnight when Alexander drew Ajax to a halt in the bailey. Despite the wild weather Hudson came running from the coach house block to take the reins, and Jarvis held the front door open. Rosalind knew that they had been waiting up for them and she felt her throat tighten with unshed tears.

'I'm so lucky to have people who really care about me,' she said shakily.

Alexander smiled as he lifted her and her baby in his arms. 'Of course we do. We all love you, Rosie. I'm no exception.' He carried them into the entrance hall.

'There's a fire in the drawing room, sir.' Jarvis pitched his weight against the door as the wind tried to prevent it from closing. 'It's a wild night.'

'Thank you for waiting up for me, Jarvis,' Rosalind called over Alexander's shoulder as he headed for the drawing room.

Hester appeared to be asleep in a comfortable chair by the fire, but she leaped to her feet. 'Rosie, are you all right?'

Alex laid Rosalind down on the sofa. 'Mother and baby doing well, Hester.' He propped two cushions behind Rosalind's head.

'I'm being spoiled, Hester,' Rosalind said sleepily. 'Come and look at my beautiful daughter.'

Hester was on her feet in an instant. 'May I hold her, Rosie?'

'Of course you may. You cared for me when I was a baby. Now you can show me how to look after Adela.'

Hester cradled the baby in her arms. 'Adela is a pretty name, and she's going to be a beauty when she grows up. I can see it now.'

'She's a lovely little doll,' Alexander said, smiling. 'I will always think of her as my little Dolly.'

Hester glared at him. 'Don't repeat that in front of her father.'

'I was there at her birth, Hester. I think that gives me the right to be a proud uncle. One day Dolly Blanchard will make her mark on the world. I don't care what my brother says. He should have been here. There's no excuse for neglecting his wife and child.'

'What's all that commotion?' Hester cradled Dolly in her arms as she moved to open the door. 'Alex, you'd best go and see. Jarvis never raises his voice.'

Alexander was halfway to the door when Ralph Lambert strode into the room, his felt hat limp and dripping with rainwater, as was his caped greatcoat.

'I know it's late, but there's something you ought to know, Mrs Blanchard.'

Rosalind dragged herself to a semi-recumbent position. 'Why are you here?'

'I'm asking you to leave,' Alexander said icily. 'If you don't I will have to eject your forcibly.'

'I wouldn't do that if I were you, Captain. I should inform you that I've been working undercover for the Metropolitan Police for the last six months.'

'I don't understand,' Rosalind said faintly. 'You were our steward.'

'I was investigating a series of crimes committed over many years, Mrs Blanchard. I came to tell you that your husband has been arrested and is currently in prison awaiting trial.'

Chapter Nineteen

The baby began to cry and Hester stepped forward, chin out and an aggressive set to her jaw. 'What are you talking about, Lambert? Are you out of your mind?'

'No, ma'am. What I said is true. Mr Blanchard has been pursuing illegal activities.'

'That can't be true,' Rosalind said weakly. 'Piers repaid all the people who were affected by his wrong-doings more than three years ago. He swore to me that he would never break the law again.'

'I'm afraid he broke his promise, ma'am.'

'Are you sure about this, Lambert?' Alex demanded angrily. 'Can't you see that you're upsetting Mrs Blanchard?'

'I didn't have to come here tonight, Captain. I felt I owed it to Mrs Blanchard.'

Rosalind fell back against the cushions. 'I had a

feeling that something was terribly wrong, but you tricked your way into our household, Lambert. We treated you well.'

'That's why I came here even at this hour of the night. You deserve better than this, ma'am. I'm sorry to have deceived you, but there was no other way. I'll say this to you, Mrs Blanchard, your husband is a clever man. It's a pity he didn't put his talents to better use.'

'You've said your piece, Lambert.' Alexander clenched his fists at his sides.

Hester placed the squalling baby in Rosalind's arms. 'Can't you see that this isn't the time to upset Mrs Blanchard?'

'I'll see you out.' Alexander made a move towards the door. 'You can give me the details outside. Mrs Blanchard needs rest and quiet. This is a very difficult time for her.'

Lambert nodded. 'You will be kept informed, Captain. If it's worth anything at all, I'm sorry for the deception, and I regret having upset the Widow Madge, but Blanchard was getting suspicious and I had to prove that I was doing my job.'

'You've said enough.' Alexander ushered him out of the room.

'He's gone, poppet,' Hester said softly. 'You must put all that out of your mind. The little one needs putting to the breast, and then I'll help you upstairs to your bed.'

'You're right, of course, but Piers is my husband.

I can't believe that he's lied to me for the past three years.'

'Lambert said that Piers is very clever, Rosie. It looks as if he's deceived us all.'

'There must be some mistake.' Rosalind shook her head. 'He wouldn't risk losing the clay mine for whatever gains he's made illegally. Maybe Lambert was lying. We don't know that he's working for the police.'

'Why would he lie about it? We would soon find out if it weren't true, so what would he gain by making up such stories?'

'I don't know, Hester. I can't think straight at the moment. I need to speak to our solicitor as soon as possible. I can't go to the prison until I'm back on my feet, but Mr Mounce would be able to see Piers.'

'You mustn't upset yourself, Rosie. You have little Adela to think of now.'

Rosalind smiled fondly at her daughter. 'She will be christened Adela, but I think she'll always be Dolly to me.' She looked up at the sound of the door opening and Alex walked into the room, but was met halfway by Hester.

'You can't come in here now, Alexander.'

'I held her hand while she was giving birth, Hester. Surely I can see her for a while. I won't tire her out, I promise.'

'That's not the point.' Hester barred his way. 'You are not her husband. Your position in this household will be in question now.'

346

'Hester, don't.' Rosalind spoke more sharply than she had intended. 'I'm sorry, but Alex is right. I don't think I could have borne the pain if he hadn't been there to give me courage. Please let him stay for a while.'

'I'll turn a blind eye this once, but you two will have to be careful. It was one thing for Alexander to stay here while Piers was at home, but the gossips will delight in spreading malicious stories about your relationship if your husband is convicted and kept in prison. Do you want to ruin the family name?'

'I don't care what people say,' Rosalind said tiredly.

'You will care when you find that Adela is cold-shouldered by society. You have a child to think of now, Rosie.' Hester glared at Alexander. 'If Adela was your daughter, would you want her to be the centre of scandalous tittle-tattle?'

'I need to speak to Rosie alone. Give me five minutes, Hester, and I will do exactly as you say.'

'Yes, Hester. Please do as Alex asks.' Rosalind met Hester's worried look with a warm smile. 'I know you mean well, but please leave us. Then I promise I'll go to bed.'

'All right,' Hester said grudgingly. 'Five minutes and then Alexander can carry you upstairs to your room. It's surprising how well a lame man can manage stairs if he puts his mind to it.' Hester stalked out of the room, slamming the door behind her.

'She knows,' Rosalind said in a low voice. 'I always suspected that she knew you slept in my bed on New Year's Eve.'

'Hester isn't the problem, Rosie. I don't care what she thinks. All I care about is you and little Dolly.'

'I don't want Hester to think ill of you, Alex. She's a good person and I trust her implicitly.'

'I know, and I'm sorry if I've ruffled her feathers, but my main concern now is to find out what my brother has been up to. You, on the other hand, must concentrate on getting back to normal and taking care of little Dolly.' He smiled tenderly and stroked the baby's head as she suckled at her mother's breast. 'I couldn't love her more if she were my own child, and I'm proud of you, Rosie.'

'I can't believe that Piers could have deceived us all for so long, Alex.'

'I'll visit the prison tomorrow. I want to hear it from his own lips, not from Lambert or anyone else.'

'I'll give you the address of Mr Mounce, our solicitor. We need his help, too.'

Alexander nodded. 'I'll do anything you ask. You know my feelings for you, Rosie. Nothing will ever change that.'

'I know, Alex, and I feel the same, but it can never be.' Rosalind raised her hand to caress his cheek just as the door opened and Hester cleared her throat as she advanced on them.

'I'll take Adela, if you'll help Rosie to her room, Alexander.'

'I can walk, but it would help if I can lean on you, Alex.' Rosalind wrapped the shawl that Dora Greep had knitted around the sleeping baby.

'Don't think I'm unsympathetic,' Hester said as she lifted Dolly in her arms. 'I loved your grandpapa for many years, but it would have caused a huge scandal had our affair become public knowledge.'

'He married you eventually, Hester.'

'I was lucky, but forbidden love doesn't often end so well.'

Despite Hester's pleas, Rosalind refused to observe the customary lying-in period. She was up and about three days after Adela's birth in order to receive Mr Mounce, who had travelled from Exeter at Alexander's request.

Dolly was left in Hester's care, aided by Nancy, who had taken to the baby as if she were her own sister. Tommy was vaguely curious, but preferred to remain in the school room with Louise where he diligently practised his reading and writing or learned his tables.

Rosalind had chosen to see Mr Mounce in the library, where she could be certain that they would not be interrupted, but it seemed odd to sit behind the same desk where Walter had spent so many hours writing his stories and poems. Alex took a seat at her side and Mr Mounce was comfortably ensconced in a padded leather chair with a cup of tea and a plate of cake on a table at his side.

'First of all, Mrs Blanchard, might I offer my condolences,' Mr Mounce said hesitantly. His teacup rattled as he replaced it on its saucer with a hand that shook. 'I find the whole business very upsetting, mainly because I know what privations you suffered before your marriage. I really thought that everything was settled and your husband's dealings were above board.'

'So did I, Mr Mounce. Please tell me everything you know. My brother-in-law went to the prison but he wasn't allowed to see Piers.'

'Yes, I realise that, Mrs Blanchard. I'm afraid your husband is being treated as if he were a dangerous criminal, a gang leader, even.'

'But that's not true,' Rosalind said anxiously. 'Piers would never condone violence.'

'I'm sure you are right, but there is a great deal of money involved. Over the last two years Mr Blanchard has been shipping goods from abroad without declaring them, and he is suspected of having connections to several illegal operations abroad. His dealings on the Continent have been subject to investigation in France and Spain. I've spoken to him briefly but he is reluctant to give me any further information, and he doesn't seem willing to co-operate.'

'I don't understand,' Rosalind said slowly. 'Surely all this can't be true. Piers promised me before we got married that his criminal activities were all in the past.'

'It seems that he's lied to all of us.' Alexander laid his hand on her arm. 'But I'd want to hear the full story from his own lips. Perhaps someone is threatening him. I don't believe that my brother is a criminal.'

'Neither do I,' Rosalind added fervently. 'Please try to make him see sense, Mr Mounce. Did he give you a message for me?'

Mr Mounce shook his head. 'No, ma'am. I'm sorry.'

Rosalind turned to Alexander, grasping him by the hand. 'You left word for Piers informing him of Dolly's birth, didn't you, Alex?'

'Yes. I tipped the guard handsomely to pass on the good news.'

'I know he wanted a son,' Rosalind said miserably, 'but I thought he might at least acknowledge the birth of his daughter.'

'I'll mention it when I see him again.' Mr Mounce produced a gold half-hunter watch from his waistcoat pocket. 'I really should be going now, Mrs Blanchard. I have a meeting later this afternoon, but I'll call in at the prison and make another appointment to see your husband.'

'Yes, please do, and if you can find out when his trial is likely, or if they will allow bail, that would be very helpful.'

'Bail has been denied, I'm afraid. I think the magistrate was of the opinion that Mr Blanchard would leave the country.' Mr Mounce stood up, eyeing Rosalind with a curious gaze. 'Tell me, Mrs Blanchard, did your husband go abroad on business very often?'

Rosalind nodded. 'Yes, he was away most of last year and again this year until the shipwreck. When he recovered from his injuries he assured me that he would do as much work from home as possible.'

'And did he?'

'At first, but he's been travelling more and more recently.'

'I'll see myself out.' Mr Mounce acknowledged Alexander with a nod and he gave Rosalind a sympathetic smile. 'I am sorry to see you plunged once again into such desperate problems. I'll do my very best to find a way round this. Good day to both of you.' He hurried from the room.

'I'm beginning to see why Piers was so keen to train me in the china clay business,' Alexander said thoughtfully. 'I couldn't understand why he travelled so much, but now I do, and it worries me.'

'Do you think he was using the business as cover for his illegal dealings, Alex?'

'It appears so. I'm beginning to wonder if Pedrick is involved, and how much of the company's finances are tied up in the ships that Piers used to transport whatever it was that earned so much money. It certainly wasn't just china clay.'

'You're not planning to visit Trevenor, are you?'

'Not yet, but I will have to very soon. I need to see Piers first.'

'Do you believe that he's been lying to us?'

Alexander grasped her hand. 'I hope not, but I really don't know what to think. I will get to the bottom of this, one way or another.'

*　　*　　*

Piers continued to refuse to see his brother, although Mr Mounce was able to report a brief interview during which Piers was less than cooperative and told him nothing that he did not already know.

It was no surprise to Rosalind when Lady Pentelow and Aurelia arrived unannounced, together with half their household. There was a flurry of activity amongst the servants at Rockwood as they made rooms ready for the unexpected guests and Rosalind braced herself for a series of lectures from Piers' grandmother. However, the sight of baby Dolly seemed to put all such thoughts out of Lady Pentelow's head and she insisted on cuddling the baby at every possible opportunity. Aurelia was not so impressed.

'She doesn't look much like Piers,' she said, frowning.

'All newborn babies look like little old men, Aurelia.' Lady Pentelow rocked Dolly in her arms. 'But Adela will grow into her looks. With Pentelow blood in her veins she will become a beauty and she will be clever, too.' She turned to Rosalind. 'I don't understand why you insist on giving her such a common nickname. I believe she is to be christened Adela, and that is what I will call her.'

'It was Alexander who called her Dolly.' Rosalind realised her mistake the moment the words left her lips.

Lady Pentelow gave her a searching look. 'I don't know what you have to do with it, Alex. You're only the child's uncle.'

'I am entitled to love her, nonetheless,' Alexander said calmly. 'I was there at her birth, and—'

'You were present while Rosalind was confined?' Lady Pentelow's voice rose an octave. 'Explain yourself, Alexander.'

'It happened by chance, Lady Pentelow,' Rosalind said hastily. 'I was visiting a tenant and there was a terrible storm. I was quite far gone and Mrs Madge sent for help. Alexander came, it was as simple as that.'

'Well, it's not the sort of story that would go down well if it became public knowledge. It would have been bad enough had Piers been present at the birth, but totally unacceptable for his brother to witness such an intimate moment.'

'All I did was to hold her hand, Grandmama.' Alexander winked at Rosalind.

'I saw that, Alexander. I suppose you think it's amusing, but you always did exactly the opposite to what was expected of you.'

'As if it isn't bad enough having one brother about to be sentenced to a long prison term,' Aurelia cried passionately. 'If this gets out we'll be shunned by society, Grandmama. People will think that Alexander is the father.'

'That's enough, Aurelia.' Alexander rose from his seat, glaring at his sister. 'Don't say things like that, even in jest, unless you want to create a scandal that really would ruin your chances of finding a husband.'

Dolly began to howl and Lady Pentelow thrust the baby into Rosalind's arms. 'You had better go somewhere quiet to feed her, or better still you should hire a wet nurse. It's a good thing that I came here. I can see that you need someone to organise your household, Rosalind. You really should be lying in so soon after the birth.'

'Lady Pentelow, I am most grateful for your concern,' Rosalind said slowly and deliberately. 'But my household runs perfectly well.'

'We'll see about that. Anyway, my main objective is to visit my grandson in prison. I imagine there has been some terrible miscarriage of the law. Piers will be proved innocent at the trial and I will have him out of that dreadful place in no time at all. He will then come to live with me at Trevenor, where I can keep an eye on him.'

Rosalind stood up, holding Dolly in her arms. 'This is Piers' home, ma'am.'

'Trevenor belongs to him. The clay mine is his life and he would never have become embroiled in whatever he's been accused of had he been living at Trevenor. You are his wife and you are very welcome, too. But you must cease this nonsense of insisting that this old pile of stones depends upon your management.'

'These are matters that are strictly between my husband and myself.'

'We'll see about that. Now I suggest you go to another room and feed the infant. Tomorrow I will advertise for a wet nurse, and I will also visit the prison.'

'Piers won't see you, Grandmama,' Alexander said firmly. 'The prison isn't the sort of place for a lady to go to.'

'Which is why I intend to demand that Piers be allowed out on bail. I will speak to the magistrate myself.'

Rosalind knew from experience that to argue with Lady Pentelow when she was in this mood was pointless. She took her squalling baby to Hester's parlour and closed the door.

'Have you had enough of her already?' Hester asked, chuckling. 'I keep out of her way as much as possible.'

Rosalind sank down on the sofa and unbuttoned her blouse. Dolly latched on immediately and Rosalind sat back against the cushions. 'Lady Pentelow is impossible, Hester. She wants to take over completely. She even had the gall to say she would hire a wet nurse for Dolly. The cheek of the woman.'

'You should have known that she would arrive sooner or later, but you don't have to let her have her own way.'

'Don't worry, I have no intention of allowing her to tell me what to do in my own home. She thinks she can get Piers out of prison and she wants to take him to Trevenor to live with her. I am welcome as long as I do exactly what she says.'

'She doesn't want to admit that her beloved grandson might actually be a criminal.'

'Neither do I, Hester. I'd go to the prison myself if I thought that he would speak to me, but I know him as well as anyone. Piers is stubborn and he won't want to admit that he's done wrong, even if it's true. I suppose I should have suspected something, if only because he always seemed to have unlimited funds. I never questioned whether the mine could have made so much profit. Maybe I should have done so.'

'You can't blame yourself, poppet. Piers is a grown man who can make his own choices. Unfortunately it looks as if they were the wrong ones, and now we will all suffer the consequences.'

Lady Pentelow set off next morning for Exeter prison, accompanied by Alexander, who had tried to dissuade her and failed. Rosalind was adamant that she did not want her daughter fed by a wet nurse and nothing Lady Pentelow could say made any difference. Aurelia made it plain that she found babies distasteful and boring, but she was eager to learn about Patricia's engagement to Sir Michael. She insisted upon Gurney driving her to Greystone Park to visit her old friend. Rosalind was only too happy to oblige as it gave her a day of relative peace and a respite from the questions with which Aurelia bombarded her.

'It isn't the done thing to have Alex living here

while Piers is away,' Aurelia said as she admired her reflection in one of the long mirrors that adorned the walls of the drawing room. 'Grandmama is quite shocked by it, and I think that Alex still has feelings for you, Rosie.' She tied the ribbons on her bonnet in a jaunty bow. 'How do I look?'

'Very elegant,' Rosalind said automatically. 'Just one thing, Aurelia. I don't want you spreading gossip about me and your brother. I'm very fond of Alex and I think he returns the affection, but we are both loyal to Piers, no matter what he's done.'

Aurelia turned to her with a bright smile. 'I wasn't suggesting anything untoward, Rosie. But it would be obvious to anyone that Alex hasn't forgotten that you two were once engaged.'

'Almost engaged,' Rosalind added hastily. 'It was never official and we both realised our mistake in the nick of time.'

'Then you were together all that time in a creepy château in France last Christmas. It must have been very romantic.'

'Aurelia, you are letting your imagination run away with you. It was a horrible place and we were trapped there because Piers was so ill, and Alexander couldn't walk. I don't know why you think that was romantic. It was all I could do to look after them both.'

'Nevertheless, you need to be very careful where Grandmama is concerned. She is very sharp and she is also suspicious. She will do anything she can to preserve the family name, and a scandal like this has put her very much on guard. I pity the magistrate if she manages to get an interview with him.'

Jarvis appeared in the doorway and cleared his throat. 'Your carriage awaits, Miss Aurelia.'

'I don't know when I'll be back, Rosie.'

'Send a message if you're going to be out after dark. You know your grandmama will worry if you don't arrive in time for dinner.'

'I'm sure Sir Michael will send me home in his carriage. Try not to let Grandmama bully you, Rosie.' Aurelia left the room, trailing her fur-trimmed velvet cape carelessly across the floor.

That evening at dinner Lady Pentelow was visibly angry. Piers had refused to see either of them and she seemed to be taking her frustration out on Alexander. She snapped at him several times during the meal, and she was annoyed that Aurelia had sent a message informing them that she was staying at Greystone Park for dinner, despite the fact that Sir Michael had promised to send her home in his carriage.

'I'm let down by all my grandchildren,' she said bitterly.

'The prison isn't the sort of place that your grandson would wish you to enter, Lady Pentelow,' Hester said calmly. 'Piers was probably thinking of your wellbeing.'

'I'm sure you would know more about that than I.' Lady Pentelow glared at her over the top of her wine glass. 'And I think I know Piers better than you do.'

'Grandmama, there's no need to take it out on Hester.' Alexander tempered his remark with a smile.

'Did I ask for your opinion, Alexander?' Lady Pentelow put her glass down on the highly polished table.

'Piers doesn't want to see any of us,' Rosalind said firmly. 'I think we will have to leave it to Mr Mounce to liaise between the family and Piers. I don't like it any more than you do, ma'am, but we do not have any choice in the matter.'

'You don't seem unduly upset that your husband has been falsely accused, madam. I would have expected some show of emotion or distress. Could it be that you are relieved that Piers is incarcerated in that dreadful place?'

'How dare you say such a thing?' Rosalind pushed her plate away. 'Why did you come here, Lady Pentelow? You've done nothing but complain and criticise since you arrived.'

'I am the head of the family, I'll have you know. I never approved of you marrying my grandson and I blame you for his misfortune. You wanted to renovate this tumbling pile of masonry and he had to find the money to do so.'

Alexander rose to his feet. 'Grandmama, that's enough. Piers is his own man and he chose the path he's taken in life. It had nothing to do with Rosalind.'

'Sit down, Alexander. You and she are far too cosy for my liking. Perhaps you would both be delighted to see Piers sent to prison for a lengthy term.'

'You are an evil old witch.' Hester jumped to her feet. 'You should be helping Rosalind through this difficult time, not accusing her of being the cause of the trouble. Piers followed in his father's footsteps. Your son-in-law was a criminal and Piers has inherited his father's bad traits.'

'You are a common woman who coerced a feeble old man into marrying you. Your place is in the servants' quarters, not at the master's table.'

'Lady Pentelow, that is quite enough.' Rosalind clutched the edge of the table, her knuckles whitening from the pressure. 'This has got quite out of hand. You are upset because Piers won't see you and Aurelia has dared to defy you. I suggest we all sit down and finish the meal that Cook has prepared for us like civilised human beings. We are not fish-wives, ma'am. We do not screech at each other or exchange insults simply because we are frustrated.'

Lady Pentelow collapsed back onto her chair. 'I'm appalled.'

'As am I, Grandmama.' Alexander glared at her angrily. 'Tomorrow I'm taking you and your servants back to Trevenor. Piers was supposed to be training me to manage the business. There's very little we can do for him if he refuses to see us, and it's time I took stock of the company. Who knows what I will find?'

Chapter Twenty

Aurelia strolled into the drawing room with a smug smile, which vanished when her grandmother reprimanded her for staying at Greystone Park that evening. Lady Pentelow gave vent to her temper, taking out her frustration on her granddaughter. Aurelia seemed genuinely shocked to discover that they were to return to Trevenor next day. Rosalind sat with her empty coffee cup still clutched in her hand, and she felt sorry for Aurelia, who had done nothing wrong.

'I don't understand.' Aurelia turned to her brother. 'What has happened, Alex? Why are we returning to Trevenor so soon?'

'Because your brother says so, and I agree with him.' Lady Pentelow rose from her seat by the fire. 'This place has a bad effect on people, and I include you in that, Aurelia. I don't want you to associate with Patricia Carey. She's unmarried and living in the same house as her fiancé. That simply isn't done.'

'They're getting married in less than a fortnight, Grandmama, and I am going to be one of her bridesmaids. I've already agreed so I can't go back on it.'

'Nonsense. You're coming home with Alexander and me.'

'No, Grandmama. I intend to stay here with Rosalind until after the wedding, or if she won't have me I have been invited to stay at Greystone Park.'

'Over my dead body,' Lady Pentelow said angrily. 'Patricia is no better than she should be. Are you willing to throw away your chances of making a good match by remaining here simply to act as her bridesmaid?'

'Weddings are a good place to find a future husband. That's what you've always told me, Grandmama,' Aurelia said sweetly. 'Besides which, Sir Michael is a Member of Parliament, and he has very wealthy and influential friends. Surely you approve of his connections?'

Lady Pentelow rose majestically to her feet. 'I am going to my room. You must do what you wish, Aurelia, but I wash my hands of you. My grandchildren are a huge disappointment to me.' She strutted out of the room with her head held high.

Aurelia sank down on the sofa beside Rosalind. 'Oh dear. I've never seen her so upset. Perhaps I ought to go to her.'

'No, leave her to think about what she's doing.'

Alexander shook his head. 'I never wanted to be the head of the household and I don't intend to take my brother's place, but I need to see the books and speak to Pedrick. I have a feeling that what I find won't be good.'

'Do you think that Pedrick was involved in Piers' crimes?' Rosalind asked anxiously.

'There's only one way to find out and I'd like to get there before the police start investigating the business, if they haven't already done so.'

'May I stay here with you, Rosie?' Aurelia asked eagerly. 'I do so want to be a bridesmaid.'

'Of course, but only if you're sure. Your grandmother won't approve.'

'I've been a dutiful granddaughter for long enough. I'm twenty-one now and I'll be on the shelf in a few years' time if I don't get away from Trevenor. Patsy has promised that I can stay with them in London when they're married. Just think of the balls I could attend, and the theatres I could visit, not to mention soirées and dinner parties. I'm being stifled in Cornwall.'

Rosalind smiled. 'I understand. Of course you may stay here. I'll be glad of the company. I can't go far until Dolly is weaned, and I refuse to hire a wet nurse. Which reminds me, it's time for Dolly's next feed. I left Nancy in the nursery keeping an eye on her while we had dinner. The poor child must be ready for bed herself.'

'Perhaps you should take on a nanny,' Alexander

said gently. 'You'll have enough to do just keeping this place going while I'm away.'

'Are you planning on returning then, Alex?' Rosalind made an effort to sound casual, but his decision to leave for Trevenor had come as a shock.

'Of course. I won't leave you to struggle along on your own. I'll be back in time for the trial and then we'll know how things stand.'

'I managed this place on my own before I married Piers. I can do it again, Alex. I don't want you to give up your life for us.'

Aurelia laughed. 'Alex has never put anyone or anything before his own wants and needs. I wouldn't worry about that if I were you, Rosie. Anyway, it's Bertie who should come home. After all, he holds the title, and he owns Rockwood, not Piers.'

'Of course, you're right. He also has a son. I wrote a letter and posted it to the address you gave me, Alex. I hope it catches up with Bertie, wherever he is at present. I'm sure that he'll love Tommy just as we all do.'

'It may take him some time to come to terms with the fact that he's a father, but I'm sure you're right, Rosie. Tommy is a lovable child and very intelligent. It's amazing how well he's settled in here.'

Rosalind sighed. 'He still has nightmares of being trapped in the darkness of a chimney and he thinks he's suffocating. I think he'll have those fears for the rest of his life.'

'Then we'll do our best to make him forget the

past,' Alexander said firmly. 'When I return from Trevenor I'll take the little chap in hand. I'll teach him to ride and take him fishing.'

Aurelia threw her head back and laughed. 'You two sound like doting parents. I'm sure Piers wouldn't concern himself over the wellbeing of one small sweeping boy.'

Rosalind rose hastily to her feet. 'It's time I went to the nursery, so I'll say good night.'

'It's still quite early,' Alexander said with a worried frown.

'I'm tired. It's been a trying day.' Rosalind gave Aurelia a beaming smile, but she walked past Alexander. Aurelia might give the impression of being flighty and only interested in herself, but Rosalind had a feeling that her sister-in-law suspected something. She made her way to the nursery where she found both children already in their night clothes. Nancy was attempting to soothe the crying baby by rocking the wooden cradle, and Tommy was sitting on the floor playing with a battered set of lead soldiers that had once been Bertie's pride and joy.

'Your baby cries a lot,' Tommy said, frowning.

'I can't pacify her.' Nancy jumped to her feet. 'I think she's hungry.'

'I should have come sooner.' Rosalind bent down to lift the squalling infant in her arms and she sat down to feed her. 'There, you see, now she's quiet, and it's time that both of you were in bed. Did Tilly bring you some supper?'

Tommy looked up, grinning. 'I had a bowl of bread and milk and a slice of cake.'

'And I had bread and milk and a jam tart,' Nancy added, smiling. 'I never got food like that in the orphanage, nor the vicar's house.'

'Into bed with you, Tommy,' Rosalind said firmly. 'And you, Nancy.'

'Will you tell us a story like you did last night?' Tommy asked eagerly.

Rosalind could see that she was not going to get away easily. 'All right. Settle down in bed and I'll sit here by the window, looking out at the stars. Did you know that you each have a special star that looks after you all night? It twinkles happily in the sky, watching and guarding you from anything that might scare you.'

'Which one is mine?' Tommy asked sleepily. 'Does it have a name?'

'It's waiting for you to give it one, Tommy. The same goes for you, too, Nancy.'

Nancy climbed into bed and pulled the covers up to her chin. 'How do I know which one is mine?'

'You look for the one that shines the brightest and remember it's shining just for you.'

Nancy yawned. 'I like the sound of that. Will you tell us a story about the stars?'

Rosalind lowered her voice and started to make up a story about two stars who could not get on together and kept arguing. At first Tommy asked questions every time she stopped for breath, but gradually his breathing grew more regular and his eyes closed. Rosalind looked from one rosy face to the other and smiled to herself – they were both sound asleep. She would have to remember where she left off the star story because Tommy would be sure to put her right if she forgot. Dolly was also asleep and Rosalind adjusted her blouse before standing up and extinguishing all the candles except one. She understood Tommy's night terrors and she insisted that a candle was always left burning in the children's room, although it had to be placed away from draughts and anything flammable.

She left the nursery and was on her way to her own room when Alexander waylaid her.

'I just wanted to say goodbye in private, Rosie. You and I know that we're behaving as honourably as we can in this situation, but I think Aurelia is suspicious.'

'Yes, I agree.'

'I won't stay in Cornwall a minute longer than necessary.'

'Alex, if it would make things easier for you I would understand if you decided to live at Trevenor. If you're really going to run the business it would be the sensible thing to do.'

He smiled and brushed a stray lock of hair back from her forehead. 'When did I ever do the sensible thing, Rosie? My brother has let you down and I'm going to protect you and Dolly, no matter what. If Bertie decides to leave the army and return home,

I'll move on, although it will break my heart to do so.'

'We will have to part sooner or later, Alex. I don't want it any more than you do, but we both know that we can never be together. My rational mind tells me that you ought to leave and find someone you can love, but my heart begs you to stay, which is very selfish.'

He leaned towards her and claimed her lips in a kiss that threatened to overwhelm her, but a whimper from Dolly made her pull away. 'Good night, Alex. I might not be up when you leave in the morning.'

'I'd rather remember you like this, Rosie. One day I hope and pray I'll be able to tell you that I love you without fear of creating a scandal that will ruin both families. I'll do what I have to in Cornwall and I want you to take care of yourself and little Dolly.' He bent down to kiss Dolly on the top of her downy head. 'Sleep well, little one.' He turned on his heel and disappeared into the darkness, leaving only the familiar scent of him in his wake. Rosalind sighed and continued on her way to her bedchamber, alone except for her small daughter.

The days that followed Alexander's departure with his grandmother and their servants might have proved too much to bear but for Aurelia, and Patricia's imminent wedding. Rosalind had not been consulted in the preparations at the start, but she found herself being drawn into them whether she wanted to help or not. Christina was more interested in her engagement to Oscar, but her plan to outsmart Patricia with arrangements to have her nuptials first met opposition from her father and from Glorina Cottingham. Christina did not approve of her friend living at Greystone Park before the wedding, but Patricia had staked her claim and nothing and no one was going to make her back down and return to Rockwood. However, she found herself lacking the guidance of an older woman and it was to Rosalind that she turned whenever problems arose. Aurelia was only too pleased to be involved, and the fittings for the wedding dress, the bridesmaids' gowns and Patricia's extensive trousseau were all conducted at Rockwood. There was a constant stream of carriages or delivery vehicles every day, so Patricia might as well have moved home, for the amount of time she spent there. However, she was not going to stay away from her fiancé any longer than necessary and Sir Michael himself seemed quite happy with the arrangement.

Sylvia was the chief bridesmaid and this caused a little tension with Aurelia, who did not appreciate being second best in anything, but she was forced to acknowledge that Sylvia had a prior claim. They were the only attendants, due mainly to the short amount of time between the announcement and the actual ceremony, but Patricia had to admit that she lacked female friends, having always preferred male company. However, she decided that Nancy was to be flower girl and Tommy could be a page. Nancy was thrilled, but Tommy had to be bribed with a promise of riding lessons from Hudson and a wooden fort for his lead soldiers. All this caused a flurry of activity, with more fittings, and a miniature military uniform was ordered from London in the hope that it would fit Tommy.

To complicate matters even more, Mr Mounce sent word that Piers' trial would take place less than a week after Patricia's wedding. Rosalind had asked twice for an interview with her husband and both times she had received a firm refusal. She decided to take matters into her own hands and, using the excuse that Nancy had to have a final fitting for her wedding outfit, Rosalind instructed Hudson to drive them to Exeter. Despite arguments from Hester, Rosalind took Dolly with her and she declined Hester's offer to accompany them, even though she knew that she would be angry and offended. However, Hester would have been even more outraged if she had known that the real reason for the trip was to visit the prison. Rosalind was determined to see Piers even if she had to wait all day.

Meggie Brewer had the gown wrapped and ready for collection and if she wondered why Rosalind did not insist that Nancy tried it on, she was too polite to say so. Nancy sat in the carriage fingering the delicate material with a rapt expression on her face, and Rosalind ordered Hudson to drive on to the prison. He shot her a worried glance but he did not argue, although he did question Rosalind's decision to go to the gates on her own.

'I won't be long, Hudson. Just stay there and keep an eye on Nancy and my baby. I'll be as quick as I can.' Rosalind could hear him muttering as she marched up to the prison gate and rang the bell. A guard appeared but her request to see her husband was refused, no matter how hard she pleaded, even when she insisted on seeing the chief warder himself. She was almost in tears when the gate was finally slammed in her face and the prison warder turned his back on her and walked away. She was about to climb into the carriage when someone tapped her on the shoulder.

'Well, if it ain't Madam High and Mighty Blanchard. Don't tell me that your old man is in stir.'

The unwelcome sound of Ezra Trimble's voice made her spin round to face him. 'Mind your own business, Mr Trimble.'

'Arrogant to the last, but I heard on the grapevine that Piers Blanchard finally got his comeuppance. We all knew that he was crooked.' He placed himself between Rosalind and the carriage.

'I'm in a hurry, Mr Trimble. Let me pass.' Rosalind could hear Dolly's mewling cries. She was due for a feed and Nancy was having difficulty in pacifying the hungry infant.

'So you've got a little 'un now.' Trimble leaned

into the carriage. 'That's a tiny one. Give it here, girl.'

'Leave my baby alone.' Rosalind beat her fists on his back. 'Don't touch her. Hudson, don't just sit there, get down and help me.'

Hudson leaped from the box and tugged ineffectually at Trimble's coat but was shaken off with a single shrug of Trimble's massive body. He made a grab for Dolly, clutching her in his grimy hands.

'I reckon I should take this one, since you stole our boy. I reckon that would be fair.'

'Give me my baby.' Rosalind's voice rose to a scream and Nancy began to howl.

'Do as the lady says,' Hudson gasped, holding his chest as if he had been winded by Trimble's sharp movement.

'No, I think this is a fair swap. You took young Tommy from us, so I'll have this one. He'll fetch a good price when he's a bit older. The missis will take care of him until then. She's a tender mother, all right.'

'You will not take my daughter from me.' Rosalind faced him. Her heart was hammering against her ribs and she was finding it difficult to breathe, but she was ready to fly at Trimble and fight with every ounce of strength to free her baby. She would die rather than allow Trimble to harm a single hair on Dolly's precious head.

'Trimble.' A stentorian voice from the prison yard made Trimble freeze, and the sound of the gates clanging open caused him to thrust the baby into Rosalind's arms.

The prison warder strode towards them.

'Do you know this man, ma'am?'

'Only to my cost, sir. He's just tried to steal my baby.'

'You've only just left your cell, Trimble. I see you haven't changed your ways. I'm arresting you for trying to abduct an infant. It's not the first time, is it?'

'It's all a mistake, sir,' Trimble said, cowering. 'I just done my time. I'm going home.'

'Not yet, you aren't. You were only on parole so you'd better come back inside and let the governor decide what to do with you.' The warder beckoned to a guard, who marched Trimble back into the prison yard. He came to a sudden halt.

'Her old man is coming up for trial next week. I got information on him that will put him away for the rest of his days. You think about that, lady.' Trimble was dragged off, still shouting.

'This isn't the place for a lady like yourself, ma'am,' the warder said grimly. 'I'd advise you to keep away from people like Trimble.' He handed Rosalind into the carriage. 'Coachman, drive on.' He slammed the door and stood back as the carriage lurched forward.

Rosalind huddled on the seat next to a sobbing Nancy, her own eyes filled with tears. 'It's all right now, Nancy. We're safe. That man won't bother us again.'

'He won't come to the castle and take Tommy, will he?'

Rosalind gave her a hug. 'No, of course not. We're well protected there. No one will hurt you or Tommy, and that's a promise.'

The day of the wedding dawned grey and stormy. Rosalind could only hope it was not an omen for the forthcoming marriage of her sister to Sir Michael. The ceremony itself was in the village church and the reception was at Greystone Park, which left her with little to do other than to make sure that the children were dressed in their wedding finery and ready on time. Hester, who had refused to order a new outfit, was dressed in her customary black bombazine, although she wore it with a handsome bonnet trimmed with red roses and a fur cape that smelled of mothballs, which she refused to replace with a newer model. Rosalind had a new gown in lilac silk taffeta, which was stylish but unadorned with frills or lace, worn with a frogged velvet mantle and a bonnet trimmed with forget-me-nots and rose-buds. Hester and Aurelia went in the landau with the children, which left Rosalind to travel on her own in the barouche. She knew that the guests would be watching her closely for signs of discomfort. It was common knowledge that Piers' trial was in a few days' time, and for the first time she was nervous of entering the church on her own, although she told herself that she would be amongst friends and the few who chose to spread gossip were not worth bothering about.

She was waiting in the front entrance of the castle for Hudson to arrive with the barouche when she heard the sound of galloping hoofs and a horseman rode through the gates and swerved to a halt.

'Alex!' Rosalind gasped with a mixture of shock and delight as he handed the reins to Pip Hudson, who had run from the stables ahead of his father driving the barouche.

'I couldn't bear the thought of you attending Patsy's wedding on your own,' Alexander said breathlessly. 'Have I got time to change out of my riding clothes?'

She gazed at his mud-spattered state and laughed. 'Only if you're very quick. Have you ridden all the way from Trevenor?'

He nodded. 'It's taken me the best part of three days, but I'm here now. Wait five minutes and I'll be with you.'

The church doors were about to be closed when they arrived, but the verger opened them wide, staring curiously at Alexander, who had hastily changed into his smartest frock coat, pin-stripe trousers and a grey waistcoat. Even out of uniform he cut a dashing figure, and Rosalind was aware of the envious glances of unattached females. However, she focused her attention on Patricia, who was standing with her attendants, poised and ready to walk down the aisle.

'I thought you were in Cornwall, Alex.' Patricia eyed him warily. 'I hope you haven't come to cause trouble.'

He shook his head. 'Of course not. If anything, I've come to wish you well.'

'Surely you're not going to walk to the altar on your own,' Rosalind said in a whisper. 'That's unconventional even for you, Patsy.'

'What do you suggest?' she demanded fiercely. 'My male relations are noticeable by their absence. Walter was supposed to be here but apparently he's been delayed. What alternative do we have?'

'I'll give you away.' Alexander proffered his arm. 'It will be a pleasure.'

'You abandoned me at the altar once before, Alexander Blanchard. I'm not going to give you the satisfaction of making a fool of me for a second time.'

'I am sincere in my regard for you, Patsy.' Alexander lowered his voice. 'Do you want to make a display of yourself?'

'Rosie, are you going to allow this?' Patricia asked angrily. 'If my former fiancé gives me away it will make me a laughing stock.'

'The organist is waiting for his cue, Patsy,' Rosalind said in a whisper. 'The guests are growing restive, so perhaps you would do better to put your differences aside for a few minutes.'

'I might have known you'd say that. You always had a soft spot for Alex.'

Aurelia nudged Patricià in the ribs. 'For goodness' sake get on with it, Patsy. No one will notice anything untoward if you don't make a fuss.'

'Yes, Patsy. Just act as if it's nothing unusual,' Rosalind added urgently. She glanced at Sir Michael, who was standing stiffly by the altar with his best man. He was not the husband she might have chosen for her sister, but perhaps an experienced older man might be able to deal with Patsy's mercurial temperament.

'I'd rather do it on my own,' Patricia said, pouting.

Rosalind sighed. 'It's up to you, but I'm going to take my seat in the front pew.' She walked off quickly without giving her sister a chance to argue, and at a signal from the vicar the organist struck up a solemn march.

Alexander led Patricia up the aisle preceded by Nancy strewing dried rose petals in their path, with Tommy walking beside her, looking very proud in his rented military uniform. Rosalind had a lump in her throat when she saw him and she wished with all her heart that Bertie could have been there. The family likeness was more pronounced now that Tommy was clean and well fed, and there was no doubt in her mind that he was her brother's son. Bertie would be so proud if he could see him now.

Alexander handed the bride to the groom and moved back to sit beside Rosalind. They exchanged smiles and he reached for her hand, clasping it in a firm grasp, which was hidden from view by the velvet of her mantle. The ceremony went off without a hitch and when the bride and groom had signed the register they processed back down the aisle followed by the guests. Carriages were waiting outside to take everyone to Greystone Park and Rosalind made sure that the children were safely ensconced in the landau with Aurelia and Sylvia before she went to find the Rockwood barouche. She could see Alexander waiting for her but as she passed through the graveyard she was accosted by a woman wrapped in a dingy black cloak.

'Mrs Blanchard, ma'am.'

Rosalind came to a sudden halt. 'Who are you?'

The woman glanced round nervously before pushing her hood back so that Rosalind could see her face. 'Do you remember me, ma'am?'

'Of course I do. You're Mrs Trimble. What can I do for you?'

Emmie Trimble glanced round again. 'I mustn't be seen. Trimble will kill me if he finds out I've been to see you.'

'Tell me what's wrong. Is it about Tommy?'

'No, missis. It's your husband who's in danger. He knows too much and they're out to silence him.'

'I'm sorry, but I don't know what you're talking about, Mrs Trimble.'

'No, you wouldn't, I suppose.' Emmie backed behind a tombstone. 'I'm risking my own life by coming here, ma'am. Trimble is mixed up with a smuggling gang from Plymouth.'

'But surely the gangs were broken up long ago, and smuggling as such doesn't exist these days.'

'The government thinks they have it under control but they don't know the amount that goes undetected. There's a lot of money in it and your husband has been involved for a long time, but if he turns Queen's evidence he could put the gangs away for a very long time, and that includes Trimble.'

'Your husband is in prison, I believe, Mrs Trimble.'

'He was due out on parole when he spotted you and the baby. My friend saw it all, ma'am. I don't hold no blame on you, but Ezra is back in prison and your old man is in danger.'

'Are you telling me that Mr Trimble is intent on harming my husband?'

'Not him personally. He's not a killer, but he knows them as will do the deed, for the right amount of money.'

'What can I do about it? How can I save my husband?'

'Get to him before the trial, ma'am. Warn him what will happen if he gives names and details. That's all I can suggest. If it means he does a longer stretch it's better than what will befall him, if you get my meaning.' Emmie looked over her shoulder. 'I got to go, ma'am. Think about what I said.'

Chapter Twenty-One

'Rosie, is everything all right?'

Alexander had come up behind her without Rosalind noticing. She turned her head to meet his anxious glance with a smile. 'Nothing to worry about, Alex.'

'Who was that woman?'

Rosalind looked round, but Emmie had vanished into a stand of yew trees. 'She's Trimble's wife. The man who sold Tommy to the chimney sweep.'

'I remember, but what did she want with you?'

'She said that Piers will be in danger from the gangs if he turns Queen's evidence.'

'I really don't know what he's got himself into, Rosie, and that's the truth.'

'He swore to me that he would never break the law again. I can't believe that he's been lying to me for the last three years.'

'I wasn't going to tell you until later, but the business is in a sorry state. Piers has been using the profits from the mining company to fund his excursions abroad, and whatever money he's made from illegal dealings, he hasn't been putting it back in the company. Pedrick seems to have been party to his dealings, and I was forced to sack him, and give his job to Martin Gibbs, the young under manager, on a temporary basis. I should have stayed in Cornwall, but I wanted to come home in time for the trial. I really need to speak to my brother.'

'I went to the prison but he refused to see me.'

'I'm not surprised by that. Anyway, it's not the sort of place you should go, Rosie. You are the innocent party in all this, and as far as I'm concerned my brother can rot in prison for the rest of his life.'

'We don't know his side of things, Alex.'

He glanced over his shoulder. 'We should make a move. I left Hester in the barouche. The children went on with Sylvia and Aurelia, but Hester wouldn't leave without you.'

'I suppose we'll have to go to the reception, although I really don't feel like it.'

'Come on, Rosie. There's nothing we can do today. We have a wedding breakfast to attend and Patsy won't want to see you looking sad. It's her big day, after all.'

'All right, Alex, but I'm going to see Piers before the trial and nothing will prevent me.'

* * *

The reception was, as Rosalind had anticipated, lavish almost to the point of vulgarity. Sir Michael had spared no expense when it came to introducing his new bride to friends and political colleagues. Rosalind could see that the guests from London were quietly impressed, although the local gentry obviously thought that Sir Michael had gone too far, and many of the older members of society frowned on the match anyway. Patricia, however, seemed oblivious to any undercurrents of disapproval and she wore the mantle of Lady Greystone as if it had been made solely for her. Rosalind knew that her sister was acting the part but Christina did not seem to be amused. She clung to Oscar's arm as if she were afraid to let him go and it was obvious that she resented having a stepmother similar in age to herself. After her mother's early demise Christina had taken on the role of hostess, and it was clear that she evidently did not like being usurped by her old friend. Sylvia bore the change in circumstances with better grace.

Louise and her parents were guests but Louise had volunteered to look after Tommy and Nancy, and keep an eye on Dolly, who had been left in the care of Ivy, one of Sir Michael's most trusted housemaids. This left Rosalind free to enjoy socialising without having to worry about her baby, and confident of knowing that she would be called upon when Dolly awakened for her next feed.

She was on her way to the nursery when Hester

waylaid her. 'You really should think about hiring a wet nurse, poppet. I know you adore the little scrap, but you will be tied to her until she is old enough to be weaned.'

Rosalind smiled. 'I wouldn't have it any other way, Hester. To tell you the truth I'm glad of the excuse to leave the party for a while. I've had quite enough of Patsy acting as if she's been crowned Queen of England, and Sylvia is following Alex like a devoted puppy.'

'He's an eligible bachelor, Rosie. That's a fact you shouldn't forget. I doubt if he'll remain your devoted admirer for the rest of his life.'

'Hester! That's uncalled for.'

'Maybe, but it's true nonetheless. You are married to Piers, and even if you were divorced or widowed you still couldn't marry his brother. It's against the law.'

'I know that. You don't have to remind me again, Hester. Alex is my good friend and I want it to stay that way. If he finds someone to love and who returns his feelings I'll be happy for both of them.'

'Forgive me if I don't believe you.' Hester gave her a quick hug. 'Go and look after the little one, and then come back and enjoy the party.'

Rosalind had nothing to say to this and she made her way to the old nursery where she found Louise rocking Dolly in her arms.

'You should be dancing the night away, Louise.'

'I'm not much of a dancer to tell the truth. I might

venture on the floor if Walter were here, but he couldn't get permission to return home so soon after the start of the new term. His professor is very strict.'

'He'll be taking his finals next year and then he'll come home for good.'

'I don't expect anything from him, Rosie.' Louise placed Dolly gently in Rosalind's arms. 'She is a beautiful baby. You are so lucky to have her.'

'I am, but one day you'll have your own children and you'll think they are the most beautiful babies in the world.'

'I hope so.' Louise blushed rosily.

'Walter will propose, I'm sure of it. He's just waiting for the right time, Louise.'

'I'm older than him.'

'Only a few years. Look at Patsy and Sir Michael – he's old enough to be her father. If it doesn't matter with them why should a few years worry you?'

Louise giggled. 'Well, if you put it that way, I suppose it's immaterial. I do love Walter and I think he loves me, but he's never said so.'

'Walter isn't very demonstrative, but I'm sure he cares for you deeply.' Rosalind looked up as the door opened and Alex strolled into the room.

Louise leaped to her feet. 'Perhaps this isn't a good time, Captain Blanchard.' She glanced anxiously at Rosalind, who had Dolly clasped to her bare breast.

'I promise not to look,' Alex said cheerfully. 'I'm escaping from Miss Sylvia Greystone, who seems to have developed a crush on me.'

'Who could blame her?' Rosalind said, laughing.

'I'd better join my parents.' Louise made for the door. 'I can come back if you need me, Rosie. I sent Ivy to get some refreshment, but she should be back soon.' She shot a wary glance at Alexander as she left the room.

Rosalind laughed. 'You continue to shock people, Alex. I believe you do it on purpose.'

'Why shouldn't I be present? We are family, after all, and I adore the little mite. She has your eyes, Rosie.'

'Alex, be serious for once. What are we going to do? If Piers is convicted and sent to prison and the clay mine has to be sold, Rockwood is going to be in the same financial state as it was three years ago.'

'All the more reason for Piers to turn Queen's evidence in return for a shorter sentence. He created this mess and he's the one who knows how to restore the finances of the clay mine and Trevenor. I refuse to allow him to bankrupt the estate. It would kill Grandmama if she lost everything because of my brother's criminal activities.'

'Then we must see Piers before the trial. We only have a couple of days, Alex.'

'You're not to go on your own. If you want to see him I'll go with you.'

The bride and groom left next day for their brief honeymoon in London. Patricia had expressed a desire to visit Paris or Rome, but Sir Michael would hear none of it. It would, he said, be prudent to establish themselves in the town house. Patricia boasted that he had given her unlimited funds with which to purchase a whole new wardrobe, and she intended on visiting all the fashionable couturiers in London, as well as furniture warehouses to make up for being denied a luxurious honeymoon.

Rosalind was glad that her sister was happy, but she herself had other matters on her mind, and that afternoon she and Alex left for Exeter prison in the barouche, leaving Dolly in Hester's care. It was the first time that Rosalind had been parted from her baby, but after her shocking experience outside the prison on her last visit, she had no intention of placing Dolly in danger. The trial was due to begin in two days' time, and although they were at first refused admission, Rosalind made an impassioned plea to see her husband, which would have melted the hardest heart, and the warder hurried off to gain permission from the prison governor.

Rosalind and Alex waited in a small, cold room with bars at the window and hard wooden chairs. It was not the most welcoming place and the smell of urine and excrement was faint but still sickening in its intensity. The noxious smells grew worse when the warder returned and, having gained assent from the governor, he led them through a maze of corridors divided by locked doors. The sound of men crying was new to Rosalind and she found that more shocking than the shouted insults and oaths that followed them wherever they went.

Piers was in a tiny cell with only a wooden bed frame, a bucket and a single chair to provide for his needs. He was in need of a shave, his hair was tangled and his clothes filthy. Rosalind was shocked by his appearance and he turned away when he saw them.

'I said I didn't want to see anyone,' he said gruffly.

'You've got ten minutes, no longer.' The warder locked them in the cell and the sound of his boots thudding on the flagstones echoed off the walls.

'We had to see you, Piers.' Rosalind barely recognised this scarecrow of a man as her debonair husband. She clasped her hands firmly in front of her in an attempt to stop them trembling. 'I'm so sorry to see you like this.'

He shot her a sideways glance. 'You shouldn't have come. I didn't want you to visit this place. You should know better than to bring her here, Alex.'

'Piers, old chap, you have to listen to her. Trimble accosted her last time she tried to see you and he threatened your child. You are responsible for their lives, not just your own.'

'Trimble is back in his cell. I can hear him ranting away at night. There's no sleeping in a place like this.'

'And you'll spend the best part of your life here if you don't turn Queen's evidence, Piers.' Rosalind lowered her voice. If they could hear the other prisoners it was possible they could be overheard too, and all would be lost. 'I know it's dangerous, but you will clear your name and we can be a family again.'

'And if I do that I'll be putting you all in danger as well as myself. I'm in too deep to get away with it, Rosie. I was fool enough to get mixed up with the gang in Plymouth. Our ship was wrecked by rivals in France. I was lucky to survive then but they will get me for certain if I turn against them, and not only me. You and the child will be in danger, too.'

'The child has a name, Piers. Your daughter will be christened Adela, but we call her Dolly. She is so beautiful – you must try to shorten your sentence in any way you can. Otherwise she won't know you.'

Piers shook his head. 'It isn't that simple, Rosie. I'm sorry to have let you down so badly. I wanted to make us rich, but all I've done is to ruin everything.'

Alex grabbed him by the shoulders and shook him hard. 'Stop feeling sorry for yourself. You have made a mess of things, but you can at least come out of this with some dignity if you turn Queen's evidence against the gangs. If the police catch them, or at least disperse them, you'll be safer than if you remain in this place.'

'Trimble is out to get you, Piers,' Rosalind added tearfully. 'His wife came all the way to Rockwood to warn me that they are planning to kill you.'

Piers sank down on the hard board that served as his bed. 'Maybe that would be a kindness to all of you. I've done you nothing but harm. I should never have married you, but I did love you, Rosie. I want you to believe that.'

'I do believe you, Piers. I don't want to leave you in this awful place. Please collaborate with the authorities so that we can get you out of here.'

Alex shook his head. 'I can hear the warder approaching, Piers. Stop being a stubborn fool and agree to do what your wife asks.' He put his hand in his pocket and drew out a leather pouch that jingled convincingly as he dropped it onto the bed. 'There's enough money there to get you tidied up for your court appearance.'

'Thank you.' Piers buried his head in his hands. 'I'm grateful, but please don't come here again, and I don't want to see you at the trial, Rosie. Remember the good days, if you can.'

Before Rosalind could speak the door opened and the warder beckoned to them. 'Time's up. You have to leave now.'

'Take care of her, Alex,' Piers mumbled as the warder ushered them out, slammed the door and turned the key in the lock.

Alexander placed a protective arm around Rosalind's shoulders as they retraced their steps through the foul-smelling corridors to the main entrance.

Rosalind took a deep breath of fresh air as she stepped outside. 'That is the most horrible place imaginable. I hate seeing him like that, no matter what he's done.'

'I know, Rosie. Try to put it out of your mind, if you can. We have a good lawyer to speak up for him and I'll attend the trial.'

'I want to be there.'

'You heard what Piers said. He doesn't want you to witness his humiliation, and I for one can understand that. You should honour his wishes.'

'I suppose so, but you'll tell me everything?'

'Yes, I promise I will.' Alexander handed her into the waiting carriage. 'Home, Gurney.' He climbed in beside her and she laid her head on his shoulder. Whatever Piers had done, she had a feeling that he had already paid dearly for his wrongdoings.

Aurelia was waiting for them when they returned to Rockwood. She demanded to know the truth about the conditions in which Piers had been confined, and although Rosalind tried to make it sound better than it was, Aurelia was genuinely upset and in floods of tears.

'How can you talk about it so calmly?' she demanded, sobbing. 'Poor Piers, he might have done bad things but he doesn't deserve such treatment.'

'I agree,' Rosalind said gently. 'No one should be kept like that. We treat our animals better.'

'What are you going to do about it then? Why should my brother suffer so?'

'Stop being so melodramatic, Aurelia,' Alex said sharply. 'Can't you see how hard this is on Rosie?'

'You never think about anyone else,' Aurelia cried

angrily. 'Anyone would think she was your wife and Piers meant nothing to her.'

'That's not fair.' Rosalind sent a warning glance to Alexander. 'We were both very distressed, but we didn't want to upset you any more than necessary. Piers has his trial coming up the day after tomorrow, and we both begged him to turn Queen's evidence and have his sentence commuted.'

'Even that has its dangers,' Alexander added seriously. 'He might serve less time in prison but the gangs are run by vicious men and if Piers followed that path he might endanger our lives as well as his own.'

'I can't believe that my brother could have dealt with such dreadful people.' Aurelia mopped her eyes with her handkerchief. 'I want to go home to Grandmama, Alex. I don't want to stay here.'

'I have to attend the trial,' Alexander said patiently. 'But as soon as it's over I'll take you back to Trevenor. There was precious little money left to run the mine, but I'll see what I can do to restore it to its full potential.'

On the day of the trial the hours seemed to last twice as long as they did normally. Rosalind did her best to keep busy. In the morning, after Alex had left for Exeter, she did her rounds of the tenants on horseback with Dolly strapped to her chest in a sling. Hester had done her best to dissuade her from taking the baby but Rosalind was determined to make Dolly as much a part of Rockwood as possible from the very earliest age. When her child was old enough to ride a pony she would take her on a leading rein, and everyone in Rockwood village would know Miss Adela Blanchard. But for now Dolly was still a tiny baby and as such she drew admiring comments from the farmers' wives and anyone Rosalind met during her travels. It seemed that the whole village knew about the trial and she received sympathetic glances, although very few people took it upon themselves to wish for a successful outcome.

At the end of an exhausting day, Rosalind arrived back at the castle in time to feed Dolly and put her to bed, leaving her under the watchful eye of Molly Greep, whose position as lady's maid had ended abruptly when Patricia decided to live at Greystone Park. Molly had been used to caring for her younger siblings and she clearly adored Dolly, which made her an ideal nanny. Rosalind emerged from the nursery and met Louise coming out of the school-room.

'I thought you would have gone home ages ago, Louise.'

'I like to make sure that Nancy and Tommy get a proper supper. I don't think Mrs Jackson takes them seriously. Sometimes she forgets them altogether and they have to go down to the kitchen and ask for food. I'm afraid she doesn't see them as members of the family.'

'I'll have another word with her and explain their position, but you shouldn't have to give up so much of your time to us, Louise. You have a life of your own outside the walls of Rockwood.'

'I don't mind. In fact I rather enjoy acting as surrogate aunt to the children. They need as much attention and affection as we can give them. I can't imagine what it would be like to have suffered as they did before you rescued them.'

'You're right, of course. I sometimes forget that they haven't always been with us. I love them both and I want the best in life for them. You put me to shame, Louise. I should give them more of my time.'

'You have enough to worry about.' Louise eyed her warily. 'Do you expect Alexander to return this evening?'

'He said he would come home the moment he knew the verdict. I won't be able to sleep until I know what's happening.'

'Would you like me to stay? I could send a note to my parents to tell them I'll come home later.'

'No, but thank you all the same. I'll dine early and I'll sit with the children until bedtime. I'll tell them more of the star story I made up to amuse them.'

Louise smiled. 'That's a splendid idea. They are really good company when you get them talking. But if you're certain you don't need me I'd better make my way home. Mama worries if I'm out after dark.'

'I'll say good night then, and I hope I have some good news when I see you in the morning.'

Louise nodded and walked away, leaving Rosalind standing in the draughty corridor with the candles flickering and the sound of the wind buffeting the stone walls outside. She shivered and wrapped her shawl more tightly around her. She knew she would not get a wink of sleep until Alex returned, and she would wait up all night if necessary.

Rosalind ate little at dinner that evening and Aurelia barely touched the food on her plate. The only person who enjoyed the saddle of lamb was Hester, whose appetite seemed undiminished by the tension in the room.

Aurelia threw down her napkin and jumped to her feet. 'I can't sit here and watch you stuffing yourself, Hester. How can you be so calm when Piers might be facing a life sentence or even transportation?'

'Starving yourself won't affect the outcome of the trial either way,' Hester said calmly. 'Sit down and finish your food, Aurelia.'

'I can't stand it here any longer. As soon as Alex returns I'm going to make him take me back to Trevenor.'

'If that's what you want, then you must do so.' Rosalind managed a smile with difficulty. 'It's entirely your choice, although I will miss you and so will Dolly.'

Aurelia shrugged. 'Dolly is a tiny baby. She won't even know I've gone.'

'At least sit down and finish your meal,' Hester said crossly. 'You won't bring Alexander home any faster by pacing the floor.'

'I have a headache. I'm going to my room.' Aurelia opened the door. 'I want to know when Alex arrives. Please send a maid to tell me.' She left the room and the door swung slowly on its hinges, closing with a loud click.

'I for one shan't be sad to see the back of that young madam,' Hester said, wiping her lips on her napkin. 'Lady Pentelow has spoiled her.'

'Perhaps, but she's as anxious about Piers as we are.'

'I would be more worried about the criminals who will be causing us problems if the trial doesn't go their way. Piers is to blame, Rosie. You need to stop forgiving him and make him take responsibility for his actions. He's been nothing but trouble since that day when he first landed in the cove with the smugglers. You were almost killed when you fell onto the rocks.'

Rosalind laughed in spite of everything. 'I had a bump on the head, and Piers carried me home. We were children then.'

'Well, he's not a child now, poppet. He's a married man with a wife and child to support. Even if he turns Queen's evidence it's likely he will still have to serve part of his sentence. The judge is unlikely to set him free.'

Rosalind rose to her feet. 'I challenge you to a game of backgammon, Hester. Let's do something to pass the time, although I'm not sure I'll be able to concentrate.'

'All right, if it takes your mind off everything I'll play, but I warn you I intend to win.'

The candles in the drawing room were guttering after they finished the last of three games, and Hester kept nodding off between throws of the dice. Rosalind shook her gently and suggested that it was time for bed.

Hester yawned. 'I'm happy to wait up with you, poppet. Although you really should try to get some sleep. Alex might not arrive home until tomorrow, or the trial might not have ended.'

'I'll stay up a bit longer, Hester, but I want you to go to bed. You look exhausted.'

Hester heaved herself from her chair. 'I must admit I'm tired, but if you need me in the night just call me.'

'I will, of course. Good night, Hester. Sleep tight.'

'That's a very vulgar term, Rosie. Your mama would not think it proper.'

'Mama barely acknowledges our existence. At this moment she's probably singing her heart out in Italy. Heaven knows when she and Claude will return to Rockwood.'

'Felicia always did what she wanted and I'm sorry to say that Patricia is the same. Good night, poppet.'

Hester made her way slowly from the room, and the draught from the door extinguished the candles on the mantelshelf.

Rosalind sat by the dying embers of the fire and felt herself nodding, but she was determined to stay up until Alex returned. She was awakened in the early hours by Molly, who deposited a squalling baby on her lap.

'I'm sorry, ma'am, but she's ready for a feed.'

'That's all right, Molly,' Rosalind said sleepily. 'I'll look after her for the rest of the night. You may go to bed.'

Molly bobbed a curtsey and hurried from the room. Rosalind settled down with Dolly at her breast, but eventually the chill in the room forced her to take the baby up the grand staircase to her bedroom. The fire in the grate had also burned down to embers, and she laid the now sleeping baby on a pillow while she undressed and climbed into bed beside her daughter. No matter how hard she tried to keep awake it was not long before Rosalind's eyes closed and she snuggled up beside Dolly, breathing in the delightful milky scent of her baby.

She was awakened by the sound of the door creaking as it opened and in a shaft of light from an oil lamp she saw Alexander, still dressed in his outdoor garments.

'What happened in court? What was the verdict, Alex?'

Chapter Twenty-Two

'It couldn't have been worse, Rosie.' Alexander peeled off his leather gloves and shrugged off his greatcoat. 'It wasn't something that any of us were expecting.'

'For heaven's sake tell me, Alex.'

He sat on the edge of the bed, taking her hand in his. 'Transportation to Australia, Rosie. Piers was sentenced to seven years in a penal colony.'

'But that's not fair – he didn't murder anyone or rob a bank. He's done wrong, but he didn't deserve such a harsh sentence.'

'Trimble was amongst others who threatened him if he turned Queen's evidence. I think in that case this was probably the best option. If he obeys the rules he could get a ticket of leave in four years.'

'But Australia is so far away. Is there no way he can appeal against such a harsh sentence?'

'I spoke to his lawyer but he seemed to think that it would be a waste of time. In the circumstances he said that Piers would be safer in the penal colony than he would in prison here.'

'If only he had been honest with me from the start. Maybe the curse of the Careys has come back to haunt us.'

Alexander raised her hand to his lips. 'I don't believe in that sort of thing, and neither should you. I'd better go and let you get some sleep, if the little maid will allow it.'

'Don't leave me, Alex.' Rosalind caught hold of his hand. 'No one knows you are here. I just don't want to sleep on my own tonight.'

When Rosalind awoke next morning she was alone in her bed except for Dolly, who was starting to cry. For a few moments Rosalind wondered if she had dreamed that Alex climbed into bed with her in the middle of the night, and then she remembered the devastating news that her husband was to be transported to the colonies. She took care of Dolly's needs before rising from her warm bed. It was still very early, but there was a sliver of light dividing the sky from the land in the east. She could only be grateful to Alexander for rising before the housemaid came to light the fire, and she washed in cold water before dressing and putting up her hair. She picked up Dolly and was about to leave for the nursery when Jennet Madge, the new housemaid, staggered into the room with a bucket of coal and a bundle of kindling.

'Good morning, Jennet. You may light the fire. I'm just taking Miss Dolly to the nursery.' Rosalind stifled a sigh of relief. Asking Alexander to sleep in her bed had been a stupid mistake, but the comfort of his strength and nearness had kept away the night terrors, and made the bad news easier to bear, for the time being at least.

She hurried to the nursery where Molly was up and preparing to look after the baby. Having left Dolly in her capable hands, Rosalind made her way to the dining room where Tilly was laying the table for breakfast.

'Captain Alexander came home very late last night, Tilly. Have you seen him this morning?'

'Yes, ma'am. He's in the kitchen eating his breakfast. I said I would bring it to the dining room but he said it didn't matter. I had to take a cup of chocolate upstairs for Miss Aurelia.'

'I expect she'll be down in a while. Will you tell Mrs Jackson that I'll just have a boiled egg and some toast for breakfast, and a pot of coffee, of course?'

'Yes, ma'am.' Tilly bobbed a curtsey and hurried from the room.

Rosalind took her seat at the table. She knew that Alexander would join her when Tilly passed on the message to Cook, and she was not disappointed. Minutes later he entered the room.

'How are you this morning, Rosie?'

'I don't know, Alex. I feel quite numb. I suppose I was expecting bad news after the trial, but I hoped that if Piers gave evidence against the other criminals the judge might commute his sentence.'

'Seven years is better than life. Maybe it will do him good in the long run. Piers has been cheating us all for years, especially you. I hate to think how Grandmama will take the news. He was always her favourite, apart from Aurelia, of course.'

'Are you going to take her to Trevenor today?'

'Yes. I promised that I would and I need to make sure that Martin Gibbs is doing his job well enough to leave him in charge.'

'You don't intend to stay and run the business yourself?'

'I still know virtually nothing about running a clay mine or selling the product. I'm a soldier, Rosie. I doubt if I could ever be anything else, despite my gammy leg.'

'What will you do, Alex? Will you live here?'

He took a seat beside her at the table. 'That's what I want most in the world, but it's even more difficult now. I have your reputation to consider and I would never do anything to harm you or Dolly. Whether you like it or not you have had the responsibility for this old pile of rocks thrust upon you by Bertie's absence. He's the one who ought to give up the army and take over the running of Rockwood.'

'The army is Bertie's life.'

'I know that, and it was mine until the accident changed things for ever.' He reached out and caressed her cheek. 'But if that hadn't happened we would never have been reunited as we were in the château. It was just you and me then, Rosie.'

She smiled. 'And Hester, of course.'

'You know what I mean. But we can't live like that here.'

A sudden stab of fear hit her as forcibly as a blow from a fist. 'You're leaving for good?'

'There's no other way. Last night I held you close, but that mustn't happen again.'

'You're right, of course. But I don't want you to leave. Where will you go?'

'I might be able to get my job back at the War Office. Ideally I'd like to rejoin my regiment, but I doubt if they'll take me back in the army.'

'You'd risk your life in the Crimea to get away from me?'

'Not you, my love. You will always be in my heart wherever I go. I want you to believe that, but if I stay here it's not only your reputation that will be tarnished. Think of Dolly growing up in a home tainted by scandal. I love her as if she were my own child, and I wouldn't want her to suffer because of something I had done.'

Rosalind turned away, unable to look him in the face. The truth was there, trembling on her lips but if she spoke it could spell disaster. The Rockwood curse seemed to be fulfilling itself with a vengeance. 'You're right, I suppose.'

'Look at me, Rosie,' Alexander reached for her hand and held it in a tender clasp. 'Tell me to my face that you understand why I must do this.'

She shot him a sideways glance. 'I do. I know you're right, but it still hurts.'

His reply was lost as the door burst open and Aurelia rushed into the room. 'Oh, there you are, Alex. Why are you lolling about in here when we should be on the road to Trevenor?'

'You must have some breakfast before you go,' Rosalind said firmly. 'It's a long journey.'

'I'm not hungry. Come on, Alex. I should think Rosie has had quite enough of us to last a lifetime.'

'Don't you want to know what happened at the trial?' Alexander pushed back his chair, but he did not release Rosalind's hand. 'Aren't you concerned about our brother?'

'Of course I am, but as he isn't here I suppose they must have locked him up. I think he deserves it anyway, for bringing shame on the family.'

'The judge sentenced him to seven years' transportation.'

Aurelia shrugged. 'Oh, well, I suppose it could be worse. Piers broke the law and he's paying for it, but Grandmama is going to be very upset, which is why we should leave immediately.'

'Sit down and have some breakfast, Aurelia,' Alexander said firmly. 'I'll send for the carriage. I suppose you're packed and ready to go?' He gave Rosalind's hand a final squeeze before rising to his feet. 'Eat something, Aurelia. I don't want you fainting away on the station platform because you were too lazy to have breakfast.'

'I'm not lazy, I'm just not hungry. Anyway, what time did you return last night? I waited up for hours.'

'I stayed up playing backgammon with Hester,' Rosalind said casually. 'Alex hadn't come home by the time I retired to my room. Anyway, does it matter? You have a long journey ahead of you so please just eat some toast and have a cup of coffee. I can hear Tilly coming now.'

Alexander opened the door and Tilly hurried in carrying a laden tray, which she set down on the sideboard.

'I'll go to the stables myself,' Alexander left the room before Aurelia had a chance to question him further.

'Is that boiled egg for me?' Aurelia took it from the tray and went to sit in her usual seat at the table. 'I might as well eat it as it's here. Pour me a coffee, Rosie. I might not get a chance for refreshment until we reach Plymouth. I know what Alex is like when he sets his mind on getting somewhere. He forgets that we lesser mortals need sustenance. You'll be glad to be rid of us, I dare say.'

Rosalind filled a cup with coffee and passed it to her. 'I will miss you all equally.'

'Maybe you'll miss one of us more than the rest?' Aurelia said with a knowing smile.

'Of course. It will be a long time before I see Piers again, unless he gets remission for good behaviour.'

'I wasn't thinking of that brother, but I could be mistaken, I suppose.'

'If you're referring to Alex, then yes, I will miss him, too. He's been so supportive since Piers went to prison.'

'And he's devoted to Dolly. I would never have imagined that my soldier brother could be so fond of a squalling infant.'

Rosalind could stand no more of Aurelia's very unsubtle hints and she stood up. 'It's time for her next feed. Thank you for reminding me. I probably won't see you again before you leave, so I hope you have a good journey. Say goodbye to Alex for me and please give my kindest regards to your grandmama.'

Rosalind hurried from the room, choking back tears. She knew that if she allowed herself to cry she would not be able to stop.

The next few weeks passed in a haze of numbness whereby Rosalind felt no pain nor any pleasure in anything other than caring for her baby. It might have been easier had Alex stayed to share the burden placed upon her, but he had not returned from Trevenor. Although she knew in her heart that this was for the best, it felt like a bereavement. She lost her appetite, which worried Hester so much that

Rosalind pretended to eat, although nothing tasted as it should. She fed most of her meals to Bob, who obligingly sat beside her chair in the dining room, looking up at her with adoring and hopeful eyes. At the beginning of December she had lost a visible amount of weight and, worse still, her milk had all but dried up, leaving Dolly constantly hungry and crying miserably.

Hester watched Rosalind's attempts to feed her child with a worried frown. 'We all sympathise with you, Rosie. It's hard knowing that Piers will be away from England for such a long time, but you must try to get over the shock, if only for Dolly's sake. You need to eat and sleep well if you're to provide her with sustenance.'

Rosalind shook her head wearily. 'I know. I'm trying, Hester.'

'It's time to consider a wet nurse, poppet. I think a change of scene would do you the world of good, too.'

Rosalind looked up, startled. 'What do you mean? I'm not going to Trevenor, if that's what you're suggesting.'

'No, of course not. You've done well to send Alexander away and that's where he belongs. I was thinking more of London. Patsy has invited you to stay in their smart new home, so why don't you accept?'

'Leave Rockwood? Who would look after everything here?'

Hester pulled a face. 'I managed very well when

I was housekeeping for your dear departed grand-papa. I didn't oversee the estate, of course, but I think it could run on its own for the amount of time you would be away. Winter is here and soon it will be Christmas.'

The idea had not occurred to Rosalind until now, but suddenly a few days or even a couple of weeks in London seemed like a good idea. She was exhausted and at every turn there were reminders of Alexander and the happy times they had spent together. Dolly was demanding and feeding times often ended with Rosalind in tears and Dolly squalling in frustration.

'All right, Hester. I agree.'

'You agree to a wet nurse or the visit to London?'

'To both. I can't look after Dolly as I should and it's breaking my heart. Do you know of a suitable person?'

'As a matter of fact I do. Widow Madge has just given birth again.'

'But she's not married.'

'Precisely, and because of that she needs money. There's no poor relief now, especially for unmarried mothers, but she's a good woman. Men take advantage of her nice nature, and she has little enough to live on as it is.'

'She delivered Dolly. I probably owe her my life.'

'So you will take her on?'

'But that means I can't take Dolly with me when I go to London.'

'Be sensible, poppet. You need to get away from here or you will fall sick and you'll be no use to any of us, least of all your daughter. Widow Madge knows more about babies than most and she'll be like a second mother to Dolly. Go for a week at least – two weeks would be better. Forget about everything here and enjoy yourself for a change.'

Before Rosalind had really come to terms with the idea she found herself on the train to London. Hester had taken over the household as she had in the past, and a letter had been sent by special messenger to Lady Greystone at her home in Duke Street. The same messenger had returned with a reply, and everything had been arranged without Rosalind having to do anything. She was met at the station by a liveried footman who took care of her luggage and led her to a waiting carriage.

The streets of London flashed past the window, bringing back memories of her first visit when she and Patricia had been desperate for money and had ventured to the capital to ask their mother for financial help. It was then that she had met Piers for the first time as an adult. She had not recognised him as the boy from the smugglers' ship, and it was during that visit they had formed a mutual attraction. Now, over three years later, she was in London to forget the misery that he had caused by his failure to reform. Her arms ached to hold her baby, but common sense had convinced her that she was here to recuperate and regain her equilibrium. Dolly had settled down in the care of Eliza Madge with surprising ease, leaving Rosalind slightly jealous but also relieved.

The elegant Georgian terraced house in Duke Street was in an ostentatiously affluent area. Private carriages stopped at the kerb to allow well-dressed house owners and their guests to alight, while road sweepers worked tirelessly to keep the surface of the road free from dung and detritus so that those wealthy enough to give generous tips could walk without soiling their boots or dainty shoes.

The footman leaped down to open the carriage door and assist Rosalind to step onto the pavement. Foster, Sir Michael's butler from Greystone Park, stood in the open doorway.

'Foster, it's good to see you here,' Rosalind said wearily. It was something of a relief to see a familiar face.

'Welcome to Duke Street, Mrs Blanchard. Will you follow me, please? Lady Greystone is expecting you.'

The marble-tiled entrance hall was square with a staircase leading up to a galleried first-floor landing. The drawing room was on this floor overlooking the street with two tall windows draped in grey velvet curtains. It was mid-afternoon but almost dark, and there were dozens of candles shining brightly in wall sconces as well as those in two ornate crystal chandeliers.

Patricia rose from a damask upholstered sofa in front of the fire and she rushed towards her sister.

'I am so delighted to see you, Rosie. I've really missed you.' She held her at arm's length. 'But you look awful. Hester said you were upset by the result of the trial and everything, and I can see what she meant.'

Rosalind managed a tired smile. 'It has been a trying time, but I had to leave Dolly with Widow Madge, that's the worst thing.'

'Yes, Hester told me in her letter, but she also said it was for the best. You've been wearing yourself out and I am to look after you and make sure that you eat properly. You're all skin and bone, as she would say.'

'You look blooming, Patsy. Married life obviously suits you.'

'It really does.' Patricia laughed merrily. 'To be honest, I'm quite surprised myself. I admit I married Greystone for his money and position, and he knows that, but it suits us both. Neither of us expects to be starry-eyed and romantic, and I have everything I could possibly want. I have a carriage at my disposal and I have a most generous dress allowance. Greystone and I attend dinner parties and soirées almost every night. We go to the theatre and mix with the most interesting people, and because I'm such a young bride I'm spoiled by the gentlemen. The ladies love to think they're taking me in hand and teaching me to survive in the world of politics. It's all a big romp.'

'I'm so happy for you. I was afraid it might not work out so well.'

'You worried needlessly. It's you who has had a bad time and you are by far a better person than I am.' Patricia sank down on the sofa and patted the seat beside her. 'Sit down and tell me everything that's been going on in that draughty old castle.'

'You know, I suppose, that Piers has received a hefty sentence.'

Patricia nodded. 'Yes, Greystone told me. He kept an eye on the proceedings. He tried to divert a scandal because it affects me as well as you, and if I'm involved it reflects badly on him. Politics is all a game, Rosie. If you're here long enough you'll find out.'

'I suppose it is. Nothing really has changed at Rockwood. Walter came home a week or so ago and I fully expect him to announce his engagement to Louise. She's been such a help to me, especially with the children. She adores Dolly and she's very fond of Nancy and Tommy. They're coming on so well with her tuition.'

'So you're going to keep them both, then?'

'Of course I am. Tommy is definitely Bertie's son. He gets more like him every day, and Nancy is a dear child.'

'I suppose Aurelia has gone back to Trevenor.'

'Yes, she went soon after the trial. Alex took her there himself. He wanted to check on the state of the clay mine that Piers almost bankrupted, but as he said, he's a soldier, not a businessman.'

'You don't know then?' Patricia put her head on one side. 'Alex returned to London. He tried to get a job at the War Office, but all the positions were filled. Greystone is friendly with most of the senior officers there.'

'He didn't succeed?'

'Alex is not a deskbound type of person. I could have told them that. The army rejected him again because of his leg injury, which he must have known would happen, but typical of Alex, he thought he could convince them that he was fit.'

Rosalind felt her head swim as the heat from the fire seemed to burn her like a fever. 'Where is he then? Did he return to Trevenor?'

'How would I know? I don't care what happens to him, and if he's fallen on hard times it's entirely his own fault. You were always too fond of him for your own good. It's fortunate he preferred me, because he would have led you a merry dance. Are you all right, Rosie? You've gone even whiter than when you walked through the door.'

'It's just fatigue after the long journey. I hated leaving Dolly, even though Widow Madge will be there to feed and comfort her. I feel as though I've left part of myself in Rockwood.'

Patricia laughed. 'You are Rockwood, silly. If you love anything it's that old pile of stones. You'll never escape from it, no matter how hard you try, but I'm going to do my best to take your mind off things. We're going to enjoy ourselves.'

'Yes, I suppose you're right.'

'I'll take you shopping in Peter Robinson, the departmental store that everyone is talking about, and we'll buy presents for everyone at home, even Hester, who's never approved of me.'

'Hester loves us all but in different ways. You do her an injustice, Patsy.'

'Perhaps, but it's you I'm concerned about at the moment. I expect you'd like to change out of your travelling costume and then we'll have afternoon tea. It's very popular amongst ladies of quality. Anyway, enough chitter-chatter, I'll show you to your room.'

'Thank you, Patsy.' Rosalind rose to her feet. 'I do need to unpack or my garments will be very creased.'

'Nonsense,' Patricia said airily. 'I've assigned a maid to look after you while you're here. Fletcher isn't a very experienced lady's maid, but even she knows how to unpack luggage.'

'There's really no need. I'm used to looking after myself.'

Patricia paused in the doorway. 'There's just one thing I should tell you before you meet Fletcher. She is one of Greystone's experiments in rehabilitating offenders.'

'She's been in prison?'

'Don't look so alarmed. Fletcher isn't dangerous, but she does know her way round London, and I'd advise you to take her with you should you wish to venture out on your own.'

'What did she do to end up behind bars?'

'She stole several items of jewellery, which she gave to her male friend who was a convicted felon. She was caught but he got away and disappeared south of the river. Anyway, she's part of a programme that Greystone hopes will be carried out nationally.'

'So I'm to be part of this experiment?' Rosalind sighed. 'You never fail to surprise me.'

'Well, you can hardly disagree with the plan, especially now that Piers is in prison for far worse offences. Anyway, you haven't any jewellery worth stealing so you're quite safe. Come with me, Rosie.'

Rosalind followed her sister along the wide landing to another flight of stairs, which led to the second floor. Her room was at the back of the house with a view of the small garden and the backs of yet more terraced town houses. Smoke from hundreds of tall chimneys billowed up into the sky, forming dark clouds, and desultory pigeons perched on slate rooftops, fluffing out their feathers in an attempt to keep warm.

Rosalind's luggage was piled up by the door and most of the valises and boxes had already been emptied. Tidy piles of garments were spread out on chairs and stools, and gowns were laid neatly on the bed, ready to be folded and placed in the mahogany clothes press. In the midst of this organised chaos stood a tall, thin woman with sharp angular features and an uncompromising expression. Her sleeves were rolled up, exposing muscular forearms as if she had been used to manual labour in the past, and her iron-grey hair was ruthlessly confined in a bun at the back of her neck. The frilly white cap she wore was tilted slightly to one side, giving her an odd unbalanced appearance.

'Rosie, this is Fletcher. She's going to look after you while you're in London.' Patricia gave Rosalind a gentle shove. 'If you have any particular instructions about how you want your clothing put away, you'd better say so now.'

'No, really. It looks as though you have everything in hand, Fletcher.'

Fletcher sketched a curtsey, eyeing Rosalind beneath pale lashes as if weighing her up.

'I'll leave you to get changed then, Rosie. Come down to the drawing room when you're ready.' Patricia backed out of the room, closing the door behind her.

'If you don't trust an old lag you'd best say so now, ma'am. But I ain't going to pinch nothing off you. I learned me lesson in stir.'

'Everyone deserves a second chance, Fletcher. As far as I can see you're very efficient and I'll be glad of your services.'

Fletcher nodded. 'You look done in, ma'am. Why don't you sit down and I'll find something for you to wear? Although you haven't much of a choice, if you want my opinion.'

'I live in the country, Fletcher. It's not so formal.'

'It ain't none of my business, anyway. But if I was

you I'd get her ladyship to treat you to a few new duds.'

Rosalind stifled a giggle. 'Thank you, Fletcher. Tell me, have you been a lady's maid before?'

'No, not me. I had a clothes stall in Rosemary Lane. I knows the difference between silk and shoddy.'

'I'm sure you do, and I'm perfectly happy to take your advice, but if you'll take a tip from me – it's not done for servants to speak to their masters or mistresses unless they are spoken to first. Even then it's best to keep one's opinions to oneself. I'm only telling you this so that you don't lose what might be a good job.'

Fletcher glared at her for a few seconds and then her stern features cracked into a half-smile. 'That's a polite way of telling me to keep me trap shut. I got you.' She selected a pale pink afternoon gown. 'You don't want to look even more washed out than you are. Sorry to be so bold, ma'am.'

'No, you're right. That will do nicely. Thank you, Fletcher.'

'Strip off, then, ma'am. We'll get you tidied up and ready to socialise.'

Rosalind took off her blouse and skirt and stood, shivering in her undergarments. Fletcher eyed her speculatively. 'You've given birth not so long ago.'

'Yes, I have a beautiful baby girl, but I had to leave her with a wet nurse.'

'I had a baby but she died young. That's what

happens when you live like what I done and go for days without food. You're lucky, ma'am.' Fletcher dropped the gown over Rosalind's head, dressing her as if she were a helpless child. 'You don't want to stay here too long, ma'am. London ain't the place for you. Take it from one who knows.' She fastened the tiny buttons at the back of Rosalind's bodice with surprisingly nimble fingers for one who had such large hands. 'There you are, ma'am. Now sit down and I'll do your hair. We don't want to send you downstairs looking as if you've been dragged through a hedge backwards, now, do we?'

'Thank you, Fletcher.' Rosalind sighed. 'It looks as if I'm going to need your help to survive in London society.'

'That's right, ma'am. If anyone does you down you just tell Cora Fletcher. They won't argue with me. Now take a seat at the dressing table, if you please.'

Twenty minutes later Rosalind entered the drawing room to find Patricia seated at a small table with a dainty afternoon tea spread out before her.

'You took your time, but you certainly look better now. Did Fletcher put your hair up?'

'Yes, she has surprisingly clever fingers. I thought I might be scalped, but she's very capable.'

'Don't let her talk to you like an equal, Rosie. She has to learn her place or she'll end up back on the streets. Remember, she is an experiment.'

'Yes, indeed. Are those cucumber sandwiches? They smell delicious.'

'You need to eat. You look as if you've been starving yourself and it isn't becoming.'

'I was plump after I had Dolly, but I'm back to normal now.' Rosalind helped herself to some tiny sandwiches.

'Greystone is dining out tonight, so we can have a quiet evening at home, but tomorrow night we're going to the theatre and we'll dine afterwards. We lead a very busy life, which suits me perfectly. Do try one of Cook's fancy cakes – she's a marvel in the kitchen.'

Rosalind smiled. 'You really are a new woman, Patsy. I think marriage suits you.'

Chapter Twenty-Three

Patricia insisted that they go shopping next day and they set off in the Greystone barouche. Their first stop was Peter Robinson, the recently opened departmental store, which was decorated in readiness for Christmas, as were most of the shops in Regent Street and Oxford Street. Patricia spent what to Rosalind was a fortune, but her sister carelessly wrote it off as petty expenses. She insisted on treating Rosalind to several new gowns and a lace shawl, and for herself Patricia bought a random selection of gloves, scarves and anything that caught her fancy. In the afternoon they visited Noah's Ark, Mr Hamley's shop in High Holborn, where Rosalind purchased toys for the children, including a new set of lead soldiers for Tommy, and a rather beautiful French doll with a china face and hands for

Nancy. She took her time in choosing a large rag doll and a colourful rattle for Dolly.

That evening they attended the Lyceum Theatre, just off the Strand, to watch a performance of *The Haunted House*, a farce that Rosalind found surprisingly entertaining, although she was exhausted after her shopping expedition with Patricia, who seemed completely tireless. They dined afterwards at Simpson's and Rosalind enjoyed the thrill of eating in such a prestigious restaurant, which Patricia assured her was frequented by eminent personages. They were just finishing their meal when Rosalind spotted a familiar face. She smiled and waved, receiving a disapproving frown from Patricia.

'It's Colonel Munday, Patsy,' Rosalind said hastily. 'We became acquainted in France when we were staying at the château.' Despite her sister's obvious annoyance, Rosalind rose to her feet and was immediately wrapped in a warm embrace by Colonel Munday.

'My dear Mrs Blanchard, this is a pleasant surprise. What brings you to London?'

Rosalind drew away, aware that they were causing a stir amongst the other diners.

'I'm staying with my sister and her husband, Sir Michael Greystone.' Rosalind shot a wary glance in Sir Michael's direction, but he stood up, holding out his hand.

'I believe we met recently at a charity ball, Colonel?'

'Yes, sir, so we did.' Colonel Munday shook his hand.

'May I present you to my wife, Lady Greystone?' Sir Michael inclined his head in Patricia's direction and she smiled sweetly.

'How do you so, Colonel? I think you attended the reception at Guildhall, but I don't think we were introduced at the time.'

'I would have remembered you, my lady,' Colonel Munday said gallantly.

'Won't you join us for coffee, Colonel?' Sir Michael resumed his seat and signalled to a waiter who was hovering nearby.

'Thank you, but I am with friends. Another time, maybe, Sir Michael.' Colonel Munday drew Rosalind aside. 'My dear, are you aware that Alexander is back in London?'

Rosalind shot an anxious glance at her sister, but Patricia had turned away to speak to her husband. 'Yes, Colonel. Do you know where he is?'

Colonel Munday shook his head. 'It's a bad business, Rosalind. He refused to return to Devonshire or his old home in Cornwall, and he's taken a poorly paid job as a clerk in Doctors' Commons.'

Rosalind stared at him in horror. 'But he's a professional soldier.'

'What are you talking about?' Patricia demanded, breaking into their conversation. 'Rosie, please sit down. You're making a spectacle of yourself.'

'Yes, yes, in a minute,' Rosalind said impatiently. 'Where is he living, Colonel?'

'He has a room above a printing shop in Hanging Sword Alley. I haven't been there myself, but I know the area and it isn't a suitable place for anyone to live.' He put his hand in his pocket and took out a silver case from which he produced a visiting card. 'My address in London, if you would care to contact me. I have to go now, but I hope we meet again soon.'

Rosalind watched him walk away with a feeling of dread. She had hoped that Alexander might have found some kind of employment commensurate with his abilities, but the information given by Colonel Munday filled her with horror. She knew that she would not rest until she had seen and spoken to Alex at least once more.

'Please sit down,' Patricia said crossly. 'What are you thinking of, Rosie?'

'I'm sorry. Colonel Munday was good to me when we were forced to spend so much time in France.' She sank down on her chair and sipped the coffee that the waiter had just placed in front of her.

When they arrived back in Duke Street, Rosalind pleaded fatigue and went straight to her room. Fletcher was waiting for her and she gave her a straight look.

'What's up with you?'

It was not the greeting Rosalind might have expected from a servant, but she ignored Fletcher's rudeness. 'Do you know where Hanging Sword Alley is, Fletcher?'

'I do, and you don't want to go there.'

'I've just heard that a good friend of mine, my brother-in-law in fact, is living in what sounds like squalid accommodation in that street.'

'I wouldn't call it a street, ma'am. It's a narrow alley between warehouses and printing shops. It's a rough area.'

'So I've been told, but I want to go there. If I can get away from here unnoticed, will you come with me?'

'Well, ma'am, put it this way – you ain't going on your own.'

Next day, as luck would have it, Patricia announced at breakfast that she had an appointment with a modiste in Bond Street.

'You'll find it very tedious, Rosie. I suggest you take Fletcher and visit the British Museum or the National Gallery. I hope you don't mind, but we can meet up this afternoon. Perhaps we'll go to Gunter's and sample their delicious ice cream and cake.'

'I don't mind at all,' Rosalind said casually. 'I would love to visit the National Gallery or the museum.'

'Good, that's settled. Tonight we're dining with some of Greystone's political colleagues so I hope there are no other old acquaintances likely to turn up.'

'Last evening was a coincidence. I hardly know anyone in London so it won't happen again.'

'I should hope not. You used to lecture me on my behaviour and now I find I'm having to keep you in order. Mama would find that very droll.'

'I'm sure she would.' Rosalind finished her breakfast with more of an appetite than she had displayed recently. She knew exactly what she was going to do this morning, and it was not spending hours gazing at beautiful works of art.

She waited until Sir Michael had left for his office and Patricia had taken the barouche to Bond Street. Fletcher had Rosalind's fur-lined cloak, bonnet and gloves in readiness, and they managed to leave the house without Foster spotting them. Fletcher hailed a cab and Rosalind sat back, doing her best to control her nerves. Colonel Munday's description of Alexander's work and the place in which he lived had preyed on her mind during a sleepless night. She had awakened even more determined to see him and demand an explanation.

The cab dropped them off outside Doctors' Commons. Fletcher went first, glaring at anyone who did not instantly move out of her way. She was head and shoulders taller than most women and her black bombazine gown and cloak gave her the appearance of a carrion crow. With her aggressive attitude she seemed ready to attack anyone who had the nerve to stand in her way, and Rosalind entered unchallenged. The old building smelled of dusty books and ancient vellum, and they were guided to the Prerogative Office, where she spotted Alexander hunched up in one of the small booths along one side of the room. The walls were lined with shelves from floor to ceiling, each one crammed with documents in ancient leather bindings that must have been there for a couple of centuries, at a guess. An official barred their way but a steely glance from Fletcher made him change his mind and he sidled off to speak to a gentleman who was requesting information.

Rosalind crossed the floor and leaned into the booth. 'Alex.'

He looked up with a start and for a moment he simply stared at her, but a sudden smile of recognition was wiped away by a worried frown. 'Rosie! What in the name of heaven are you doing here? This isn't the place for you. How did you know where I was?'

'Colonel Munday told me. Don't blame him, Alex. I would have come looking for you anyway.'

'Blanchard, get on with your work.' A small plump man wearing a green-tinged jacket and trousers padded up to them, glaring at Alexander. 'May I be of assistance, madam?'

'No, sir. Thank you, but I need to speak to Captain Blanchard.'

'He's not a captain here, ma'am. We do not encourage our clerks to have visitors.'

Fletcher moved towards him. 'Who says?'

The small man quivered. 'It's the law.'

'Go away,' Fletcher hissed.

'I'll have you evicted, miss.' He spoke boldly but he backed towards the door.

'Don't anger me, friend,' Fletcher said between clenched teeth. 'I ain't nice when I gets cross.'

'I see you have a champion,' Alexander said, chuckling. He put down his pen and folded the document he had been copying. 'We can't talk here.' He stood up and edged free from the narrow space. 'Let's go outside.'

The small man cleared his throat noisily. 'If you leave now you won't come back, Blanchard. This is a place of law and you should respect your position.'

Alexander reached for his coat and unhooked it from a many-branched coat stand. 'As Mr Dickens said in *Oliver Twist*, the law is an ass – an idiot. Good day, sir.'

Fletcher chuckled. 'I couldn't have said it better meself, cully.'

'I'm glad you approve.' Alexander shrugged on his coat and ushered them out into the freezing winter air. Their breath curled around their heads, forming clouds that wafted away in the cold east wind. 'You'd better come to my room so that we can talk, but I warn you it's not what you're used to, Rosie.' He hurried them through the bustling streets to Hanging Sword Alley.

Alexander opened the front door and Rosalind covered her nose and mouth with her hand as the smell of damp, filth and rotten food made her want to retch.

'Ain't no one here heard of soap and water and

a bit of elbow grease?' Fletcher said caustically. 'I wouldn't keep pigs in this midden.'

'Very true.' Alexander led the way up the narrow staircase. 'No self-respecting pig would want to live here. Take care because some of the treads are in a bad state.'

Rosalind picked up her skirts and followed him, keeping to the wall where there was less damage to the splintered wood. Fletcher came last but as she reached the top she handed part of the banister rail to Alexander.

'It come away in me hand, guv.'

He laid it on a milking stool that seemed to have been abandoned in the middle of the landing. 'The whole building is in danger of collapsing. It's not the sort of place I would wish to bring ladies, but it's too cold to stand outside for very long.' He unlocked a door to his right and stepped inside.

Fletched grunted. 'It's the first time I've been called a lady. Most people ain't so polite. Anyhow, you got a lot to talk about, I can see that. I'll look out of the window and admire the view.' She picked her way across the floor, stepping over discarded boots and empty beer bottles. 'You could do with a house-keeper, guv.'

'I apologise for the mess,' Alexander said humbly. 'I wasn't expecting visitors.'

'Never mind that.' Rosalind met his gaze with a questioning look. 'Why, Alex? Why are you working in that dreadful place? Surely you could have found somewhere better to live than here?'

'I'm sure that Greystone will have told you that I'm not fit for anything else. He seems to have taken a particular interest in my affairs, which is why I couldn't get anywhere with the War Office.'

'Are you saying that he used his influence to stop you finding work?'

'I think he had a hand in it, Rosie. I can't prove it, of course, but when I returned to London there was a chance that the powers that be could find me something, perhaps even send me out to the Crimea in an advisory capacity.'

'Why do you think that Greystone had anything to do with them turning you down?'

'Do you really need to ask? I dare say Patsy has told him all manner of things about me. I know my failings, but I was a good soldier.'

'I'm sure you were, but why didn't you return to Rockwood or even Trevenor? Why put yourself through all this, Alex?'

He shot a wary glance at Fletcher's back but she seemed to be intent on watching a noisy altercation in the alleyway below. 'You know why I must not return to our old life. At least not until Piers is a free man again.'

'Your grandmama would welcome you home with open arms.'

'Grandmama always held back when it came to me. I was never her favourite.'

Rosalind lowered her voice. 'I would do anything to help you.'

'That's just the trouble. I don't trust myself, Rosie. I'm not such a selfish brute that I would put you in an impossible position, nor am I a leech who would choose to live off the woman he loves. You know very well that I can't return to Rockwood Castle to live.'

'Shh.' Rosalind glanced anxiously at Fletcher. 'One thing is obvious. You can't stay here and you've probably lost your position at Doctors' Commons anyway.'

'That's true, but it's not your problem, Rosie. I'm a grown man and I can look after myself.'

'I don't care what you say. There must be some way out of this, Alex. Perhaps Colonel Munday could help.'

'I'm not going round asking for favours or begging for work. I got myself into this, and it's up to me to sort out my problems. You have enough to do without worrying about me.' He took her hand in his and held it close to his chest.

'But I do worry about you, Alex.' Rosalind closed her eyes, she could feel his heart thudding to the same beat as her own. 'Especially now. I simply can't walk away.'

Fletcher turned her head. 'Look here, it ain't none of my business, and I know my place, but you two need your heads banging together.'

'What did you say?' Alexander demanded angrily.

'Who are you, anyway? No servant would behave the way you do.'

'Fletcher is my friend,' Rosalind said firmly. 'She may not be a polished diamond, but I like her and she speaks common sense.'

'All right, then.' Alexander slipped his arm around Rosalind's waist. 'Since you seem to know everything, what do you suggest, Fletcher?'

'Well, if it was me I'd take you back to my drum and devil take the hindmost, but that's for people like me. As you're gentry, I'd still say you should take him back to wherever you came from. If he can't live with you he could find somewhere nearby. The rest is up to you. I ain't no arbiter of morals.'

Rosalind stared at Fletcher in amazement, hardly able to believe her ears, but Alexander threw his head back and laughed. The sound echoed round the small room and a large chunk of plaster dropped from the ceiling, shattering to tiny pieces on the bare boards.

'Your new friend speaks sense, Rosie.'

'Then you'll return to Rockwood with me, Alex? Fletcher is right: you don't have to live in the castle, and there are plenty of cottages on the estate that would be infinitely better than this.' Rosalind eyed him intently. 'I need a steward I can trust. It would serve until you decide what you really want to do.'

'There you are then,' Fletcher said triumphantly. 'The lady speaks good sense, guv. If I were you I'd accept and be done with it.'

'Please, Alex.' Rosalind grasped his hand. 'Say you'll consider it, at least. If you agree we'll return to Rockwood tomorrow or the next day. I miss my baby and I want to go home.'

Alexander smiled reluctantly. 'It seems that you're always coming to my rescue, Rosie. What would I do without you?'

Fletcher shook her head, uttering a snort of contempt. 'Men! The lot of you are just big babies. He'll agree, missis, and I just done meself out of a job.'

'Do say yes, Alex. Come home to Rockwood and help me to run the estate.'

'When you put it like that it's hard to refuse.'

'Lord give me patience. Say yes, you fool.' Fletcher shook her finger at him.

Alexander eyed her thoughtfully. 'You have a lot to say for yourself, Fletcher.'

'If you take up my lady's offer you'll need someone to look after you, guv. I can cook and I can tidy up better than you can, if this is an example of your housekeeping. I fancy a trip to the country meself. I got a few people here in London who would like to skin me alive, if you know what I mean.'

'I sympathise with them,' Alexander said with feeling. 'Are you a good cook?'

'I am, as it happens. At least, I can boil an egg or a bit of salt beef, and no one overcharges me when I go shopping.'

'I'm not sure that Rockwood is ready for someone

like you, Fletcher.' Rosalind turned to Alex, smiling. 'Does that mean you accept my offer?'

He raised her hand to his lips. 'I'd be a fool not to. Besides which, you need someone to take care of you while Piers is away. I think Fletcher will be a great help to us both. I'd pit her against Trimble or his criminal friends any day.'

'Then we can go home,' Rosalind said, heaving a sigh of relief. 'Maybe it's best if I don't tell Patsy and Sir Michael that you're planning on returning to Rockwood. They might think it odd if I take you with me, Fletcher, so we'll say that you're going to be my personal maid. There's always work at the castle if you get tired of looking after the captain.'

'Thanks, ma'am, but I don't see meself living in a castle. I'll look after the captain as if I was his batman. That I can do.' Fletcher looked from one to the other and grinned. 'I'll wait for you outside, ma'am. It's brass monkeys out there so don't keep me waiting too long.' She stomped out of the room, slamming the door behind her.

'She's going to be a handful, Alex,' Rosalind said warily. 'Are you sure you want to take her with you?'

'It adds a bit of respectability if I have a house-keeper, and no one is going to argue with Fletcher. I know I should go away and get out of your life for ever, Rosie, but I can't do it. At least this way we can see each other legitimately.'

'Yes, but it's still going to be difficult, Alex. I won't pretend otherwise.'

'I tried and failed to make a life without you. The fault is all mine.'

'No, it isn't. I came looking for you and now I've found you I don't want to lose you again. It would be different if I knew you were doing something that satisfied you and made you happy, but I can't bear to see you living like this.'

He held both her hands and then released her, stepping away. 'You'd better go or Fletcher will be after my blood. Let me know when you intend to travel and I'll meet you at the railway station.'

'I will. Now I just have to tell Patsy that I'm going home. She won't like it but it's not up to her.'

Patricia stared at her in dismay. 'But, Rosie, I thought you were enjoying yourself here.'

'And I am, Patsy. It's been wonderful, but I miss Dolly and the others. I shouldn't have left my baby. You'll understand when you have children.'

'Indeed I won't. Greystone doesn't want to start another family and I never intend to have children, so we agree entirely on that subject. Look at you – you're a slave to that baby. You should stay for a week at least and leave all your problems at Rockwood.'

'I'm sorry, Patsy. I know you've done your best to entertain me, and you and Sir Michael have been most generous, but I want to go home.'

Patricia tossed her head. 'Well, you can't travel on your own. Whoever heard of such a thing? You'll have to stay at least until we can find someone to accompany you on the journey.'

'That is all settled,' Rosalind said hastily. 'Fletcher is going to come with me. I've decided to take her on as my personal maid.'

'You can't mean that, Rosie.'

'But I do. She's intelligent and quick to learn, and I feel safe with her. She lacks polish but that will come in time.'

'I don't know what Greystone will say about that. The woman has been in prison.'

'My husband is in prison, in case you've forgotten. Piers is serving a seven-year sentence for something much more serious than what Fletcher did.'

'Well, if you're quite sure. It was only an experiment, after all.'

'And it's obviously worked. You may tell your husband that Fletcher is to be employed by me and she will no longer be a danger to anyone, least of all herself.'

'Perhaps it's as well you're going back to the countryside. Heaven knows what sad cases you might take on should you have decided to remain in London for any length of time.' Patricia sighed. 'But I will miss you, Rosie.'

'You could always return to Greystone for Christmas and then we can share the festive season. After all, Sylvia will be on her own if Christina decides to spend Christmas with the Cottinghams. I'm sure Sylvia would be delighted to see you.'

'Oh, didn't you know? Sylvia has been invited to spend Christmas at Trevenor. It seems that she and Aurelia are the best of friends. My sister-in-law could have come to London, but she chose Cornwall, so I know where her loyalties lie. Now you are abandoning me, too.'

'Honestly, Patsy. You have so many parties and social functions to attend, you won't have time to feel lonely. You know you can always come home to Rockwood if you really miss your family.'

'Thank you, but I think I'd be better off here than in our draughty ancestral home. Are you sure you want to leave tomorrow?'

Rosalind gave her a hug. 'There are preparations for Christmas to be made. I can't leave them all to Hester. I'll miss you, Patsy, but I have to go home.'

'You won't be getting any Christmas gifts from me. I think I've been very generous as it is. I'd keep the gowns I bought for you but they wouldn't fit me. Greystone says he likes a woman with a bit of meat on her bones. It's very vulgar but it pleases him to say so. Anyway I'm going to my room to change for dinner and you'd best do the same. We're dining at home tonight.' Patricia left the room with the air of a martyr walking to the stake.

Rosalind sighed. She could not blame her sister for being angry, but she had found Alexander, and the fact that he was willing to accept her offer of employment at the castle was almost too good to be true. She hurried to her room where she found

Fletcher sorting out garments to be packed ready for an early departure.

'I can do that, Fletcher. I want you to take a message to Captain Blanchard for me.'

'We're leaving tomorrow?'

'Yes, I questioned Foster and he told me that there is a train at ten o'clock in the morning. Please tell the captain to meet us at the railway station. We'll purchase the tickets so he can join us on the platform.'

'So you're going ahead with it, ma'am. Good for you, that's all I can say. I ain't never been in a castle, but I imagine it's not too different from prison – the building itself, I mean. Cold and damp, I should imagine. I can't wait.'

Rosalind managed a half-smile, wondering whether Rockwood Castle was ready for someone like Fletcher. She could imagine Hester's face when they were introduced.

Chapter Twenty-Four

Hester met them in the entrance hall. She glared at Alexander, but colour flooded her cheeks when she came face to face with Fletcher. They studied each other like duellists preparing for a battle.

'What's up with you, missis? Have I got two heads or something?' Fletcher demanded angrily.

'It's Lady Carey to you, woman. Who are you, I'd like to know.' Hester narrowed her eyes. 'What have you brought home now, Rosalind?'

'Now, now ladies.' Alexander stepped in between Hester and Fletcher. 'There's no need for this. Miss Fletcher is my housekeeper, Hester. We're not going to be here for long.'

'That's right,' Rosalind said hastily. 'Alexander has had some bad luck in London and so I've offered him Lambert's position as steward. He'll live in the

438

old keeper's cottage and Fletcher is going to keep house for him.'

'I thought we'd seen the last of you, Alexander,' Hester said in a low voice. 'If you cause trouble you'll have me to answer to.'

'Here, Captain, are you going to let her talk to you like that?' Fletcher shot a hostile glance in Hester's direction. 'She's no lady. A title don't alter nothing. A book has a title and a play in the theatre has a title but you can't imitate breeding.'

'Yes, thank you, Fletcher. I'll send for Tilly and she will show you your room.' Rosalind sent a warning look to Hester. 'The luggage will be sent up later.'

'All right, but I might as well make meself useful.' Fletcher picked up several valises, tucking one under each arm and grabbing the handles of the other two. 'Oy, cully.' She jerked her head in Jarvis's direction. 'You may be old, but you look strong enough to bring the rest. You can show me the way.'

'Jarvis is the butler here,' Hester protested. 'We have a footman to do the heavy work.'

'Waste of time and money.' Fletcher started off up the grand staircase. 'Come on, butler. Show us you ain't too feeble to carry a couple of cases.'

'I'd better follow her, my lady,' Jarvis said apologetically. 'I know her sort. She'll purloin the silver if I let her roam freely about the castle.'

'Watch what you say, old man.' Fletcher cast him a quelling glance. 'I done me time and I ain't going back to prison for a few odd bits of silver.'

'She's your guard dog, Alexander,' Hester said icily. 'You'd better muzzle her before she causes some real trouble. Come with me, Rosalind. I want to talk to you.'

Rosalind followed Hester to her parlour and closed the door behind her. 'How is Dolly? I couldn't bear to be away from her any longer.'

'She's well and thriving. Eliza Madge will be staying here with her infant until Dolly is weaned. I take it that's all right with you, Rosie?'

'My milk has dried up or I wouldn't consider it, but who's looking after Mrs Madge's other children?'

'Jessie Wills lives in the cottage next door to Eliza. Her girls are grown up and in service so she's on her own with Saul still serving time in prison. It seems she's fond of the young ones and happy to have something to do other than taking in sewing and mending.'

'I must go to the nursery before I do anything else.'

'You'll tell me first why you've brought Alexander back to Rockwood, let alone that harridan he says is his housekeeper.'

Rosalind drew herself up to her full height, meeting Hester's gaze with a steady look. 'Whatever you may think, Alexander is my brother-in-law – he's part of the family and he's fallen on hard times. I need a steward and who better than someone I can trust absolutely?'

'People will talk.'

'Let them. I can't be responsible for what the gossips think or say. They'll soon get tired of the subject and start on someone else. I have to look after the children and the estate, and I can't do it all on my own.'

'You have me, Rosie. Doesn't that count for anything?'

Rosalind gave her a hug. 'Of course it does, Hester. You are the one person in the whole world I could trust with my life. Now let's forget about Alex and start planning for Christmas. We have the children to consider and the servants, too.'

'What do you suggest?'

'Rockwood might have been poor in the past, and our fortunes probably won't recover from Piers being sentenced to transportation, but it was always a happy place. I intend to make it like that again. Now I'm going to the nursery and I'll see you at dinner. Could you let Cook know that we have two more mouths to feed?'

The door opened before Hester had a chance to respond and Walter walked into the room. 'What's going on? I just saw Jarvis staggering upstairs behind a strange woman. She looks how I imagine the curse of Rockwood would appear if it were a person.'

Rosalind laughed. 'I think you might have something there, Walter. That person is Cora Fletcher – it's a long story and I'll tell you at dinner – but she's going to be Alexander's housekeeper.'

'So you found him in London?'

'Yes, in the most degrading circumstances. I couldn't leave him to suffer like that. Piers would have done the same, had he been able.'

'You brought Alex back to Rockwood?'

'I've given him Lambert's position as steward. I need someone to handle the tenants and the rent collecting for me, and Alex seems like a good choice.'

'Is he going to live here? You know that will make tongues wag.'

'I've thought of that, Walter. He's going to have Lambert's cottage and Fletcher is going to live there, too. It's all quite respectable.'

Walter wrapped his arms around her. 'You're a woman to be reckoned with, Rosie. I admire you tremendously. I hope when Louise and I have children that our daughter is just like you.'

'I wouldn't say that in front of Louise,' Hester said, chuckling. 'You never were very tactful, Walter.'

A dull flush spread from his thin cheeks to his neck above the cravat he had tied so badly. 'I didn't mean to disparage Louise. I was so scared she might refuse when I asked her to marry me, but she said "yes". It was the happiest day of my life. I love her dearly.'

'Of course you do.' Rosalind kissed him on the cheek. 'Congratulations, Walter. The sooner you marry her, the better, as far as I'm concerned, but wouldn't you like to announce your engagement with a party?'

'No, we both shy away from things like that,

Rosie. I was thinking we might marry at the end of the Easter term. I'll have finished my degree course by then, and who knows? I might have had some luck publishing my book of poems.'

'A June wedding will be wonderful,' Rosalind said happily. 'It's something to plan for and look forward to. That is what we must do now, Walter. We need to look to the future.'

Next morning, having satisfied herself that Dolly was thriving in Eliza Madge's care, Rosalind rode Sheba and Hudson saddled up Piers' horse Warrior for Alexander. They rode to the cottage in the woods, with Fletcher following in the dog cart driven by a reluctant Gurney. In less than twenty-four hours Fletcher had managed to alienate most of the servants both indoor and outdoor, and Rosalind was convinced that she enjoyed creating a stir. However, when they arrived at the cottage in the clearing, where evidence of the fire many years ago was still to be seen in the burned and blackened tree stumps, Fletcher seemed as thrilled as a child. She sprang down from the cart and stood with her hands clasped, gazing at the cottage with shining eyes. There had been a hard frost overnight and every blade of grass and each individual dead leaf sparkled in the pale winter sunlight.

'I never seen nothing so quaint,' she said in a low voice. 'It reminds me of a picture book me dad stole for me when I was just a nipper.'

Alexander opened the front door. 'Well, don't

stand there in the freezing cold. Come inside, Fletcher, and light a fire. Do something useful.'

Rosalind followed him into the main room, which served as both kitchen and parlour. Despite a recent coat of whitewash on the newly plastered walls, there was still a lingering smell of charred wood. It was quite obvious that Lambert had left hurriedly without even bothering to clear away the remains of his last meal. Used cutlery was scattered over the table, together with empty beer bottles and plates with the congealed remnants of food. Mouse droppings littered the newspaper that Lambert had used as a tablecloth and ashes spilled onto the tiled floor in front of the range. It was hardly a welcoming sight. Rosalind was beginning to wish that she had sent some of the cleaning women to make the place habitable, but Fletcher marched into the room with a delighted smile on her face. She shrugged off her woollen cape and rolled up her sleeves.

'I'll soon have this place shipshape. I likes a challenge. Out of me way, please. I got work to do.'

'You'll need supplies,' Rosalind said, backing towards the doorway. 'There's a good shop in the village that sells everything you might need.'

'Give us the money then and I'll go there when I'm done here.'

Alexander took a leather pouch from his jacket pocket and laid it on the table in the only space that was rubbish free. 'Don't spend it all at once. This has to last for a few days.'

'Dora Greep, the farmer's wife, supplies us with eggs, butter, cheese and milk. The farm is not far from here, Fletcher. Tell her to charge whatever you purchase to the Rockwood account.'

'I don't need charity, Rosie,' Alexander said gruffly.

'You'll earn it, Alex.' Rosalind laughed. 'Maybe it would be a good idea if you visited the Greeps' farm first of all. Your charms will work to your advantage with Dora. She likes a good-looking man, so I've been told.'

'I suppose I have to start somewhere. Anyway, I think I've met her husband in the Black Dog. Perhaps I'll start with him.'

'Whatever you think, Alex,' Rosalind said sweetly. 'Now, I'd better go home. We've only got a few days left until Christmas and nothing has been done to make the castle look festive. I'll get Nancy and Tommy to help me bring the decorations down from the tower room.

'One thing you could do for me, Alex, is to call on Abe Coaker and ask him to cut down a fir tree for the entrance hall and a slightly smaller one for the drawing room. If he's not at home he'll probably be in the kitchen garden.'

Fletcher seized a besom and began sweeping the floor, sending dust and dried leaves swirling around in eddies. 'Out of me way, please.'

Outside in the cold air Rosalind wrapped her cape more tightly around her. 'You will be quite comfortable here, I hope, Alex.'

He lifted her onto the saddle as easily as if she were a child. 'Of course. I'm a soldier, Rosie. I can bivouac anywhere, and this is luxury indeed, especially compared to that dreadful room in Hanging Sword Alley. You can't imagine how grateful I am for all this.'

She smiled. 'You might not say that when you find out how much work is entailed in your new position.'

He held onto the reins, frowning thoughtfully. 'Are you sure this is what you want, Rosie? You don't have to look after me, you know.'

'It's you who'll be looking after me indirectly, and you have Fletcher to take care of you.'

'I'm not sure I can cope with the thought of living here with the Queen of Darkness.'

'Don't let her hear you say that. She really is just trying to make you comfortable.'

'I think Fletcher can take a joke. But seriously, we have to be careful how we behave for Dolly's sake, if not for our own.'

'Your presence here might cause a bit of a stir at the outset, but people will get used to the idea.'

'My brother is a fool. He's thrown away the greatest gift he could ever have.'

'Let's not talk about it now.' Rosalind wheeled her horse round. 'On second thoughts, perhaps I'd better go and see Dora Greep first and pave the way. She is the world's biggest gossip so I don't want her making up the information she spreads round the village. I just wish I could be there when she first meets Fletcher.'

'Let me come with you. I expect she's seen me around anyway, but it would be better if we're formally introduced. Maybe I can find her husband on the farm and have a word with him, too.'

'Perhaps you're right. Maybe we're both worrying about nothing. Who better to be my steward in times like these than my husband's brother?'

As Rosalind had expected, Dora Greep eyed Alexander curiously and with a certain amount of suspicion, but he exercised his considerable charm and she was soon won over. Alexander left with a wheel of cheese, a dozen eggs and a pound of butter wrapped up in muslin and cabbage leaves. Dora promised to send the dairymaid to the cottage with a pail of milk, although Rosalind suspected that it would be Mrs Greep herself who turned up at the door. Dora would then have first-hand information to pass round about the stranger from London who was the captain's housekeeper. Rosalind could not help wondering who would win that particular battle of wills, but if she were a betting woman she would put her money on Fletcher.

Rosalind parted from Alexander at the farm gate. He rode off to take the food to the cottage and she returned to the castle. It was a wintry scene with the bare branches of the trees silhouetted against a cold grey sky, and the mournful cries of gulls circling overhead. It would be a long winter, and after an indifferent harvest there would be hardship amongst the villagers by the time spring came.

Rosalind reined in Sheba and gazed over the silvery surface of the backwater as an idea came to her. Everyone needed a lift in their spirits and she knew just how to accomplish that. She rode to the stables and left Sheba in Hudson's capable hands before making her way to the kitchen where she found Mrs Jackson preparing luncheon. As luck would have it Hester was there supervising, or as Rosalind suspected, interfering with the arrangements for dinner that evening.

'I'm glad I caught you both together,' Rosalind said cheerfully. 'I've just introduced the captain to Dora Greep at the farm, and it occurred to me that we should revive our old custom of giving a Yuletide party for the servants and all those in the village who serve us as well, including the tenants. It would be an excellent way of introducing the captain as our new steward. Times have been hard since my husband was sentenced, but we have to go on.'

'A party?' Hester raised her eyebrows. 'This is Wednesday and next Monday is Christmas Day. There's no time to arrange such a festivity, let alone pay for it.'

'Let me worry about the finances, Hester. What do you say, Mrs Jackson? I was thinking about something along the lines of a simple harvest supper. We'll hold it in the largest of the barns so there won't be any need to have everyone indoors. We'll have music and dancing and a hog roast. Piers saw to it that our cellar was well stocked so there will be ale, cider, mulled wine and fruit cup to drink.'

'I could bake a ham, ma'am,' Mrs Jackson said warily. 'And I'll make mince pies. That's if Annie could help me. She doesn't have so much to do in the house at the moment, and she's a good cook.'

'It's a lot to ask of you, Edna,' Hester said slyly. 'It's not like the old days when we had plenty of help in the kitchen.'

Mrs Jackson bridled. 'There's nothing I can't do if I put my mind to it, Hester – I mean, Lady Carey. I can call in help from the village and Joe Hannaford could order pasties from the bakery in Dawlish, as well as bread rolls. I've already made two batches of mincemeat and my pastry is second to none. I'll roast a couple of capons and make some frumenty.'

'Then I'll do the sherry trifles,' Hester said firmly. 'My trifle is good enough to serve on the royal table at Windsor Castle, let alone here at Rockwood.'

'Excellent.' Rosalind clapped her hands. 'I knew I could rely on both of you. We'll celebrate Yuletide as we did when I was a child, and introduce the captain to the village at the same time.'

'They know him already,' Hester said grimly.

'This is different.' Rosalind spoke more sharply

than she had intended. She softened her words with a smile. 'We're all working together now, Hester. We have to rebuild Rockwood's reputation and our relationship with the village.'

Hester nodded. 'You're right, of course. You can rely on me.'

'And me, ma'am,' Mrs Jackson added eagerly. 'What day do you suggest?'

Rosalind thought quickly. 'Sunday is Christmas Eve, so what about Saturday? It only gives us three days to prepare, but I'm sure we can do it in time.'

'I'll call in help from my sister Maud from the Black Dog. She's famous for her beefsteak pies so maybe we could add those to the list, and I'll send Jennet to Hannaford's shop and Joe will order in the pasties from the bakery. We'll soon get organised, ma'am.'

'Don't forget our Christmas dinner,' Hester said grimly. 'I don't want to eat leftovers from the party.'

'There's no danger of that, Hester, I mean your ladyship. I have had Christmas planned for months, despite everything going topsy-turvy around us. Begging your pardon, Mrs Blanchard.'

Rosalind managed a smile. 'I knew I could rely on you, Mrs Jackson. I'll leave the catering in your capable hands. I'm going to the nursery now, and then I'll be helping the children to decorate the main rooms.'

'I saw Abe and the captain in the main hall just now with a huge fir tree. I think it's the largest we've ever had.' Hester placed the list she had been compiling on the table. 'That's for you, Edna. It's a list of things we'll need from Hannaford's. You may add whatever you need.'

Rosalind smiled as she left them chatting amicably – at least that was one crisis averted. There had always been an element of competition between Hester and Cook, mainly due to the fact that Hester could not quite give up control of the kitchen, but the arrangements for the Yuletide celebrations seemed to have given them a common aim. Rosalind hoped that it would be so with the rest of the servants, both indoors and outside. She knew she was taking a chance by employing Alexander, but she hoped the party would bring everyone together.

'Invitations,' Rosalind said out loud as she crossed the entrance hall.

'Talking to yourself now. It's a bad sign, Rosie.' Walter emerged from the library, making her turn with a start.

'Walter, you're just the person I need. I'm inviting the whole village to a Yuletide celebration to be held in the largest barn, and on reflection probably a couple of the smaller ones as well. I need invitations to be sent out, or perhaps posters to be placed around the village. Can I leave that to you and Louise? She's not giving the children any more lessons until after Christmas.'

'That sounds like a good idea. What brought this on?'

'It's partly to introduce Alex to the wider community, but it's also to show that we're not hanging our heads in shame. Everyone knows about Piers' sentence, but that doesn't alter the fact that Rockwood has been here for centuries and scandals have come and gone.'

'I'll work on some posters before dinner and I'll get Tom Hannaford to put one up in his father's shop window. Louise will help me and we'll go round tomorrow spreading the word and delivering invitations. The news will go round like wildfire anyway. A party at Rockwood Castle is something that no one will want to miss.'

'I knew I could depend upon you.' Rosalind blew him a kiss as she mounted the stairs and hurried on her way to the schoolroom, where she found Tommy and Nancy busy making paperchains.

'Look what we're doing.' Tommy jumped to his feet, holding up a length of rather sticky pieces of paper glued together with flour-and-water paste.

'That's beautiful, Tommy.' Rosalind smiled. 'Perhaps we should leave them to dry while we go up to the top tower room and look for the decorations.'

'Yes, please.' Nancy laid her work carefully on the nearest table.

'Coaker has brought in a large Christmas tree for the entrance hall,' Rosalind said as she led them out of the room towards the narrow servants' staircase. 'And I'll ask Captain Alex to find a smaller one for the drawing room. We're going to be very busy for the next few days.' She stopped on the top landing. 'And we're having a big Yuletide party for the whole village on Saturday evening.'

'May we come?' Nancy asked breathlessly.

'Of course you may. It's almost Christmas and we're going to celebrate.'

An hour later the large tree in the entrance hall was decorated with the carefully unwrapped glass balls, scarlet bows and tinsel. Nancy and Tommy did most of the choosing and hanging of decorations, but twelve-year-old Noah Coaker, Abe's grandson, had been called in to climb the ladder and put the star on the topmost spike of the fir tree, as he was head and shoulders taller than Nancy. The children's excitement began to wane when they thought they had finished, but Alexander appeared with a smaller but still reasonably large tree for the drawing room. They followed him as if he were the Pied Piper and the three children watched eagerly while Alexander secured the tree in a large tub of soil, strategically placed by Abe himself. Rosalind stood with Dolly cuddled in her arms as she watched the proceedings with a smile on her face. Alexander made the children laugh, but he was able to control their excitement with a single word and they behaved beautifully. When the tree was safe he allowed them the freedom to place the decorations where they wished, even if the result was slightly lopsided and Tommy was more interested in the wooden soldiers than the prettier tree ornaments.

Eliza Madge had come down from the nursery with her baby boy in her arms, and she watched the children's antics with a smile on her face.

'The captain is so good with the young ones,' she said appreciatively. 'I'll never forget how he stayed by your side when Dolly was born. Not many men will do that, let alone someone who isn't the baby's father.'

Rosalind shot her a suspicious glance. 'He likes children,' she said casually.

'He most certainly does. He crept into the nursery this morning to see Miss Dolly. I think he's embarrassed to be seen making a fuss of her, but I told him he's the child's uncle, it's perfectly natural for him to love her just as much as her real papa.'

'Yes, indeed. Family attachment is very real.' Rosalind kissed Dolly's soft cheek. 'And she is a beautiful baby.'

As if in answer Dolly opened her eyes, screwed up her face and began to cry.

'I think she's hungry, ma'am. Shall I take her to the nursery?'

'Yes, of course.' Somewhat reluctantly Rosalind allowed Eliza to take her daughter. 'I'll be up later to give her a cuddle. I don't want her to forget me.'

Eliza chuckled. 'No fear of that, ma'am. Babies are like little animals: they know their ma by her scent.' She bustled off, carrying a baby in each arm.

'Dolly is the most beautiful baby, isn't she?'

Rosalind looked round to see Alexander standing

too close to her for comfort. 'You didn't tell me that you visited the nursery.'

'Do I have to report my every movement? I love my little niece, or isn't that allowed either?'

'Shh,' Rosalind said in a low voice. 'Don't say things like that.'

'I'm sorry, Rosie. I'd better go.'

'No, wait. I've decided to celebrate Yuletide in the old way by throwing a party for the whole village as well as the servants. It's as much to introduce you as the new steward as it is to honour Christmas. Everyone loves a party.'

'You'd do all this for me?'

'It's for myself as well, Alex. I don't want Rockwood to suffer for what Piers has done. The Carey family have survived worse scandals over the centuries. We'll get through this together.'

'You really are the most remarkable woman I've ever met,' Alexander said in a voice that throbbed with suppressed emotion. 'My brother should have loved and treasured you and your child. He should have protected you . . .' He broke off as Jarvis entered the room.

'I'm sorry to interrupt, ma'am, but Lady Pentelow's carriage has just drawn up outside.'

Chapter Twenty-Five

'Grandmama!' Alexander met Rosalind's startled gaze with a question in his eyes. 'Did you invite her for Christmas?'

'No, of course not. She went off in a fit of pique and I haven't heard from her since.'

He pulled a face. 'Grandmama never could resist a party. She must have had a message from above or, knowing my grandmother, maybe the devil himself told her what to expect.'

Rosalind giggled in spite of herself. 'Hush, Alex. Don't say such things.' She glanced at the children who had stopped what they were doing and were staring at them wide-eyed.

'That's really lovely.' Rosalind walked towards the tree, clapping her hands. 'You've done a splendid job, and thank you in particular, Noah. You've been a great help. Well done.'

Noah blushed scarlet and nodded. 'Thank 'ee kindly, ma'am.'

'You may go now, Noah, but you and your family are all invited to our Yuletide celebration on Saturday. Please pass the message on to all outdoor servants as well as those in the stables.'

Noah tipped an imaginary cap and hurried from the room. Rosalind turned to Tommy and Nancy. 'I suggest you go to the nursery and have your luncheon, and afterwards you may wrap up warmly and go out to collect holly and ivy for the house.'

'I haven't much to do this afternoon.' Alexander turned to Tommy. 'Wait for me and we'll go together. We'll take the governess cart and then we can pick as much as we can find. We have the barns to decorate as well.'

'Yes, Captain.' Tommy clicked his heels together and saluted.

'At ease.' Alexander patted him on the head. 'I'll see you in an hour or so. You, too, Nancy. We need you to keep us in order.'

Nancy giggled. 'Yes, Captain.'

Rosalind smiled at their eager faces. 'Before you go, Alex, you'd better deal with your grandmother. I can't think why she's come here so close to Christmas, but—' She broke off as the door opened and Lady Pentelow made a dramatic entrance.

'Thank you, Jarvis, but I think I know my way to the drawing room.'

457

'Good morning, Grandmama,' Alex said warily. 'This is a pleasant surprise.'

'I'm afraid we weren't expecting you, ma'am,' Rosalind added hastily. 'Your rooms haven't been made ready.'

'I'm not staying, Rosalind. Sylvia has invited Aurelia and myself to spend Christmas with her at Greystone Park instead of travelling to Cornwall. She is unsure whether her father and your sister will return home, or if they would choose to remain in London for the festive season. The poor girl has been all but abandoned.'

Rosalind shot a wary look in Alexander's direction, but he remained impassive. 'I see. Well it's good of you to call. May I send for some refreshments?'

'No, thank you. I just wanted to let you know that we are in the vicinity.'

'That can't be the main reason for calling here now, Grandmama.' Alexander ushered the curious children from the drawing room and closed the door. 'Why have you travelled all the way from Cornwall at this time of the year?'

'I came specifically to see you, Alexander. You are a huge disappointment to me. I was hoping that your return to London would be permanent. You do realise, I suppose, that your continued presence here is creating yet another scandal to be borne by those closest to you.'

'I don't live here now. I have a cottage on the

estate and a housekeeper, so it's all very proper, as you would say.'

'Alexander has taken the position of steward. Lambert left under a cloud and I can't manage everything on my own.' Rosalind faced Lady Pentelow with a defiant lift of her chin. 'You have no right to criticise him for trying to help his brother's family.'

'The business is failing.' Lady Pentelow sat down abruptly on an upright chair. 'Matters have reached such a peak that the mine will almost certainly have to be sold.'

'I am next in line to Piers. I'll do anything I can to prevent that happening.' Alexander eyed his grandmother closely.

'You have nothing to do with the mine. It belongs to Piers, not you, Alexander.'

'I thought it belonged to the family.'

'Then you were wrong. Piers is the sole beneficiary of your late grandfather's will. If I can find a buyer the money will cover the debts incurred due to Piers' mismanagement.'

'But how will you manage, Lady Pentelow?' Rosalind asked anxiously. 'Will you lose your home?'

'No. I will keep Trevenor, although my income will be very much reduced. Aurelia has a small annuity, which will allow her to live in moderate comfort but is not large enough to attract fortune hunters.'

'And yet I have nothing.' Alexander walked slowly

to the window, staring out at the bleak winter garden. 'Not that I care, of course, but it makes me curious. I remember hearing once that there was some sort of scandal in the family, which is why I think you are so afraid of public scrutiny of our affairs.'

'It happened a long time ago, Alexander. You were an innocent child. Your grandfather and I decided that it was best to keep the truth from you. It's a secret that lies heavily on me these days.'

'Don't you think that Alexander deserves to know what you've been keeping from him, ma'am?' Rosalind could feel the tension building in the room and she was growing even more anxious.

'If it concerns me directly I need to know,' Alexander said firmly.

Lady Pentelow sighed, shaking her head. 'I agree, although it hurts me to relate the sad tale. It's not something I really wish to talk about.'

'You can't stop there,' Alexander protested. 'Please go on.'

'Very well, this isn't easy to say, but you are not my grandson. Your mother was my niece, Penelope Teague.'

Alexander stared at her with a perplexed frown. 'What are you saying?'

'Penelope was the only child of my late brother and sister-in-law – just a girl of sixteen when she fell in love with a dashing cavalry officer. They eloped but my brother gave pursuit and brought Penelope home, despite her pleas that she be allowed to stay with Julius. Some months later she died giving birth to you, Alexander.'

He regarded her with a dazed expression. 'Then you are my great-aunt, not my grandmother.'

'That's correct. My husband and I decided it would be better for everyone if you were taken into the family and treated as our grandchild.'

Rosalind took a step towards him, holding out her hand. 'Alex – I'm so sorry.'

He shook his head. 'Let me get this straight. My mother was your niece and my father was an army officer who apparently took advantage of her and then left her to die alone. Is that right?'

'No, not exactly,' Lady Pentelow said reluctantly. 'To be honest I never liked Julius Hampton. He was too confident of his looks and charm for my liking, but Penelope fell under his spell. He did offer to marry her but her father would have none of it. If he had known that she was with child he might have acted differently.'

'What happened to my father, the cavalry officer?'

'He died less than a month after your mama passed away. He was thrown from his horse and he never recovered consciousness.'

'Did he know about me?'

'I don't know the answer to that, Alexander. He was serving in the East India Company Army and he died in India. His family were informed but they wanted nothing to do with you.'

'Have you met my family? Where do they live?'

'I met your paternal grandfather once. He came down from London to see Penelope's parents. He contributed towards your education.'

'But he wanted nothing to do with me personally,' Alexander said bitterly. 'In other words, he paid you to keep me away from my other family.'

'I'm sorry, Alexander. This would never have come to light in my lifetime but for the present circumstances. If it's any consolation I've always thought of you as my grandson.'

Alexander was silent for a moment. Rosalind could see that he was struggling with a maelstrom of emotions and she felt his pain, but she knew this was not the time for an outward display of sympathy on her part. She bit her lip and remained silent with difficulty.

'Does Piers know about this?' Alexander said at length.

'No, but I feel bound to let him know before they ship him off to the penal colony, which must be any day now. I want the family affairs put straight.'

'And Aurelia?'

'I don't intend to tell her. Aurelia loves you dearly and it would break her heart. Besides which, she has given me another problem, which I must face on my own.'

'What has she done now?' Rosalind moved to Alexander's side and grasped his hand. 'What else have you to tell us, ma'am?'

'Aurelia has been seeing too much of Martin Gibbs, the mine manager. He's obviously set his sights on her, no doubt thinking that if he marries the mine owner's sister he'll be made for life. Unfortunately she has taken a liking to him, too.'

'He's a decent fellow, Grandmama. I mean Greataunt – I don't even know what to call you now,' Alexander said wearily. 'I wish you'd told me all this sooner, but now it's out in the open it explains a great deal. I always knew that you had reservations when it came to me. Now I know why.'

Lady Pentelow rose from her seat. 'That's unfair, Alexander. I treated all you children equally, and one after another you've all let me down.'

'Alex hasn't done anything wrong, Lady Pentelow,' Rosalind said angrily. 'He is the injured party, not you.'

'Really?' Lady Pentelow gave her a frosty look. 'I suppose carrying on with his brother's wife is honourable behaviour, is it?'

Alexander raised Rosalind's hand to his lips. 'All right, I'll admit that I've been in love with Rosalind for a very long time, but we've done nothing to be ashamed of.'

'And yet here you are, once again, holding hands with Piers' wife. Sadly I think you must take after your father. Julius Hampton was a philanderer and Penelope fell for his charms. I'd advise you to be very careful, Rosalind, or you may fall into the same trap.'

'Don't involve Rosalind in this, Aunt,' Alexander said angrily. 'She is above reproach, and I do love her, but we've accepted that we can never be together.'

'I've no time for this sentimental nonsense. I think it best if I leave now. We won't speak of this again, do you understand, Alexander?'

Lady Pentelow rose from her seat and walked to the door, hesitating for a moment to look back over her shoulder. 'Such a pity. I once thought you had potential, Alexander, but I see that you are content to be this woman's lackey.'

'That remark was unworthy of you, Aunt.' Alexander turned away to stare out of the window.

'We're giving a Yuletide party on Saturday.' Rosalind made an effort to sound calm, even though she was inwardly fuming at the humiliation that Lady Pentelow had heaped upon Alexander. 'My sister, Aurelia and Sylvia are invited, even if you choose to stay away, Lady Pentelow. I'm sure you wouldn't want to set tongues wagging by forbidding them to attend.'

Lady Pentelow left the room without deigning to answer.

Rosalind twined her fingers around Alexander's hand. 'I am so sorry, Alex. I don't know what to say.'

'I think I always knew that I was different, and now I understand why.'

'It's so unfair. You are being punished for something that was none of your doing. Your father might have been a libertine or he might have been deeply in love with poor Penelope. It seems to me that they weren't given the chance to live their own lives, with tragic consequences for you as well as them.'

'It's a shock, I must admit, but I'll get over it. I'm more worried about what will happen to Aurelia if the business is sold. The trouble is that I can't do anything to help.'

'I suggest you ride over to Greystone Park now and invite the girls to the party on Saturday. You are probably the best person to talk to Aurelia because she'll listen to you, whereas she might not take any notice of what Lady Pentelow says, especially with regard to Martin Gibbs. I remember meeting him and I think he's someone to be reckoned with.'

'I may not be related to Aurelia and Piers in the same way, but we're cousins, and that gives me the right to have my say. I do care about them, Rosie. I really do.'

'I know you do, Alex. None of this alters who you really are, and it won't make any difference to those who love you. Now go, before Lady Pentelow has had time to get into her carriage.'

He nodded. 'You're right. Aurelia is still my little sister and I won't allow anything to come between us. I'll protect her from the truth for as long as I can.'

The next couple of days were spent in a frenzy of activity. The aroma of baking permeated the ground floor of the castle, which was decorated with boughs of holly, trails of ivy and scarlet ribbons. The huge tree in the entrance hall glittered with tinsel, glass balls and strings of beads, as did the smaller tree in the drawing room. The children did their best to help make everything ready for the party, whether it was toting bales of hay from one barn to another in order to make room for the revellers, or hanging paperchains from the beams, together with swags of holly and ivy. Dora Madge's older children were also eager to help, and Rosalind found tasks to suit everyone. The entire village were expected, apart perhaps from some of the fishermen, who preferred to sit in the Black Dog and nurse a pint of ale rather than socialise. However, all the local farmers and landowners had accepted their invitations, as had Squire Cottingham and his wife. Oscar and Christina had indicated that they would attend. It seemed a pity that Aurelia and Sylvia were not to be included, but Lady Pentelow was adamant that they would not grace the occasion with their presence.

The preparations on Saturday continued until winter darkness swallowed up the deer park and surrounding countryside, although it was only half past four in the afternoon. In complete contrast, the avenue leading up to the castle gates was lit by flaming torches. The barn doors were left open to greet the guests and fiddlers played energetic gigs accompanied by Jarvis's sister, Minnie, who hammered the keys on an ancient harmonium. The temperature had plummeted and frost was already sparkling on the hedgerows and tussocks of grass in the meadow. The scent of mulled wine, spices and citrus peel welcomed the guests and a tempting aroma from the hog roast and chestnuts cooking on several braziers filled the cold air.

Rosalind and Hester stood in the entrance to the largest barn, welcoming the early arrivals, but as the guests began to arrive in greater numbers it was impossible to speak to each one individually, and Rosalind chose to mingle with the crowd. She had decided that informality was the key to an enjoyable evening and the dancing commenced immediately, with couples jigging about on the compressed earth floor, and children chasing each other around the hay bales. As the drink flowed, the party spirit grew more rowdy, but it was all good natured and everyone seemed to be enjoying themselves, even Fletcher, who had beaten Albert Yelland, the village blacksmith, at arm wrestling in full view of the assembly and was being plied with glasses of strong cider by the appreciative onlookers.

Rosalind chose to turn a blind eye to this over-exuberant behaviour and was chatting to the vicar and his wife when she looked up and saw Lady Pentelow at the entrance, together with Aurelia and Sylvia, and close behind them were Patricia and Sir Michael. Rosalind edged her way through the crowd of dancers to greet them.

'This is a pleasant surprise, Lady Pentelow.'

'Is it? I'm not here for pleasure, I can assure you of that. I'm merely keeping tongues from wagging.'

'This is all so rustic and quaint,' Sylvia said excitedly. 'I love mixing with the villagers, but I can't imagine that Papa finds it so charming.'

'Your papa is a politician, Sylvia. He'll shake hands with the pig man and kiss grubby babies if it gets him a vote.' Aurelia grabbed her friend by the hand. 'I'm hungry. Let's go and get some food. I love eating with my fingers – it's so common.' They walked off arm in arm, giggling like schoolgirls.

'Good evening, Rosie.' Patricia stood beside her husband, looking far too elegant for such an informal occasion, diamond earrings sparkling in the light from the lanterns hanging from the rafters, and her ice-blue satin gown would have been more appropriate for a ball in a great house.

'This is a nice surprise. I thought you were spending Christmas in London,' Rosalind said happily. 'Good evening, Sir Michael.'

He inclined his head, smiling, but his eyes searched the crowd as if he were looking for likely voters. Rosalind could have told him that very few of the local people were eligible for the franchise. Patricia seized her by the arm and drew her towards a table at the side of the dance floor.

'This was a splendid idea, Rosie. This sort of thing is very good for Greystone's career.'

Rosalind stifled a giggle. 'I didn't organise a Yuletide party to further your husband's political ambitions, Patsy.'

'I know you didn't, but it really does help. Moreover, Greystone has plenty of money, so if you need financial help I'll make sure you get it.'

'Thank you but we're not bankrupt yet.'

'Things must be tight with Piers destined to serve his sentence on the other side of the world. Who knows when he'll return, or if he'll survive? Who will look after you and little Dolly if he doesn't return?'

'I ran Rockwood single handed before I married Piers. We survived and I can do it again.'

'I know you will, Rosie. All I'm saying is that we can help if need be. I might be Lady Greystone now but we are still sisters and we look after each other.'

'At one time it was me advising you, Patsy,' Rosalind said with a wry smile. 'Now our situations are reversed.'

'Yes, and I'm enjoying every minute.' Patricia laughed. 'Alex is looking for you, I think.' She lowered her voice. 'Don't say I told you, but I overheard Greystone and Lady Pentelow talking about the possibility of Alexander returning to the army. I'm not his greatest admirer, but I know they're not doing it for his good. It's to avoid further gossip, if you know what I mean.'

'Oh, yes, I do. I know exactly how their minds work. The army was Alexander's life and he wanted to rejoin his regiment but they rejected him on medical grounds.'

'You should have married Alex. That was your biggest mistake, Rosie.'

'It's too late to think about that.' Rosalind glanced over her sister's shoulder. 'I need to talk to him.'

Patricia unfurled her fan and held it in front of her face. 'Lady Pentelow told us everything about Alex and his true identity, but Aurelia mustn't know and she's coming this way. She adores Alex, and it would break her heart if she found out that he's not her brother.'

'I think it will be up to Alex to decide if and when to tell her.'

'Yes, I agree. Anyway, I see that Greystone has been cornered by the lovely Glorina. I need to rescue him.' Patricia snapped her fan shut and sashayed off in her husband's direction.

Rosalind waited for Aurelia to make her way through the throng of people.

'Are you having a good time, Aurelia?'

'Actually I am having a much better time than I thought I would.' Aurelia turned and beckoned to a tall young man whom Rosalind immediately recognised.

'Isn't that Martin Gibbs? What's he doing here? I don't think your grandmother will approve.'

Aurelia giggled like a naughty child. 'No, she won't. Isn't it fun?' Her smile faded. 'I knew that Martin had followed us from Cornwall and he's staying in the village, so I sent word to ask him to come here. I want you to meet him properly and perhaps you can use your influence to convince Grandmama that he's a good man. I love him, Rosie, and he loves me.' She beckoned to Martin and he hurried to her side.

'Good evening, Mrs Blanchard. I hope you don't mind that I came here without an invitation.'

'Good evening, Martin. You are most welcome.' Rosalind had met him briefly when she first visited Trevenor, and she liked the look of him despite Lady Pentelow's damning indictment of him as a fortune hunter. His plain face was creased into a worried frown but when his eyes rested on Aurelia his expression changed subtly. Rosalind knew instantly that this was a man deeply in love. He might be ambitious but she did not think that would drive him to marry simply for money and position. Besides which, he must be aware that the clay mine was about to be sold.

'You will put in a good word with Grandmama, won't you, Rosie?' Aurelia put her head on one side, waiting for an answer.

'I don't think Lady Pentelow would take notice of anything I have to say, Aurelia.'

'Oh, but she will. I know she will. After all, you own a castle and many acres of land. You are an important person. Well, perhaps not as important as Sir Michael.' Aurelia cast a glance at Patricia and Sir Michael, who were seated with the vicar and his wife.

Rosalind turned to Martin. 'You do know that the mine is up for sale, don't you, Mr Gibbs?'

'Yes, ma'am, but the interested buyer has promised to keep me on as well as the other miners. My position is assured. I was hoping to talk to Lady Pentelow this evening. Do you think you could put in a good word for me, ma'am?'

'I think the best person to represent your case is you yourself, Martin. Lady Pentelow appreciates honesty and forthrightness. Why don't you approach her together? She's never denied you anything you really wanted in the past, has she, Aurelia?'

'No, I suppose not,' Aurelia said doubtfully. 'But this is different.'

'Not entirely. If you can show her that you are sincere, Martin, she will listen to you.'

'Alex is coming to speak to us.' Aurelia clutched Martin's arm. 'Maybe he will stand up for us with Grandmama.'

'It would be better if you and Martin spoke to her first,' Rosalind said firmly. 'Let her see how much you care, and, Martin, you need to know exactly how you're going to support a wife and family. That is very important.'

He nodded. 'Yes, I realise that. You're right, Mrs Blanchard. I need to be honest and show her how sincere I am, and that my intentions are entirely honourable.'

'Yes, that's exactly what you need to tell her. She's just walked away from the squire's table, so why don't you speak to her now? She's smiling, Aurelia. You just have to pick the right moment.'

472

Aurelia dragged Martin through the throng of dancers and revellers to where her grandmother was standing, momentarily on her own. Rosalind crossed her fingers. She could only wish them well. If she had followed her own heart in the first place she might have avoided all the pain and difficulties in which she found herself now.

Alexander approached her, holding out his hand. 'May I have the pleasure of this dance, Mrs Blanchard?'

She met his warm gaze with a smile. 'I'd be delighted, Captain.' She allowed him to lead her into an energetic polka. He held her firmly round the waist, whirling her around and somehow managing to avoid crashing into the other less expert dancers.

'Your party is a great success. Everyone seems to be enjoying themselves, even Grandmama. I'll have to continue calling her that, if only for Aurelia's sake, but one day I'll tell my sister the whole truth as I know it.'

'It's a sad story, but your mother and father would be proud of you, Alex. I know I am.'

'Really?' He held her closer. 'That matters to me most of all, Rosie.'

They came to a sudden halt at the sound of a disturbance outside the barn doors.

'I'd better go and see what's happened.' Alexander released her. 'Stay here. It could be a drunken fight.'

Rosalind followed him from the dance floor. 'It

doesn't sound like that to me.' The cold night air came as a shock after the fug in the barn.

'What's going on?' Alexander demanded.

A rider, muffled by a scarf and a caped greatcoat, dismounted with a sharp command to Hudson to hold the horse's reins. 'I have a letter for Mrs Piers Blanchard, sir. I have to give it to her personally.'

Rosalind stepped forward. 'I am Mrs Blanchard.'

He took a sealed document from his inside pocket and placed it in her hand. 'I need a reply, urgently, ma'am.'

Chapter Twenty-Six

Rosalind broke the seal with trembling fingers. 'Hudson, bring the lantern closer, please.' She studied the spidery writing accompanied by several large ink blots.

'What does it say, Rosie?' Alexander asked anxiously. 'Who sent it?'

'It's from Bertie, but it's not his writing. I think he must have dictated it to someone else.'

'What's happened? Where is he?'

'He's in the Railway Hotel, Exeter. He says he was badly wounded and he can't ride. It's all a bit vague and I can't read some of it for the blots and bad spelling. We must go there and bring him home, Alex.'

'Of course, but it's late. We won't get there until the early hours of the morning even if we leave immediately.'

'I don't care.' Rosalind turned to the messenger. 'Please tell my brother that we're on our way to fetch him.'

'Yes, ma'am.' The man mounted his horse and rode away.

'We have to go to Exeter right away, Hudson. I know it's late but I want you to have the barouche made ready and brought round to the front entrance as soon as possible. We have to bring my brother back home.'

Hudson snapped to attention. 'I'll drive you myself, ma'am.'

'I'm coming with you, Rosie.' Alexander placed his arm around her shoulders. 'You'd better change into some warmer clothes. It's going to be a long cold night.'

'What's going on, ma'am?' Fletcher appeared in the doorway clutching a pint mug in her hand. 'What's all the fuss?'

'It's all right, Fletcher,' Rosalind said with a dismissive wave of her hand. 'Please tell Lady Carey that I've been called away. We're going to Exeter to fetch Sir Bertram. He's been sent home from the Crimea because of his injuries. Heaven knows what state he's in if he can't write the note himself.'

'You mustn't allow your imagination to run away with you, Rosie,' Alexander said gently. 'He's managed to survive the long journey so he must be on the mend.'

'I hope so, but it doesn't sound too good.'

Fletcher stepped outside. 'You need to change your garments, ma'am. I'm coming with you. I know how to deal with all manner of wounds and broken bones. I can help.'

'All right, if you're sure, but you might have to ride on the box with Hudson on the way home.'

'Do I look like a shrinking violet?' Fletcher turned to Alexander. 'You'd better tell Madam Hester where we're going. She can sort out the drunken chambermaids and make sure that Sir Bertram's room is made ready with a good fire and aired bedsheets. Come on, ma'am. I'll see you safely back to the castle.'

It was still dark when they arrived at the Railway Hotel early next morning, but the ostlers were ready to take the horses to the stable and the chambermaids were going about their business, lighting fires and making the public rooms ready to welcome weary travellers.

Alexander ordered breakfast for them all but Rosalind insisted on being shown to the room where Bertie had spent the night. The chambermaid knocked gently and entered first. She lit a couple of candles and stoked the fire before leaving.

Rosalind walked over to the bed, hardly daring to breathe, but Bertie seemed to be sleeping peacefully and apart from the thick stubble on his chin and dark shadows under his closed eyes, he looked almost the same as the last time she had seen him.

She decided to let him wake up in his own good time, and she was about to creep away when he opened his eyes.

'Rosie? Is that you?'

She grasped his hand as it lay on the coverlet and raised it to her cheek. 'Yes, Bertie. I've come to take you home.'

'Where's Wolfe? He's usually here with me.'

'Wolfe? Who is that, Bertie?'

'My soldier servant. He's carried me through this, quite literally. I'm a cripple, Rosie. I was shot in the back and I'm paralysed from the waist down.'

Rosalind went down on her knees beside the bed. 'Oh, Bertie, I'm so sorry. Are you in much pain?'

He laughed, but it was a hollow sound. 'I can't feel a thing, that's the trouble. The army surgeons say I'll never walk again.'

Rosalind choked back tears. Why did such a dreadful fate befall someone like Bertie, who had always been so active? 'That's dreadful. I don't know what to say.'

He squeezed her fingers. 'You're here. That's all that matters. I'll try not to be a burden to you and Piers.'

'You'll never be that, Bertie. You are Sir Bertram Carey and Rockwood is yours. When you are fully recovered you will run the estate and I'll be there to help you.'

Bertie grinned ruefully. 'What will Piers say to that?'

'It's a long story, Bertie, but Piers has gone away and he won't be home for a very long time.' Rosalind rose to her feet as the door opened and a giant of a man with a scarred face and a patch over one eye stomped into the room.

'What's going on? Who are you, lady?'

'Wolfe, mind your manners,' Bertie said sharply. 'This is my sister, Mrs Blanchard. She's come to take me home.'

'You must have written the letter to me,' Rosalind said, smiling. 'I'm very grateful to you for taking such good care of my brother. It must have been a very difficult journey all the way from the Crimean Peninsula.'

'Aye, it was. But you came here quick enough. I'll grant you that, ma'am.'

'We travelled through the night, and we're ready to leave when the horses are rested.'

'Did anyone accompany you, Rosie?' Bertie beckoned to Wolfe. 'Prop me up, there's a good fellow.'

Wolfe obeyed with surprising gentleness, even going so far as to plump up the pillows to ensure Bertie's comfort.

'I don't want to tire you,' Rosalind said anxiously. 'Alexander came with me and my maid Fletcher.'

'I spotted a cove in a smart suit with an old crow of a woman dressed in black. If looks could kill I'd be stone dead.'

'Fletcher is all right.' Rosalind stifled a nervous

giggle. It seemed ludicrous that a ferocious-looking man like Wolfe would be scared of a woman half his size. 'She's my maid and she came with us to see if she could help, but I see that you have all the assistance you need, Bertie.'

'Wolfe saved my life on the battlefield. I couldn't have made the journey without him.'

'You will come home with us, I hope, Mr Wolfe.' Rosalind eyed him warily. 'You would be more than welcome. We have plenty of room.'

'Of course he'll come with us, Rosie. I can't manage without Wolfe. I told you, I'm a useless cripple.'

'Now, Lieutenant, there's no cause to talk like that,' Wolfe said severely. 'If you'll kindly leave us, ma'am, I'll see to your brother's needs and then I'll fetch his breakfast.'

Bertie managed a weak smile. 'At least I can feed myself, Rosie. I'm not a complete baby. Anyway, I don't suppose you've eaten so you should look after yourself. We'll have plenty of time to talk later, and you can tell me everything that's been happening at Rockwood.'

'Yes, of course.' Rosalind rose to her feet and walked to the door. 'You'll have a hero's welcome when we get home, Bertie.'

'Is it Christmas Eve? I've quite lost track of time.'

'Yes, it is. We'll have a proper family Christmas, and it will be all the better because you are with us.' Rosalind blew him a kiss as she left the room.

Alexander and Fletcher were in the dining room about to tuck into a hearty breakfast when Rosalind joined them. A maidservant hurried into the room with a plate of bacon and egg with devilled kidneys and two racks of toast.

Fletcher reached for the coffee pot. 'Shall I pour you some, ma'am? I know it ain't me place, but you look done in.'

Rosalind took her seat. 'Thank you, Fletcher. I am a bit tired but I'm so glad we came. Poor Bertie is being very brave but I can see how his injury has damaged him in mind as well as body. The doctors have told him he'll never walk again.'

Alexander put down his knife and fork. 'I am so sorry, Rosie. That's terrible news. It was bad enough for me to discover how limited my choices are with a gammy leg, but I feel for Bertie. I really do.'

'I suppose that great hulk of an ugly brute is his servant.' Fletcher passed a full cup of coffee to Rosalind.

Rosalind chuckled in spite of everything. 'Fletcher, you say the most outrageous things. For heaven's sake don't repeat that in company.'

'I don't mix with company normally, ma'am. I know that you and the captain are different, but I mind me manners when I has to.'

'Quite,' Rosalind said drily. 'Well, I hope you'll try to get along with Wolfe because he'll be travelling with us, and for Bertie's sake I hope he'll agree to stay on at Rockwood. Bertie will need all the help he can get.'

They left at midday, the horses having had ample time to feed and rest. Wolfe carried Bertie to the carriage and set him down next to Fletcher, with Alexander and Rosalind on the opposite seat. Wolfe rode on the box beside Hudson, who eyed him warily but did not raise any objections. Rosalind suspected that very few people would argue with Wolfe, although she suspected that Fletcher was merely biding her time and would not bandy words if it came to an argument. Fortunately it was a reasonably pleasant journey back to Rockwood, although by the time they reached home Bertie was extremely pale and obviously very tired. It was almost dark and Hester had thought to have the flambeaux lit to create a welcoming sight. Bertie revived a little when he saw the castle lit up against a purple sky, and he gasped with delight when he saw the Christmas tree in the entrance hall and the swags of berried holly and fronds of ivy that deco-rated the grand staircase.

Walter was the first to greet them and his eyes filled with tears at the sight of his older brother being carried in the arms of a giant of a man.

'Bertie, I'm so sorry, but it's good to have you home all the same.' He gave Bertie a gentle hug. 'We've got your old room ready and Hester has made your favourite rabbit stew. She thought you might not feel like a big meal after travelling so far.'

'Thank you, Walter. That all sounds wonderful. Will you lead the way to my room? I'd like to rest a while.'

'Of course, and then I'll take Wolfe to the servants' quarters. I'm sure they have a room for him fairly near to you.'

'No. Wolfe has to stay close so that he's there when I need him. He can sleep in my dressing room tonight.'

Rosalind had been watching the brothers' reunion with tears in her eyes, but she managed a smile as she caught up with them. 'Perhaps tomorrow you'd like all your things moved to Grandpapa's old suite of rooms. Jarvis used to occupy one of them so that he was always on hand. I think Wolfe will be quite comfortable there. After all, you are the master of Rockwood now, Bertie.'

'I'm not even the master of my own body, Rosie,' Bertie said with a rueful grin. 'However, it is a good idea. I'll sleep in my old room tonight and tomorrow I'll move. It's good to be home for Christmas.'

Rosalind smiled. 'You're safe, Bertie. That's all that matters.' She watched Walter mount the stairs, followed by Wolfe with Bertie in his arms. It was a bitter-sweet homecoming, but she knew she had to be thankful that her elder brother had survived when so many others had lost their lives in the fighting or from disease. She turned to Alexander with a sigh.

'I know you wanted to return to your regiment, Alex, but I'm so glad they wouldn't take you back. I know it's selfish, but that's how I feel.'

'There's nowhere I'd rather be than at your side, Rosie. I would have done my duty and returned to the battlefield, but this is where I want to be.' He glanced over his shoulder at the sound of running feet and cries of delight from the children. Tommy rushed at him and clung to him like a burr.

'You've come home. We thought you'd gone away again, Alexander.'

Nancy stood back, smiling shyly. 'It wouldn't have been a proper Christmas without you.'

'Have you had your tea?' Rosalind asked gently. 'You know you have to hang your stockings on the mantelshelf or Father Christmas won't visit you.'

'I didn't do that at the vicarage,' Nancy said sadly.

'Nor at the sweep's house. Us boys lived in the attic with the rats and spiders.'

'Well, Tommy, that's all behind you now.' Rosalind laid her hand on his thin shoulder. 'I have a big surprise for you both tomorrow, but you won't get any presents unless you go to bed now.'

Fletcher had been standing quietly but now she stepped forward. 'No nonsense now, young 'uns. I'll see you upstairs and make sure you get into bed.'

'We're going.' Nancy seized Tommy by the hand and dragged him towards the staircase, followed by Fletcher.

'I'll send Jennet up with some warm milk,' Rosalind called after them. 'Good night.'

Their responses were drowned by excited giggles as they raced on ahead of Fletcher, whose heavy boots echoed off the ancient oak treads.

Alexander laughed. 'I can see Fletcher as the nursery maid from hell. They won't dare play around if she's there.'

'Don't be mean, Alex. Fletcher has a kind heart beneath all that black bombazine. Maybe I can persuade her to change her style of dress so that she doesn't look like a professional mourner.'

'You always think the best of people, Rosie. That's been your trouble all along. I'm afraid we ordinary mortals are bound to disappoint you every time.'

'If you're thinking of Piers, I suppose it's true, but we *were* happy at first. Then his desire to make money seemed to take over and things went wrong. Anyway, I'm going to the nursery to see Dolly, so why don't you go and find Hester and tell her we're home? I'll be down directly, and when the children are asleep I'll fill their Christmas stockings.'

'Will it start tongues wagging if I help you?'

'It's Christmas Eve. Peace on earth, goodwill to men. I think it's a magical time. Bertie is home safe and we'll make sure he has everything he needs. The children are well and happy, and you're here with me. I couldn't ask for more.' Rosalind stood on tiptoe to kiss him on the cheek.

'I'm afraid I'm not so easily satisfied. More than

anything in the world I want to be by your side to take care of you and protect you from everything that's not good and beautiful. I've never wanted to take responsibility for anyone in my life until I met you, Rosie. I may never get the chance to prove myself to you, but whatever happens I'll never be far away.'

Rosalind was awakened next morning by two small people jumping on the end of her bed. She opened her eyes, blinking as the pale wintry sunlight filtered through a gap in the curtains.

'Merry Christmas,' Tommy shouted, bouncing up and down excitedly. 'Look what we had in our stockings.' He emptied the woollen sock onto the coverlet, sending sugared almonds tumbling after boiled sweets, nuts and an orange. He held up a bar of Fry's chocolate. 'I've never had one of these before. I can't wait to taste it.'

'Put it back, you bad boy,' Nancy said firmly. 'We have to have our breakfast first, you know that. Lady Carey is very strict about meals and so is Mrs Jackson.'

Rosalind sat up in bed. 'I'm sure one little piece won't spoil your appetites. I won't tell anyone, and it is Christmas Day.' She wrapped her arms around them. 'We'll have a lovely day with just our little family.'

'And Fletcher,' Nancy added hastily.

'And Wolfe.' Tommy wriggled away from Rosalind's affectionate hug. 'He's a proper soldier. I'm going to join the army when I'm old enough, just like Sir Bertram and Wolfe.'

Rosalind swung her legs over the side of the bed. 'We'll have breakfast early and then we'll all go to church, but first I'm going to the nursery to see my baby.'

'I love Dolly,' Nancy said dreamily. 'She's beautiful, just like you, ma'am.'

Rosalind grasped Nancy's hand. 'If you had just one wish what would it be for, Nancy?'

'A Christmas wish, you mean?' Nancy's eyes brightened. 'Well, I would wish that you were my mother, ma'am.'

'Yes, I would, too,' Tommy added eagerly. 'But I'd also wish for a new set of lead soldiers. Half of mine are missing.'

'I can't be your mother,' Rosalind said thoughtfully. 'And I'm too old to be your sister, but perhaps you could call me Aunt Rosie. I feel as though you've both been with me for ever. We're a family and I hope for great things for you both.'

At that moment Fletcher burst into the room without bothering to knock, although this was her usual way of entering and no matter how many tactful hints she received to the contrary. She placed a steaming jug of water on the washstand.

'What are you two nippers doing here? Mrs Blanchard wants to get dressed in peace. Off you go and make sure you wash behind your ears, young Tommy. I got eyes in the back of me head so I'll know if you have or you haven't.' She shooed them out of the room. 'I brought hot water for you to wash. They're all at sixes and sevens below stairs, getting dolled up for church.'

Rosalind stood up and stretched. 'Will you be attending church with us this morning, Fletcher?'

'Me? No, missis. The gargoyles would jump off the roof if I walked into a church. I'll stay here and keep me eye on Wolfe. I don't trust him. He's got a shifty eye.'

There was no answer to that and Rosalind took advantage of the rapidly cooling water to have a wash before getting dressed. It was easy to slip into the old routine and she went to the nursery first to have a cuddle with Dolly and discuss her baby's progress with Eliza. Having satisfied herself that all was well, Rosalind made her way to Bertie's room, where she found him propped up against a pile of pillows, sipping a cup of coffee. Wolfe eyed her warily, saying nothing.

'How are you this morning, Bertie?' Rosalind stood at her brother's bedside. It was wonderful to have Bertie home, but his crippled condition was heart-breaking. She managed a bright smile. 'Merry Christmas.'

'I never imagined I'd be spending it here at Rockwood, but it's good to be home.'

'We're going to church later on, but after that we'll spend the rest of the day quietly. Perhaps you would like the day bed moved into the drawing

room. There's a beautiful tree that the children decorated.'

'Where did they come from, Rosie? Are they one
of your good causes?'

She perched on the edge of the bed, taking his
hand in hers. 'Didn't you get my letter, Bertie?'

'No. I hadn't had any news from home.'

'You have a son, Bertie. That's what I told you in
my letter.' Rosalind glanced at Wolfe and he retreated
into the dressing room. 'It came about by accident,
but I saved Tommy from a brutal chimney sweep.
The poor child was half-starved, beaten and burned.
He would have died if I hadn't intervened.'

Bertie stared at her in amazement. 'He looks like
a fine fellow, the little I saw of him last evening, but
how do you know he's my son?'

'Do you remember Sally Farthing, Bertie?'

'Of course,' he said warily. 'We were desperately
in love, but we were very young.'

'Did you know she had a child?'

Bertie's eyes widened. 'No, I didn't. What are you
saying, Rosie?'

'It's a long story, but I met Sally's sister and she
told me everything. Sally died when Tommy was
two and Emmie Trimble raised him as her own, but
her husband, who is a complete villain, sold Tommy
to the sweep. That's how I found him.'

'I loved Sally, but I was sent back to school and
I was told she had married. How can you be so sure
that Tommy is my son?'

'You only have to look at him, Bertie, but apart from that, Sally had him christened and your name is on the register as Tommy's father. I have no doubts that he is your son.'

Bertie's eyes filled with tears and he dashed his hand across his face. 'I can't believe it. Poor Sally.'

'Our grandfather paid her to go to live in Exeter. It's a sad story and I would have raised him as your son even if you hadn't returned. He's a bright little boy and he deserves a chance in the world.'

The cup and saucer shook dangerously in Bertie's hand and Rosalind took it from him, placing it on a table close to the bed. 'I think a son like Tommy is the best Christmas present you could wish for, Bertie.' She leaned over and kissed him on the forehead. 'I'll leave you to think it over.'

'Does the boy know about me?'

'No. I haven't told him anything. I wanted it to come from you, but only if you feel you can love him as your son.'

'What sort of father can I be?' Bertie indicated his motionless lower limbs. 'A boy needs a father who can teach him to ride and do all the things that a good parent does.'

'Bertie, look back to our childhood. Our father was absent most of the time, but you grew up to be your own man without his influence. You have the opportunity now of concentrating all your energies into helping Tommy through the difficulties of growing to manhood. Think what Sally would have wanted for the boy.' Rosalind patted his hand as she rose to her feet. 'You don't have to decide right away. Get to know Tommy first and I'll support whatever decision you make.' She left the room, happy to have passed on the news and certain in her own mind that Bertie would make the right choice. She did not know the full extent of his injuries but it seemed likely that her brother would never be able to father any more children. In Tommy he had a son and heir, and a child who desperately needed the love and guidance of a father.

Later, in church, Rosalind barely heard the words intoned by the vicar. She automatically repeated the prayers and sang the hymns, but her mind was elsewhere. She was still thinking about Bertie and the decision that faced him when she left the church, closely followed by Hester, Alexander and the rest of the household. Rosalind was walking slowly towards the lychgate when Sir Michael stepped out in front of her.

'Might I have a word in private, Rosalind?'

She glanced anxiously at Patricia, who merely smiled and walked on with Lady Pentelow and Sylvia. Christina and Oscar had stopped to talk to the vicar, while the squire and Glorina chatted amicably to a group of acquaintances.

'What is it, Sir Michael? You haven't stopped me to wish me the compliments of the season, I'm sure.'

'I do, of course, but this is much more serious and

pertinent to your current situation.' He drew her aside into the shelter of one of the ancient yew trees. 'I realise I haven't always been the best friend to you, Rosalind, especially after you spurned my advances. But I realise now that you were right, and I am extremely happy with your sister. Patricia and I are cut from the same cloth, and we understand each other.'

'I'm so glad, sir, but what has this to do with me?'

'I'm coming to that and I'll be quick because I can see Alexander eyeing me warily. This, I believe, affects him, too. Anyway, I visited Piers in prison at his request. He realised how badly he had treated you and he wanted to make amends.'

'He's being punished by the law, Sir Michael.'

'This isn't a question of justice – he wanted to set you free from a marriage that he knows he has ruined by his selfishness and criminal behaviour.'

'I don't understand.'

'Piers asked me to put through a Private Member's Bill so that you could be divorced and set free.'

'He divorced me?'

'He used the fact that he is a convicted criminal, due to spend the next seven years in a penal colony and he paid a considerable sum to make sure the bill passed without anyone contesting it.'

'But the money, Sir Michael – where did he get enough to pay for such a thing?'

'That isn't for you to worry about, Rosalind.' Sir Michael put his hand in his inside pocket and took out a folded, sealed document. 'This leaves you free to marry again, should you choose to do so. It was the only gift that Piers could think of that would make up for his cavalier treatment and the disgrace he brought upon you and your family.'

Rosalind took it from him, shaking her head. 'I don't know what to say.'

'It works to my advantage, too, Rosalind. If you and Alexander had decided to go against the mores of society it would have created a scandal that would have affected the whole family, and that includes me and my career.'

'Yes, I see that now.'

'It's Christmas Day, so we should celebrate together. Patricia is desperate to see Bertie so we will bring your gifts this afternoon.'

'Thank you.' Rosalind could think of nothing else at that moment other than the fact that this slim piece of parchment meant she was once again a free woman. It was a sad end to the marriage that had promised so much at the beginning, but had failed to bring happiness to either party. When she looked up Sir Michael had walked away to join his wife and they were climbing into their carriage.

'What was that all about, Rosie?' Alexander took her by the hand. 'Are you all right? You're very pale.'

She met his anxious gaze with a tremulous smile. 'I've just had the most surprising piece of news. I'll tell you when we get home, but I still can't quite believe it.'

* * *

A fire roared up the chimney, sending sparks flying and filling the air in the drawing room with the scent of burning apple wood, which mingled with the sharp and refreshing pine aroma from the Christmas tree. The children had opened all their presents with cries of delight and Rosalind handed gifts to everyone, including the items she had purchased in London. The servants were having their own Christmas party in the servants' hall, including receiving the presents that Hester had organised for them. However, both Fletcher and Wolfe had refused to join their colleagues below stairs. Wolfe insisted that he was the only person strong enough to lift Bertie and carry him wherever he wished to go, and Fletcher simply stood her ground, arms folded as she stood at the back of the room, watching the proceedings. Rosalind had tried to persuade her to sit down and enjoy herself, but Fletcher continued to stand, even when she was handed a glass of sherry and a plate of Mrs Jackson's famous Christmas cake.

Hester rose to her feet and marched over to Fletcher. 'It's Christmas Day, woman. Stop acting like a martyr being burned at the stake. Come and sit by me and stop scowling. You're frightening the children.'

Fletcher managed a faint smile. 'Ta, Lady Carey. Just this once. After all, you and me are sisters under the skin, ain't we?'

Rosalind had been close enough to overhear this

exchange and for a moment she thought Hester might slap Fletcher, but Hester remained calm.

'I wouldn't go so far as to say that, Fletcher. But sit down anyway.'

Fletcher manoeuvred herself onto a chair beside Hester and took a swig of sherry. Lady Pentelow raised her eyebrows and sighed heavily, but Bertie clapped his hands, chuckling.

'I've missed all of you so much. It's almost worth the injury to be home with you on Christmas Day.'

'I'm sorry we didn't get you a present, Bertie,' Rosalind said, clasping Alexander's hand out of sight of the rest of the company. 'But we had no idea you would be home.'

Bertie was reclining on the day bed that Wolfe had brought down from one of the tower rooms, but he raised himself on his elbow. 'I want to make an announcement as I have all of you here. Even my brother, Walter, who has abandoned his books for long enough to share this moment with us. I have had the most wonderful news today, and the finest Christmas present ever.' He beckoned to Tommy, who ran to his side and squatted on the floor. 'This young man and I have been getting to know each other. Fate separated us years ago but today I have found out that I have a son. Tommy, tell them who you are.'

Tommy leaped to his feet again. 'I was Tommy Trimble, but now I'm Tommy Carey and I have a father and a real family. Merry Christmas to you all.'

There was a moment of silence and then everyone began clapping.

Walter grabbed Louise by the hand and led her to stand with him by the tree, which was lit by dozens of tiny candles. 'I have equally wonderful news to add to that. Louise has done me the honouring of agreeing to be my wife.' He held up her left hand on which sparkled a diamond engagement ring.

The applause grew louder until Alexander moved into the centre of the gathering, holding up his hands for silence. 'Grandmama, Aurelia, you have been my family since I was born, but recently I discovered the sad story surrounding my birth. Grandmama is actually my great-aunt, and Aurelia and Piers are my cousins.'

Aurelia clasped her hands to her mouth. 'Don't say such things, Alex. You are my brother.'

'You will always be my little sister to me. I love you and nothing can alter that.'

Aurelia sniffed and wiped her eyes on a handkerchief that her grandmother passed to her. 'I love you, too, Alex.'

'There is still another obstacle in your way, Alexander,' Lady Pentelow said icily. 'The woman you want is still married to my grandson.'

Rosalind shook her head. 'That's not true, Lady Pentelow. Piers has given me my freedom. Sir Michael will give you the details, but an Act of Parliament has dissolved my marriage to Piers. For once he acted like a true gentleman.'

Alexander went down on one knee in front of Rosalind, clutching her hand. 'Rosalind, I've loved you for so long that I can't even remember my life before we met. You are my one love and I want to spend the rest of my days with you. Will you do me the honour of becoming my wife?'

A murmur ran through those seated around them. Aurelia mopped tears from her eyes, although Lady Pentelow remained outwardly unmoved. Hester clasped her hands tightly in front of her, while Walter and Louise stood together by the window, smiling happily. Sir Michael reached for Patricia's hand and raised it to his lips. It was Nancy who leaped to her feet, clapping her hands.

'Say yes, Aunt Rosie. Please say yes. We love you and Captain Alex. Dolly would say yes if she knew how to talk.'

Rosalind curled her fingers around Alexander's. 'I do love you, Alex.'

'Oh, for goodness' sake, say yes, woman.' Fletcher rose from her seat, standing arms akimbo. 'You were born to marry the captain. Anyone can see that.'

Wolfe cleared his throat. 'If that crone doesn't shut her mouth I'll carry her outside and leave her in the snow.'

'Is it really snowing?' Tommy rushed to the window, followed by Nancy.

'I'm the head of the family, so I believe,' Bertie said, smiling. 'I give you both my blessing.'

Rosalind leaned over to kiss Alexander on the lips. 'I will marry you, Alex.'

He stood up and swept her into his arms, kissing her soundly.

'There's a carriage pulled up outside,' Nancy cried excitedly.

Walter looked out over their heads. 'Good heavens, it's Mama and Claude.'

Rosalind laid her head on Alexander's shoulder. 'I couldn't be happier, Alex. We are all together as one family. Life is wonderful.'

Read on for a sneak peek of the next book
in The Rockwood Chronicles . . .

Runaway Widow

Coming February 2022!

Duke Street, London

Patricia Greystone stood by one of the tall
windows in her elegant London home, gazing out
into the nothingness that was a London Particular.
The thick, greenish-yellow peasouper had blan-
keted the city from early afternoon with no sign
of clearing. The only glimmer of light came from
the streetlamp directly in front of the house, but
even that was diffused to nothing but a soft glow.
Outside there was silence as if the world had come
to a sudden end, and the smell of sulphur and
soot seeped into the room. A soft rap on the
drawing-room door made Patricia turn away from
her vigil.

'Enter.'

The door opened to admit the Greystones' long-
serving butler, Foster. In his hands was a silver salver
on which lay a folded and sealed document. 'A boy
brought this for you, my lady.'

Patricia crossed the floor to snatch up the sheet of paper. She recognised her husband's seal and her fingers shook with impatience as she unfolded the brief note written on paper with a House of Commons heading. 'Thank you, Foster, there's no reply. The House is sitting late and Sir Michael will not be home for dinner.'

'Very well, my lady. Will you be dining at home?'

'Yes, I suppose so. That will be all, Foster.' Patricia sighed and turned away. Yet another evening ruined, although this time it was the fog which made it impossible to attend the dinner party at the home of Lord and Lady Stanton whose lavish entertainments were legendary. Greystone was probably debating something utterly thrilling like the proposed sewage works east of the city, which had become a vital necessity after the Great Stink that summer. In July and August, the Houses of Parliament had been evacuated because of the pervading smell from human and manufacturing effluent. However, her husband's late-night sittings were coming a little too often these days, curtailing their social life to an ever-increasing extent. Had it not been for the fog Patricia would have attended the Stantons' soiree on her own, but it was doubtful if anyone would venture out in these adverse conditions. She went to sit by the fire, watching the glow fairies sparkle and then die away on the sooty fire back, and the orange, red and blue flames licking around the lumps of jet-black coal. Suddenly and unexpectedly she was thinking of her childhood home. Rockwood Castle in Devonshire had not been the most comfortable place to grow up with its draughty corridors and dampness seeping through the stone walls. There had been a time when they were forced to live off the land, but at home there had always been love, laughter and companionship spiced by squabbles and differences of opinion. She smiled as she recalled her rebellious youth. She must have tried her elder sister's patience to the limit, but Rosalind had always been there to support her when she needed her most. Their relationship had been strained by their mutual involvement with Alexander Blanchard, whom Rosalind had once spurned, and Patricia had almost married. Rosalind had eventually married Alexander after a stormy marriage to his cousin Piers, which ended in divorce. But sisterly love had triumphed and now Rosalind and Alexander were proud parents, devoted to each other and their growing family.

A glowing ember bounced onto the hearth, but Patricia chose to ignore it. She had a small army of servants to do menial tasks, leaving her with nothing to do other than to change her clothes three times a day with the help of her personal maid. There were always invitations to accept and others to send out, but Patricia's life nowadays was one of socialising, entertaining and being entertained. With a husband many years her senior she was used to being treated as delightful and decorative by his contemporaries, who either patronised her or flirted outrageously, which did not amuse their matronly wives. Patricia had learned as a bride of twenty to parry the gentlemen's advances with a fluttering of her long eyelashes or a sweet smile, whilst inwardly writing them off as pathetic old men. She stretched her feet towards the comforting blaze, smoothing the satin skirts of her emerald-green dinner gown. She knew this colour suited her and it was Greystone's favourite. The décolleté neckline flattered her youthful figure and brought a sparkle to her husband's eyes. She loved Greystone, but she was not in love with him and never had been. She had married with her eyes open and her sights set on wealth and position, but she had kept her side of the bargain and her husband had nothing with which to reproach her. They had agreed from the start that there would be no children from their union. Greystone had two grown-up daughters, Christina was now married to the local squire's son in Rockwood village, and Sylvia, as yet unwed, who lived in the family home Greystone Park, chaperoned by her formidable cousin, Martha Collins and her timid companion, Miss Moon. Patricia was fond of her stepdaughters, although they had found it difficult to accept their father's decision to marry someone less than half his age, but they had gradually come round. Perhaps, she thought dreamily, she ought to bring Sylvia to London at the start of the Season. Sylvia at the age of twenty-three was too old to be a debutante, but there might be some eligible bachelors who would find her naïve charms attractive. Miss Collins and Miss Moon would not be included in the invitation. Patricia had had enough of domineering women, her mother and Hester, their former housekeeper, included.

Patricia jumped at the sound of someone knocking on the door. 'Enter.'

Foster appeared in the doorway with his usual impassive expression. 'Begging your pardon, my lady, but there is a gentleman at the door who wishes to see you.' He approached Patricia's chair, once again proffering the silver salver on which sat a deckle-edged visiting card. 'Shall I tell him that you are unavailable?'

'Who on earth would have braved the fog to visit at this time in the evening?' Patricia studied the copperplate writing with a sigh. 'Tell Lord Eldon that I am otherwise engaged.'

The words had barely left her lips when a tall, handsome man with dark auburn hair and a wicked twinkle in his grey eyes strode past Foster. He came to a halt and with an exaggerated gesture he swept off his top hat and bowed.

'Forgive the intrusion, Lady Greystone.'

Patricia made a determined effort to look casual as she rose to her feet, but she was always pleased to see Larkin Eldon, despite the fact that he was a notorious flirt with questionable morals. She was fully aware that he had a tendency to gamble recklessly, cushioned by the huge fortune he had inherited from his late father. It was said that he could drink the hardest toper under the table and still present as being reasonably sober, but despite his raffish reputation he was immensely popular with both men and women. He could charm the sternest matron, should the necessity arise, and one look from him would set the debutantes' hearts aflutter. Patricia was not so naïve, but there was something irresistible about Eldon and she genuinely enjoyed his company.

'My husband has not returned from the House, Eldon,' she said primly. 'The sitting has gone on longer than expected.'

'So I believe, my lady.' Eldon handed his top hat, gloves and greatcoat to Foster. 'I trust you won't send me out into the peasouper without allowing me to recover from the exertion of walking here this evening. I had to feel my way along the railings outside the houses to reach your home. The fog is so thick I almost had to crawl on my hands and knees.'

Patricia knew she had lost the first round in the battle, and if she were to be honest with herself she was delighted to see Eldon. She was fully aware that his ardent pursuit of her company was a reaction to her refusal to be one of his many conquests, but Eldon could make her laugh and he was an excellent guest at a dinner party or a soiree. He excelled as a dancing partner and he had introduced her to the excitement of card games such as Faro and Baccarat, and the thrill of picking the winning numbers in Roulette. He had made flirtation an art.

Foster cleared his throat. 'My lady?'

'It's all right, Foster. Lord Eldon is welcome to stay until he feels he can brave the weather again.'

'Will his lordship be dining tonight, my lady?'

Patricia met Eldon's amused look with a shake of her head. 'I don't think so, Foster.'

Foster bowed and left the room, straight-faced as ever but somehow managing to express his disapproval.

'Aren't you going to offer me a brandy? I did come all this way just to see you, Patricia.'

'Eldon you never do anything unless it is for your own amusement or pleasure. If you want a glass of brandy you know where to find the decanter and a glass.'

He laughed. 'You know me so well, my dear.' He strolled over to a side table to select a decanter and he poured a tot into each of two glasses. 'You will join me, won't you?' He handed one to her with a persuasive smile. 'Come now, don't frown at me, Patricia. You'll crease that lovely alabaster brow.'

'I might have preferred sherry. You should have given me the option, Eldon.' Patricia accepted the drink anyway.

He took a seat opposite her and raised his glass. 'I know you better than that, Patricia. You say all the correct things, but you enjoy a tot as much as

I do, although admittedly not in quite the same quantity.'

'I should hope not.' She sipped the brandy and the warming effect of the alcohol made her relax a little. She sat back in her chair. 'Why are you here, Eldon? You must have known that the Stantons' dinner party would have been cancelled because of the fog.'

'Of course I did, and I also knew that your husband would be delayed at the House. Surely the fact that I braved the terrors of the London Particular to come here this evening must convince you of my utter devotion to your beautiful self?'

Patricia eyed him over the rim of her glass. 'I think you were bored, Eldon. You simply wanted to create mischief by coming here and compromising my good name.'

'You do yourself an injustice, Patricia. I came here because I care about you. Besides which, you are the one woman in London with whom I can be myself. You speak your mind and you are good company, added to the fact that you are extremely beautiful and utterly desirable.'

'And you are a rogue and an arch flatterer, but I must admit I was a trifle bored.'

'I knew it and I've come to rescue you from a long and extremely dull evening. If I had my way we would always be together.'

Patricia downed the last of the brandy. 'Are you telling me you wish to marry me, Eldon?'

He placed his empty glass on a drum table at

the side of his chair. 'If you weren't already married to Greystone that is exactly what I would wish.'

Patricia met his earnest gaze and began to giggle. 'You are such a liar, Eldon. If I was unmarried we wouldn't be having this conversation.'

'Do you doubt my feelings for you, my angel?'

'Quite frankly, yes, I do. How old are you, Eldon?'

His eyes widened in surprise. 'I'm thirty-three. I'm in my prime.'

'I think if you had wanted to marry you would have done it many years ago. After all, you have all the assets that any matchmaking mama would consider requisite.'

'Tell me about them, Patricia.'

'You are quite presentable and you are extremely wealthy. You have a title and a country estate even larger than Greystone Park. Added to that you have a mansion in Grosvenor Square.'

He put his head on one side. 'All true, of course, but is that how you chose Greystone? Did you assess his assets in a similar fashion?'

'Of course I did, Eldon. On the other hand, I do love my husband. He gives me everything I want and more. We understand each other perfectly.'

'But you remain faithful to him, even though he's a cold fish.'

'Don't call him that. You know nothing about our relationship. I wouldn't disgrace the family name by having affairs, so you will never know me better than you do now, Eldon.'

He clutched his hand to his heart. 'You wound me, my dear. I am not a philanderer, my regard for you is genuine.'

Patricia rose to her feet and tugged at a bell pull. 'You are a roué and lies trip off your tongue without any effort on your part, but you are the most amusing man in London and that is the only reason I tolerate you.'

He pulled a face. 'I'm being dismissed? Or are you inviting me to dine with you?'

'If you're worried about finding your way home in the fog, I'll send one of the footmen to guide you with a flaming torch.'

'No, that won't be necessary. I admit defeat tonight, but I won't give up, Patricia. One day I will make you mine, married or not.'

Patricia turned to Foster as he entered the room. 'Lord Eldon is leaving, Foster.'

'Unwillingly, I should add.' Eldon rose to his feet. 'But I will see you at the opera tomorrow evening.' He took Patricia's hand and raised it to his lips, looking her in the eyes with a gaze that left nothing to her imagination.

'Yes, providing the fog lifts.' She snatched her hand free. 'Safe journey, Eldon. I'll give my husband your regards.'

He smiled and blew her a kiss as he allowed Foster to usher him from the room. Patricia sank back onto her chair. Eldon's suggestive glance had made her pulse race, but she was not going to allow him to win. She had made a bargain with Greystone and she intended to keep her word.

'Shall I inform Cook that you will be dining soon, my lady?'

Foster's voice brought her back to the present with a jolt. 'Yes, Foster. I'll be dining on my own.'

When dinner was announced, Patricia went to the dining room and sat in state at the head of the table. She picked at her food, although it was delicious and beautifully presented. For the first time in her married life she felt lonely. Perhaps it was the feeling of being isolated by the penetrating blanket of foul-smelling fog that had unsettled her, but she went to her room as soon as she had finished eating. She rang for her maid and within minutes Betsey hurried into Patricia's elegant bedchamber, slightly out of breath.

'I'm going to bed now.'

'Very well, my lady.'

Patricia waited while Betsey undid the tiny fabric-covered buttons at the back of her dinner gown, followed by the laces on her stays. Despite the fire blazing up the chimney, the room felt damp and Patricia shivered when Betsey slipped the fine lawn nightgown over her head.

'Has my husband returned from the House, Betsey?'

'Not to my knowledge, my lady. The fog is getting thicker by the minute if that's possible.'

'Then I hope it's an all-night sitting. It would be madness to attempt to get home in these conditions.'

'Shall I do your hair, my lady?'

Patricia nodded and sat on the dressing table stool. 'I hope it's lifted by morning.'

'It generally does, my lady.' Betsey took the pins from her elaborate coiffure one by one, placing them in a silver pin tray.

Patricia closed her eyes while Betsey brushed her long golden hair in smooth soothing strokes, but after a while she raised her hand. 'Thank you, Betsey. That will be all.'

'Goodnight, my lady.' Betsey curtsied and hurried from the room, leaving Patricia alone once again.

The silence in the street below was eerie and with the servants' quarters far away below stairs, Patricia felt suddenly that she was the last person on earth. She climbed into bed, pulling the covers over her head. Sir Michael had his own room but tonight she would have willingly shared her bed with her husband. His conjugal visits were infrequent, and Patricia suspected that he kept a mistress hidden away somewhere, but she accepted this as part of life. Most of the married women she knew had husbands who enjoyed the favours of others, and for the most part they chose to ignore such peccadilloes. Patricia sighed. She had chosen this life with her eyes open and she did not regret her decision. It must be the winter weather, but tonight she felt lonely. She almost wished that she had invited Eldon to stay for dinner, but she knew in her heart that would have been a mistake. Eldon was too attractive to be safe, and too amusing to be ignored. She huddled down between the sheets and drifted into a dreamless sleep.

Next morning, Patricia was in the middle of eating her breakfast when Sir Michael strolled into the dining room, bringing with him the smoky smell of the lingering peasouper.

'Good morning, Patricia. I trust you slept well.'

'Yes, thank you, Greystone. You didn't come home last night.' It was a statement rather than a question, and Patricia eyed him warily. She knew that his latest mistress lived in one of the more squalid streets in Westminster, and she wondered if he would make an excuse or if he would tell her the truth.

'It was too dangerous to travel far. The session continued for most of the night and what little sleep I had was in my office.' Sir Michael examined the selection of dishes on the vast mahogany sideboard. 'I'm devilish hungry.' He selected bacon, sausages and a couple of fried eggs before taking his seat at the table. 'What did you do last evening? I assume that the Stantons' dinner party was called off.'

'Yes, it was and I would have hesitated to go on my own, although Eldon called in with some ridiculous story about feeling his way along the railings to get here.'

'That sounds about right. It was one of the worst peasoupers I've seen for a long time. What with the smoke from the manufactories and domestic chimneys and the terrible stink from the river last summer, we really need to think about cleaning London up before we suffer even further outbreaks of disease.'

'Yes, of course. I suppose a new sewage system is very important. Will you be free to attend the opera this evening?'

'I hope so, but if not I'm sure Eldon will be only too happy to escort you.'

Patricia eyed him curiously. 'Doesn't it worry you that Eldon is a terrible flirt?'

'Not at all. I trust you implicitly, Patricia. We had an understanding when we married and it suits us both to honour it. Don't you agree?'

'Yes, of course, I do.'

'Then you won't be too upset when I tell you that I have to go away for a while.'

'Go away? Where?'

'It's a diplomatic mission abroad, but I'm not free to divulge any details, even to you.'

'But you know I wouldn't say anything, Greystone.'

'I do, but there are plenty of people who are very clever at extorting information. It's their job and they do it very well.'

'I see. How long will you be away?'

'I don't know, but I hope the business in hand will be dealt with quite quickly.'

'Am I to stay here in London on my own?'

Sir Michael smiled indulgently. 'You have a houseful of servants to take care of you, my love.

But if you feel you would like to spend time in Devonshire, that is quite all right, too.'

'It sounds as if you expect to be away for some time.'

'I have to be prepared for a longer stay than I would wish, but I will keep you informed by letter. I can't tell you any more than that.'

'When do you leave?'

'Tonight. I'm sorry it's such short notice but I had no say in the matter.'

'We are attending the opera at Covent Garden.'

'I will escort you there, but I will leave before the interval. Everything must look normal. I'll make sure that Eldon sees you home safely.'

Patricia stared at her husband in disbelief. 'You put your trust in him?'

'No, my love. I trust you to behave as the wife of a prominent politician should, and I know you won't let me down.'

'So if I understand you, Greystone, I may remain in London and accept invitations to dine or to go to the theatre, and you are quite happy for Eldon to stand in for you?'

'I wouldn't put it like that, but you are very young, my dear. I can't expect you to go into a convent simply because I have been called away on business. Eldon might be a bit of a rake, but he is a gentleman and he knows how far he can go. You will be safer in his company than some others I could name.'

'Why can't I come with you? I would love to travel abroad, wherever it is.'

'This is a serious diplomatic mission. I have to go on my own, apart from Maynard, of course. He's busy packing my things as we speak. You can always go home to Greystone Park. I'm sure Sylvia would be delighted to have your company. You and she were always chatting and giggling together when you were girls.'

'Is that how you really see me, Greystone? Am I simply a friend of your daughters whom you happen to have a fancy for?'

'What nonsense you talk sometimes, Patricia.' Sir Michael ate the last slice of bacon with obvious enjoyment. 'I will miss my English breakfasts. Let's hope I can complete my duties quickly and efficiently and be home before Easter.'

Patricia rose abruptly to her feet. 'You'll excuse me, Greystone. I have an appointment with my modiste this morning.' She left the room without waiting for his response. Shocked by his sudden news and annoyed by her husband's casual dismissal of any feelings she might have, Patricia went to her room and put on her outdoor garments. She would have no compunction in spending as much money as she pleased – her modiste was excellent but not cheap, although a whole new wardrobe would be a little compensation for the disruption to her social life. The gossips would be kept busy when she attended functions without her husband, but they would delight in spreading rumours anyway. Sometimes her mischievous spirit won and she deliberately gave them something to talk about, but Greystone was always there to act as a buffer against the harsh realities of London society – Patricia had a feeling that things would be very different with her husband out of the country.

Look out for the third enthralling novel in The Rockwood Chronicles series . . .

Runaway Widow

Coming February 2022 . . .